KT-149-975

ST.HELENS COMMUNITY LIBRARY
3 8055 01310 1365

THAT LIVERPOOL GIRL

In the backstreets of Liverpool, Eileen Watson lives with her mother Nellie, daughter Mel and three tearaway sons. Life isn't great, but they have each other, and family can get you through anything. Or can they? Then, Britain declares war on Germany and their lives change forever. The children have to be evacuated, but Mel refuses to go, and so Eileen says goodbye to her mother and sons, moves from the street they love and faces a future without most of the people in her precious family. Thus begins a journey for them all, filled with forbidden love and tragedy.

THAT LIVERPOOL GIRL

THAT LIVERPOOL GIRL

by

Ruth Hamilton

Magna Large Print Books
Long Preston, North Yorkshire,
BD23 4ND, England.

British Library Cataloguing in Publication Data.

Hamilton, Ruth
That Liverpool girl.

A catalogue record of this book is
available from the British Library

ISBN 978-0-7505-3630-1

First published in Great Britain in 2011 by Pan Books
an imprint of Pan Macmillan, a division of Macmillan Publishers Ltd.

Published in Large Print 2012 by arrangement with
Pan Macmillan Publishers Limited

Magna Large Print is an imprint of Library Magna Books Ltd.

Printed and bound in Great Britain by
T.J. (International) Ltd., Cornwall, PL28 8RW

For Billy Guy, who walks my dogs and reads every word I write, though not simultaneously.

This book is a celebration of Liverpool's spirit, her defiance and determination through some terrible years. With respect and pride, I praise a tough generation who managed to remember to laugh.

If I have shifted things round a bit, forgive me. After thirty-one years in my chosen city, I beg some licence. In this place my forebears arrived from Ireland a hundred years ago. They moved inland, but I returned here with my sons in 1979. I have never regretted that journey.

God bless Liverpool, and God help my football team.

Ruthie.

ACKNOWLEDGEMENTS

I welcome into my life
Wayne Brookes (editor) and
Ryan Child (Wayne's assistant),
both fabulous people.
Thanks for all the help, boys.
Oh, and the laughs.

PART ONE

1939

One

'She's got one. She's always had one. Her face might favour a stewed prune some of the time, like, and she's a cut above us lot, but she's definitely got one in that there posh front room.' Nellie Kennedy leaned against the door frame and stared across at number one, Rachel Street. 'Her mam and dad had it before her, and I'll swear Henry Brogan picked up the wotsname to be charged up last week.'

'Wotsname? Do you mean the battery?'

Nellie awarded Kitty Maguire a withering look. Kitty, at the grand old age of twenty-nine, owned very few teeth, a pale grey face, virtually no flesh on her bones, three kids and a husband who could take gold if beer drinking ever became an Olympic sport. 'I'm not asking her,' Kitty said. 'She looks at me as if I should get back under a stone. No, I'm not asking her about nothing. She never talks to nobody.'

'Neither am I asking her.' Nellie shook her turbaned head. 'At a time like this, I think she should come out and tell us what's been said. It's like what you'd call a neighbourly duty in my book. She knows we're all stood here waiting like cheese at fourpence.'

There was only one wireless in the street, and it belonged to her at the end. Her at the end was a spinster of indeterminate years who had stayed at home to care for her parents, a pair of sad, colourless people with not much to say for themselves towards the end of their lives. After running a Scotland Road shop for many years, they had eventually retired, shrunk, and dropped like autumn leaves, but in the middle of winter. Arthur and Sarah Pickavance had shuffled off within days of each other, leaving Miss Pickavance to return to her position as ironer in a Chinese laundry, a situation that appeared to give her airs, as she never got dirty.

Few could understand why she remained in the Scotland Road area, because she wasn't a Catholic, wasn't Irish, and wasn't poor by most standards in these shabby parts. Her clothes were always nice, since she got them done at work, and she had proper furniture with a sofa and matching chairs in the parlour. It wasn't easy to see into her parlour, as thick lace curtains covered the bottom half of the sash window, while an aspidistra blocked more of the view, but she kept herself nice. And she did have matching furniture. In an area where a proper pair of boots with laces was a novelty, two brown chairs and a brown sofa were wealth indeed. She was supposed to have carpet squares and a real canteen of knives and forks, plus a proper tea set with saucers, cups and plates decorated with red roses and a bit of gold on the rims.

Nellie Kennedy, eyes and ears of the world, had been heard to opine on many occasions that Hilda Pickavance thought she was too good for round here. 'One of these days she'll have her nose that far up in the air, she'll come a cropper under the muck cart, and that'll be her done.' But today Nellie wasn't saying much. Nobody was saying much, because a heavy, if invisible, weight rested on the shoulders of every man and woman in Britain. Eleven o'clock had come and gone; at approximately eleven fifteen, Chamberlain was going to broadcast. This was not a good day for anyone of a nervous disposition.

Rumours were rife, and had been developing with increasing speed for a month or more. The chap who sold newspapers door to door said he'd heard that France was joining the anti-Nazi stance, that Australia, New Zealand and Canada were loading up ships, while America couldn't make up its mind because it didn't need to be bothered worrying about Europe. Ernie Bagshaw, who had just one eye and a limp from the Great War, was going about telling anyone who would listen that the Luftwaffe had already carpet-bombed London, so there'd be no broadcast. But no one listened to him, as he was just being his usual cheerful self.

'My Charlie thinks Hitler'll win,' announced Kitty. 'We'll all be walking daft and talking German by next year, he says.'

'Hmmph.' Nellie's 'hmmphs' were legendary. She didn't need to use words, because Kitty Maguire knew what was going through her next-door neighbour's mind. Charlie Maguire was mad and pickled. He was mad enough to have taken a sample of his wife's urine for testing in order to hide his drinking, and pickled enough to believe the doctor when told he was the first pregnant man in that particular area of Liverpool. Yes, the 'hmmph' was adequate, because Charlie definitely wasn't.

'We could have let the kids go on Friday,' Kitty said. 'Maybe we should have sent them on the trains, Nellie.' She left unspoken the reason for the corporate if unspoken decision not to send the children on the evacuation trains. Asked to provide a change of clothing, pyjamas or night-dresses and extra underwear, the mothers of Scotland Road were stymied, since few children owned much beyond the rags on their backs. What was more, many from large families carried wildlife about their persons, and a visit to the local bath house would have proved expensive.

But Nellie agreed with Kitty's statement. All they had were their kids, and Scottie was near enough to the docks to warrant flattening by Hitler's airborne machines. 'I know, love,' she sighed wearily. 'And if wishes were horses, beggars would ride. But you're right, because if London cops it, we'll be next. No way will Liverpool be left out of this lot.' Nellie was old enough to remember the last bit of bother. It had left her widowed, and the intervening twenty years had been beyond hard. Life was still far from easy, because Nellie shared a house with her daughter, also widowed, and four grandchildren, three of whom were wild, to say the least. Half the time, nobody knew where the lads were, and the other half, Nellie, her daughter and her granddaughter wished they'd leave the house and get up to whatever they got up to when nobody knew where they were, because of the noise.

'Did you get the horse back to the carters'

yard?' Kitty asked.

Nellie sighed heavily. 'Jimmy Leach came for it. I don't know what our Bertie was thinking of. A carthorse is a bit big to hide in a back yard.' She shrugged. 'He was going on for days about wanting a horse, and he took one. Thank God it was docile. But getting to the lav wouldn't have been easy, not with that great big article tied to me mangle.' She sighed again. 'Trying to hide a nineteen-hand carthorse between a tin bath and a mangle. I ask you.' She shrugged.

'You have to laugh, though,' said Kitty.

'Have you? With what's going on in Germany, I can't even manage a smile these days. Ooh, look. I don't believe it.' The lace curtain in number one had disappeared, the sash window was being raised, and a wireless had taken the place of the aspidistra. Drawn like bees to pollen, adults and children began to congregate until the small crowd outside number one was at least four deep and two houses wide. No one said a word; even babies sat silently while waiting for their fate to be decided. Hilda Pickavance fiddled with a knob till she found the right station. She turned up the volume as high as it would go, then stood next to the instrument, hands folded, head bowed, as if she waited for Holy Communion. The broadcast began at eleven thirteen precisely.

And they heard it. No one spoke or moved while the Prime Minister made a brave effort to hide sorrow and bitter disappointment. His little piece of paper, the one that had fluttered in the breeze only months before on cinema screens, was now all but screwed into a ball and deposited in the rubbish cart. 'This country is at war with Germany.' He asked for God's help to be given to the righteous, then went away to do whatever Prime Ministers did at times like this. The crowd emitted a synchronized breath before beginning to disperse. War. Husbands, fathers and brothers would disappear, and some would never return.

It was ridiculous. On a beautiful late summer morning, everybody's life changed in the space of a few minutes. Even here, where poverty was king, sunlight washed over the houses, birds sang, and fluffy white clouds drifted across a perfect sky. Good weather was one thing that didn't happen just to the rich. Good weather came from God, and He gave it to all His children.

The stunned silence continued. Although shelters were being built and children moved up and down the country in search of safety, the news remained incredible. Should they have let their kids go, and bugger the shame that accompanied poverty? What now? In every female heart, a little devil prayed for their menfolk to be declared unfit to serve. If they weren't well enough to be picked for work on the docks, surely they could not be expected to defend their country?

Nellie Kennedy, as tough as old hobnailed boots, began to cry. She sank to the ground, where she was joined by Kitty, her neighbour of several years. No longer young, no longer as resilient as the front she presented, Nellie felt she couldn't take any more. She'd been on the planet for only fifty-odd years, yet she felt ancient, worn out and unbelievably sad. It was happening again.

It wasn't supposed to happen again.

'Come on, queen,' whispered Kitty. 'Don't let go. We've got to hang on, girl. No point in giving up before we've even kicked off, eh?'

The onlookers moved closer, unwashed bodies and dirty clothing removing the earlier freshness of the day. But they soon cleared off, because a wailing sound invaded the area, a noise to which they would need to become accustomed for years to come. They scattered, leaving Nellie and her neighbour on the cobbles.

Hilda Pickavance came into the street to break the habit of a lifetime. 'Mrs Kennedy,' she said. 'Would you come into my house, please? I think the siren's just for practice. Would you kindly come in too, Mrs Maguire?'

Kitty shook her head and walked away. Much as she would have loved to get a glimpse of the matching furniture, she had to go back home and see what her children were up to. Did they have their gas masks? Was this really just a practice on the sirens?

But Nellie allowed herself to be led away. For the first time ever, she would be able to report properly on the state of Hilda Pickavance's home. The fear and sadness remained, but she would shortly find distractions.

Nellie Kennedy closed her mouth with an audible snap. The trouble with porcelain dentures was that they were noisy in the event of shock. Blood and stomach pills, this was a lot to take in. First, there was a war on, a fight Britain might never win, because rumour had it that Hitler was more than ready to conquer the whole of Europe. Second, she was drinking tea from a china cup in the presence of a neighbour who was landed bloody gentry. 'Are you sure?' she managed at last. 'Is it not a mistake, like?' She had a saucer. A real saucer that matched the cup. But she didn't extend her little finger, because that would have been taking the whole thing too far.

Miss Pickavance inclined her head. 'My father was cut off without a penny before I was born. My mother didn't pass muster, you see, because she was a mere cleaner. My uncle felt sorry for my father and sent money. That paid for our little shop – remember the shop?'

'I do. They were very polite, your mam and dad. And sometimes they let us have stuff on tick when we ran out of bread or something we really needed. We called it the just-about-everything corner, because your dad sold just about everything, didn't he?'

Hilda Pickavance smiled tentatively. 'The same uncle died intestate – without a will – and I am his only surviving relative. I found out properly just last week, so I've been on to the authorities and they said yes. I can use it for evacuees and farming.'

Nellie, a town girl to the core, shifted in her chair. 'A farm, though?'

'Yes, part of the estate is a farm. Livestock and arable, so quite a lot of land. Land is going to be vital, because this country will need to become as self-sufficient as possible.'

'Eh?'

'The merchant ships that import food and so

forth will come under attack. We shall have to grow our own supplies. Mrs Kennedy, this is a serious business – we need to take children with us. And I shall require someone like you, because I'm unused to children.'

Nellie had been so engrossed that she'd forgotten to study the furniture. Today had been a bit like an old silent movie – well, apart from the sirens. It had walked at a strange pace, jerking about and changing direction without warning. Bright sunlight had birthed hope, then hope had been shattered by the broadcast, now it threatened to bud once again. Would it be shot down in flames? Would this become yet another false promise? 'What about my Eileen and her brood?'

'They will come with us. She can clean and cook.'

Nellie blinked rapidly. She would wake up in a minute, surely? Somebody would start shouting that somebody else had pinched his boots and gone out in them, Eileen would be scraping together some sort of breakfast, and the dream would be over. 'So you *are* posh, then? We always knew you were different, what with not being Catholic and all that, but are you proper gentry, like?'

Hilda Pickavance laughed, and the sound was rusty. 'I was born in a room above a shop in town. Until Uncle found us, we lived hand to mouth, so I never considered myself gentry. When he sent the money, we took the shop and bought this little house, and we settled here, because the business was close by. My father was a proud man, and Uncle didn't find us again.

Perhaps he didn't try, but that's not important now. We have to deal with what's going on at the moment. I have land, you have children. We need each other.'

'And you worked in the laundry?'

'I loved my job. I was always good at ironing, so I went to work with those lovely Chinese people after our shop closed. Then I had to leave to look after my parents, and when they died I went back. A few weeks ago, I saw a notice in the newspaper, and found out that I'm a woman of substance. Yes, it's a lot to take in.'

Nellie didn't know what to say. Hilda Pickavance was not a bit stuck-up, and she was offering safety, yet the part of Nellie that belonged here, in Liverpool, was aching already. 'I don't know,' she managed at last. 'I'll have to talk to Eileen and the kids – they're not babies.'

'I know what you mean. I have envied you for such a long time.'

'Envied?' Nellie paused for a few seconds, incredulity distorting her features. 'What's to envy? I clean in the Throstle's Nest. Me husband's long dead, our Eileen cleans big houses for peanuts because her fellow died on the docks, and you envy us that? She's up Blundellsands scrubbing, I'm cleaning sick off the floor in filthy lavatories...' Her voice died of exhaustion.

'My mother was a cleaner,' said the woman from number one. 'What I envy is the fact that you have each other. I am brotherless, sisterless, parentless. I had one uncle, whom I never met, and now I am completely alone in the world. That's why I want some of you to come. I don't know you well, but I recognize you. I'm afraid, Mrs Kennedy. To be honest, I'm absolutely terrified of all this – the war, the property, everything.'

This was the morning on which Britain had gone to war, when Hilda Pickavance had shared her wireless with the neighbours, when Nellie Kennedy learned that 'her from number one' wasn't so stuck-up and different after all. 'Right. What happens next?' she asked. The woman was shy, that was all. She just wasn't used to folk.

Hilda's face was white. 'Well, I have to go and look at the place. It's been described to me, of course, and I've seen a few photographs, but nothing's real till you see it properly. Mrs Kennedy, the bombs aren't real until the body of a child is dug out. I'm sorry to speak so plainly, but–'

'No, no, you do right. There's no harm in calling a spade a shovel, no matter what it's used for. I'm Nellie, by the way, so you can call a Kennedy a Nellie while you're at it with the spade.'

'Hilda.'

'Hello, Hilda. When are you going?'

'Tomorrow. Come with me.'

'You what?'

The poor woman's hands picked at a beautifully laundered handkerchief. 'I can't do all this by myself. Had the war not happened, I'd probably have sold all the land and property and bought myself a house somewhere in Liverpool. Liverpool's all I know. Like you, Nellie, I've never lived anywhere else. I have to go and look at my new life.'

Nellie pondered for a while. 'Where is this place?'

'North of Bolton.'

Nellie's mouth made a perfect O before she spoke again. 'Bolton's a big town full of factories. It'll get pancaked, same as here.'

Hilda explained that her legacy was out in the wilds among small villages and hamlets, that Liverpool was in more danger as it was coastal, and gave her opinion that women might well be forced to work. 'Better to be on a farm than in a munitions factory, Nellie. Put your grandchildren first, and grow potatoes. Well?'

'Can I go and fetch our Eileen? I can't make a decision this big on my own. And our Mel's old enough and clever enough to make up her own mind.' Nellie sighed. 'I'll never work out where she got her brains. Top marks in that test, so she got what they call a scholarship.' She looked through the window. 'What the bloody hell's that soft lot up to? Have you seen this?'

'I have.' Hilda smiled, though her eyes remained grim. 'They're waiting for the planes, Nellie. God alone knows what they've done to Poland since they walked in. I suppose Warsaw will soon be – as you say – pancaked. Probably more like *crêpes suzette*. Flambe, or even cremated. There will be no mercy.'

The visitor gulped audibly. 'So it won't be just bridges and railways?'

Hilda shook her head. 'It will be babies, Nellie. And that's how it will be here, too. We aren't ready. If those in government had listened to Winston Churchill, we might have had more weapons and planes. The men who would have built those things will be called up to fight. Women will assemble guns, tanks and planes. Shall we stick to cabbages and onions? Shall we save some children?'

'God!'

'Is on our side. Go on. Fetch Eileen.'

Nellie stepped into the street. Eileen was one of those who stood and stared at the sky. The all-clear had sounded, yet half of Rachel Street crowded on the cobbles, every neck tilted back, each pair of eyes scanning the blue for signs of an incoming formation. Nellie whistled. Her whistles, like her 'hmmphs', were legendary in the area. Attention was suddenly diverted from heaven to earth. 'They won't come today,' she told them all. 'It's Sunday. They'll be in church praying for Hitler, their new pope.' She beckoned to her daughter, and led her into the house opposite theirs.

Forced to sit through the tale for a second time, Nellie examined the parlour. It was spotless. Cream-painted walls carried framed prints, and a grandmother clock ticked happily in the corner. Folk had been right about the suite, right about the carpet.

The wireless, now atop a well-polished desk, was still turned on, though at a lower volume. The people of Dublin were burning effigies of Chamberlain in the streets. Churchill had been summoned to the cabinet room. Survivors in Warsaw were reported to be ecstatic – they clearly expected a lot from Britain. British men aged between eighteen and forty-one would be called up in stages, while immediate volunteers would be accepted if medically fit.

When Eileen left to talk to her children, Nellie stayed, because Hilda wanted not to be alone. So she was there when Churchill was made First Lord of the Admiralty, there when reports came of ships signalling, in great joy, 'Winston is back'. She was there for lunch and for tea, was an ear-witness when King George broadcast to his empire, when the *Athenia,* with many Americans on board, was torpedoed and sunk by a German submarine. Russia was to remain neutral as part of a pact with Hitler, while Roosevelt insisted that America was not to be involved.

Australia announced its intention to fight, as did New Zealand, the West Indies and Canada. At half past eight, France declared war on Germany.

'France is in a terrible position, geographically speaking,' said Hilda.

Nellie agreed. 'Yes. They'll be in Hitler's way, won't they?'

Hilda nodded. 'The Germans will just walk in, and then there'll be nothing more than a thin ribbon of water separating Adolf and us. Imagine how the people of Dover feel, Nellie. It's only about twenty miles from Calais.'

That was the moment when it all hit home for Nellie. France would no doubt do her best, but she was probably as ill-equipped as England. Twenty miles? Some folk could swim that. That fellow Captain Webb had swum it, for a start. He was on most of the boxes of matches she bought. 'I think I'd best come with you tomorrow, Hilda. Our Eileen, too, if that's all right, because it has to be her decision – they're her kids.'

'Yes.'

Nellie attempted a smile. 'Mind you, if there's horses, Bertie'll be there in a shot. He pinched one last week from the carters' yard and brought it home. He'd have tried taking it up to bed with him if we hadn't noticed it.' She looked down at work-worn hands. 'It's all changed today, hasn't it?'

'Yes.'

'I'm not a country girl.'

'Neither am I.'

'And we're just looking, aren't we?'

Hilda nodded her agreement. 'Looking costs nothing. We'll leave at one. You'll have finished work by then?'

'Yes, and Eileen doesn't do Mondays, so she'll be ready.'

Hilda stood up and held out her hand. 'It's been a pleasure to meet you at last, Nellie. Tomorrow we'll see a completely different world, one where the harvest has just come in, children running free, fresh air, cows wait to be milked, and eggs will be plentiful.'

Nellie shook her neighbour's hand. 'You make it sound like a holiday.'

'I wish. Oh, how I wish.'

Hilda watched while her new-found friend walked across the narrow street and disappeared into a house she shared with five people. Nellie and her daughter slept in the parlour, while the three boys shared the front and larger bedroom, leaving the small rear room for Mel, the brains of the family. The mattress on which Nellie and Eileen slept was probably parked in an upright position behind other furniture during the day. Cleaner than most others, the Kennedy/Watson clan still suffered the effects of overcrowding, but they didn't smell as badly as some. They managed to get to the public bath house on a fairly regular basis, while Mel bathed when she stayed at a friend's house in Crosby. Yes, there was Mel. What would she decide to do?

Mel Watson, baptized Amelia Anne after her dead father's dead mother, was doing her Latin homework. She had fought hard for her place at Merchant Taylors', because the priest hadn't liked the idea of her going to a non-Catholic school, and tram fares were hard to come by, but she'd hung on in there. A friend at school had given her a second-hand bike, and that was a great help. It was a long way from Rachel Street to Crosby – a long way in more senses than one – but Mel was a determined girl.

The war had landed downstairs. There was no need for Hitler, since Bertie, Rob and Philip were making enough noise to wake the dead. She put down her pen, walked to the door of her tiny room and opened it. The word 'farm' was being repeated, as was 'Miss Pickavance' and 'when do we go?' It was clear that Mam had decided to evacuate the boys. Sitting on the stairs, she wrapped the skirt of her uniform round her knees. Gran was talking now, was making the boys shut up, so some sense was promised.

'We're all going,' Gran said. 'The whole of our family, and Miss Pickavance. We'll be safe, and there'll be plenty to eat, and–'

'And horses,' shrieked Bertie, who was the youngest of the three.

Mel crept back into her room. She stretched out on the bed, hands clasped behind her head.

A beautiful child was promising to become a beautiful young woman, and she would get her way. There was a spare room in Gloria Bingley's house. Gloria Bingley's father and brother were fond of Mel. Mrs Bingley, too, was fond, but in a very different way. They had given her the bike. They had bought her two dresses and had fed her many times. This might be the very opportunity for which she had waited.

But Mel would miss her family. Pragmatic by nature, she tried to go along with the flow of life, picking up whatever was wanted and available, refusing to worry about her poverty-stricken household, the vagaries of her brothers, the loudness of her grandmother. This was the situation into which she had been born, and she had made the best she could of it.

Her undeniable beauty was a tool she used from time to time. She had inherited her looks from her mother, who had stoically refused to remarry, though she had not been without potential suitors. But, as Eileen repeated with monotonous regularity, she would not wish her three boys on the worst of men, while the best had the sense to stay away. As for Mel's brain, it was just a fluke. Many clever people came from lowly beginnings, so she wouldn't be the first urchin to strut the stage with the Cambridge Footlights.

How far were they going? There were no farms round here, though a few of Lord Derby's existed over towards Rainford and Maghull. It would be further away, in a place where no housing estates had sprung up since the Great War. 'I don't want to lose my mother,' she told a statue of Our Lady.

'And what if Gloria's dad and brother want to do more than look at me?'

At thirteen, she knew almost all there was to know about sex. Gender issues were another problem, since her brothers had, from the very start, considered her bike to be fair game because they were boys, while she was a mere female. The matter had been settled by Gran: two beatings with a belt that had belonged to Dad, followed by the acquisition of a chain and padlock. Mel's bike now lived in the front room, attached to a hook in the wall that had been installed by a docker. It was the only way for a girl to survive in a house that contained members of the so-called superior sex.

Sex itself had similar rules, she supposed. In order for the species to survive, males had been furnished with the urge to invade the female body. Women and girls needed to be clever, because these masculine requirements could be utilized. A pretty face, good legs, a small waist and developing breasts were assets not to be underestimated. When manufactured innocence invaded a sweet smile, dresses, bikes and food became available. Could a bed be attained by the same means? It would be safer, she decided, if she shared a room with Gloria. She didn't want babies from Gloria's brother; she wanted Cambridge. School holidays could be spent with the family she didn't really want to lose, while term time would be a sight easier if she lived in Crosby.

The door opened. 'Mel?'

'Come in, Mam.'

Eileen sat on the edge of the lumpy bed. She told her beautiful daughter about Miss Pickavance and the inheritance, about Gran's intention to shift everyone inland, about the boys' excitement.

'I heard it,' said Mel.

'Miss Pickavance said that Bolton School might take you because of special circumstances. But it's about ten miles from where we're going–'

'Mam, I'm staying here. Somebody will put me up. Bolton School might be doing the same courses, but differently. And I don't want to pedal twenty miles a day, do I? There may be some public transport, but petrol's going to be scarce.'

'Is it?'

Mel nodded. 'It's imported, and the seas won't be safe with all those U-boats lurking.'

'Eh?'

'Submarines. We won't want to risk them blowing up the oil tankers, so petrol will be rationed, as will all imported stuff. Mam, it's going to be a nightmare. Please let me find someone who'll take me in, then I'll do my best to get to you during the holidays.'

Eileen began to weep softly. 'I don't want to lose me girl, do I?'

This was the weak link in Mel's sensible, I-can-cope-with-anything chain. She adored her mother. No matter what she achieved in life, no matter where she worked, this woman would be with her. 'You'll never lose me, and I'll never lose you till the day one of us dies, Mam.' She had watched her mother going without so that the children might be better fed. She'd seen her in the same clothes day in, day out, frayed but clean, shoes polished and full of holes. Mam's beauty was finer now, almost ethereal, because her facial skin had become translucent, allowing miraculous bones to boast loudly of their perfection. From this wonderful woman, Mel had gained life, reasonable health, and the power that accompanied good looks.

'We'd be safer,' Eileen said now. 'But I'd be worried past meself about you, babe. From the moment you were born, you were perfect. Your dad cried when he saw you, said you were the loveliest girl in the world – except for me, of course. But they'll bomb Crosby, Mel. They will. I know they'll be aiming for the docks and the ships, but Crosby's only two minutes away in a plane. How can I leave you?'

'You've the three lads, that's how and why. On a farm, Bertie can run out his madness, and the other two will learn skills like planting, harvesting, collecting eggs and milking cows. Gran will be better in fresh air. As for bombs – well, they'll just have to keep out of my way, because I'm going to Cambridge.'

'How?'

'When I get there, I'll work ten nights a week in a pub.'

'But there aren't ten in a week.'

'I'll soon alter that.'

'I bet you could, too.' If her Mel set her mind to something, it suddenly became achievable. 'All right, love. But when you decide where you're staying, I want to see the people and the house.'

'Of course.'

Eileen went downstairs to re-join the rabble. If she had to meet people from Crosby, she'd need clothes. Perhaps Miss Pickavance would lend her something sensible. But would she dare to ask?

In one sense, the day on which war was declared had become the best in Hilda's life so far. Her parents had been kind, gentle but rather quiet folk. Both avid readers, they had introduced her to books at a tender age, and she still devoted much of her leisure time to reading. The wireless was excellent company when she was dusting and sweeping, but at other times she chose books. She had never been a communicator. At work, her employers, who valued her greatly, spoke Cantonese for the most part, so Hilda's conversation practice had been sorely neglected. Today, she had broken her duck. Very soon, she would become a comparatively wealthy woman.

But this little house was part of her. She even kept Mother's last piece of knitting in a bottom cupboard, the needles stopped and crossed in the middle of a row. It had been a cardigan for Father, but it had never been finished, and he would not be needing it now. Yet Hilda couldn't part with any of it. What was the sense, though? Why should she hang on to a house in a slum, a street that might fall down or be bombed before being selected for demolition? And, if she kept it, would it be burgled and looted in her absence, or might a neighbour look after it? The cleanest people were coming with her, so...

'Calm down,' she ordered. 'You are going to look, no more and no less.' After the war, she might sell – what was it called? Willows. Willows was a large house; then there was Willows Home Farm and a little hamlet labelled Willows End.

No, Willows Edge. The place was reputed to be slightly run down, as Uncle had spent most of his time abroad. The solicitor had intimated, as delicately as he could, that Uncle had favoured the company of young men, hence the lack of direct offspring. And Hilda had blushed. She needed to stop blushing and start living.

Mother and Father were together on the mantelpiece. The photograph had been taken a few years ago during a visit to Southport. Hilda smiled at them. Sometimes, she had felt rather de trop in this house, because the love those two had shared had been enough, and they hadn't needed a child to underline their status. Yes, they had loved her; yes, they could have managed without her. To this day, she felt no resentment, since she had been raised in a stable home, one to which a drunken parent never returned, where silence was normal, and contentment seemed eternal.

It had been a sensible union. God knew there were few of those in these parts. But nothing was eternal. Mother had passed away one Christmas Eve; Father had followed her three days later. The whole of Scotland Road had turned out for the double funeral, since most of them remembered kindness and thoughtfulness. So decent had the Pickavances been that no one had ever gone over the top with a slate. Even after the shop had closed, pennies and threepenny bit had landed on the doormat wrapped in scraps of paper with a name, and a message– *Last payment,* or *I still owe you another 8d.*

Now this. What would Mother and Father have done? Had Father outlived Uncle, this problem and its accompanying wealth and responsibility would have been his. There was a farmer, there were farmhands. There was a land agent who collected rents and kept order on the whole estate. Hilda would be their boss. It was all rather daunting, but she didn't want to shame the memory of the people who had raised her. 'I'll try,' she said to the photograph. 'God help me,' she continued as she doused gas mantles in preparation for bed. She picked up her candle and walked to the stairs. This place was all she knew. From tomorrow, life might change, and she was not prepared for that.

Two

'A woman. A bloody woman!' Neil Dyson threw his cap onto the kitchen table where it narrowly missed the milk jug. 'I know I won't be one of the first to be called up, but I might have to go sooner or later unless the job here's termed reserved. Jean, you're the best wife any farmer could want, and I'd trust you with my life, but this is one blinking big farm, and you'll be answerable to a female from the middle of Liverpool. The only things she'll grow are her fingernails, and I bet she'd run a mile if she saw a cow or a big boar. She'll be as soft as putty and as daft as a brush.'

Jean Dyson poured another mug of tea for her rampageous spouse. He was ranting and raving, while she was trying to bake bread and scones. 'It's not her fault, Neil. She's just the last man standing, and she happens to be female. She didn't turn her uncle into what he was. None of it's her fault, love. You know I thought the world of Adam Pickavance, but he was never here, was he? If we saw him twice a year, we were doing pretty well. But calm down, for God's sake. We've trouble enough without you aiming for a stroke. And you know how much I hate all the shouting.'

'Adam Pickavance?' he snorted. 'Too busy chasing pretty boys all over the place, he was. He never bothered about us lot, did he? The houses down the Edge need new roofs and all sorts, Willows is slowly rotting away, and who's going to run this place?'

'I am.'

'But you'll lose most of the hands. The older ones might get left here, and a few of the very young, but anybody eighteen to twenty-five with no children will be off within weeks. You'll have to register every animal in triplicate, there'll be no meat to market without the Ministry say-so, and you'll be–'

'Oh, give over. It's not just us. Every family in the country's going to be in a bit of a mess.' She raised a hand when he opened his mouth to continue the rant. 'Neil, just stop it. I don't want anybody to go, don't want anybody to fight. You won't be called up, because you're turned forty, so stop it. Anyway, all this has to be taken out on Hitler, not me, not Chamberlain, not England. We're all frightened and in the dark, and it'll get worse before it gets better. Like I said, it's everybody from Land's End to John o' Groats, but God help them in the south, because they're nearest to hell. Now, go and stamp about on the land, because I've listened enough, and I've baking on. My bread doesn't thrive when somebody's in a bad mood, and we want to send some decent stuff up to Willows for when she comes on her visit.'

Neil picked up his cap and slammed out of the house. Not for the first time, he wished he could get his hands on enough money to buy this place. His dad had farmed it, and Neil had taken over. He knew every animal, every pleat and fold in the land, every ditch and hedge – a bloody woman? Adam Pickavance had been as much use as a damp squib, but answering to the agent of an absent man was one thing; having a woman in charge would change matters. Or would it? Perhaps she might leave everything in the hands of Keith Greenhalgh, who was a fair man, knowledgeable about the estate, and unlikely to be called up, as he was well into his forties while his occupation could sit nicely under the umbrella labelled essential and reserved.

In the top field, Neil stopped and surveyed a domain he had always considered his own. As far as he could see in any in any direction, the land belonged to Willows. The hamlet known as Willows Edge nestled in a dip, and all the houses therein were tied to the estate. Keith Greenhalgh had done his best, but the funds left in his care by Adam Pickavance had been insufficient to cover anything beyond bare essentials, and the dwellings were in need of attention. A flaming woman, though...

'Morning, Neil.'

It was the man himself. 'Keith. I was just thinking about you.'

Keith joined him and both men leaned on a fence. 'How's it going?' the agent asked.

'As all right as it can go. Conscription hangs over the field hands like a thundercloud, and a Scouse woman's taking the reins. Couldn't be better.'

Keith chuckled. 'Look. I shouldn't know this, and I shouldn't be telling you, either, but the old man left a fair sum, didn't fritter it all away. She might pull us out of ruin.'

It was Neil's turn to laugh. 'Oh, aye? And one of my pigs has just floated down tied to a purple parachute. The bloody woman'll be all lipstick and shoes, because she's a townie. I guarantee she'll think more about her perfume than she will about folk. These city women know nowt about owt.'

'If you want to know what's in her head, she's been talking about bringing evacuees from Liverpool, because they live near the docks. Seems quite a sensible type to me, and no spring chicken, or so I'm told.'

Neil shook his head thoughtfully. Down below, in the large hollow that contained Bolton, children were living among factories and smoke, but they weren't going to be brought up to the tops, were they? Oh no. The place was going to be overrun by Scousers. The invaders would be useless. They would have no idea of husbandry, because the only animals they would have seen were dray horses, and he pictured the hordes in his mind's eye running through fields and flattening crops. 'Bloody wild, they are. They pinch what they want, run about barefoot, and–'

'And that doesn't happen in Bolton? You've not

had much to do with the bottom end of Deane Road and Derby Street, then? I have relatives down yon, Neil, and they struggle. Their kids aren't perfect. Hungry children steal, because when push comes to shove we all would if we stood alongside real hunger. Get off your high horse, lad, before you take a fall.' He tapped his forehead, then his mouth. 'Keep that open, and that closed. Until she arrives this afternoon, we've no idea what she's made of. But I can tell you this much for nothing – the owld fellow loved the bones of his brother, and the lady is that brother's daughter. Open mind, buttoned lips. Think on.' Keith walked away.

Neil knew that Keith and Jean were right. He was carrying on like a two-year-old in a tantrum, when in reality he was no more than a speck in the cosmos. Everybody mattered. Everybody was the same in the sight of God. Willows Home Farm was no more important than the next, and he had been blessed with a sensible wife. Two daughters, they had. For the first time in his married life, Neil was glad that he had no son.

But behind all these worries at the front of his mind, there was a dark place he scarcely dared to visit. In spite of propaganda in newspapers and on cinema screens, the mood of the country was not good. Hitler was reputed to have thousands of fighter planes, hundreds of bombers. He could wipe out Britain in a day if he so chose. These fields, this pure, green, velvet beauty, could soon belong to a crowd of goose-stepping foreigners, so why worry about a few bloody Scousers? An invasion by Liverpool was infinitely preferable to the other possibility.

Fruit-pickers were busy denuding trees in the orchards. Cows grazed in the distance, and even further away, on higher ground, sheep looked like little flecks of cotton wool against the hillsides. In a place as beautiful and peaceful as this, it was difficult to imagine war. But he remembered war. He had fought in it, had survived, though it had taken many men from these parts. The war to end all wars had been the subtitle of the previous mess. Men had come home after doing the impossible, after climbing over dead comrades in mud-lined trenches, after losing limbs, sight, the ability to breathe... Neil nodded. They had come home to grinding poverty, had fought to their last ounce of strength to live in a country that didn't deserve them. 'And now we do the same, and we come back to the same. Land of hope and glory my bloody backside. If I go, I'll be fighting for Jean, Stella and Patty.'

Yet a small corner of Neil's heart held a picture of a good, quiet man with a stammer, a soul so fine and true that almost every Englishman admired and loved him. His brother, the one with all the airs and the swank, had buggered off with the ugliest woman imaginable, leaving a sibling in poor health to run the family shop. Bertie, now George VI, his wife and daughters, they deserved saving. But even they couldn't sort out the nitwits at Westminster. Which was just as well, in a way, because the King favoured Halifax, while the country needed Winnie. Chamberlain would have to go. Yes. The cretins in the Commons should have listened. To Churchill.

Right. He had a horse with a limp, a sow with a sore teat, and a wife who was fed up with him. He would walk to the vet's to ask for a visit on behalf of the first two, and he would find some nice apples for Jean. She made a lovely apple pie, did his Jeanie…

A car arrived in Rachel Street. A novelty, it attracted small children like flies until the driver sounded the horn, at which point they dispersed and stood in a jagged line on the opposite pavement, only to shift again when Nellie Kennedy and her daughter emerged from their house.

Hilda Pickavance, who had been waiting for her new friends to put in an appearance, gathered together pieces of shattered nerve and stepped outside. This was all getting a bit too much for her. She was to have a meeting with a Keith Greenhalgh, agent and steward for the estate known as Willows. The only men with whom she'd had contact thus far were her father and her employer at the laundry. She thanked goodness that older children were at school as she placed herself in the front passenger seat, smiling tentatively at the driver, who had left his seat in order to open the door for her. When he had settled her two companions in the rear of the vehicle, the man returned and pulled away.

Cheering children chased them as far as the Rotunda theatre, where they fell away and turned to go home.

'Miss Pickavance?'

'Yes.'

'I'm Jay, really John Collins. There was a spate

of Johns when I was born, so I got reduced to Jay.'

Hilda couldn't lay her tongue against one sensible syllable, so Nellie helped her out. 'My granddaughter's reduced from Amelia to Mel, and it never done her no harm. She's at Merchant Taylors'. That's the best public school, and she won a full scholarship. Very clever girl, our Mel. And beautiful like my Eileen.'

Eileen dug her mother in the ribs. 'Stop showing off,' she mouthed. It was always the same with Mam when she met someone for the first time. She said her own name, then waded in over her head with Mel's success. Her granddaughter was top of the class in most subjects; she was going to Cambridge if a source of money could be found, and she did lovely calliography. Time after time, Eileen had corrected the word to calligraphy, but Nellie was happier with the extra syllable, as it sounded posher. She had quite a collection of home-made words, and she used them deliberately and without mercy.

'She can sing and all,' Nellie said now. 'Voice of an angel.'

'How would you know?' Eileen asked. 'For one thing, you're tone deaf, and for another, you're biased. Why don't you brag about the other three, eh? One of them put Sally Wray's tea-rose-coloured directoire knickers up a flagpole – I don't know which of them, but I'll get to the bottom of it.'

'Or the top,' said Hilda, her back shaking with laughter. 'Flagpole? Top?'

'Oh, heck,' groaned Nellie dramatically. 'You've

woken a sleeping giant here, Eileen.' She poked Hilda's shoulder. 'Oi, clever clogs. Might be top for flagpole, but it's bottom for knickers, so hang on to your ha'penny, missus.'

But Eileen ploughed onward. 'Our Bertie and the horse – that'll go down in history down Cazneau Street and Scotland Road. I mean, I know he's only six, but per-lease. Hiding a cart-horse between a small tin bath and a bloody mangle? He has to have come from a different planet. If he hadn't been born at home, I'd swear they'd given me the wrong baby.'

The driver pulled into a kerb, dried his eyes, and swivelled as far as possible in his seat. 'You two should be on the wireless,' he moaned.

'We haven't got one,' came Nellie's quick reply. 'We had one, like, but it never worked since our Philip stood on it to reach a shelf. He's been on the wireless, but he fell off.'

Jay drummed his fingertips on the steering wheel. 'And I suppose when he tried tap dancing, he slipped into the sink? The old ones are always the best, right?'

Nellie pretended to glare at him. 'This is all we need, a clever bloody Woollyback. You talk slow, but you get there, don't you, lad?'

He sighed. 'Look. Getting there's what it's about today. We've miles to go, and we'll not get there at all if I can't see for laughing.' He pointed to the new boss of Willows. 'And this lady has business to discuss, but she'll get yonder all red-eyed and daft if you don't stop this malarkey. All right?'

Nellie and Eileen shrugged. 'Please yourself,' said the former. 'It's not every day you get free entertainment thrown in, like, but we'll shut up.'

They would probably have shut up anyway, because the journey was becoming interesting. They saw decent terraced houses in Lowton, stared at winding gear that took men down into half a dozen pits on the route round the hem of Wigan, knew they were nearing the mills when they noticed tall chimneys ahead.

Jay parked again. 'And there you have it, ladies. If you look beyond the town, you'll see hills on three sides. They protect the cotton, keep the damp in, you see. The mills have to be boiling hot and wet, or there'd be a lot of spoilage. No hills on the Manchester side, so it's more a ladle than a bowl. Anyway, look over to the left a bit, Miss Pickavance. A massive piece of land up yon is yours. Your forefathers toiled for that, just to get out of the town. So, welcome home.'

Hilda was staring at the inheritance of which her beloved father had been deprived.

'Miss Pickavance?'

'Yes?'

'Are you all right?'

'My parents would have loved to live up there. They had a hard life. Not as hard as some, but...' She put away the rest of the words. 'Let's go. I want to get this over and done so that I can go home. Because my thinking will probably start after the meeting.'

They trundled down Derby Street towards town. In shabby alleyways that ran off on each side, there was poverty that mirrored conditions round Scotland Road. Infants ran barefoot, some of them scarcely dressed. The shops on the main road were neglected and tacky, and had very few items on display in their windows. On several corners stood small covens of women in black, ancients who still dressed like Victorians, skirts reaching their ankles, grey shawls covering their blouses. They inhaled snuff from small boxes, or sucked on white clay pipes. Every other building seemed to be a public house. Yes, this bit was home from home for Nellie and Eileen.

In town, Jay pointed out the open market.

'It's not open,' Nellie said. 'It's shut.'

'Open as in the open air, and don't pretend you didn't already understand,' was his reply. 'It works Tuesdays, Thursdays and Saturdays. The enclosed market, Market Hall, is down by the side of Woolworth's.'

'Right. And where's this here Willows?'

He pointed. 'A good ten miles out that way.'

'Any shops?' Eileen asked.

'Well.' Jay rounded the corner into Bank Street to begin his climb up to the moors. 'Elsie Openshaw got herself turned into a post office. She had to pass a test for that, but the mail's not delivered. I collect the stuff for Willows, and Willows Home Farm and some of the tenant farms, but them who live on the Edge collect their own. She sells a few basics like soap and lamp oil. People from the Edge use her more than we do.'

'Ooh, I wouldn't like to live on the edge,' said Nellie. 'What if we fall off?'

Jay chuckled. 'It's just a word, just a name. When the place was first bought, them there cottages were probably on the edge of Willows land, but it's been expanded since them days.'

'Not by my uncle, I take it?'

'No. He ... er ... he lived a different life, miss. Nice chap, never upset anybody, but he didn't care about Willows. So it's all a bit on the run-down side. I do my best – I'm the jack-of-all-trades, and my wife's the jill. Funnily enough, Gill's her name. Gillian when she goes to Buckingham Palace, but– No, she doesn't go to any palace, I'm pulling your leg. Any road, enjoy the scenery. You'll miss your river, but you'll gain the countryside.'

When they crossed the ring road, the climb became slightly more serious. They left behind shops, brick-built houses and signs of movement until they reached a place where there were stone houses on one side, fields on the other. 'Look at the trees,' Eileen sighed.

'Yes. Wood and leaves.' Nellie was trying hard not to be impressed. 'What's behind the long wall?' she asked.

'Ora et labore,' Jay replied. 'Pray and work. It's a school for Church of England scholars.'

'Heathens,' Nellie sighed. 'We couldn't send her there. At least they're not all Protestants where she is now.'

They took a left fork and soon they were in real countryside. The route was interrupted from time to time by clusters of stone cottages, while the odd farmhouse sat in the distance. Cows and horses peered over hedges as if passing comment on the noise of the internal combustion engine, while bales of hay waited to be taken inside for the winter.

'This is Willows Edge,' Jay announced. 'Don't blink, or you'll miss it. The house with GVI and the post box in the wall is Elsie's. She's also in charge of making sure nobody shows a light while the war's on. Elsie seems to be in charge of most things round here. She volunteers herself for anything and everything.'

'We'll have to see about that,' Nellie whispered to her daughter. 'Nobody organizes me.'

'Shut up, Mam.'

Jay was now driving up a narrow, unpaved lane. He stopped and pointed out the farm. 'This is the main farm, also known as Willows Home Farm. You have others, but they are leased out to tenant farmers who pay you rent. The home farm maintains the estate, selling produce, cattle and so forth. Neil Dyson and his wife Jean live there. They have two daughters, Stella and Patty. Neil was born in that house, took over from his dad. Very decent people, do anything for anybody, they would. But he might go sooner or later. Army, I reckon, though he won't be called up yet, because he's turned forty.'

At last, Hilda spoke. 'This is a large leap for an ironer in a Chinese laundry. I seem to be going from a room twelve by twelve to an area that defies measurement. It's a lot to take in.' She owned several farms. Why had she not been warned about owning several farms?

Jay inclined his head. 'Too true. Had things not gone the way they did, you and your mam and dad would have been here already, and you'd be used to it. But you can depend on me and Gill, on Neil and his wife, and on those who don't get called up. After that, it'll be all women, anyway. Land Army, so I hear. Mostly females. I'll have to go soon enough. If Neil gets the call, my Gill will probably move in with Jean, and that will free up the gatehouse for the duration.'

They reached the aforementioned gatehouse, and Eileen sighed. 'Ooh, that's lovely, Mam. Built of stone, and leaded windows, too.' Then her attention was grabbed by the main building. 'Jesus,' she breathed. 'And look at all the willow trees.'

'There have to be six willows positioned like that,' Jay said. 'If anything happens to a tree, we need to get a new one straight away, or the crops will fail and we'll have no luck with cattle. This is where we breed the county's best cows and bulls; we win prizes. So we take no chances, and look after the willows. My job would be easier without them, because I cut the lawns, but there you have it. The willows stay.'

'I like them,' Hilda said. 'But I don't have to look after the grass, and I expect the lawn underneath all those weepers doesn't thrive.' She turned in her seat and addressed her neighbours. 'Your boys could use them as tents or dens.'

'They like kiddies.' Jay grinned. 'I know it's a load of old wives' rubbish, but they seem to whisper when children play under the branches. Now, the stables are at the back, between the house and Home Farm, and I reckon come spring we'll be ploughing with horses. I'll show you the rotation table, Miss Pickavance. With it being war, we won't have much left fallow – just enough for the stock. Neil and Keith will keep you in the picture. Fuel for tractors will be rationed, which is why you'll need to depend on your horses.'

Hilda hadn't yet met the agent, but her head

was already full of stuff that was foreign to her. She tried to imagine how night would be here. There was probably no gas at this distance from town, certainly no electricity. It would be all oil lamps, candles, and wood-burning stoves.

Scotland Road was a long way from perfect, but it wasn't isolated. Scotland Road would be a target for Germans who might drift a short way east; Willows would be attacked only if a pilot needed to offload his bombs in order to retain sufficient fuel to reach home. The odds were in favour of the move.

The house was big, but not massive. Water was heated by a back boiler, and there was an indoor bathroom that served four large enough bedrooms. Downstairs, there were two sitting rooms, one of which was named a morning room, so Nellie immediately christened the larger of the two 'the afternoon room'. There was also a dining room and a large kitchen. Any decay was not noticed by the three incomers, who were used to conditions infinitely worse than these. 'I'm scared,' Hilda whispered to Nellie.

'Aye, it's a big thing, isn't it? A different life, that's for sure. Safety's a big bonus, though. But then there's Mel.'

'She won't come.' It was not a question.

'Says she's going to try to get digs in Crosby, somewhere near the school.'

'I'll pay,' said Hilda.

'No need. She'll be classed as an evacuee with any luck, so they'll get paid by the government. Eileen'll miss her. So will I. And the lads are nothing but trouble. Do you realize what you're taking on, Hilda?'

Jay had led Eileen outside to look at the stables, so the other two women could now talk in private.

Hilda nodded, a glint in her eye. 'I know I'm just an ironer, Nellie, but I had a fairly decent education at Miss Millichamp's academy. I'll be their teacher to start with, then we'll look for schools.'

Nellie sighed. 'So, we're doing it, then?'

'I'm not leaving your children to die. You lost a good man in the previous conflict, and I believe poor Eileen's husband was killed by half a ton of falling cargo. Those boys of yours may be out of hand, but so is every child in Rachel Street. Nellie, I am putting my foot down for once in my life. You're coming.'

So it seemed to be settled before the agent even put in an appearance.

Nellie and Eileen stayed in the morning room while Hilda had her meeting with Keith Greenhalgh. It lasted just about half an hour, allowing a further half-hour for tea with scones made that morning by Jean Dyson and served very ably by Jay, who made an excellent cup of tea. Afterwards, the visitors were plied with more scones and bread, cabbages, tomatoes, home-grown potatoes, carrots and swedes. 'Take them home,' Jay told them. 'Give your kiddies a taste of food straight from the soil. And here's some butter from the best cows in Lancashire. You'll be back,' he said, winking at Nellie. 'They'll all be safer and better fed.'

'Except for my Mel,' Eileen sighed.

Nellie, too, was concerned about her granddaughter. She was pretty, far too pretty not to be a worry. Already, men and boys stared at her in the street, and she was much too young to be away from her family. Yet they could not, dared not, interfere with her education. She had been given a chance that was unheard of in the streets that flanked Scotland Road. And there was something about Mel that spoke of determination and single-mindedness. 'We can't force her, Eileen. She's set her heart on Cambridge, and she'll get there. It would be wrong if Hitler ruined her education.'

'Yes, but she has to come to us in the holidays.'

'She will. She might be a high flyer, but she'll not neglect you, because her mam's always been her world.'

They began the journey homeward. The days were shortening, and Hilda found herself worrying once again about the countryside and its blackness. Yet she had inherited a beautiful house, an immense acreage, several farms, and the responsibility that went along with all that. The row of houses on the Edge needed to be made waterproof for the winter, as did some parts of the main house. According to Keith Greenhalgh, the home farm was in good order, but Hilda might be responsible for some of the patching up required by the farms occupied by paying tenants. 'I won't know where to start,' she said as they made the easier journey down from the moor.

'But Keith and I do,' Jay said. 'Once you've sorted out the money, we can go from there. You won't need to do much.'

Hilda disagreed. 'I'm determined to learn,' she

said. 'I've no intention of taking this lightly. I want to know about animals and ploughing and planting and–'

Jay laughed. 'Hang on, Miss Pickavance, or you'll have us all out of work before this war kicks off.'

They heard a few sirens as they made their way back to Liverpool. All these practices might well mean that no one would react when real bombardment threatened, because it was a bit like the boy who cried wolf.

The three women had enjoyed a taste of fresh, clean air, and they began to notice how much dirtier town life was. They were sleepy, too, just as they often were after a rare day in Southport. Clean air made a person lively, and liveliness made a person tired. It was probably the way humanity was meant to be, living in freshness, and sleeping well at night.

This time, Jay drove down the dock road, because he had never seen it before. Even so late in the day, men were working hard to unload cargo and bring in for storage as much as they could, especially where foodstuffs were concerned. Sea routes would be threatened for both Royal and merchant navies. Men's lives could not be risked for the sake of a few bananas and pineapples – even molasses would be scarce, so every effort to stock up was being made. 'You can't stop here, Miss Pickavance,' Jay said. 'This lot will be a prime target, so you have to move inland. I mean, the Germans would be daft if they didn't go for these docks.'

'I know.' She sighed. She was an heiress. Very

suddenly, she had become a person of standing. And she didn't know how to feel about that. Until now, Hilda had owned nothing beyond household goods and clothing. Money left after the deaths of her parents was salted away against her old age. 'How many farms are there?' she asked.

'Only four, not counting the home farm.'

Only four. Four roofs, four families, four lots of rainwater goods, walls, doors, windows. 'Tell Keith I want to know everything about the condition of those farmhouses. I'll need written reports, and I do hope I'm not being a nuisance, Jay. So much to learn, you see.'

What Jay saw was a good woman who took duty seriously, probably too seriously. He grinned. 'It'll be a pleasure, Miss Pickavance.' How far removed she was from the expectations of Neil Dyson. Keith had told Jay about the 'all lipstick and shoes' description delivered by the home farm manager. There was little of the Chanel No.5 about Hilda Pickavance, but there was a fine business head just waiting to become informed. Yes, she would make a good fist of it. If she failed at anything, it wouldn't be for want of trying.

'And if you would kindly ask the people in Willows Edge whether they have been approached by the authorities with regard to evacuation, I'd be grateful. At the farms, too, please. As you have seen for yourself, the children in this area are perilously near to a busy dock system.'

'Certainly.' He dropped them off, smiling as he watched them distributing fruit and vegetables from the boot of the car. It was a long way home, but for Miss Pickavance the journey would be much, much further. She was, in his opinion, an excellent and genteel woman. Qualities such as hers were much needed in times such as these. Adolf had better hang on to his hat. With people like this about, Britain would not roll over easily.

Mel came downstairs to meet Gran. 'Where's Mam?' she asked.

'With Miss Pickavance. She's borrowing clothes so she can go to Crosby and look where you'll be staying. What have you done with your brothers?'

Mel shrugged. 'The hellions were not containable, and I have maths homework. They're probably chasing molasses up the dock road, or stealing from the late shop. What happened, Gran?'

Nellie told her granddaughter about the day's adventure. She spoke of acres of undulating land, beautiful greens, dry stone walls and pretty little houses, also of stone. Miss Pickavance was an extremely rich woman, and she intended to shelter as many children as possible from these mean streets. Nellie spoke about the willow trees and how they had to be placed, about Jay, their driver, and Keith Greenhalgh, who was the steward, or the agent, or some such fancy thing. 'It's out in the wilds, Mel. The sort of place where you could stick one of the poor folk with TB and watch while the disease got blown out of them. There's horses, pigs, sheep, chickens and goats. Oh, and prize-winning cattle. And orchards, and field after field of veg. It was a lot to take in, because we only stopped a couple of hours. Listen, when your mam comes home in a minute,

Miss Pickavance wants a quick word with you.'

'Right.' Mel sat down. 'Gran?'

'Yes, love?'

'What'll happen to our house? This house?'

Nellie parked herself next to her favourite person. 'We'll have to let it go.'

'So ... I'll have no home?'

Nellie closed her eyes against the pain that came with war. 'Your home will be a very grand and proper house north of Bolton. It has a back boiler and its own bathroom, mile after mile of land, a car, horses and tractors. That's where your mother and I will be, so that's your new address.'

'But what about here? I mean, I know my school's in Crosby, but this is home.'

'And you're not ashamed. I know you're not.'

Mel lifted her chin in a gesture of defiance known to everyone in this house and in several households further afield. 'Look, Gran. There are girls – and boys for that matter – all over Crosby and Blundellsands who've been to prep schools and crammers, and they still didn't get a place. I'm living proof that a person who doesn't have her own pony, a grand piano, and a twenty-roomed house on Merrilocks Road can still have the brains, the fire and the belly required to make it all the way up to Oxbridge. I'm a pioneer. And when I'm a don, or whatever, I shall still come back here and show them what can be done.'

Nellie blinked the wetness from her eyes. Mel was one in a million, and she was so proud of this granddaughter that she felt she might burst. 'But we can't pay rent on a house we're not using, love. And you mustn't live down here. That's the whole point in what we're doing – this is going to be a battle zone. Me and your mam are taking the hellions, as you call them, miles away, but we can't take you, because of the school. You could go to Crosby, which might be a bit safer, but you can't live here. So you come with us, or it's Crosby.'

'Crosby.'

'There you go, then. Now, get across and see Miss Pickavance, and tell your mam to get back here, because she's three sons missing.'

Hilda was pleased with herself. She'd found a nice grey suit, a white blouse and a pair of decent shoes for Eileen. Eileen wanted to make an impression, and Hilda understood, since she, too, had lived for many years among grime, destitution and hopelessness. If Mel was going to spend the duration in a doctor's house, her mother wanted to feel comfortable in the presence of company that probably considered itself to be elevated.

As Eileen left the house, her daughter entered.

'Well,' said Hilda while the girl sat down. 'So you're going to live in Crosby?'

'Yes, Miss Pickavance.'

'Then we can help each other.'

'Really?'

Hilda expressed the opinion that most raids would happen during the hours of darkness. 'If you can, and only if it's safe, try to let me know what's going on. I shall pay you, of course, but–'

'I don't want paying, Miss Pickavance.'

Hilda held up a hand. 'Stop the nonsense, Mel. All your friends will have spending money, and you won't.'

The famous chin came up. 'I shall do a paper round.'

'I'm sure you will. But come here when you can and look at my house in daylight. Write to me. Tell me about ... everything.'

'Even the bad stuff?'

'Yes, of course.'

From that moment, these two understood one another completely. They shared a common sense, intelligence and a terrible hunger for knowledge. Mel was to have a key to Hilda's house, and she would write a letter each week to let her benefactor know what was happening in Liverpool, and she must write the truth, or as much of the truth as she could discover. 'I won't let you down,' she said. 'Unless it's all beyond me.'

'I know.' Hilda stood up. 'So, that's that.'

Yes, that was that. Nellie, Eileen and her three boys would be living at Willows. Soon, other needful children might be plucked from these streets and from their families, but Hilda was depending on the co-operation of tenant farmers and people who lived at Willows Edge. For now, she had to wait. Like many others, she hoped that Hitler, too, was playing a waiting game.

Three

Eileen looked wonderful. In a slate grey skirt and jacket donated to the cause by Hilda Pickavance, she was elegance personified. Nellie looked at her daughter, saw what might have been, then turned away to attend to her pan of scouse. Eileen should have had a chance in life, because she was beautiful, and the white blouse, good shoes and leather bag served only to underline what had already been there. No fashion house had created the bone structure, the natural poise, the grace of Eileen Watson. She was beautiful inside, too, because she was a good, clever woman who should have received a better education. Well, she was good and clever till she ran out of patience–

'Mam?'

Nellie stopped stirring the stew. 'Yes?'

'How do I look in this lot?'

The older woman adjusted the expression in her eyes. 'Marvellous, queen.' She wouldn't cry, mustn't cry. 'I should have done more for you. After all, you were my one and only. I think God looked at you, saw perfection, and decided I'd had enough luck. You should have gone to a good school. I ought to have got you away from here so that you might have had a chance of something better than–'

'No, Mam. Our Mel will do it all. But...' She sat down. 'Thirteen, Mam. It's not just an unlucky number – it's an awkward age. If this war goes on for four or five years, she'll be a young woman. And I won't have been here for her. I know it's three against one, except it's not against, but you know what I mean. The boys need me. She needs me. But I have to go with the majority.'

Nellie knew exactly what was going through her daughter's head. Already a beautiful girl, Mel could become a target for any hungry male, and, with blackouts, bombings and panics, a young female with no family behind her might get into all kinds of trouble. It felt as if they were planning for the protection of three sturdy lads, while leaving a vulnerable, academically gifted girl to the vagaries of chance.

'Oh, Mam. Could Hitler not have waited a few years?'

Nellie nodded thoughtfully. In the house belonging to the Bingley family, there was a boy the same age as Mel. Gloria Bingley had a twin brother and he, too, would be growing up. A cold sweat played up and down the length of her spine. She remembered her own teenage years, the power of that first surge of hormones. 'Eileen?'

'What?'

'I'll take the boys to Willows. You stay and mind Mel.'

Eileen's jaw dropped for a moment. Had her beloved mother gone mad? Philip, Rob and Bertie were almost beyond retrieval, and they hadn't yet reached the terrible teen years. Quite frequently, it took all three female members of the household to find them, as they had no sense of time, no sense of much, in fact. They ran for illegal bookies, helped fence stuff stolen from the docks, were involved directly or peripherally with most minor crimes that took place in the Cazneau Street and Scotland Road areas of Liverpool, and were completely out of hand on a regular basis. They were noisy, naughty, disobedient and irreverent. 'Mam, you can't do it.'

'I can and I will. You just watch me. And there's a fair bit more to Hilda Pickavance than any of us thought.' There was more to Nellie's Eileen, too. She'd read all the classics, had educated herself to a high standard...

Eileen sighed. 'This house will be dangerous whether there are two of us or six of us living in it.'

Nellie had thought about that, too. Eileen cleaned for a Miss Morrison in Blundellsands. Miss Morrison was growing frail. With only herself and Mel to care for, Eileen might volunteer to help the elderly lady and take shelter in lieu of pay. Mel could walk to school, and Eileen would be living near to all the houses she cleaned. 'I know you're meeting Mel outside Merchants at four o'clock, but that doesn't stop you going to talk to Miss Morrison first, eh? I mean, you've nothing to lose and everything to gain.'

'But Mam–'

'But nothing. There are men up at Willows, and there are no docks, no shops, no bookies. I may not know them, but I reckon Jay from the gatehouse, that Neil from Willows Home Farm and Keith will be able to handle our three rogues. Ask yourself this, Eileen. Can you leave her? Can you walk away from that girl?'

'Oh, Mam. The boys'll kill you. They're too much. We should offer them to the government as weaponry.'

'Look, I'll have help. They can run wild where there's no damage to be done. And it'll be all hands on deck when the show kicks off, because young ones will do the work of men, men who'll be off fighting the bloody Germans.'

It was a dilemma. Eileen could stay behind with her daughter, and might save that daughter from any potential mishaps. In doing that, she could be signing her own mother's death warrant, because the three boys were hard to handle. But Mel needed looking after. She was not a parcel to be passed over for the duration, something that could be picked up from Lost Property after the war had run its course. 'Hilda's going to run a little school at the big house. How on earth will she cope with our Albert?' Albert, usually named Bertie, was the one who had stolen the horse.

'Hilda could just surprise us all yet,' replied Nellie. 'She might not have lived our life, but she's been in these parts for long enough to know what goes on. With a cane, a blackboard and a bit of chalk, she'll come into her own, I reckon. There's a streak in her, Eileen. It's something I've seen in our Mel, and I think it's called bloody-mindedness. Listen to me. Give it a try. If we can't manage, I'll let you know. Anyway, you have to speak to Miss Morrison first. Let's not make the horse jump before we've got to the hurdle, eh? Save your energy for later.'

A subdued and thoughtful Eileen Watson found herself wandering the streets of Crosby that afternoon. This, the main village, had wonderful shops, thatched cottages and pleasant, dignified people. She didn't notice the men who stared at her, failed to realize that she was causing quite a stir in Hilda's suit, blouse and shoes. But with only two hours to spare before collecting Mel, she set off up Manor Road towards the truly select houses. On St Michael's Road, she opened a gate, walked up the path, and inserted her key in the door of Miss Morrison's detached residence.

The old lady was happy but surprised to see her cleaner. 'Have I got my days wrong again?' she asked. 'I think I'm getting worse in the memory department.'

'No, Miss Morrison.' Invited to sit, she placed herself opposite her employer and laid before her the problem concerning Mel, the school, evacuation and safety. 'I'm sure Dr and Mrs Bingley are decent people. I know he's your doctor, and he's a nice man. But my Mel's thirteen and nearly forty in the head. You see, Miss Morrison, she could be seventeen or so when the war's over. I can't take her to the middle of Lancashire, because they gave her a scholarship at Merchants, and she needs to see it through. All I want is my children to be safe. If the boys are running about on a farm, I can rest easy. Mel's different, ahead of her time, very attractive–'

'Like you, then.'

'Younger, Miss Morrison. I don't want her head turned. She can be stubborn. I need to keep hold of her, because her growing up to adulthood has already started.'

Frances Morrison inclined her head. 'We've all

been young, dear. Now, I suppose you want somewhere for you and Mel, because we're all sure that Scotland Road will be less than safe. It's too near the city and too close to shipping. The answer is yes, since I'm no longer fit to be alone all the time. And a bit of life in the house will do no harm. Take the two bedrooms at the back, dear. Mine is at the front, as you know, and the one next to mine is small.'

Eileen grinned. 'It's bigger than the one she has at the moment.' This was a lovely house. It had electric lighting, a proper cooker, a nice kitchen, gardens, a hall... 'Thank you, Miss Morrison.'

The old lady's eyes twinkled. 'Er ... if you wish to be diplomatic, I don't mind if you tell the Bingleys that I invited you to stay here. He knows I now need a nurse once a day, so he'll understand that I don't wish to be alone at nights. In fact, it won't be a lie, since you didn't ask directly.'

Eileen explained that the move could not take place until the boys and her mother had left for the countryside. She made tea and sandwiches for Miss Morrison before going off to meet Mel.

As she reached Liverpool Road, a thought occurred. She hadn't consulted Mel. The girl was at the age when she considered, quite rightly, that she should have some input in decisions that impacted on her life. Oh dear. Everything had moved along at such a pace today that Eileen had failed to allow herself time for thought. War did this. War made people jump ahead without thinking. Mel was almost a woman. The area in which she lived made for early maturation, because kids who lived in poverty needed to grow physically and mentally in order to survive. Her academic superiority had also added to her development, and she was far wiser and abler than most of her peers.

Yet when Eileen met her daughter outside the gates of Merchants, the news was accepted with joy. Mel would have her mother, her own larger room, and an electric reading lamp. 'Great,' she cried. 'I'll still be able to visit my friends, but my best friend will be living with me. You, Mam. You're my best friend.'

It was at times like this that Eileen felt privileged. Mel was grounded. She knew what she wanted, what she needed, what she owed. All around her on a daily basis she saw girls from backgrounds that were rich in money and life-style. She displayed no envy and no desire to imitate what she saw. An almost inborn sense of manners, of how to behave in a multiplicity of circumstances, meant that Mel seldom felt out of place. She was already a citizen of the world and, to prove it, she spoke several languages.

Mel smiled at her mother. She had never brought friends home, because she could not imagine them accepting her way of life even though she accepted theirs. Yes, the divide existed, but she would straddle it. A canyon stretching from Liverpool to Cambridge might have been judged impassable by most, but Mel was the brightest girl in her class. She knew it, the school knew it, and her classmates were acutely aware of it. She had tamed the lion named Merchants; Cambridge would be just one more pussy cat. Perhaps a Bengal tigress, but this girl would have it eating out of her hand.

'Mel?'
'What?'
'We still have to go and see the Bingleys, don't we?'
'Yes, Mam. We do.'

Gloria wasn't here, as she had stayed behind for music lessons. Somewhere down the road, the sound of a cat being tortured would be inflicted on other people's ears, and that was fine in Dr Thomas Bingley's book. Gloria, like her mother, was an un-pretty plodder. Marianne Bingley's looks had faded rapidly after marriage, and she was now a mouse, all corrugated brown hair, light brown skin and pale eyes. At least the eyes weren't brown, but Tom wasn't the sort of man to be grateful for small mercies. Her cooking was tolerable, but unimaginative, and he thanked whichever deity was in charge that Marie wasn't learning the violin alongside their daughter.

Two of them today, then. The mother of Mel Watson was easily as beautiful as the child, so he was in doubly responsive mode. Later, he would probably make use of his wife, but in the dark. Until now, the body he had pounded had been a substitute for Mel; now, it might change identity, and he was glad of that, since he hated to think of himself as a paedophile. Marie looked even plainer today, as would any dandelion in a bed of rare orchids.

Marie smiled, just as she always did. She poured tea, handed out sandwiches and cakes, all the time wondering why the hell she stayed. She had been a good match, had brought money into the marriage, and the house on St Andrew's Road was not mortgaged. But he wasn't interested in her. Every time Gloria's friend came to the house, Tom wanted sex. It wasn't love-making; it was masturbation with a partner.

And now, here came the mother. The accent was there, broadened vowels, confused consonants, participles jumping into places that ought to have been claimed by verbs. She 'been' somewhere, she 'done' something, yet Tom hung on every syllable, even when a T bore traces of S, when D collided with a different T. As she settled and the nervousness decreased, Eileen Watson's English improved rapidly. It seemed that she had two tongues; one for the place of her origin, another for the rest of the world. She was well read...

Yes, the older of the two guests was a long way removed from stupid. Physically, the woman was ethereal, like some Victorian heroine who had survived a slight decline. Her words cracked the facade, but failed to shatter the image. That such physical perfection should be visited on a product of the slums was sad. It would be of little use unless Eileen Watson chose to sell herself to sailors, Marie thought.

But the daughter... Marie's eyes moved left and settled on the younger wraith. Whenever seated next to this one, poor Gloria looked like a bag of bricks. Not only did she trail in the wake of the creature when it came to physical attributes, but Mel was also an out-and-out winner in the academic stakes. She seemed to float ahead of the work, as if she took extra lessons, yet that could not possibly be the case. But worse by far than all that was the fact that Mel knew what was happening. The mother seemed unaware, but the daughter awarded Tom sly glances and pretty little smiles. Oh yes, she knew how to work the oversexed creature to which Marie had fastened herself.

'Marie?'

She looked at her husband. 'Yes?'

'A fresh pot of tea, perhaps?'

The smile remained in situ. The urge to break the teapot against his skull had to be carefully denied, because Marianne Bingley was a deliberately good wife. She was a good wife into whose bank account went every penny she could salvage from housekeeping. Her running-away money was safe, but she had to wait until her children were grown. Like the obedient soul she portrayed, she asked the visitors whether they might prefer coffee, and would they like a slice of Madeira.

In the kitchen, Marie Bingley splashed cold water on heated cheeks. The girl would not be living here, and that was the good news. But the bad news outweighed it, since both mother and daughter intended to settle for the duration in St Michael's Road, which was well within walking distance of this house. Miss Frances Morrison's health would now become of prime concern to Dr Tom Bingley, and Marie's anger, damped down for so long that it seemed to have turned to black ice, suddenly made her stomach ache.

She returned with fresh tea, watched her husband's eyes travelling over the bodies of two unbelievably beautiful females. Her digestive system continued in overdrive, and she excused herself rather suddenly. After vomiting in the downstairs half-bathroom, she rinsed the taste from her mouth, washed her husband from her mind. Because this was the day on which the worm would turn. There would be no healthy argument, no true fight. But from this very night, she would move herself into the fourth bedroom. The twins would notice, but the price she had been paying for peace in this house was suddenly too high. 'He will not touch you again,' she promised the plain, wholesome face in the mirror. If he wanted relief, he could find it elsewhere.

When the visitors had left, Marie forced herself to be brave before the children returned from music and chess. 'Say one word, and I shall probably kill you, Tom.' The tone was even, almost monotonous. She inhaled, closed her eyes against the sight of his shocked face, then allowed it all to pour out of her like more vomit, but without the retching. 'I'll be moving into the spare room,' she said. 'It has taken me years to work my way up to this, so try listening for once. You almost ate Eileen and Mel Watson while they were here – after undressing them with your eyes, of course. That would have impinged on me, as you would have used me later to relieve yourself of sexual tension. So I advise you to find someone else to tolerate your sad, selfish bedroom activities.'

'What the hell–' he attempted to begin.

'Hell is the right word. You're hopeless. Now, sleeping arrangements aside, life continues the same. When Gloria and Peter leave, I leave. My father has willed his house to me, so I shall not be homeless in the long term. He will take me in if he's still alive, and when he dies everything comes to me, so I am safe. Meanwhile, we keep things on an even keel for the children, and for the sake of local society.'

Tom stared at her. In fourteen years of marriage, she had never strung so many words together in one speech. Life had wobbled on its fulcrum, had shifted because of a force he had never before recognized. As a result, he suddenly felt insecure, undermined and slightly afraid. She was his wife, but she was a creature far stronger than the dull, quiet woman with whom he had lived for all this time. 'I have rights,' he said.

'So do I. What happens in our bed isn't love, isn't even sex. It's rape. You come upstairs with your hormones rampaging for Mel Watson. You give me no consideration – not even a kiss, and scarcely a word. I just lie there in pain while you make noises like a sick gorilla. Not one recognizable syllable do you utter. You were never much of a lover, but you have become a bloody rapist. So bugger off and leave me be.'

The door slammed in her wake. She never swore. She always did exactly what was asked or expected of her. The door opened for a split second. 'Oh, and the girl plays you like a fish on her hook. Stick to the mother, or you'll be in jail. I'll put you there myself.' The door crashed home for a second time.

Tom dropped into his favourite wing chair. What was it his father had said? Something about allowing a woman to win, and about allowing her to know she had won? All the time, Marie had realized that he needed sex whenever stimulated by someone other than her. Well, what did she expect? There was nothing desirable about her. She was frumpy, asexual and boring. Yet he was suddenly uncomfortable in his own skin. Was he useless in bed? Certainly not. He was an attractive man who needed a beautiful woman. Marie was not beautiful, but Eileen Watson certainly was.

The evening meal was even quieter than normal that night. Marie topped up her wine glass three times, leaving too little for her husband, who had to make do with water when his own glass ran dry. He chewed his way through lamb cutlets with mint sauce, carrots and sauté potatoes, and waited for his wife to clear away in preparation for a pudding. But she announced that there would be none tonight, and they had better get used to that, as there was a war on. She would be joining the Women's Voluntary Service, so people in this house had better buck up, clear up and wash up. After this undecorated announcement, she left the room and went upstairs.

'Is there something wrong?' Gloria asked.

Tom had his answer prepared. 'Your mother hasn't been sleeping well. She's going to try the spare room.'

'But Mel might need that, Daddy.'

'No. She'll be staying elsewhere.'

Peter was audibly disappointed. 'She's fun,' he grumbled. 'I'll be stuck here with Gloria in excelsis. I was looking forward to having a bit of life in the house for a change.'

Tom studied his children, realizing that he seldom looked closely at them. Gloria, like her mother, promised to be a brownish person with a dumpy, clumsy frame and no outstanding features. Had there been no money in the family, she couldn't have gone to Merchants Girls, because she would not have gained the marks required in order for one of the few bequeathed bursaries to be awarded to her. The only person in whose company Gloria became animated was Mel Watson, who owned life and brains sufficient for several. Unselfish for a second or two, Tom felt sorry for his daughter. She might've come out of herself had Mel been stationed here for the duration of war.

Peter was a different kettle of fish. He had inherited his father's brown eyes, yet his hair remained fair. The boy had a well-developed body, clear skin, a handsome face and, like Mel, managed to shine at school. Academically sound and with a good memory for detail, Peter also did well in a variety of sports. This was definitely Tom's son. Unsure thus far of his goal, the older twin swung between medicine and a fierce desire to play cricket for Lancashire. Tom had explained that the two were not mutually exclusive, so Peter could well do either or both.

It was as if Marie had given birth to one carbon copy of Tom, and one of herself. There was no malice in Gloria, just as there'd been none in her mother until today. He shifted in his seat. Had that been malice, or had it been natural anger? He did not wish her any harm, but he could no longer manage to want her. Like many of her sex she was wise and intuitive, and she had worked out that whenever he engaged with her she was just the nearest piece of equipment designed to receive him.

The twins left the room, abandoning their father to sit among the debris of the last supper. He named the event thus because everything would be different from now on. Marie would provide for her family, of that he was in no doubt. But he imagined her in the WVS and knew that she would make a good member of such an organization. Determinedly English, and quietly furious with Germany, she would invest her all in any job required of her. As wife of a well-known doctor, she enjoyed the respect of local people.

He stood up and walked to the window. Again, he wished that he might join up and serve in some field hospital, but that privilege would be denied him, as he had two small afflictions: his feet needed supports under their arches, and he had a perforated left eardrum. A thought occurred. Peter was thirteen; if this show continued for five years, the boy would be conscripted. He had not inherited his father's flat feet, but his twin sister had. Peter was fit. Peter was going nowhere, Tom decided as he cleared the table. His wife seemed to be on strike.

The kitchen bore a strong relationship to a battle zone. Remnants of high tea shared with Mel Watson and her mother lingered on the drop-down middle section of one of a pair of green cupboards known as kitchenettes. Saucepans, abandoned on the hob of the gas cooker, had traces of the last supper encrusted on their interiors. A grill pan contained congealed lamb fat, while peelings from carrots and potatoes occupied a colander in the sink. This was what she faced each day, and more than once. Marie was a bloody good mother who always gave one hundred per cent of herself.

Tom rolled up his sleeves and set to. He did everything properly, dealing first with glassware and cutlery, changing water for crockery, soaking pans, wiping surfaces.

'Thank you, Tom.'

He turned. 'Marie.' He was a bad man, and she deserved better. 'Men don't realize what women cope with until they're stuck with it,' he said.

'I wouldn't have left the washing up.'

He looked at her; she looked at him. After shifting her clothes from the marital wardrobe and into the spare room, she was hot and sticky and her hair was corkscrewed. Tom, in a flowery apron and damp shirt, brought to mind some henpecked character from a Charlie Chaplin film. They burst out laughing simultaneously. He remembered the girl he had married; she thought about the laughter that had accompanied their courtship. 'I don't hate you,' she said quietly.

'Same here.'

'We'll just have to muddle through, Tom.'

'Yes. You, me and the armed forces. Life's rich tapestry, what?'

She nodded and began to dry dishes.

Eileen opened the door. 'Jesus, Mary and Joseph,' she mouthed.

'Hardly,' said the policeman who held one struggling boy in each hand.

'Philip, Rob and Bertie,' said the second, who was holding on to Rob. 'Jesus and his mam and dad never turned up, said they were busy. But these three were there. I believe you are the owner of these fine young criminals?'

Eileen stepped aside to allow the representatives of the law into her parlour. There was scarcely room for family in the tiny front room, so by the time the three offenders were lined up in front of the fireplace she and her mother were forced to stand with their backs to the opposite wall, the one to which Mel's bike was affixed, while the constables had to occupy the window area.

'What now?' Nellie asked resignedly. 'Have they burned down the Liver Buildings, sunk the Isle of Man ferry, or is it something serious like high treason?'

'There's a special school opening,' said one of the men. 'It's for young delinquents, and it's in the middle of Derbyshire. We can kill two – or three – birds with one stone, because it counts as evacuation as well. They won't be bombed, but they'll be knocked into shape. God knows they need it.'

'What have they done now?' Nellie repeated.

One of the pair delivered the opinion that what these three hadn't done would make a shorter list. The other attempted a reply. 'They've been running bets for Nobby Costigan, pinching fruit from the Jubilee Stores, and when we finally caught up with them they were trying to work out how to free a barrage balloon from its moorings with a penknife and an axe. The axe is being kept as evidence, but the penknife broke and one of these heroes chucked it in the river.'

'Why?' Eileen asked.

Philip answered. 'Because it was a no-good

knife. Couldn't cut butter.'

Eileen closed her eyes for a moment. 'Not the knife, soft lad. Why the balloon? Why did you try to free a balloon that's there to protect our city?'

'We wanted to see what would happen.' Bertie swallowed hard after this admission. 'If it got loose, like, and floated off.' His voice died of terror.

Nellie sighed deeply and turned her head in the direction of her daughter. 'Eileen, go and fetch Hilda. She can explain what's going to happen to these three.' She glared at the miscreants. They looked like gingerbread men cut from similar shapes in descending sizes. Each had brown hair, blue eyes, angelic features and a devilish attitude painted over by good looks and sweet smiles. Well, Bertie's would be sweet once his adult front teeth grew in properly.

Their grandmother continued to stare at them while Eileen was away. The three lads were more trouble than a gang of drunken Orangemen at a St Paddy's day party. They were wild, daft and short of several good hidings. But they weren't going to any school for delinquents, oh no. They were bad enough already without being taught more tricks by the rest of the criminal fraternity. A couple of years in juvenile jail, and they might well return with violin cases, funny hats and Chicago accents. 'They're going where I take them,' Nellie advised the constables. 'Not to some training camp for gangsters, thanks all the same.'

The policemen removed their helmets. 'One thing's sure, Mrs Kennedy. When Hitler starts playing with his big fireworks, there'll be looting.

A direct hit on a row of houses, and these three would be in like Flynn. They can't help themselves. Their dad would be ashamed.'

'There's nothing worth pinching,' Nellie told them. 'Most round here think soap's a luxury.'

'That's not the point. War's hard enough without having to keep an eye out for the Three Stooges. They need a firm hand.'

Hilda and Eileen squeezed their way into the house. 'Good evening,' said the former. 'I understand that you are on the brink of arresting these three young boys.'

Well, I wouldn't go as far as–' The first policeman stopped when his mate dug him sharply in the ribs. 'What?' he asked, rubbing his side.

'They and some others have to be removed.' Policeman number two assumed charge of the situation. 'Yes, they have to go.'

'I see.' Hilda folded her arms. 'Removed? Like a growth? Or three growths? Over my dead body, young man. They are going to no commune for the unsalvageable.'

Eileen and Nellie looked at each other. As suspected, there was more to Miss Hilda Pickavance than met the immediate eye of any beholder.

'And you'll take responsibility?'

'I shall. They will be in rural Lancashire, and I shall deal with their education. There will be no barrage balloons, no shops and no bookmakers for whom they might run. Their mother has told me of their behaviour. The whole family is deeply ashamed, but you have to understand that these two ladies are widows, and there is no male influence in the boys' lives.'

'Which is why they could do with a special school,' said Number Two.

Number One, still busy holding his ribs, simply nodded.

'They will be farming,' Hilda snapped. 'They will be providing food for the populace. Now, unless you want to place them in a cell tonight – and I advise strongly against that – I suggest you leave us to cope with this matter.'

The three boys watched in awe as the policemen left the scene. Miss Pickavance was absolutely brilliant. They grinned at each other, rejoicing in their good fortune. But their happiness was short-lived. As soon as the uniformed men had disappeared, they got both barrels. Mam would save them, wouldn't she? For once, Eileen remained rigidly unmoved.

'Get your night things and go to my house. There is a double bed in the front upstairs room, and you will sleep in it. Tomorrow, you'll blacklead my grate and clean all windows before and after school. If and when I go out, you will be supervised by your mother or your grandmother. You will eat when we decide, speak when we decide, breathe when allowed. You will go to school, but if you are late coming home, appropriate punishment will ensue.'

'En-what?' Six-year-old Bertie was struggling to keep up with all the posh talk.

'Follow,' snapped their nice, quiet, well-mannered neighbour. 'Every moment of your lives until we move to inner Lancashire will be supervised. You are not to be trusted. I am thoroughly ashamed of you.' She turned on her heel and walked out of the house.

Philip, at eleven, was the oldest of the gang. 'I'm not going to her house,' he announced, arms folded defiantly across his chest. 'I'm not.'

Rob, at nine, was similarly decided, but Bertie, who thought there might be cocoa across the street, ran upstairs to pick up sleepwear made by his mother out of a shirt that had belonged to his beloved father. He picked up similar items that were the property of his brothers before returning to the ground floor. 'I've got your nightshirts,' he told them.

Nellie fastened her eyes to Philip's. After a few seconds, the sheer weight of her personality forced him to avert his gaze. She moved on to the middle brother, and he endured her glacial stare for a fraction of a second. Hilda Pickavance had begged Nellie to accompany her into the countryside because she needed help with children. But Hilda could manage better than most, and this evening had proved that. 'Right,' she said to the three rapscallions. 'You can't be trusted, so your mam and I will take you to Miss Pickavance. It's that or the police station. Well?'

They chose *that*. After walking the three across the street, Nellie and Eileen waited until they heard Hilda's key turning in the lock when the boys had entered the house. 'Bloody hell,' Nellie whispered. 'Talk about hidden talents.'

Eileen waited until they were home. 'She's acting.'

'I know that.'

'She's being Miss Millichamp.'

'Miss Millie who?'

'Champ. Headmistress at her school. They didn't believe in caning young ladies, but Hilda said that sometimes she would rather have had the cane. So when you sent me to fetch her, she said she was going to do a Miss Millichamp. Miss Millichamp used to get so deeply disappointed that the girls would be in tears. Psychology, according to Hilda. See, she seems quiet and polite and all that, but underneath, she's just like the rest of us, only cleverer.'

Mel came downstairs. 'Armageddon again?' she asked.

Eileen nodded. 'Police. Something to do with a pound of apples and a barrage balloon.'

Mel decided not to ask for further clarification. 'Where are they?'

'With Miss Millichamp,' Eileen replied. 'She looks like Hilda Pickavance, but actually she's a Miss Millichamp. The cops wanted to send the boys to some sort of special school for bad lads, but Hilda stepped in. Wiped the floor with a couple of constables, then waded in on Rob and Philip. Bertie was all right, being the youngest.'

Mel grinned. 'Peaceful, isn't it?'

Nellie raised her head and looked into her granddaughter's eyes. 'For some, it's going to be too peaceful, love. Out there, we have unborns who'll never see the light of day, babes in prams who won't live to learn to walk. Loads of old people won't get the chance to die in their own beds, and every man who ships out of here will be a target.'

'Sorry, Gran.'

'In 1918, I never really believed it was over. I was

right. They just had a long rest, that's all. We've enjoyed what they call a pause in hostilities, because all our young men were dead or near-dead, so we had to grow a new lot. But as long as men are in charge, Mel, there'll be war. There's always some bugger trying to prove he can pee highest, run fastest and beat folk up. Like at school. Only this time, it's a bigger playground.' She left the room.

When Mel made to follow, Eileen stopped her. 'Leave her, girl. She'll be talking to your granddad. She always does when she's frightened – she prays to him like he's a saint.'

'Oh, Mam.'

'I know, love. I know.'

Four

Keith Greenhalgh was in the morning room at Willows trying to write to Miss Hilda Pickavance. He forced himself to stop chewing the pen and start shaping words. After all, he couldn't sit here forever daydreaming about a woman who was, for the present, out of reach. How old was he? Seventeen? No, he was forty-odd and counting, so he'd best get on with things.

Dear Miss Pickavance,

The four tenant farmers have not yet been approached by evacuation authorities, and they are each willing to take two children from Liverpool, preferably older ones, as their wives will be too busy for baby-minding. I am still discussing the situation with cottagers who live in Willows Edge, but there is one house empty, and you may want to bring a family; a mother with young children, perhaps.

He threw down the pen. Elsie Openshaw was being her usual pig-headed self. No, pigs were OK people; crocodile-headed was nearer the mark. Unprepared to accept the undeniable fact that 'her' cottage was not her actual property, she was standing firm and refusing to cooperate when it came to the placement of children.

The sight of Elsie Openshaw standing firm was not a pleasant one, as she was a woman of considerable size and, with her arms folded and her face set, looked about as inviting as a midwinter funeral tea. The cheerful flowered apron wrapped round her uncomely form lost any appeal it might have had as soon as it made contact with her body. The metal from which her curlers were made echoed the state of her mind. She was fixed, unbendable, and she intended to ensure that all her neighbours took a similar stance.

Your four tenanted farms are Cedars, Four Oaks, Pear Tree and Holly. So in reality you have five farms rather than four as mentioned in your letter. It occurred to me that I hadn't told you the names of those places, but your solicitors may well have. All are occupied by decent folk, and you will find them extremely

Yet again, he discarded his pen. The cottages on the Edge were also the property of the woman to whom he was attempting to write. Elsie Openshaw, a widow whose husband had died to escape her, Keith suspected, was allowed to stay on rent-free because of the years of labour her man had put in at Willows Home Farm. Did she not realize that she could be out on her ear if she remained intransigent? 'I am not afraid of you, you old witch,' he mumbled. The letter could wait; a more pressing piece of business required his attention. 'Why is it always me?' he asked no one at all, since he was alone. It was always him because he was agent and steward, so he had better shape up, buck up and prepare to put her back up.

He pulled on cap and coat, left the house, and began the walk down the lane towards Willows Edge, his own cottage, and the abode of Mrs Elsie Openshaw. She wanted sorting out. Her kids were long fled, yet all three of them sent money for her food and other necessities. If they didn't send money, she visited them, and they avoided that like the plague. She wasn't a woman; she was a bloody government.

Elsie had been a tartar all her life, and it was time somebody stood up to her. Keith, a mature, strong man, was not in fear of her. The sudden quickening of his pulse was connected to the business of being slightly older, wasn't it? No, it wasn't. He was scared to bloody death, and he had to have a showdown. Showdowns were not in his nature, but they were required occasionally.

For many years, Keith had lived near the harridan. No one ever answered her when she ranted, but everyone in the terrace talked behind her back. Some said it was a pity she'd not died instead of poor Bill, who had been eroded by hard work and nagging to a point where he could take no more. All said she was a nasty old witch, but who would dare to tackle her? He grinned. Something about the group he termed the Liverpool girls promised that life might change. He wished he could speak directly to Nellie Kennedy, ask her to bring a large, loud family to live in the empty cottage. He wished he might speak directly to her daughter, but the reason for that was a mile away from Elsie and her lashing tongue. He paused for a fraction of a second before passing Elsie's house. He would deal with her in a minute. Yes, he definitely would.

Keith entered his own house first and laid a fire to be lit later if needed. Evening came earlier now, and there was sometimes a chill in the air. Why did he keep seeing her face? Not since the death of his darling Annie Metcalfe of Bromley Cross had he looked with real desire at any woman. Annie's death, some twenty years earlier, had left a hole in him. She had been stricken with a kind of blood poisoning after suffering a burst appendix, and she had been his soulmate. Her photograph, in faded sepia, still took centre stage on the mantelpiece. They had never married...

Her name was Eileen, and she had three sons and one incredibly talented daughter. When alone with Eileen for a few precious seconds during the visit, he had fallen hook, line and sinker for a woman who spoke what was tantamount to a foreign language, who had difficult boys, the eyes of an angel and hair like gossamer silk. She was bloody gorgeous. He did not trust his feelings. This kind of stuff happened in daft books written by daft women for daft women. Yet he was persecuted by visions of her in his bed, his house, his life. He pictured her at the sink, saw himself creeping up behind her to fold her in his arms, pull back her hair, kiss her neck. He was daft. Love at first sight? Not again!

Keith Greenhalgh almost laughed out loud. Women found him handsome; he found women silly or nasty, like the old bat he would be visiting shortly. For sex and companionship, he had enjoyed a ten-year relationship with a childless woman whose husband did not quite satisfy her hunger. It was a good friendship, and there would be little acrimony should a parting of their ways occur. So he wasn't looking for anything shallow, was not looking for anything at all. It was the same with most aspects of life. 'Search for a lump hammer, a great huge article you've owned for years, and it's disappeared off the face of the earth. When you don't want it, you fall over it in the shed doorway,' he told Annie's photo.

But Eileen wasn't a lump hammer; Eileen had heart and soul in her eyes, a delicate, beautiful face, and a body that should be on cinema screens. He was glad she wasn't on cinema screens... What if she already had somebody? No. He'd overheard Nellie saying to Jay that Eileen steered clear because of her boys. Did he have a chance? Did he? He hadn't ached like this for years. 'I want her,' he said aloud. 'I want a bloody woman I don't even know. She talks funny, she's got terrible sons, and I bet she knows as much about estate management and farming as I know about delicate embroidery. I need my head examining.'

However, none of this was useful. He should take a short walk and impose himself on Elsie Openshaw, hag of this parish, self-appointed queen of all she surveyed, miserable old woman with a black heart, a face like a giant plate of stewed tripe, and her husband's teeth. She didn't like to waste anything, so she'd taken them from the mouth of a corpse, and had spent several years trying with a marked lack of success to break them in. She was horrible.

She opened her door before he had time to knock. As usual, she had been at the window keeping an eye on her territory. 'I'm coming in,' he said, trying not to recoil too obviously when brushing past her hugeness. That was a good name for her. Her Royal Hugeness. It should be patented and hung round her neck with a bit of rope. Or a garrotte. He walked through the small shop, once a parlour, into the kitchen-cum-living room. The house smelled unclean, like rancid butter, dirty cloth and old paper. He turned and faced her. 'I'm writing to the new owner of the estate,' he began. 'I have to give an account of everybody who lives round here.'

'Oh, aye? The Liverpool woman what's dad ran off with a cleaner?'

'Yes.' He bit back the words 'at least she cleaned'.

'And?' The upper teeth dropped again. For a split second, she looked like something that lived under a bridge to frighten billy goats. She was quick, though. The set was clicked back into position in a fraction of a trice. He'd seen better-looking gargoyles acting as rainwater goods outside mansions and the like.

'And people want you out. They daren't say it to your face, and they'll deny it if you ask, because they fear you. You're a bully, and your brain's smaller than your gob. Oh, and if anyone else complains about mail being interfered with, it'll be the police that provide the transport to shift you. Stop steaming things open. Stop poking about in parcels and putting new string round them. We're all on to you. Folk aren't as daft as you want them to be.'

She dropped into a chair, which complained loudly at the sudden assault. 'Who do you think you're talking to, Keith Greenhalgh?'

'You. I'm talking to you. You're in a rent-free cottage, and we need space for evacuees.'

She almost managed to fold her arms across an upper body the size of Brazil. 'So to keep me house, I have to take a bloody Scouser in?'

He shook his head. 'Not likely. I wouldn't put any child within a mile of you, Elsie Openshaw. Your own couldn't get away quickly enough. Young Daisy threw herself at that farmhand until he impregnated her. Everyone along here knows that. They know how you treated Bill and the kids, and they know first-hand how you treat your neighbours. If I told them you were leaving, they'd have a bonfire, but the guy would be large and female. Even the blackout wouldn't stop them celebrating seeing the back of you.' There, he had done it. A peaceable creature by nature, this was hardly his forte. He wasn't shaking. There was a chill in the air, that was all.

Her mouth opened and closed, Bill's teeth

shifting nervously in a cavern that threatened to inhale them, but no words emerged. A terrible fear visited her chest. Widows of long-serving farmhands were always housed. Sometimes, they had to share accommodation, but they were never thrown out. 'Can she change things, just like that?' she finally managed.

'She can. So can I. It's part of my job, Elsie. If any tenant, whether tied or rent-paying, makes life difficult for another or others, he or she will be given notice to leave. It's in every agreement signed by a resident.'

The woman gulped.

'Careful. You'll be having Bill's dentures for dinner.' Keith sat down. 'Two conditions. One, you clean this place up – it stinks. Two, you stop yapping about everything and everybody. Don't put people off when they think about taking a Liverpool child. Those kiddies live in a huge port, and there'll be ships, explosives and God alone knows what docked nearby. Sorry. Number three is the one I almost forgot. Leave the post alone, or I'll have you out of here so fast your curlers'll catch fire before you reach Willows Lane.'

Elsie struggled to her feet. 'I've just remembered, there's a letter for you.' She went off towards the front room, which was now her precious shop.

'Did you hear all I said?' he shouted.

'Yes.'

'And?'

She returned. 'Woman's writing,' she wheezed. 'From Liverpool.'

'Right.' He stared at her. Was she the full quid,

or was she a bent farthing? 'Elsie?'

'What?'

'Did you hear my conditions if you're going to stay here?'

She nodded, and her several chins wobbled, though not in harmony. It was as if they were fighting for space above a tight collar, and no one was winning. After a few seconds, the layers of blubber reached some sort of agreement and settled down, presumably to negotiate terms of peace. 'Clean up, shut up, put up, and leave the bloody mail alone,' she barked.

She was the full quid, then. 'And stop being nasty to people and about people. Some teeth of your own might be a good idea, and all. Those you took from poor Bill are fit to frighten horses.'

Outside once more, Keith tried to contain his excitement. The writing wasn't Hilda Pickavance's. Miss Pickavance used as near as damn it to copperplate. He couldn't imagine Nellie sitting down to write a shopping list, let alone a letter. It had to be from *her*. But he left it on the dresser while he brewed tea and lit the fire. Sometimes, a treat tasted sweeter if you had to wait for it. Her lettering on the envelope was clear, though this was not the hand of a formally educated person. Well, he wasn't educated. Anything he knew had been picked up long after his escape from the confines of school.

He opened the envelope carefully with the help of some obscure item attached to a penknife of many parts, including a tool that had never in its life managed to remove a stone from an equine hoof.

Dear Mr Greenhalgh,

I am writing to let you know that I shall be staying in Liverpool with my daughter, as she is too young to be left for any length of time. It must seem terrible, because my mother will be forced to cope with Philip (11), Robin (9) and Bertie, really Albert (7 if I let him live till Friday).

Please try to put these boys of mine to some sort of work. They are quick learners, but easily led astray, and they were in trouble with the police again very recently. The farms should be ideal, because work in the fields will use up their energy. I hope you aren't annoyed at my boldness in assuming too much in view of our brief acquaintance...

He put down the page and smiled. She might talk oddly, but she was well-read, by gum. That paragraph might have been penned by Austen herself. He hadn't been wrong; there was something special about Eileen Watson. But she wasn't coming. Sighing, he picked up the letter again.

our brief acquaintance, but will you please keep an eye on them, on my mother and on Hilda? Goodness, how many eyes does one man have? Also, I beg you to come or send someone whenever possible to bring me and my daughter over to Willows at weekends. I know that cannot happen every Friday, but I should like to spend time with my family. We hope to visit at half-term and at Christmas as long as we can overcome travelling difficulties and find someone to care for Miss Morrison, the lady with whom we shall be lodging.

Travelling difficulties? If he had to steal an armoured vehicle from an army base, he would do it and be damned. And she had written 'should' like to spend time with family. So this was the source of Mel's good brain, then. Like many born in the early years of the twentieth century, Eileen had experienced only a brief and unedifying brush with scholarship, but she had remedied that.

I walked down to the river earlier on. It is very busy. There is urgency in the movement of every man, and no one stops for a crafty smoke like they do when life is normal. Beyond trains and cranes and ships, I saw the sun and wondered why God was allowing it to shine at such a time.

The warehouses are said to be bulging with imports, though we cannot know exactly what, and they are under heavy guard. As well as police, soldiers and sailors are standing watch and many are armed. As the sun went down, the river was bright red and that made me shiver. I am sure you can guess the reason for my discomfort.

I enclose on another sheet the address of Miss Frances Morrison. She has a telephone and I have included the number in case you need to reach me in a hurry after we have all finished playing musical chairs. Thank you for your kindness. Please keep in touch if you have time, because I shall enjoy reading about my fine, healthy, country bumpkin boys.

Yours sincerely,
Eileen Watson.

Oh, God. He was almost in love. The paper was

thin and cheap, so he reused the envelope as protective custodian. 'She wrote to me, not to Jay. She knew him better, because he did the driving, but she chose me.' There had been a connection, a mutual attraction. More important, her humour was on show in the letter, and where there was humour, there was intellect. 'Eileen.' He tried the name for size and shape, rolled it from his tongue into the empty room. It seemed lonely out there by itself, so he paired it off with his own forename. 'They'll have me locked up,' he advised the crackling fire. 'I'll get put away for talking to the fireback. But there's no cure for this one.'

He stepped out of the kitchen into his back garden, fed his half-dozen friendly and inquisitive hens, picked some rhubarb for a crumble to be shared with the Dysons, and dead-headed a few flowers. A good enough housewife, Keith always helped his neighbours, since cooking for one was uneconomical and no fun. Jean baked his bread, so this tit-for-tat arrangement had been born long before Hitler decided to take over the world.

There was no treatment for this. It had been the same with little Annie Metcalfe of Bromley Cross. Little Annie had retained her full title, even after death, as there had been several Annes born that year, and the need to differentiate between them had birthed extended names. Even now, he could smell the sweet breath of an angel who had died in the sort of agony from which an animal would have been released within hours.

There was no mercy for gentle human souls, was there? He had never been unfaithful to his Annie.

What happened between him and Cora Appleyard was mechanical, automatic, almost akin to breathing. He was grateful to her, as was she to him, but there was little or no pillow talk, because their joinings imitated the behaviour of animals. They had a need, and they indulged it. Until now, his heart had been the property of a dead girl.

The letter to Miss Pickavance could wait until morning, but the scribe in him itched to reply to one Mrs Eileen Watson. She had word-painted a picture of blood on the Mersey; he would return the favour by describing the gentle beauty of rural Lancashire, though he would not go over the top. What had she said? Something about not assuming too much after so brief an acquaintance. 'And I'm sitting here with a daft grin on my face,' he said. 'But by heck, I'll drag that one up the Willows, even if she has to come kicking and screaming.' God, he was stupid.

Still laughing about the child who would be seven if Eileen allowed him to live until Friday, he toasted bread and scrambled a couple of eggs. A man who lived the country life had to keep his strength up. A cup of tea and a bit of music on the wireless, and he was set for the night. Keith Greenhalgh might be as mad as a frog in a box, but that was normal, since real love made a man crazy. He knew that. Because he'd been here before.

A flabbergasted Jean Dyson closed her mouth with a snap. She didn't believe what she had just heard, yet she must believe it. Neil had a chance. There was a possibility – even a probability – that his occupation might be judged essential and reserved, because somebody had to show the Land Army what was what, so many of England's farmers would be kept at home. 'Why?' she asked softly. 'Why volunteer? If you sit it out, you'll be too old to get called up.' There was no point in screaming at him. If she shouted, he would go and sit with his cows in the shippon.

'We got talking, me and Jay, and we decided it's what we want. There's no saying we'll be picked anyway, so don't start worrying yet. There's every chance we'll be psychologically unsuitable, or we won't get through training for one reason or another. Then, as you said, there's my age. If I volunteer, I'll be considered.'

She cleared the table and began to clatter supper pots on the counter. She should have been in bed at least an hour ago, but she'd started knitting and lost track of time. 'So you're down the pub playing pat-a-cake with Jay, and you both come home fighter pilots.' She poured hot water into the washing-up bowl. 'How drunk did you have to be to get off the ground? I know he's a daft beggar, but you should–'

'Stop it, love.'

'What was your fuel? Guinness or bitter?'

'Jeanie–'

'Don't you Jeanie me.' She waved a tea towel under his nose. 'Leave this house voluntarily, Neil Dyson, and you won't get back in. If you did get called up, you should have the sense to keep your feet planted on the ground. At sea, if the Germans don't get you, the water will. In the air, you'll become a ball of fire with two hundred bullets up your rear gunner. The army's the only lot with a small chance. I knew I'd married a daft so-and-so, but it takes the whole cream cracker, this does.'

'I've been reading, Jean, and–'

'Then stop bloody reading. You've two daughters upstairs. Don't you want to live for them?'

'Course I do. I don't want them raped by invaders either, don't want them shoved into some prison camp then on to a breeding programme because they look Aryan.'

'And?'

'It'll be fought in the air, Jean. They'll fly in to bomb, to drop troops, to invade. It's because of my children that I want to shoot the buggers out of the sky.' He didn't say the rest of it, because it would sound too soft and maudlin. In a way he didn't properly understand, he was keen to fight for the King. George VI had suffered enough through getting lumbered with a job he'd never wanted; now the poor chap had to come over all positive and determined, because a war had arrived to ice the cake for him. 'I want to serve my country,' was all Neil allowed himself to say.

'Oh aye? And growing cabbages and spuds isn't serving your country? What's the flaming matter with you? Somebody has to keep the home fires burning and the ovens filled. I'll be here ripping guts out of chickens and knee-deep in feathers while you go and save the world? Right.' She tore off her apron. 'That's it. You are manager of Willows Home Farm. I am not. I shall take the girls to my mam and dad's up Bury Road, seeing as they've got a couple of spare rooms. You can please your bloody self, but the farm will have no boss.' She stalked out of the room. After a few seconds, she reappeared briefly. 'This kitchen is shut due to illness. I am bloody sick of it. The farm is shut, too.'

He waited, tapping his fingers on the table, walking round the room a few times, drinking a small bottle of ale, glancing at headlines in an old newspaper. When the clock told him she'd been gone for twenty minutes, he followed her upstairs, undressed and slipped into the bed. 'Jeanie?'

'Bugger off.'

'Hit me, and I will.' He dragged her into his arms. 'Do you think I like the idea of some ugly, sweaty Kraut doing what I'm about to do? Would I want a Nazi general touching you like this, or like this?'

'Stop it.'

'You know you want me. You always want me.'

It was no use, she told herself resignedly. She was his happy plaything, and she loved him. When she got her breath back, she dug him in the ribs. 'Oi, you.'

'What?'

'Come back dead, and I'll kill you.'

'OK, love. I'll remember that.'

Jay Collins was rather less fortunate than his partner in drunken crime. He told his wife of his intentions regarding the air force before going out to fill the log basket. When he returned to the house, all the doors and windows were locked, and he was rendered homeless. This new circumstance was disconcerting, as he had enjoyed a roof over his head for all of his thirty-two years, so he waited to see what would happen next. What happened next was extremely damp and uncomfortable, because his wife opened an upper window of the gatehouse and poured a bucket of water on his head. The water was cold, and he moved away in case a repeat performance might be in the script.

'Gill?' he spluttered.

'They won't take Neil,' she yelled. 'He's well turned forty, and his eyes are funny. In case you haven't noticed, his arms need to grow longer so that he can read the newspaper properly. But they'll take you, because you're nobbut a handyman. Why don't you wait to be called up? You will be called up, because we've no kiddies, but why go now?'

'Because I want to choose what I do in the war.'

'Huh.' The window slammed.

'Gill?'

Nothing happened.

'Gill? Let me in.'

Nothing happened again. He considered his options, which were few. The idea of sitting outside and dying of pneumonia didn't appeal, even though it would make her sorry. He could break in, but she would kill him. Neil kept farmer's hours, in bed at nine and up and about by five except for one night a week – tonight – when he went to the pub and Jean took over morning duties on the following day. She still had to be up by five, so that was a nonstarter. Which left only the boss, who was a man of understanding and discretion, and therefore won hands down.

Jay, feeling a real idiot, jogged down the lane until he reached Willows Edge. He hammered on the door, and was almost overcome by relief when it opened. 'Thank God,' he said from the heart.

'Bloody hell in a handcart,' the boss exclaimed. 'Who got you dressed and ready? Neptune? Have you been paddling in Blackpool? Did you take your bucket and spade? Where's my stick of rock?'

Jay rushed to the fire. 'Don't start, Keith. I'm not in the mood. She threw me out. I can't break windows that are antiques, can I? Get that bloody kettle on, my bones are frozen and my teeth won't keep still.'

'This isn't like Gill. What happened to make her carry on like that?'

'Me and Neil happened. We were in the Red Lion, because it's Neil's night off, and we made a decision. We want to be fighter pilots. And we even went home early, but a man can't do right for doing wrong as far as Gill's concerned.'

Keith, doing a pale imitation of a saddened man, put the kettle to boil. 'On a scale of one to ten, how drunk were you when this decision made itself?'

'About seventeen. Put it this way – the landlord wouldn't let us play darts, and we both got lost on the way home, ended up in a cow shed just off Willows Lane. It was Neil's cow shed, so we got our bearings after that. Nice, aren't they?'

'Eh?'

'Cows. Very comforting. I'd never noticed that before.'

'Jay?'

'What?'

'Sit down and shut up. I'll find you a towel and some pyjamas.' Shaking his head slowly, Keith walked up the stairs. Hitler had a lot to answer for, and one of his first victims was downstairs, teeth chattering so hard that they threatened to break. Fighter pilots? Jay couldn't navigate marriage or his way home, while Neil had no chance. He'd been in the last war, Lancashire Fusiliers, so he'd already trained in the army, and if they did start taking older men they wouldn't want him as an airborne hero.

Keith came down, throwing a towel and some pyjamas at his visitor before airing his views. 'Neil and I were both in the Lancs Fusiliers,' he said. 'No way will a man our age get to train as a pilot. But you might. And if it's what you really want, go for it. She'll calm down. They take it as personal, as if you can't wait to get away. Gill thinks you don't love her any more.'

'I love the bones of that girl.'

'I know you do. She knows you do. But she's annoyed.'

Jay stared at his boss. 'I'd no idea,' he said sarcastically. 'I thought she was playing water fights or cleaning windows. I only went out for some wood, and she locked that house down like the Tower of bloody London. If they ever need somebody to mind the Crown Jewels, she's their man.'

'Gill's frightened.'

'And I'm not? We're all afeared, Keith. There'll be folk called up who don't want to go. Leading them in won't be easy, because their hearts aren't going to be in the job. I want to save Britain for the British, and I've always wanted to fly.'

'Pilots will die like bluebottles, lad. Exactly like flies. They'll fall to earth or into the sea as if they've been hit by a giant fly-swatter with a machine gun as backup. As soon as you take off in a Spitfire, it'll be nearer my God to thee in more ways than one.'

'I know.'

'So why?'

Jay shrugged. 'Because I have to.'

A few seconds strolled past. 'Then go to it. Neil knows he's too old. He can try lying about his age, but his eyes won't pass muster. I'll have a word or three with him tomorrow. Now, dry off and go to bed – back room. I've a letter to finish.'

'Thanks, boss.'

'One more thing.'

'Yes?'

Keith pondered for a while. 'I know it's none of my business, but get Gill to the doctor's, will you? I know it's not supposed to happen for her, but she's put a bit of weight on, and there's a little dark mark under both eyes. It may be nothing, but, before you volunteer, get a pregnancy test. Her hormones might be in a mess. I could be wrong, but better safe than sorry, eh? A woman's body knows it's pregnant almost from day one, a long time before the brain gets the message. You might find there were two of her chucking water.'

Jay's jaw moved south. 'Bloody hell.'

'Bloody hell is right. Now, stop dripping on my rug. A friend pegged that for me years ago.' He walked into the kitchen. A sudden desire to weep like a child was drowned by a cup of water. The tea was brewed, and he carried into the front room a pint pot filled with the steaming beverage.

Jay, pyjama-clad, was huddled over the fire. 'If she is, what shall I do?'

'Wait till you've crossed a bridge or two. If the doc says she's having a baby, ask how she'll be, but even a doctor can't really predict that. If she is carrying, you might want to wait and see for yourself how she is. On the other hand, the thought of becoming a dad could make you even more determined to fight. I don't have a magic wand, Jay. It's your life – live it.'

Jay took his pint of tea upstairs. There would be little sleep for him tonight. For a start, the bed was lumpy, and it wasn't his. And he remained chilled, mostly because he was used to sharing with a warm body. A baby? It was all she wanted. Her motherless state was a huge source of disappointment for Gill Collins. In her opinion, a woman without children was scarcely a woman at all. And she loved kids, was even planning to take an evacuee or two. He hoped she understood what she'd be living with, because if the women were anything to go by, Scouse kids promised to be several handfuls of mischief.

'Three pages already,' Keith said aloud. 'A letter of this length when I hardly know her?' But he did know her. She'd been in his head, his bed and his dreams for days. He hadn't been to visit Cora, didn't need her. There was something distasteful and impolite about using one woman while seeing the face of another. Should he throw in the job, move to Crosby and find work there? No. Because he knew how to woo her, and the key was three boys. If he could tame them and get them to behave sensibly, he might be halfway to winning her.

The chap who drove you here has just arrived wet through to the bone. He's been half drowned and locked out by his wife, because she doesn't want him to join the air force. It seems he got drunk with one of the farmers, so drunk that they were both ordered by the landlord not to play darts. They ended up in a shippon and decided to fly. I think they were flying already, because they couldn't find their way home. I believe navigation will not be a strong point for either of them.

I seem to have overstayed my welcome with this letter, as it will take up your time, but it's wonderful to be able to indulge in correspondence unconnected to business. Please don't worry about the boys. I shall make it my goal to ensure that they are occupied and out of trouble. It will be my pleasure to bring you to Willows as often as possible. I may change horses if you have a carter, and I can pick up Nero in exchange for the borrowed horse when I return you to base. There may be a shortage of petrol, so it'll be back to horses and carts for all of us.

He reread the whole letter, wondering whether he had gone too far in mentioning how pretty she was. It had been the same with Annie, God bless her. One encounter, and he'd been lost. And here he was, twenty years older and wiser, two decades dafter, with a fool in bed upstairs. No matter what went on around him, no matter which piece of work he was tackling, Eileen was there in his mind, right at the front where business should sit. So where was the real fool? Upstairs or here, sweating over a letter?

The answer entered the room. In striped pyjamas and work boots, Jay Collins looked as mad as a spring hare. 'I'm just … er … the lav.' He walked out through the kitchen.

Life, Keith told himself, was weird. One minute he felt like weeping, and the next he was practically doubled over at the sight of his handyman in boots and sleepwear. Was Keith the pregnant one? Were his hormones in turmoil? 'Perhaps I'm having an early menopause. I must tell the quack about my poor nerves.'

Jay returned. 'Bloody raining now,' he muttered as he climbed the stairs.

The rain was the last straw. As mirth rose in his throat, Keith Greenhalgh damped the fire, turned off the lamps and went upstairs. It was time for bed. He had given up on today; it was a hopeless case…

Five

'We could decorate a Christmas tree with that grin of yours, Eileen Watson. It's all the letters, isn't it? They've been coming through that door by the sackful. I seen you stood there yesterday with a gob on because there was no letter.' Nellie sighed like a ham on stage. 'Isn't love wonderful? Ooh, I can see it now, hand in hand through buttercups and daisies, tossed over the wall by a bull, landing side by side in a cowpat. Lovely.'

Eileen shrugged and changed irons, setting the cool one to heat near the fire, picking up the hotter one and spitting on it to make sure it sizzled. 'Stop it, Mam. You're getting on my nerves, so give it a rest. He's just a nice fellow, a decent man. It's good to hear about the place where you'll be staying with our three musketeers. I see that stain came out of our Philip's shirt.'

'And you've gone red.'

'So? What are you, counsel for the Crown Persecution? Because that's what this is, Mam. It's perse-bloody-cution. Would you rather I went a nice shade of green?'

'Well, it would suit, seeing as you're half Irish.' Nellie wandered off for a brief segue down a different avenue. 'She's give you some lovely clothes. Funny, isn't it? When she wore them, they looked dowdy. You look like a film star in Hilda's stuff. It's that figure of yours. She's straight up and down, but you're curvy.'

Eileen continued to iron her children's clothes. They were lucky, because Miss Pickavance had kitted them out with decent stuff for their evacuation. They had strong boots and good trousers, and they even had pyjamas. Some kids round here slept in their school clothes for weeks on end, no vests, no underpants, no breakfast. She felt guilty about those who wouldn't get the chance of evacuation, which was why that side of things was being left firmly in Hilda's court. And Hilda was coming out of herself while searching for candidates, so it was a good thing all round.

'He's handsome, I'll give you that. One of the

best-looking blokes I've seen in a long time. Lovely head of hair, tanned skin, laughing eyes. And he won't get called up. About ten years older than you, I reckon, and a Woollyback, but that can't be helped. There's always one fly in the ointment, but, taken all round, I dare say he'll do for you.'

'Mother!'

Nellie chortled. When Eileen called her Mother, the water was definitely warming up a bit. If she didn't jump soon, it could boil. Because Nellie's Eileen had limits. This angel could become a real little virago if pushed an inch too far in the wrong direction. 'But you like him, though, don't you? I mean you did take a fancy, I can tell.'

The iron was slammed down onto a couple of roof slates that served to protect a table that was well past redemption. Eileen glared at her mother. 'Listen, Sherlock. It's elementary, and I'm Watson. He's a penfriend. So stick that in your pan and fry it with a couple of onions.'

'Ooh, look,' Nellie exclaimed. 'Our Eileen's come over all Mae West in a mood.' She was talking to nobody, as the children were at school, and she and her daughter were the only people in the house. 'You've had a letter today, though. I can tell you've had a letter today, because it's wrote all over your face.'

'Written.'

'Eh?'

'Written all over my face. And it was on paper, actually.'

'Was it? Actually?'

'Yes.' The ironing continued. Today's was a brilliant one. He'd told her about his childhood down in Bolton, his mam and dad, brothers and sisters, little Annie Metcalfe from Bromley Cross, dead for over twenty years. And he'd sent a parcel this time. Thank God Mam had been out cleaning the Throstle's Nest, because she would have made a symphony out of it rather than a mere song and dance. Mam was a caution. Mam was happy, because her Eileen might have found a good man. Might have. It was early days.

'Eileen?'

'What now?'

'I know we hardly met him, but he's lovely.'

'Yes.'

'You'll take it slow, though?'

'Course I will. He's got to meet my boys yet. We could have five farms ruined by Christmas with no help at all from Hitler. Our Bertie can start a war in a shoe box.' She sniffed. 'I'll miss you, though.'

'Same here, queen. It'll be like ripping one of me arms off, only this can't be helped. You have to stay with her. My granddaughter's special, and I don't want nobody wiping their feet on her front doormat.'

'You being vulgar again, Mam?'

'I am. Anyway, I'm going next door to see Kitty. Charlie went out for a packet of cigs last Friday, and she's seen neither hide nor hair since. I know she's used to it, but she's gone worser with her nerves this last month. Ever since Chamberlain come on the wireless, she's been like a cat on hot bricks.'

Alone, Eileen dug out her parcel from behind the upended mattress on which she and Mam slept. There was the letter, a photograph of

Willows, and a copy of Shakespeare's sonnets. He was making love to her. From a distance not far short of forty miles, he was caressing her soul. Inside the book, tissue thin enough to be transparent held dried flowers between a dozen or more pages. All her life, Eileen had waited, however unconsciously, for a relationship like this. It was a fairy tale, and she was Cinderella. There was no carriage, no glass slipper, no midnight deadline, but the hero had a gentle heart, humour, and a good brain. It was all too quick, too quick because war loomed.

At the age of thirty-three, this mother of four children had been washed ashore on an island named Hope. Her Lazzer had been a wonderful man, and she was not betraying him. Keith had a memory of a girl he had loved, so they were equal on that score. For the first time, she smiled while thinking of Laz. After baptizing him Lawrence, his family had shortened that to Lawrie, which sounded a bit like the name of a large vehicle, so Eileen and he had made up Lazzer. They'd been happy. To this day, Eileen missed the weight of a man, the power, the loving and whispering. But she'd pledged herself to her children, and three of those children were ... on the wild side. Keith would straighten them out. It was silly, placing faith in a bloke she hardly knew, and yet... He could do it. He would do it. 'Slow down,' she muttered.

The scream came at that moment. Eileen shoved her treasures out of sight and ran into the street. Kitty Maguire was lying face down on the pavement, balled fists battering the flags, a blood-curdling sound escaping from her throat. Over her stood Nellie Kennedy and two policemen. Other neighbours came out of their houses, mostly mothers with children too young for school. Eileen interpreted word-shapes on her mother's lips. Charlie Maguire was dead. A constable advised Eileen that the body had been washed up on Ainsdale beach, just another piece of flotsam tossed about by the Mersey's unpredictable rips. 'She's taken it bad,' he said unnecessarily. 'Mind you, he was never sober, so we're not surprised he's come to grief. Poor woman.' He shook his head sadly.

Days later, Eileen remembered how she had thought of herself coming ashore on an island named Hope. While she had been pondering that, Kitty's husband had been thrown up by the tide, and a whole family had been stranded on a shore entitled Despair. Life took, and life gave. Because on that first day, Hilda Pickavance rode in on her white horse and promised Kitty a cottage in Willows Edge. The true hero of the piece was a quiet woman with a spine of steel, a person who, when blessed with good fortune, insisted on sharing it. Charlie was dead, but his wife and children would be safe.

For several nights, Eileen and Nellie took turns to sit up with Kitty. Weeping continued till the early hours of every morning, after which whoever was on duty dozed fitfully in an uncomfortable chair. Poor old Charlie had been doomed anyway. According to the doctor, his life sentence was always going to be commuted to early release, since his liver was fit only for saddlery and bootsoling, not for cleansing blood. He had been a long way past retrieval, and his illness showed in every corner of the disgusting house he had inhabited. From where she sat, Eileen could hear wildlife in the kitchen. She recalled one of the babies, now grown, being taken to the hospital after eating 'currants' from the kitchen floor. That dried fruit had been produced by rodents, and the child had suffered the consequences. The smell in here was almost unbearable.

Cockroaches scuttered about. These creatures, along with mice and silverfish, were frequent visitors in Nellie and Eileen's house, but Nellie kept on top of them and was merciless when it came to methods of dispatch. Mel had once termed her gran a murderer of mice, but the job had to be done. Poor Kitty had lost hope and energy; perhaps both might be reborn once the funeral was consigned to the pages of recent history.

Eileen closed her eyes. By now, Mam had discovered the letter, the book, the photo and the dried flowers. It didn't matter. If Mel should ever be on the receiving end of a man's dedicated attention, Eileen would want to know. Age scarcely came into it, because Eileen was Nellie's child, just as Mel was Eileen's.

Kitty woke again. 'Will I like it up there, Eileen? Do you think we'll be all right out in the wilds?'

'I hope so, love. There'll be fresh air and probably no bombs, so it has to be an improvement.'

'I'm scared.'

'Yes. So am I.' Kitty was better off, though she didn't know it yet. Her husband had been difficult, and occasionally violent, a fact that accounted for several of Kitty's absent teeth. He had failed to provide, so his young had scarcely thrived, and he would not have been fit for any kind of war service. By falling into the Mersey when drunk as a lord, he had done his wife and children a favour, since they could now be rescued. Hilda Pickavance would not have allowed Charlie into one of her cottages, and Kitty would have continued down the slippery slope for many years to come.

'I know what you're thinking. He was no good, and I'm better off.'

Eileen shook her head. 'He's better off, Kitty. He suffered. You know he suffered, because you told us about the bleeding. Remember? That was real pain, you see. And when he turned on you or the kids, it was the booze, not him. Part of him was screaming to get well, while the rest of him knew it was too late. Even so, whatever Charlie was, he was yours and you'll miss him. But my mam will be with you over at Willows. My mam will look after you.'

Kitty stared into a feeble fire. 'Know what I'm looking forward to, Eileen?'

'No, what?'

'Teeth. For the funeral. Proper teeth fitted by Mushy Goldberg. He does a good pair, tops and bottoms, for a couple of quid. People have been so kind.'

Eileen smiled to herself. The locals had gone without their pies and their pints so that Kitty's blackened stumps could be removed. The gums were currently being given a few days to heal in order to be replaced by some Mushy Goldberg specials in time for Charlie's big send-off. 'Try to have a little doze,' was all she said for the time being.

Morning struggled to be born some time after six. This was going to be the end of Kitty's first full week as a widow, and Eileen knew from personal experience how hard that would be. She couldn't eat or prepare food in here, so she crept next door to make tea and toast. Mam was asleep on the parlour floor mattress, the book of sonnets in one hand. She was struggling a bit in coming to terms with Shakespeare, but she had brains enough to give the bard a chance. 'I've been lucky,' Eileen whispered. 'We've made it this far, you and me, Mam. Yes, I've been a lucky girl.'

A sort of polite friendship had developed between Tom and Marie Bingley. She, more relaxed now that she had her own bedroom, threw herself head first into the development from scratch of a local WVS and, when she wasn't reading government literature and attending meetings, she was knitting khaki socks and telephoning headquarters about bandage sizes and food parcels. She continued to nurture and provide for her family, but cooking and shopping had ceased to be the focus of her life. Marie was needed by the community, and her war work became the core of her existence.

Tom's spare time was less gainfully employed. He did his duty, helped the sick, tended the dying and the newborn, but he was restless. Then he saw an article in last week's newspaper, the story of a washed-up body found on a nearby beach. Next to this item was printed a grainy photograph of the widow standing in a street with her neighbour. Even here, in patchy black and white, the neighbour shone. Dear God, Eileen Watson was seriously beautiful.

He showed the paper to his daughter. 'Where exactly do they live, Gloria?'

'Rachel Street, number two, I think, so that poor lady whose husband drowned must be number four. It's quite near the Rotunda theatre, round about where Cazneau Street meets Scotland Road. Why?'

'It's just that we know Mel, don't we? And now that I've met her mother, well ... I thought I might help the bereaved family.' He watched her smile as it arrived to illuminate a face that seemed to be improving somewhat.

'That's a nice thing to do, Daddy. But Mel never takes anyone home. I can't say she's ashamed, because she probably isn't; she's too ... organized for that. It's just that she keeps her two worlds apart, because they wouldn't mix. Even the poor have their rules.'

'Rules don't buy a coffin, Gloria.'

'No, but some things are bigger than money.'

For a few seconds, Tom looked at his daughter. She was a sensitive soul, then. She would probably grow up to be like her mother, dutiful, correct and capable. No beauty had been promised, yet something was happening. Cheekbones. Yes, they had started to show through disappearing puppy fat. 'When are they moving to Crosby?' He attempted to dress the question in casual clothes.

'Very soon. Miss Morrison's having their rooms painted. She has a soft spot for Mel's mother, so she's trying to get everything nice for them.'

'Good, good.' Tom left his daughter to her homework and went into the study. He had to see Eileen Watson. But he owned the grace to feel some shame, since he was considering using a dead man as a stepping stone, and such an intention did not sit comfortably on his conscience.

Marie entered the room, a piece of white paper in her hand. 'I wonder,' she began, her tone offhand, 'whether you might do me a favour, Tom.'

'If I can, of course I shall.'

The paper was a five-pound note, and she passed it to him. 'I read that the other day,' she said, pointing to the newspaper. 'And I thought we might go down and visit Mrs Watson and her neighbour. But I simply haven't time today, because there's a committee meeting early this evening. Please give the poor young widow that money. God knows she'll need it.'

There was an unfamiliar expression on Marie's face, a cross between challenge and a sort of triumph. She was telling him that she'd lost the key to her chastity belt, that he could look elsewhere, that she had better things to do, wool to wind, women to organize, a war to win. The balance of power had certainly shifted on this bit of St Andrews Road.

He felt strangely hurt. She was married to a successful, respected, handsome man, but all she offered was politeness and a kind of comradeship. 'A civilized arrangement' was what she wanted. After the war, depending on how long it lasted and how old the twins were at the time, she might look for divorce or separation. The disgrace of that would ruin his practice, so he must try to change her mind. At present, that mind was rather like Stonehenge; any change would arrive as a result of centuries of erosion.

She left the room, smiling to herself as soon as the door was closed in her wake. Taking the upper hand was strangely exhilarating. Having been the first to contact the relevant authorities, she was, by default, in charge of the WVS. Although no ranks existed within the service, she was the first to receive an official blouse with that badge on the pocket, red and white, a crown at its top, and W.V.S. embroidered above the words *CIVIL DEFENCE* and *CROSBY.*

In accordance with the dictates of its founder, the Women's Voluntary Service undertook a duty to familiarize locals with the dos and don'ts in case of bomb attack. Members were instructed to hammer home the necessity of keeping light from showing, as well as provide comforts for displaced persons at home and for troops employed in battle. She had a reason to live, a reason all her own. No longer was she just a wife and a mother; she had lists to type, telephone calls to make, women to manage. The war was her saviour.

Then there was home. She had assumed command here, too. By removing herself from the marital bed, Marie had taken charge. This also had been by default in its own way, as she had never fully understood the power of sex. It was something one did in order to procreate, and it was a nuisance. But when it stopped, the male became very odd. Sometimes, he looked almost crazed, eyes shifting from side to side, occasionally fixing on her breasts or her legs. She wasn't a handsome woman, but the breast and leg departments were adequate. Was he going insane? If that were the case, he could travel the road alone, because she had no intention of losing her own mind.

Anyway, she'd seen all she wanted of the damp patch on the main bedroom ceiling, had wasted more than enough time waiting for him to groan and flail before collapsing on her like a lump of boiled fish. The whole business was moist and rather unwholesome. He needed it, though, especially when a pretty woman or girl had visited. Well, he could manage without her. Men were designed literally to please themselves, and she had just given him unspoken permission to turn his attention to some other female.

So that was that. Now, where had she put the instructions about how best to pack a shoebox with goodies for a soldier? And should Muriel Crabtree be in charge of bandages? Muriel kept horses, and there was usually a whiff of manure about her person...

The edge was keener in Liverpool than in Crosby and Blundellsands. People scuttered to and from the docks, humour less audible, faces set in lines that spoke volumes about what was dreaded. Barrage balloons, pretty and silver, bobbed about in the cool evening air. Older men wore the garb of wardens and fire-watchers, while younger males went about their business in a hurry, as most would soon be gone into the hungry maw of Europe. The invisible, silent wind of change howled behind expressionless eyes. Afraid yet determined, this tough, valiant breed prepared to bomb and to be bombed. Grey ships moored in shallow water were being edged out by tugs, as they were sitting too low and in danger of becoming silt-bound. What was their cargo? Why were there so many Royal Navy uniforms about?

They were no doubt loading missiles, and it was all suddenly very real. Tom drove past guns whose huge nostrils pointed skyward as if in immediate readiness to spit rounds of flak at German fighters and bombers. Thousands of sandbags were piled on pavements waiting to be taken to their final resting places. Windows bore criss-crossed tape applied so that glass would not fly too freely once the show began in earnest. Little trains chugged across the road, and a smell akin to cordite danced skittishly on the breeze.

He stopped the car and watched a different world, one that was a mere seven miles from his home. Used to houses with garden gates, a stranger to organized and heavy industry, Tom was cushioned, and he knew it. And he suddenly understood Marie's obsession with socks and bandages. While the contribution of one small arm of civil defence might seem paltry, it could be vital to a man who bled in a ditch, to another whose extremities were unbearably cold and wet. Little shoeboxes crammed with sweets, biscuits, cigarettes, socks, a scarf and a greeting would mean the world to an injured man in some damp and undermanned field hospital.

He left the docks and drove a short distance inland. No longer wishing to see Eileen, he knocked at the door of number four. But Eileen opened it. He followed her into the kind of hell he had read about, though this was his first real sight of it. The need to stop breathing had to be overcome, though there was very little oxygen in the place. Eileen Watson looked like a diamond set in tin, though Mrs Maguire fitted her surroundings well enough. 'I'm Dr Bingley,' he said to the new widow. 'My wife's at a civil defence meeting but she asked me to bring you this. We saw the article in the paper.' He handed over the five-pound note. 'We know Mrs Watson and her daughter, so...' He ran out of words.

Kitty Maguire's hand shook as she accepted the note. 'Me teeth,' she said through tears. 'God bless you, doc. I've never had hold of a fiver before. I can pay for me new teeth so I won't show me kiddies up.'

He didn't know what to say, because mind and throat were suddenly dry.

Eileen led him out. 'She's not herself,' she said quietly. 'All she goes on about is her teeth. Mushy Goldberg took out the bits that were left a few days back, and he's making her a set of falsies. They'll be ready in the morning, just before the funeral. We had a collection to pay for them, but she can use that for other essentials. I'm afraid she's coming out with some odd things.'

'Shock,' he managed.

'Yes, I suppose so.'

They stood on the pavement. He fiddled with his trilby while she stared at her shoes. 'It's a bloody mad world,' he said eventually. 'And I think it'll get worse before it gets better.'

'No doubt. Thanks, anyway.' She went back to Kitty.

Tom drove home. He knew he couldn't offer his services as fireman, warden or driver, because he was going to be essential. If a baby was coming, it wouldn't hang on while he manned a phone in town. Perhaps he might be allowed to roll a few bandages. Perhaps he could learn to knit socks. Whatever he could or couldn't do, he felt seriously inadequate.

Fortunately, Kitty Maguire had managed by the skin of her few remaining teeth to keep up her insurance payments, so Charlie could have a decent enough send-off. He was in a closed coffin, as the Mersey had done its usual thorough job, but he came home and spent his last night in his own house, as was traditional in Catholic families. The final vigil had to be sat by men. Charlie's widow went upstairs to bed while three male neighbours occupied the front room and drank Guinness in an effort to make the situation more bearable. This was a filthier than normal house, so alcohol was required to take the edge off things.

They played cards, drank, dozed, played dominoes, dozed again. Even seasoned navigators of Scotland Road life were unused to conditions as bad as Kitty Maguire's, and they slipped outside occasionally to clear their heads and noses of a stench that defied description. In the mix were dried urine, the droppings of rodents, decaying food and piled-up house dust, all topped by the musty aroma of damp mould. They felt sorry for poor Charlie, whose last night on the earth's surface had to be spent in so malodorous a place. Yet they all knew that Kitty had tried her best until it all got on top of her, and that the man in the box had not done right by his family. He was a drunk, he was dead and, with the help of Miss Pickavance, Kitty and her three kids might get a fresh start.

When morning came, the men stood by the coffin until Kitty put in an appearance. She shot through the shabby parlour like a bullet from a gun, her expression similar to one visiting the face of a child who expected a decent Christmas. 'He's opening up early,' she told them. 'Just for me.' She had scarcely delivered this announcement before she left the house. Three bedraggled children appeared, all dirty, all hungry. One of the neighbours took them home for a slice of bread, a drop of milk and a wash, while another announced his intention to gather borrowed clothes for them.

'They've got clothes,' he was informed by his companion. 'Miss Pickavance will bring them across in a bit.'

Charlie couldn't be left on his own. Even now, dead as a dodo, the poor beggar continued to be a nuisance. The remaining two men stood in the doorway to wait for Kitty to come home. When she finally returned, she had happy eyes, tidy hair and a mouthful of bright, white teeth. While she explained that Mrs Goldberg had done the hair, the two remaining keepers of Charlie's final vigil stood open-mouthed on the pavement outside number four, their eyes riveted to her mouth. Her words seemed to struggle while being born, because they had to find their way past obstacles that were almost impassable. Her face was bigger, taller, different.

'I've got teeth,' she said proudly, though with difficulty.

This might have provided a subject for debate had circumstances been different. Because Kitty didn't have teeth; the teeth had Kitty.

So sorry about your neighbour, Eileen. It's sad when a man loses his life at such a young age, and tragic for his family. Let's hope they have a better time when they get to Willows Edge.

Have you noticed how people talk about a 'very nice funeral'??? I mean, what's nice about shoving some poor devil in a box under damp earth with worms and moles and God alone knows what else? And afterwards, when you stand in a pub trying to eat a ham sandwich, you realize you can't because the place stinks of men's urinals, stale beer and tobacco smoke.

Eileen shook her head and giggled out loud. He was describing the Throstle's Nest to a T, and yes, people had talked about the nice funeral.

I know it doesn't seem right, but I have been laughing my head off about Kitty and the teeth. The date will be remarked upon not as the day on which Charlie was buried, but the occasion when the teeth moved in. How I pray your doctor friend will attend to Kitty's mouth furniture, otherwise I won't be able to look at her without chuckling when she gets here.

Dr Tom Bingley had been very kind. Not only had he attended church, burial and funeral tea, he had also asked Kitty whether the teeth hurt. Kitty had admitted that talking was difficult, eating impossible, so the good man had invited her to visit a friend in Crosby who specialized in the adjustment of dentures. There would be no charge. Tom hadn't brought flowers, so this small service would have to suffice in lieu.

Eileen put down her letter and walked to the window. Some of Hilda's parents' bits and pieces were being taken by the local carter up to Willows. Hilda, Mam, Philip, Rob and Bertie would leave in a few days, while Eileen and Mel would be bound for Crosby. And he would be there, just round the corner.

It had all seemed so innocent, that meeting in town. He had come to talk to her about the work his wife was doing, had taken her to a headquarters in Liverpool, had asked whether Eileen would consider doing the job, but here, on Scotland Road, just once or twice a week. And she had said yes, and he had kissed her. He was not for her. She'd been plagued by sexual desire for other men, had always managed to escape before indulging her weakness. But this man was powerfully attractive and ... and she was a damned fool. He was not, not, not for her. Keith was nearer the mark, yet Tom Bingley was a magnet, and she was scrap iron. Difficult. It was the war, she reminded herself for the umpteenth time.

For a few minutes, she was back in the car with him, her open mouth crushed against his, tongues meeting and playing, her body melting under the touch of clever hands. She needed... She wanted... His warm breath caressed her ear as he used words to praise her body, while his expertise brought her to a state of pleasure for which she had decided never again to search. It was wonderful and terrible, and she was now awakened once more. Had Laz lived, their family would have been huge. 'He's not for me,' she repeated for the hundredth time.

She thanked God – if God would listen to so pathetic an argument – that full intercourse had been an impossibility in a motor vehicle. Like many others, Eileen had caught the war disease. Make love while you can, for tomorrow...

Then there was Mam. Mam had noticed the glow, had listened to moans in the night while her errant daughter had relived in dreams what had happened to her in the front seat of a doctor's car. But it wasn't love; it was sex, and that was different, a sin to be confessed to a priest, except that she couldn't, because she was ashamed. She needed, wanted... Damn the bloody war!

Nellie entered. 'Daydreaming again? About that Keith one?'

'No. Just watching Hilda's stuff being taken. It's getting real now.'

Something was getting real, Nellie Kennedy mused, and it was nothing to do with a tallboy, a wardrobe and a clock with a brass pendulum. 'Eileen?'

'What?'

'Is it that doctor?'

After a brief pause, the reply was delivered. 'Yes.'

'Blood and rabbit innards, he's a married man. His daughter's our Mel's best friend. Have you ... you know?'

'No.'

'But you will?' So many hurried weddings and unwanted pregnancies. 'Don't let Hitler push you into something you'll regret.'

Eileen bit her lip. 'I thought I'd be all right. I mean, this isn't the first time I've been tempted, because it's only human nature, isn't it? Then I thought some kind of love might happen with Keith, because he's lovely. But Tom... He brings out my best and my worst, Mam.' She turned and faced her mother. 'How many people can talk like this to their mams, eh? And who will I turn to when you've gone? I mean, he'll be living yards away from me. His wife's...'

'What?'

'Living in a different part of the house. Sleeping on her own, I mean. And I don't want to repeat what happened in that car. He's like some kind of master of the art, and he bloody well adores me.'

'You're pretty. You're like one of them Stradi-wotsit violins, and he's a good fiddler, knows how to get the best tune out of you. Listen, girl. You know damned well Lazzer only had to look at you and you fell pregnant. How will you explain a big belly to your daughter, eh? So he'd better be careful what he does with his bow, or he can fiddle off. I'll kill him.'

'No, you won't. And he knows ways of making sure I don't get a big belly. I understand it's all physical. I'm not daft. But he thinks she'll want divorce or separation when the kids are older, and by then I might love him for more than the tunes he plays on my strings. He's clever. I like clever people.'

'Eileen–'

'I'm thirty-three!'

'So was Jesus, and look what they done to him. I'm going out.' The door slammed.

The letter was lovely. Keith was lovely. He described early morning frosts, the birth of piglets, geese skeining over the moors, the fresh, cutting air of early evenings. He gave her the crow of a cockerel, communication between cats domestic and feral, a cow seeking the milkmaid who usually tended her, awarding her a flick of the tail, a gentle reminder that hot, painful udders needed relief. He brought her into the barn, where she inhaled the comforting, sweet scent of stored hay. Keith stroked her soul, but Tom had ignited her flesh. And Eileen's flesh was a force to be reckoned with.

Nellie marched into Crosby like a Valkyrie with a severe headache after a long night on the mead in Valhalla. In the manner of one of those females from Norse mythology, she was here to decide who would die in battle. Dr Tom Bingley didn't know he was engaged in combat, but she would inform him very soon. After stopping several people, she finally found a woman who was a patient of Dr Bingley. 'He's not open till four,' she said. 'But there's a little coffee and tea place next door to his surgery. Just down there on Liverpool Road, it is.'

'Ta, queen.'

Nellie rattled round in her purse until she found the price of a cuppa. Placing herself in the window, she waited for his car to pull up, thanking God that he didn't practise from home. That wouldn't have stopped her, but it would have been awkward. This was about protecting women from scavengers, and Marie Bingley was one of the number who required saving. Nevertheless, Nellie would have gone and done whatever... Here he came. She walked out of the cafe and stood, arms akimbo, outside his place of work.

'Mrs ... er ... ?'

'Kennedy. I'm here about me daughter.'

He blinked a couple of times as if trying to remember where he had seen her before. 'I'm sorry?'

'Eileen Watson's mother. You'd best get me in there before the sick start to form a queue, because you'll be one of them if I get my way, lad.'

'Oh. Right. Very well.' He unlocked the door with an unsteady hand before ushering her through the waiting area into the surgery at the rear of the building. He sat down and, with a sweep of his hand, indicated that she should occupy the patients' seat.

'No, ta,' she said. 'You never know who comes into places like this. I might catch something.' She waded in at the deep end, scarcely stopping for breath while she berated and insulted him in the age-old way of those who had lived the hard life. The air was stained by words that should never have visited the tongue of a woman, and the diatribe was not delivered quietly.

Then she got to the point of her visit. 'Now, don't be getting me mixed up with them who're all wind and piss, because you'll be wrong. My girl lost her husband to an accident five or six years back. Since then, she's kept herself to herself, because she has four kids. And along you come, a married man, an educated bloke, and you want your way with her.'

He folded his arms. 'Are you threatening me?'

'Yes. Too bloody right I'm threatening you. If you don't leave our Eileen alone, you'll be just a little bit dead. All right? And if I and a few good lads have to go to hell for murder, so be it. Because I'm telling you now, if you get into her knickers, you *will* find yourself starting a new fashion, a six-inch blade worn just about where your heart would be if you had one. I'm not kidding. Touch her, and you'll rue the bloody day. You'll be watched. She'll be watched. Wait till I tell our Mel about her best pal's dad, eh?'

'You wouldn't!'

'Wouldn't I? I am putting the Dockers' Word out on you, mate. The old lads won't be called up, and they're stronger than any mee-mawing quack from Crosby. Don't be surprised if you wake up dead with a docker's hook sticking out of your throat.'

'That would definitely be a hanging offence.'

Nellie laughed, though the noise she created sounded grim. 'Are you confusing me with somebody who gives a monkey's arse what happens to you, your daughter, your fancy flaming life? Or to me? See, I'm not impressed by them what think they're better than us common folk, because us common folk know how to fight wars, how to kill, where to stick the bloody knives, and how to scare seven shades of shite out of Hitler. We'll be the ones that do that, Dr Bingley. Oh, and in case you're still not hearing me, I'll leave you a small

deposit just as a sign of goodwill, eh?'
'Pardon?'
'Granted.' She dropped her bag, balled her right fist and thrust it forward with all her might until it made contact with his left cheek. His head shot back and hit the wall. For once, she thanked God for all she had learned during a difficult life that had made her keen-eyed and street-smart. 'That's just the start. Leave her alone!' she screamed before abandoning him to his pain.

He heard the outer door slam, and walked across the surgery to see if anyone had overheard the fracas. The waiting room was empty, and he was grateful that his receptionist was running late yet again. He placed the *SURGERY CANCELLED* sign in the doorway and shot home a couple of bolts. Anyone who needed urgent treatment would be seen by Dr Clarke, who was just a few yards along the road. Back in his consulting room, he surveyed the damage. By tomorrow, he would have a very black eye; right now, he might be in need of immediate help. The hag had possibly broken his cheekbone.

Six

Neil Dyson, who had been more than slightly drunk on what was now named 'Flight Night', had been talked out of his Guinness-fuelled decision to become a fighter pilot. He was too old, too daft, and he returned quickly to the old religion, which was pale ale and darts. He'd served in the last war, he had a good wife who needed a husband in one piece, and two daughters who adored their dad. Drunkenness didn't suit him, and he intended to live life in a safer mode in future, because his three girls required a sober head of household. Furthermore, he would be wanted at home, because he was the main farmer, and he knew every inch of his acreage better than the back of his own hand.

His companion in lunacy, Jay Collins, adhered loyally to the black stuff, as it seemed to make him just a little stronger while he waited to hear whether the rabbit had died. Men didn't talk much about pregnancy, as it was the domain of women, but he required an anaesthetic while he sat not talking about it. He'd no idea what a rabbit had to do with any of it, but he seemed not to be in full control of his life any more, because it was all beyond his reach. Between rabbits and Spitfires there was a very large chasm, and he was doing his level best to decide what was going to be his next move.

'Jay?' Neil said for the third time from the other side of the table. He was clearly flogging a dead horse and a comatose handyman. Oh, at last. Here came an answer.

'What?'

Not an answer, then. 'Gill's talked a few times to my Jeanie, so I know why you're wearing a miserable face. You just have to get through it; it's as simple as that. You look like you've lost a quid and found a tanner.'

'Oh.'

'No news, then?'

'No.'

'Is she being sick of a morning? Is she eating daft stuff like pickles with jam or bacon with treacle?'

'No.'

'But the doc said he thought she was probably expecting?'

'Yes.'

This was yet another thoroughly riveting conversation, thought Neil as he drained his glass. 'Pint of Guinness, is it?'

'No.'

'Are you going to say anything other than yes and no?'

'I don't know.'

'Bugger.' Neil went to the bar for a refill. Jay was about as much fun as a rainy Methodist picnic these days. Over in the opposite corner, Keith Greenhalgh was nursing a pint of brown. He wasn't much of a drinker, but he wandered into the pub from time to time just for a bit of company and noise. He should have got wed, because he was a good man and would have made a fine husband. There was a story to him, and rumour had it that he'd never recovered from the death of a fiancée. Damned shame, it was, because the lad needed something to paint a grin on his face.

But Elsie Openshaw was putting about a new tale concerning a very pretty woman who had visited Willows with Miss Pickavance. This woman was writing to Keith, and he was replying on a regular basis. 'Three or four a week,' Elsie had said. 'And they've only seen each other once.

Too fast, them Liverpool floozies are. She'll have her feet under his table and her nightie on his pillow before you can say knife.' Thus had the oracle spoken, though Neil would have preferred to hear the news from the horse's mouth.

He paid for his pint and carried it to Keith's table. 'All right if I sit here?' he asked. 'Only Jay's turned into the strong, silent type and I can't cope – it's like talking to the wall. I swear he's in a world of his own. He needs a foot up his backside, that's certain sure. There's hardly one word of sense coming out of his gob.'

Keith inclined his head. 'Yes, park yourself here by all means. The lad's worried. That mad Dr Stephenson didn't need to do a test – I reckon she's near three months gone, and I'm no doc. It's as plain as a pikestaff to most of us. All Stephenson needed to do was lay his hands on her abdomen, but no, he had to go for a pee test.'

Neil laughed. 'My Jeanie says the same. And if Stephenson was sober, Gill's sample will have gone off for testing in some lab; if he was drunk, it could be anywhere from his back pocket to the medicine cabinet. Jean says she'd rather get the vet any day, because Stephenson doesn't know whether he's coming or going. It's time he stopped practising, cos he'll never reach perfect this side of Judgement Day.'

Jay, having finally noticed his solitary status, wandered across and joined them. 'I wondered where you'd gone,' he complained. 'I was sat there all by myself like somebody with smallpox. You could have said.'

Neil shook his head sadly. 'We're right opposite

you. You couldn't miss us if you'd just try to focus; there's only three tables in here. But you're hearing nothing, seeing nothing, and saying next to nowt. You've a face like a smacked bum, and it's getting on my bloody nerves. She's...' He lowered his voice, as the topic was not going to be suitable for a men's bar. 'She's having a baby. Jean thinks so, Keith thinks so, and Gill knows so. So. Go home and look after her while you can. Be with her, Jay.'

Jay stared down into his drink. 'I'm thirty-two years old. I'm married to a woman who makes me happy, and she wants a baby. It looks like she's having one, and I don't know what to do.'

Keith frowned as if concentrating hard. 'You're thirty-three, I think. Boil a lot of water and find piles of towels and clean sheets,' he said with mock seriousness. 'Tell her to breathe, pant and push, but not necessarily in that order. Pick the kid up and make sure it's screaming, slap it if it isn't, then give it a wash and–'

Jay banged on the table with a fist. 'I don't mean that, you daft pair of lummoxes. The war. It's my war, this one. You lot have had yours, and it's my turn. If I wait to be called up, I could be shoved in the army. It's an airman's war. It's all going to be happening over our heads, and I want to be there with the boys in blue, not stuck in a ditch with a gun, no ammunition, no cigs and salt beef butties for me tea.'

'Very deep,' said Neil. 'I've told you, sit tight and go where you're sent.'

Keith thought differently. 'Listen, we'll look after her. Go and do your pilot training, and we'll see to Gill. I promise we'll make sure no harm comes to her or your baby.'

'If I go off voluntary, she might lose the kiddy. If I sit, wait, and end up in the Fusiliers, my long face could be enough to cause a miscarriage. I can't win either way.'

'Don't let anybody wearing a swastika hear you say that,' Neil advised. 'Now, get home and talk to her properly. You're neither fish nor bloody fowl till you get this lot worked out. And we have to get that house ready for Miss Pickavance and–'

'I'm gone.' Jay walked out of the pub, almost colliding in the doorway with Mrs Elsie Openshaw. He blundered out into darkness, his head swimming after only two pints of Ireland's nectar. He couldn't carry on like this. That bloody doctor wasn't worth the bloody ink on his bloody birth certificate, and that was an undeniable bloody fact. Was the rabbit dead, or was it still faffing about doing what rabbits did, which was getting pregnant themselves? The world seemed to be moving away from him. Sometimes, he felt as if he wasn't really here, as if a thick blanket sat between him and everything else. It was weird. There was something he had to do, and he needed to remember.

He was fed up. If he turned right, he'd be on his way home; if he turned left, he'd be ... he'd be going for Collie. Andy Crawford, better known as Collie because he always had a sheepdog, knew his onions. Then there was wotsername. Elsie Openshaw. He'd seen her a minute ago, and she'd been completely out of context. That was right, because Elsie had been in the taproom, and women didn't go in there, as there weren't many chairs and tables, since serious drinkers imbibed on their feet at the bar. He shoved his head through the door. 'Mrs Openshaw?' he shouted.

'Yes?'

'Will you stop here with Keith and Neil? I'll pick you up on me way back.'

'Your way back from where?' Keith asked. He turned to Elsie. 'Wait a minute while I try to get some sense out of him.'

'You and whose army?' Neil asked, his face deliberately grim.

Outside once more, Jay took a few deep breaths. He would get this sorted out if it killed him. That blinking doctor should have the sack. He was neither use nor ornament. The uselessness had started years back, and residents of several villages suffered as a result. As for ornaments, Jay had never seen one with such a big, red nose. The man was semi-retired, and he should be in a field with the rest of the worn-out horses who never did any harm.

'Jay?'

'Hello again, Keith.'

'Where are we going?'

'Eh?'

Keith repeated his question.

'You're going back in there to look after Mrs Openshaw. I'm going... I'm going somewhere.'

'Where?'

'Somewhere else.'

The words blood and stone paid a brief visit to Keith's mind. Jay had shut up shop and was no longer open for business. 'All right. See you later, then.' He went back inside and bought Elsie a port and lemon.

'What's he up to now?' Neil Dyson wanted to know. 'I've had better conversations with cows and pigs at the farm. In fact, even the wife makes more sense than Jay.'

'He's confused,' Keith said.

'Confused?' Neil took a swig of ale. 'I've seen balls of wool in a straighter state after the cats have been at them. There's something wrong with yon fellow.' He slapped some coins on the scarred table. 'Here, get Elsie another one of whatever that is while we wait for our fighter pilot to make up his mind where he'll be landing next. Let's hope he's packed his bloody parachute.'

Elsie, who had come only to give Keith a letter from Miss Pickavance, was enjoying herself. She was sitting in a pub with free drinks, and she was needed. Keith Greenhalgh hadn't called in for his mail today, and Elsie, who had recognized the copperplate writing of the new boss, had decided to follow Keith to the pub before going to bed. The message might be important, so she'd wanted to put it in his hand rather than through his letter-box. It was also a chance to eavesdrop, and she could never resist that temptation. And here she sat, on the cusp of something eventful; she could feel it in her bones. Against a background of conversations ranging from tupping through turnips all the way up to a war that didn't seem to be happening, Elsie waited for the main event.

The curtain rose some fifteen minutes later. Jay's head appeared once more. 'Keith, Elsie? Can you follow me, please? Neil, you stop here, or there'll be too many of us.' So Neil stayed, while the other two walked out of the pub.

Jay was ready for them. 'Don't start,' he said to Keith. 'I'm not in the mood. You walk up behind us. Mrs Openshaw can get in the back of Collie's car with the dog.' He left unspoken the obvious fact that no one else would fit on the rear seat once Elsie was established as cargo. 'You may as well set off walking now,' he advised his boss. 'You'll be a witness.'

Keith blinked several times. Life had taken on a surreal edge, and Jay Collins, handyman and occupier of the gatehouse, had appointed himself producer and director of this particular scene. One thing was certain. Gill would hit the roof.

Gill, clad only in her nightdress, was drinking cocoa near the fire when her husband walked in. Her 'Hello, love' died during its third syllable when two more people and a dog followed him into the room.

'Don't start,' Jay repeated for the umpteenth time. 'I'm not in the mood.'

Gill picked up a shawl and covered herself.

'Lie down on that sofa,' ordered Elsie. 'Then I can see what's what before this man of yours goes mad with worriting. He's about as much use as a nine-bob note while he's this way out.'

'Bugger off,' was the only reply Gill could manage as she turned on her beloved husband. 'Listen, you. I know you're bloody daft, but I don't need a midwife, and I certainly don't want a vet. Sorry, Collie,' she told Andy Crawford. 'I know it's not your fault. This stupid article I married needs brain surgery. Have you brought your kit? Do him on the kitchen table. There's a drill in the shed if you need help to get through his thick skull.'

'I warned you,' the vet said. 'I don't deal with humans, Jay.'

'I do,' Elsie announced. 'She's a good two months gone.' She sidled up to Gill. 'Just let me put a hand on your belly, love.'

Gill marched across the room and flung herself in a supine position on the sofa. Jay was in a bad mood? Murder sat in her heart while the local blabbermouth prodded her abdomen. 'Well?'

'There's a babby in yon,' announced Elsie. 'Collie?'

The vet joined the unqualified midwife. He placed both hands on Gill's belly and the smile on his face was answer enough. After listening to the sounds of her innards through an instrument usually employed on pigs and cows, he spoke to Gill. 'You'll farrow in about seven months, perhaps six,' he announced. 'And yes, Stephenson should retire–'

Everything stopped when Keith entered just in time to catch the suddenly legless body of a father-to-be.

Gill sat up. 'See? See what I mean now, Keith? Bloody fighter pilot? He goes into shock because his wife's expecting, so how will he manage with half of Germany up his back end?' She stood up. 'Put him on here, Keith. Elsie, get brewing tea, will you? Collie, toast some bread. He's always hungry when he comes round after one of these carryings-on.'

The vet stood over Jay. 'How often does this

happen, Gill? Every day, once a week, or what?'

Jay's wife pondered for a moment. 'It happens, then it stops. He has phases. He can't drink much beer or he goes peculiar, sort of white and shaky, and faints now and again. No pattern to it, except it's tied up with food and ale. He passed out on our wedding day, showed me up good and proper, and he sometimes loses what I call his thinking-in-a-straight-line if he hasn't eaten enough.'

'Does he drink a lot of non-alcoholic stuff?'

Gill nodded vigorously. 'Water, tea and pop by the gallon. Why?'

Collie reminded everyone that he was not a doctor. 'But I'm taking him to Bolton Royal tomorrow whether he likes it or not.' Recent research had discovered that diabetes came in at least two types, and Jay, who was relatively young and on the thin side, seemed to be suffering from type one. Either his body was producing insufficient insulin, or his system was failing to make use of it. 'He needs looking at.' And if Collie should be proved right, Jay would not be serving his country in any conventional way.

The eyes opened. 'What happened?' Jay asked.

Elsie arrived with tea. 'Drink this when you sit up,' she ordered. 'I've put sugar in it. Sometimes they need sugar. His breath smells like pear drops. Oh, yes. I've seen it all before.'

'Be quiet, Elsie,' Collie urged.

'What?' Gill's antennae were on red alert.

Elsie ignored the vet and motored on, in her element now. 'Could be suffering from the sugar diabetics,' the queen bee pronounced. 'It means injections and a special diet and a review at the hospital from time to time. This'll be why you think he sometimes doesn't make a lot of sense. They go funny and they smell of pear drops. So it's not his fault, the way he carries on, love. If it's diabetes, they do act a bit daft from time to time, and they can't drink beer.'

Gill swallowed hard. 'Will he die?' she asked.

'We all will,' was Elsie's smart reply. 'But there's a farmer over Harwood way who's the same road out, and he copes. It just depends. The food you eat has to balance with the insulin you put into your body. It can be a bit hit and miss at times, but he'll get there, love. See, there's a fair whack more to it than the food you put in, because if you work harder than you did yesterday, you'll burn more off. They always have to carry sugar or sweets or a biscuit. He ... er ... he won't be a fighter pilot, Gill. But I reckon he'll make a good dad. You'll have to keep an eye on him, though.'

Jay, who had eaten a bit of toast, decided it was time to speak up. They were all talking as if he wasn't here, and... Yes, sometimes he was here but not here. There was definitely something up, and it needed sorting.

Gill burst into tears, though she laughed through the fear. 'Look at the cut of him,' she sobbed. 'He even steals my big moment when I find out I'm going to be a mam. Elsie, Collie, I'd like you two here at the birth. Not for me, I can manage, I'm sure. But you'll have to hang about and catch this bugger when he keels over.' She knelt on the floor and hugged her husband. 'A baby, Jay. We've done it.'

Jay, whose blood was now better balanced,

realized that his head was no longer full of Spitfires and Lancasters. There were times when he got fixated and angry, and there were occasions when he forgot the simplest things: a word, a name, a task that ought to have been automatic. 'I don't think I should drink black beer,' he told Gill. 'It turns me into a fighter pilot.'

She kissed his cheek 'We'll get you right, lad. Me, Collie, Keith and Elsie, we'll see if somebody can find a spare brain for you.'

Jay blinked. 'What's wrong with me?'

'Nothing,' she answered. 'You're just mad, that's all. Join the club.'

Keith was by himself, because his usual assistant, one Jay Collins of Willows Gate House, Willows, Near Bolton, had gone to hospital with his wife, the vet and a collie dog. The dog would be left in the car, but Jay and Gill would be examined, one for diabetes, the other for pregnancy. Collie had expressed to Keith the private opinion that Jay would be kept in so that his condition could be monitored. 'He's probably got more sugar in him than you'd find in a pound of dolly mixtures,' the vet had said. 'And when it burns off, he turns into a rag doll. But don't sack him, please. We have to look out for each other.'

Keith had no intention of sacking anyone, because Willows folk looked after Willows folk; it was their eleventh commandment. At least he knew now why Jay sometimes lost the plot. Furthermore, the lad shouldn't be driving the car until he got straightened out, because what Collie termed a hypo could become the cause of death for several people. So Keith had to take over the chauffeuring job as well. He hoped Gill would be all right. She'd waited years to get pregnant, and she needed an easy time.

There were four bedrooms in the big house, all a decent size. Neil's wife was coming in later, as she had washed bedlinen and towels, but Keith was in charge of furniture. Miss Pickavance, a very thorough type, had sent a rough drawing of the upstairs, so he knew how to allocate each room. The two slightly smaller ones were for herself and Mrs Kennedy, mother of Eileen, grandmother to the three boys. The lads were to occupy the largest front bedroom, while the second biggest was for Eileen and her daughter, who would visit whenever possible.

The beds were built, thank goodness. He and Jay had put them together yesterday, so today was mattresses, sheets and blankets. Wardrobes, dressing tables and drawers were all clean and in place, and a fire would be lit in every room, since the house, long neglected, had not been aired in years. Roofers had begun work on cottages and farms, as the new owner wanted every tenant to be warm and dry this winter. For too long, the estate had been an orchestra with no conductor, but she would tune them up and give out the sheet music. Whatever she undertook, she would throw herself in and do her level best, and Keith had known that after sitting with her for no more than a few minutes.

Apart from the war, life was looking up. But there was one other niggling worry: the timbre of Eileen's letters had changed slightly. It was almost as if she had placed a sheet of frosted glass over the messages, creating a small distance between herself and him. She wrote a great deal about Crosby and Blundellsands, about the old woman with whom she and Mel would be lodging, and about a family named Bingley. The husband was a doctor, the wife a homely type who ran the local WVS, and both children were pupils at Merchants. Eileen, too, was going to help occasionally with a different arm of the Women's Voluntary Service, because Tom had introduced her to some committee or other in town. Tom. The name seemed to jump out from the page every time he looked at it. She mentioned him so casually; too casually.

He sat on the bed that would be Eileen and Mel's. She would sleep here, breathe here, dream here. Would she dream about Tom with the homely wife, the qualifications, the good job? Was she about to offer herself to married man? If Keith could feel a pang of jealousy at the thought that these windows might have the privilege of misting over with the exhalations from a mouth he needed to kiss, hating Tom Bingley was going to be a very easy task. He was being silly, and he knew it. Eileen Watson was a virtual stranger, yet he was allowing himself to become tangled up in thoughts of her that would probably take him nowhere.

Jean Dyson arrived. She stood in the doorway, hands on hips, mouth set in a grim line. 'What happened?' she demanded. 'And why was my Neil left out of it? He sat in that pub waiting for someone to tell him what the hell was going on, but he never found out, did he?'

Keith rose to his feet. 'It was Jay's show, not mine. I wasn't doing the choreography. Collie Crawford and Elsie Openshaw confirmed that Gill is pregnant, then Elsie decided that Jay has diabetes. So they're all at the infirmary, dog included, which leaves just you and me to get this place ready. And now you know as much as I do.'

It was Jean's turn to sit down, though she used the dressing table stool. 'Bloody hell. No aeroplanes for him, then.'

'No.'

'Can he work?'

'Probably. Whatever happens, I think Miss Pickavance will look after him. She's not the type to penalize somebody for getting ill. She's too decent for that.'

'I hope so. For long enough, it's been me and Neil at Home Farm, Jay and Gill at the gatehouse, you down on the Edge. Gill's supposed to be housekeeper when the house is up and running, but can she do it with a passenger? She wasn't supposed to be able to have kids.'

Keith shrugged. With Jean and Neil, with Gill and Jay, there was no holding back, none of the social awkwardness that often existed between the sexes. Pregnancy and other delicate matters didn't belong in the public domain but, between friends, all was fair. 'She could carry well, Jean. Conception was the problem, but she might not have a bad time while she carries. There's no way of knowing, is there?'

Jean studied her companion for a few moments. 'I'm amazed you never got wed. You've a lovely nature, Keith Greenhalgh, and I reckon some poor girl's missed out on a happy life.'

'Set in my ways. A bit of a bore most of the time. I have my breakfast, work, get a snack, do my crossword, work, light a fire, have my tea and read the rest of the paper. Floors get swept twice a week, and I flick a duster round on Sundays, wash the kitchen floor, get–'

'Give over. You left one thing out.'

'What?'

She smiled. 'You read your letters from that young woman me and Neil never saw, the one who came with Miss Pickavance.'

Keith laughed. 'Just a friend who likes writing. I enjoy writing letters, too.' He swallowed. 'In fact, I think she might have met someone in Liverpool, so you can cross that name off the non-existent list.'

'Aw. I am sorry, lad.'

He was sorry, too, but he mustn't let it show. He had to check on the kitchen, the woodshed, the coal. There were brass and silver to be polished, crockery to be rinsed of dust, furniture to be rescued from the imprisonment of protective coverings. Normally, he would be working in a supervisory capacity only, but with Jay and Gill at the hospital, he and the home farmer's wife had been forced to step into their roles. They made up all the beds, and Keith laid a fire in each room. 'Right,' he told his companion. 'And that, as they say, is that. Time for a break, love.'

When they sat down in the kitchen for a well-deserved cup of tea, Jean asked Keith whether he would be taking an evacuee. 'I might,' he said. 'If there's one on his own. But the three lads up here are going to need a firm hand from what I've heard. If any of them starts bother, I'll move him in with me. Are you getting one?'

'A girl,' she said. 'With already having the two girls, we're more used to females.' She stood up. 'Right, I've a meal to do. Will you be eating with us tonight? You'll be very welcome.'

He shook his head. 'Thanks, but no. I've a few things to do.'

Alone once more, he allowed a long, sad sigh to surface. Thoughts of Eileen had been keeping him going. He couldn't return to Cora Appleyard for sustenance or relief, because he was fixated. Again. And there was no one with whom he might share his thoughts and fears, since most would see his weakness rather than the strength of his feelings. Should he stop writing to her? Was a clean break less painful than an extended goodbye? And anyway, this foolishness could be part of an overactive imagination. Eileen and Tom might be no more than friends...

He went out to talk to the horses. His favourites, the large cart-pullers, were out in the field acting daft. A carthorse at play was a magnificent sight, owning the same silliness as an untrained polo pony but carrying about his person the weight of a small steam engine. The sight of four feathered feet waving in the air while an equine giant rolled in the grass was one to be treasured.

Keith whistled, and they stopped their foolishness to follow him into the yard. Behind them trotted a little palomino. Keith had plans for Pedro. The youngest of Eileen's boys liked horses, and he would be taught to ride. There was still a chance. If he could tame her sons, he might just get her to look at him again. And life at Willows needed to be as easy as possible for Miss Pickavance, so the management of those children was of prime importance.

He settled the horses and returned to the house, surprised when he found Gill sorting out cupboards and crockery. 'How did it go?' he asked. 'Has Collie gone home?' He had not expected to see her, but she told him that the ward sister had ordered her home, as Jay needed to settle. 'I have to take pyjamas and stuff tomorrow, because he'll need them.'

'And Collie brought you back?'

'Yes, he's gone. He's a couple of cows need attention over at Pear Tree. And I'm pregnant, and Jay's having blood tests, but they're ninety per cent sure it's diabetes. So that's his dream of being a pilot finished. He can fly a kite, but that's about it.'

'And you're upset, but you're hiding it.'

She nodded and carried on wiping saucers. 'I'm not upset about having a baby, because it's what I've always wanted. It's Jay. They gave me a booklet, and on one page it warns about heart attacks and blindness while further on it tells a diabetic to carry on as normal. So it's not just Stephenson that's mad; it looks like the whole medical profession could do with a fortnight in Blackpool for rest and recuperation.'

'They'll be keeping Jay in for a while, then?'

'Yes. They have to get his food points to balance with his insulin, then try to calculate how much work he does in a day, multiply the points, adjust the insulin accordingly, then go back to the number they first thought of. It's like some warped game. They've no idea what they're doing, and I'll have to pick up the pieces when their guesswork goes wrong. I'll be following him around all day.'

'I'll help. You know I'll do anything I can, Gill. So will Neil and Jean. Do you want to sleep at Home Farm tonight? I'm sure they wouldn't mind.'

'No, no. I'm all right.' She wasn't. She didn't want to sleep at Jean's house, but she wasn't all right. There was the worry about Jay, for a start. Bolton Royal Infirmary seemed not to know whether to starve him or feed him, and she was afraid in case the little one in her belly might never see its dad. But there was a bigger anxiety, and he was standing very near to her. Gill had no idea how or when it had happened, but she seemed to have grown rather too fond of the land agent. She hadn't fallen in love, because that was a sudden thing; she had slid into it smoothly and easily. Trying to climb out was no use; it was like struggling in quicksand, as she seemed to sink further whenever she attempted to free herself.

'What is it, Gill?'

'Tiredness,' she answered.

'Then go home and rest. I can finish off here.'

She walked towards the door, stopped and turned. 'Why did you never marry, Keith?'

He raised his shoulders. Everyone kept asking him the same question. 'No one would have me? Oh, I love too well, Gill. There was a girl, and she died. Her ghost stayed with me for a very long time, and I'm no spring chicken now. But there's a lot to be said for living alone. I please myself and only myself. I can get away without shaving at weekends, and no one nags me.'

'Do I nag Jay?'

'Yes, of course you do. And Jean nags Neil, because that's the way it works. Women nag, and men ignore them.'

She loved Jay. She did, she *did*. This Keith Greenhalgh business was a flash in the pan, no more than that. It was a bit like when she was at school, and Jimmy Schofield held her hand during long multiplication. At the age of twelve, she'd had her wedding planned; she and Jimmy would marry, get a farm and have four children. It was all connected to hormones, and her hormones belonged to the man she'd married. She had to make herself fall in love with Jay all over again.

'Gill?'

'It's all right, Keith. I just got a bit fed up with Jay the super-pilot. Not easy living with someone who doesn't know whether he's coming, going, or falling on the floor like a sack of logs. I love him, I'm sure, but it's been hard wondering which one of him would be coming home.' She paused. 'The being in love doesn't last, does it?'

'I don't know. I expect it lasted for me because I turned her into an angel. The dead are always perfect, but we aren't. You've a lot to face up to. There's a baby coming, and your man's ill. Don't stop loving him because he's less than perfect. Now's the time for a deep friendship to be formed. When you locked him out that night and he came to me, he was a sick man. We didn't know that. We thought he was a natural clown who couldn't hold his drink. He's your husband, Gill. In sickness and in health, remember?'

She smiled. There were many kinds of love. Red hot desire usually burned itself out, and unless replaced by something more substantial it disappeared like steam pouring upwards into the atmosphere. Romantic love that depended on poetry and posturing was not to be trusted, either. Love needed to come from the mind as well as from the soul. Real love was loyalty, laughter, and conversations in which minds met even though they didn't necessarily agree.

Gill wasn't sure what she felt for Keith Greenhalgh, so she decided that it was some kind of combination of all three. She wanted to touch and be touched, might have enjoyed a bit of Wordsworth, and the man was an intelligent communicator, when he chose to talk. He was a passing fancy, or so she hoped. She said goodbye and left.

Keith continued to deal with crockery and pans. Something about Gill had moved him. She wasn't pretty, wasn't ugly, was a good woman. She had mid-brown hair and blue irises, and the skin beneath her eyes was currently stained like bruising on a peach. Other than that, her complexion was good, her figure pleasing... He cleared his throat. She had been talking to him, and beyond the words sat something he neither wanted nor needed.

Kitchen knives and meat cleaver went into a top drawer. Was a meat cleaver suitable company for Philip, Robin and Albert? They had to learn what not to touch, how to behave properly, or their mother would never again give Keith the time of day. 'God help me,' he whispered. He couldn't bear the memory of the expression he'd seen in

Gill's eyes. Nor did he wish to contemplate a life without a chance to be with Eileen.

Should he talk to Gill? What might he tell her? She'd made no declaration, and what was he going to say about a look on her face? Nothing. Gill would need to frame the words, and she wouldn't, as she was a decent human being with a family to care for. Perhaps if Jay got balanced and a bit more sensible, she would learn to value him again, because he was a good lad underneath the daftness.

Life was hard. Keith locked up Willows and went home for something to eat. Later on, he might go to the pub for a couple of pints. Sometimes, a man needed his comforts.

Seven

There was something terribly wrong. Whatever it was crackled in the air like undischarged lightning, and Mel wished with all her heart that it would show itself in a blaze of temper before going away and leaving in its wake a clearer atmosphere. This was a local war; the real one waited while Hitler entrenched himself in France. Only then would he be capable of bombing the north of England; he could get to London from Germany, but not much further. Yet it would come; oh yes, it would come. This quiet period was not to be trusted, and people should not become complacent, because the planes might already be lined up on the

French coast. Meanwhile, the Battle of Rachel Street had begun.

The three lads, whose recent brush with the law was being taken extremely seriously, were sleeping in Miss Pickavance's house. They were unusually quiet, untypically clean, and they wore a corporate expression that might have sat well on the face of a hunted animal being chased towards unfamiliar territory. But that was not the problem. The awful truth was that Mam was not speaking to Gran, and Gran's features were set in grim lines that spoke volumes on the subject of disharmony.

They never quarrelled. Occasionally, there would be a small disagreement about the lads and their mischief, about when the family would go to the public bath house, about ordinary, everyday things that niggled and caused small amounts of tension in many households. This was different. This was enormously different. It was enough that her country was waiting with bated breath for the inevitable onslaught by a foreign power; that her mother and grandmother should be daggers drawn was ghastly. Ghastly was the favourite word at school these days; war, uniform and the creatures at the boys' school were all too, too ghastly, and the vowel had to be a long, tall 'ah' rather than a flat Lancashire production.

Mel stretched out on her bed after doing battle with the subjunctive mood in French. She had won, but small victories were suddenly meaningless, because all was far from well on the home front. There'd been an enormous, earth-shaking fight, but Mel had no idea of its subject. She didn't need to know, yet she wanted all to be well before the imminent parting of ways. 'It would be ghastly,' she told the ceiling.

Gran, having disappeared for several hours a few days ago, had returned with bruised knuckles and a visibly altered attitude. Since then, a cloud had settled over Rachel Street. It was heavy, black, and it promised to deliver a storm of enormous proportions, since Mam and Gran seemed unwilling to negotiate a peace treaty.

Mel dared not interfere directly. Born with an innate sense of when to speak and when to hold her tongue, she had the intelligence to stay out of this. Whoever stepped into the field of battle would only make matters worse. Such an intruder might also get burned by the temperature in the arena. Homer's *Iliad* screamed for attention, but Mel had bigger and British fish to fry. She had to make something happen while remaining outwardly detached.

The whole neighbourhood was affected. Gran was doing a lot of hmmphing and Mam was walking about with a face like a bad knee, as Gran might have termed it had she been using language. Everyone was due to move in a couple of days, and it would be sad if the two adults in the family parted on bad terms, especially during a war. Not that there'd been many signs of conflict thus far, but men in uniform were marching and driving through Liverpool in their hundreds. This quiet time could not last for much–

Ah. The front door slammed. Mam didn't make such a noise, even when in a bad mood, so Mel identified the incomer as Gran. Minutes later, her mother came home. Latin could wait, Mel decided. She would visit her brothers and Miss Pickavance, as nothing would happen here unless all potential referees and linesmen had left the field of play. She jumped up, ran downstairs and called out her intention to visit number one.

When Mel entered the house across the street, Miss Pickavance asked a question by raising an eyebrow, and Mel shook her head sadly. There was no progress. Everything was changing: Philip, Rob and Bertie sat at the table doing homework; that, in itself, was a rarity to be treasured. The quiet, gentle woman who was meting out their punishment had proved that she was a force to be reckoned with. Her deep disappointment was far more effective than a stroke from a cane or a cuff round the ear.

Hilda led Mel into her kitchen. 'It can't go on,' she mouthed.

Mel nodded. 'It won't,' she answered in a whisper. 'Otherwise I'll knock their heads together.'

They drank tea while the boys giggled in the next room. Mel hoped that Mam hadn't gone straight upstairs. She slept in the boys' room now, leaving Gran the luxury of a mattress all her own in the downstairs front room. 'Fingers crossed,' she said.

'Yes,' agreed Hilda. 'May good sense prevail.'

'Keep your voice down,' Eileen ordered. 'Kitty next door's had enough trouble lately without having to listen to you roaring like a bull at a locked gate.'

The older woman attempted to rein herself in. Her daughter was on the route to perdition, and

Nellie was trying to set up a roadblock 'He's married,' she hissed. 'You know damned well he's a married man, because Mel's his Gloria's best friend. How can you even think of such a thing? You're supposed to confess sins of thought, you know.'

'Can you not play a different tune?' Eileen folded her arms and tapped an angry toe against the floor. 'You walk in there and try to take his eye out – did you know he had to be checked for a broken cheekbone? As for putting out the Dockers' Word ... I despair. He should sue you.'

Nellie dropped into a chair. 'You've seen him,' she accused. 'You've met him while you were supposed to be at work.'

'Course I have. Somebody had to apologize for your behaviour. I saw him the day after you hit him, if you must know. His face was all the colours of the rainbow, and he'd been at the hospital after you punched him.'

Nellie shrugged. 'At least I told you what I'd done. And he daren't bloody sue, because it would all come out. As for you, I am ashamed to death. Sleeping with a man who's a father, a husband and a doctor? What about when you get pregnant, eh? Don't come running to me with a bastard on board. Then there's Mel. Do you think nobody'll notice? You'll stop her being top of the class, I can tell you that for no money.' She paused for effect. 'So you've made your mind up to ruin your little girl's life. Give yourself a pat on the back.'

Eileen inhaled deeply. 'I will, Mam. Because when I went to see him, I said sorry for what you'd done, and I told him he'd get nowhere with me. What I object to is you trying to be in charge of a thirty-three-year-old woman. I shouldn't have told you I had any sort of feelings for him. We've always been able to talk, you and me. It seems as if I can't ever tell you anything again.'

Nellie's lip quivered. 'Don't say that, girl. You're my world. You're everything to me, Eileen. I just want to keep you safe.'

'I know. But I promise you here and now that I'll do nothing to hurt our Mel.' She paused. 'And I know well enough that I could come to love a man ... perhaps a sensible one like Keith Greenhalgh. I'm not a fool, you know. I just have a lonely body. And Keith is very, very special. I had a dream about him last night. It was ... lively.' But she mustn't make the hurry-up mistake, mustn't develop war fever...

When Mel returned from her unscheduled visit, she heard them both weeping. As prearranged, she bounded up the stairs, went into the front room, removed the blackout screen and held a lighted candle near the window. That was the signal for which Miss Pickavance would be waiting. The storm had passed and the air was clearer. It was Germany's turn now.

The swelling had subsided somewhat, but Tom still looked as if he had gone several rounds with a champion boxer. Mrs Kennedy packed a fair punch, and she was hefty in the verbal department, too. How she had managed to produce a daughter as elegant and dainty as Eileen beggared belief. Even Eileen's accent had improved, and her tendency to abuse English grammar seemed to be disappearing fast. But she was backing off, was becoming determined to concentrate on Mel, who was her sole reason for remaining in Liverpool. He wanted her more than ever. The war had enlivened her sexuality, and he was prepared to serve her in any way she might require.

He looked at himself in the bathroom mirror. A black eye did not sit well on the face of a doctor, whose prime concern was supposed to be the physical integrity of his patients. The official explanation was that he had argued with a door and had come off second best, but he'd seen a few glances that spoke of disbelief.

The door opened. 'Will you be long?' Marie asked.

He continued to look in the mirror, though his gaze now travelled past his own image and settled on her. She looked different. There was tousled, carefree and newly styled hair, and a rosy glow on her cheeks. 'You look well,' he remarked. The war seemed to be suiting women, then.

Marie nodded, backed out, and closed the door. She crept into the spare bedroom and perched on the edge of a narrow, single bed. He must not be encouraged to find her attractive. She was having a wonderful time, and he was not going to be allowed to spoil it. The business she chose to name rape was now a thing of the past, and she intended to keep it that way. Tom and his pot of petroleum jelly could stay in the master bedroom, thanks very much, because she neither needed nor wanted more children, as she had done her duty by delivering two for the price of one. He wouldn't come in here. He was too proud a man to chase her in order to have his way.

But ... Norman had arrived in her life. Norman carried the keys to the church hall in which Marie's WVS people met several days a week. He was a good Christian man, a widower whose offspring had flown the nest, and he treated Marie with a deference to which she was becoming happily accustomed. Norman had beautiful hands, and he played the piano. He was over fifty, wealthy enough after selling a string of chemist shops, and he was clearly attracted to Marie. For the first time in her life, she felt something that was no stranger to desire. When he touched her arm, she shivered, and her nice, middle-class core prayed that no one noticed.

Marie Bingley now knew that she had never completely loved her husband. The marriage had been a sensible liaison encouraged by both families, since the Bingleys had a clever son but little money, while Marie's family had given her a dowry sufficient to house their daughter, her gifted husband and the children when they arrived. Tom had been paid to marry a girl who was moneyed, but not pretty. However, she was prettier these days, and the man in the bathroom had noticed that.

Marie had no idea what was happening to her. All she knew was that a day without Norman was cold and empty, that his smile fed her, that his quiet playing on the piano while 'his' ladies knitted, chatted and drank tea was soothing and pleasurable. He was of the old school, had been raised by elders who taught him to treat females with near-reverence, and to run the family business sensibly and with the welfare of customers at the forefront of his mind. Norman liked her, enjoyed talking to her about his time in the army, his war, the shops he had supervised.

She heard Tom going downstairs. After claiming the bathroom, Marie soaked in water perfumed by crumbled bath cubes, washed her hair and prepared to deliver a lecture on first aid. Her ladies would be involved in battle once the bombs came and, as the wife of a doctor, Marie was deferred to when medical matters surfaced. She was in charge, and Norman had kindly helped her in the preparation of the lecture.

It wasn't love, she reassured herself. It was a decent man treating a woman properly. Nevertheless, before leaving the house, she applied to her mouth a discreet shade of lipstick. There was nothing wrong with trying to look her best, was there?

The two rooms were beautiful. Eileen touched an eiderdown, pleased beyond measure when she felt its smooth, silky cover. Her room was mainly green, while Mel's was in several shades of pink. They each had a wardrobe, a tallboy and a chest of drawers. Eileen's electric reading lamp had a tasselled shade, as did Mel's in the other room. Mel also had a real desk with a roll-back top and sections for all her work. There was a bookcase, too, and a good chair on which she would sit to do her homework. After Rachel Street, this was a palace.

Eileen checked the blackout screens, making sure that she understood the mechanisms that held them in place behind the pretty curtains. When both screens were back under the beds, Eileen began to clean the bathroom. Miss Morrison was downstairs enjoying a bowl of homemade soup. The old lady seemed content and a great deal less worried now that she knew she would not be alone throughout the war. Then, just as she was rinsing the washbasin, Eileen heard his voice. 'How are you today, Miss Morrison?'

She shuddered. There was nowhere to run, and there would never be anywhere to run while she lived in this house. The owner had a heart condition, and was his patient. Mel and Eileen would both be here, and the man downstairs was a bold, needful creature. His idea of courtship was roaming hands and battling tongues. She wanted him, couldn't lie to herself about that, but all the same he was a creature to be avoided, and avoidance was not an option now. The thought of hiding in a wardrobe allowed her a humorous moment, yet she didn't even smile. He was here, and he had come for her rather than for Miss Morrison.

When he entered the bathroom, Eileen continued to polish taps. He closed the door, and within seconds his hands were round her waist and travelling north. 'I told the old dear I'd take you home in the car,' he whispered.

She turned in his arms. 'Do you want a matching pair?' she asked. 'And I mean black eyes, not my breasts. I nearly lost the love of my mother because of you.' Desire and anger were a difficult combination. She wanted to kill him, needed to kiss him, and was as confused as a blind man in a maze. But she had known this before, had battled with and beaten several desirable men who had tried to wear her Lazzer's shoes since his death. Tom Bingley was just another toy she didn't need.

'Then learn not to confide in her,' he suggested.

'I may confide in the woman downstairs,' she threatened. 'And she's one of the few who can afford to pay your medical bills. She likes Dr Ryan. Dr Ryan's been here when you've been unavailable, and women prefer a female doctor. Miss Morrison wouldn't approve of your behaviour.'

Tom stepped back. 'I like a feisty female,' he said. 'Though I could take or leave Ryan, I have to say. But you smell of tomorrow, my darling. A magic urchin, you are. So I can't give you a lift home?'

'No.'

He stood near the door. 'This Dockers' Word,' he began.

'Stands indefinitely,' Eileen snapped. 'They've had to stick together, because the ones who got work had to help the poor buggers that didn't get chosen. They're close-knit, welded and bolted together like steel girders. You make a move on me, and they'll have you.'

'Bollocks,' he answered through a smile.

'They have those, too,' Eileen advised him. 'They're not likely to be afraid of a doctor with a black eye and a toothbrush sticking out of his ear.'

'Toothbrush?'

She held the weapon aloft. 'It's all right, this is an old one, so I won't be wasting much. I use it to clean round taps. Which ear would you like me to choose? I noticed you have two of them.'

'The one with a perforated tympanic membrane. That's spelt with a Y or an I, by the way.'

'Thanks for improving my education. Now, bugger off.'

He chuckled softly. 'She made it up, didn't she? That Dockers' Word business is a figment of your ma's fevered imagination. Though I have to say she probably picked up her colourful language on the waterfront. Your mother has a mouth like a sewer.'

Eileen crossed her fingers behind her back. 'She may be a lot of things, but Nellie Kennedy's no liar. I've known her all my life, and she never lies, never steals. My mother is an honest woman. You're going to need eyes in the back of your head. Oh, and if you want to mend your ear drum, you can borrow our Mel's puncture kit.'

His eyes narrowed. This one was a bright little bugger, and she wanted taming. 'You enjoyed what I did to you, what we did together,' he said.

'Like everybody else, I have animal instincts,' she replied. 'The difference between you and me is that I can control mine.'

He nodded very slowly. 'Can you? Can you really?' He left the room.

Eileen sank slowly onto the lavatory seat. She couldn't control her limbs, let alone the sensations that rippled through her body whenever he was near. There was a sixth sense, and she was its victim. That extra faculty was nothing to do with looking into the future or talking to spirits. It was a two-way traveller, and very difficult to ignore. He was suffering, too, because his extra sense had met hers halfway across the space that separated them. There were better men than him; there was Keith, for a start. She hadn't spent enough time with him yet, but he was definitely interesting, because even his letters made her innards melt. 'Why do I suddenly need a blasted bloke anyway?' she asked the door.

Tom was telling Miss Morrison that Eileen hadn't quite finished her work, and that he had more patients to see. For the sick and elderly, he used a different tone, but it was genuine. Tom Bingley was perhaps oversexed, but he actually cared about his patients. Miss Morrison thought the world of him, and he came and went as he chose in this house.

'He's not a completely bad man,' Eileen whispered to herself. 'But Mel matters a damned sight more than he does.' There was no turning back now; she and Mel had to move from Rachel Street. Rumours of dogfights over Hastings and other southern towns were rife. She couldn't give back word to the lady downstairs, couldn't stay in her own house, was going to be living within reach of Tom for as long as the war lasted. He had in his possession a potion that could guarantee her freedom from pregnancy. It had come from abroad, and very few knew of its existence. Oh, God. She should not be thinking like this.

Having regained the ability to walk properly, she finished her work and went downstairs. A neighbour would come in later to heat thoroughly the meal she had prepared for her precious old lady. Frances Morrison was sweet, partially deaf, and as bright as a new button. She was looking forward to having Mel in her house, as she approved strongly of the public school system. She was a member of the Conservative Party, an ex-headmistress of a small and very exclusive primary school, and she had objected strongly when advised to lower the union flag from its post in her garden.

'Are you going, dear?'

'Yes. We'll move in at the weekend if that's all right with you.'

'Good, good. I shall get the chance to converse in French.'

Eileen laughed. In her day, Frances Morrison must have been the subject of gossip, as her bible held a commandment stating that all children should begin a second language by the age of nine. The pupils of Abbeyfield School had entered secondary education with a smattering of French, and they usually outstripped all others in that subject, a fact that was much mentioned in this house.

Eileen bent and left a kiss on a soft, papery cheek. 'The minute this war's over, I'll run your flag up myself. God bless.'

'And may He bless you, my dear.'

Tom was outside, car parked at the pavement's edge, his person propped casually against a garden wall. He couldn't have done a better job had he actually set out to advertise his intentions. 'Get in,' he ordered.

'No.' Her heart was doing about ninety miles an hour in a built-up area, and there was a war on. Fuel, she told herself irrelevantly, should be saved.

'Get in, or I shall kiss you now in full view of the inhabitants of St Michael's Road. My wife will be told, and you will be co-respondent in the ensuing divorce. Come along, hurry before a docker spots me.'

Fuming, yet hungry for him, she placed herself in the passenger seat. He closed her door, walked round the vehicle, then sat next to her. The engine roared as he turned and drove towards the river.

'You're wasting petrol and your time,' she said. 'You're also attracting attention with all that noise.'

He slammed on the brakes, and a shard of fear entered her chest, because they were still in a residential area.

'Damn you.' The words were forced between clenched teeth. 'It's not just about sex any more, is it? I have fallen in love with you, my little urchin. And you are a mere inch from returning the compliment. If I were free, I'd marry you tomorrow.'

'No, you wouldn't.'

'I would. You know I would.'

'Get me away from all these houses. Now!'

He carried on until he reached a quiet stretch of river before parking again.

She told him straight. 'I have three sons who can curdle custard just by staring at it for a few seconds. Because we live in a poor area, and because they have no dad, they're very wild. Only last week, all three were arrested, and there was talk of them going into an institute for young offenders. Instead, I'm sending them with my mother to a farm on the moors outside Bolton. Whoever marries me gets lumbered with them. All three of them. Mel's no trouble, but Philip, Rob and Bertie are nightmares. You wouldn't last a week.'

'I love you, Eileen.'

'That can soon be killed by three lads who think nothing of stealing, running bets and making enough noise to rip the skin off your rice pudding.'

'I don't like rice pudding. Or custard.'

'Neither do I, but that's not the point. You know Mel. You can see how she is: clever, polite and kind. They are the exact opposite. But they're my lads, and they go where I go once we get Hitler sorted out.'

He stared ahead at the grey, angry water. 'Then we'll live in the countryside. We can move as soon as you like.'

'I have to stay with Mel. Mel is my real bit of war work. She's going to Cambridge if I have to drive her there with a whip, Tom. How do you think she'd cope if you and I were found out? She'd fall behind. Your daughter would lose her best friend, and I'd lose what's left of my self-respect. Oh, and a Catholic can't marry a divorced person. It would mean excommunication.'

She could build all the barriers she liked, but he would not give up. 'I can't live without you. Wouldn't it be murder if I popped off?'

'No. It would be suicide, and that's a prosecutable offence. If you survived, you'd be charged.'

He laughed mirthlessly. 'You're a clever girl.'

'I read a lot. I don't resent my daughter, yet I know I would have done well if I'd had her chances. But I didn't, and that's that. Then there's my mother. You've met her. You know how she is. As long as she's alive, she'll be with me. I'd have gone with her to the country except for Mel. I had to choose, and I picked my daughter, because she's too beautiful and clever to be left to chance. You must have looked at her yourself, because she's me all over again. And yes, I know I'm pretty, and false modesty is pointless. If and when I want a man, I'll find one with no ties and plenty of patience, because he'll have to put up with the boys and my mother.'

He studied her face hard. 'And you've someone in mind?'

She nodded. 'But it's early days. He's a good man, a hardworking man. Like me, he's educated himself, and he will help Mam with the boys.'

'So he's a farmer?'

Eileen shook her head. 'No, he isn't a farmer. He supervises half a dozen farms and a load of houses. That's the sort of man I'll go for. He's also promising to be adorable.'

Tom was angry. Why had he married Marie? Why had he married for money? 'Then just allow me a little time before you commit to him. I'll take care of you. Who knows who'll come out alive when the bombing starts? Let's grab what we can while we can. I know you want me, Eileen. I could repeat now what I did last time we were in this car, and you'd let me. In fact, you'd encourage me. Am I right?'

'Yes, but it would be wrong. It's the war, that's all. This isn't real.'

He told her that Tuesday and Thursday nights would be her time to be in Scotland Road at her post. But he had informed the ladies of the WVS that she would be caring for the sick in Crosby, so she wouldn't be required to go. She could walk instead to the flat above his surgery on Liverpool Road. 'I'll be waiting,' he threatened. 'A nice fire, double bed, bathroom, small kitchen. We can make toast afterwards and feed each other. I'll lick the butter from your fingers, Eileen.'

'Stop it.'

'Your daughter need never find out.'

But Eileen didn't believe him. If Mam could notice a glow on her daughter's skin after a quick fumble in a car, surely Mel would catch a glimpse of the same? 'It shows,' she told him. 'In my face.'

'You miss lovemaking.' It was not a question.

'Of course I do.' But she'd learned to cope, had never met a man who lit her up quite as readily this one did. 'We had a good life, Laz and me. We weren't wealthy by any stretch of the imagination, but he always worked, didn't drink, and we were very close. Lovemaking was something we learned together, and it was private and special. That was real love, you see. This isn't, and it never could be, because I think you're greedy and ... unwholesome, I believe the word is. You'll become a dirty old man who pays for sex.'

He could manage no reply. She was insulting him, yet he could not for one moment doubt her honesty. Eileen said what she felt, and delivered her opinion unadorned by dressing. It was this earthiness that made her so appealing, because her raw, almost visible sexuality was rooted in directness and lack of inhibition.

'Take me to the tram stop,' she said now. 'And my war work will be of my choosing, not yours. I'll be on my feet, not on my back in your double bed dripping with butter.'

'Eileen–'

'No. If you play on my baser side and get me to do what you want, I'll never forgive you or myself afterwards. Mel comes first. She leaves the rest of her class standing for brains and for beauty, and you know it. Do you really think you've a claim on me while she's parked in the way? Do you?'

Tom lowered his head. To get the better of Eileen, he would need to dispose of Marie, Mel, three boys and Eileen's mother. Since mass murder was not in his nature, he seemed to have come up against six insurmountable barriers. He took her to the tram stop.

Just weeks earlier, everything Mel and Eileen owned would have fitted into a couple of medium-sized boxes. Now, with clothes, shoes and bags kindly donated by Hilda, the carter would be needed to take their possessions to St Michael's Road. Eileen, the proud owner of a Singer sewing machine, property of the deceased Mrs Pickavance, planned to make over some items for Mel, who was growing at a rate of knots she described as ghastly. 'Nothing fits,' she pretended to complain. 'And I need a brassiere, Mam. Can you adapt one of yours?'

'I'll try when we've moved,' Eileen promised. 'Go and help your brothers with their homework. It might be half-term before you see them again.'

'And that is not ghastly.'

'Mel!'

'I know, they're my flesh and blood, and the priests say I have to put up with them. It's all right for priests in their nice, quiet presbyteries.

They don't have to live with three monsters and half a police force, do they?'

'Your gran and Hilda will straighten them out.'

'And your penfriend?'

'Stop being ghastly, Mel.'

The girl laughed. 'Gh*aaah*stly, Mother. You have to get the ah into it.'

'So it's not just my Ps and Qs, then? I have to get my Rs right, too?'

'That sounds rude.'

'Good. Go and help the poor woman who's lumbered with the junior branch of the Al Capone fan club.' Eileen paused. 'I'll miss round here, you know. People think Scottie Road's all bad news, but it's not. We'll not find a community like this ever again.'

'Oh, you will. Just do a burglary and you'll meet half of this lot in jail.' Mel left the house before her mother could reply.

Eileen sat for a while waiting for Nellie, who was next door trying to comfort Kitty. Kitty Maguire had decided to panic again about moving, and Nellie was trying to calm her down. The calming down involved tea, brandy and many words of wisdom, and the ensuing period of peace seldom lasted long.

Alone, Eileen looked round the front room of number two. She knew every crack in the plaster, every mark on the walls. Her children had been measured near the outer door, four sets of lines with names near the floor. There they were, step by step, all four of them caught, held still, a pencil drawing a line level with their heads. Two and a half was the significant one, because when doubled, it gave the approximate height of the end product, the adult. Her boys were all going to top six feet, while Mel promised five feet and eight inches, which would be tall for a girl.

The fireplace was small, as was the room. There was always a fire in the kitchen, and when one was required in here Mam would carry through a shovel filled with burning coal and pour it into the little iron basket. Cupboards built in at each side of the chimney breast were battle-scarred, paint that was years old flaking off, two handles missing, one door drunk because of a failed hinge. Eileen and Laz had set up home here, and she would soon close the front door for the final time. He would never come back. Sometimes, in the early days of widowhood when she had heard tuneless whistling in the street, she had imagined... But Laz hadn't been the only bad whistler in these parts, and he had never burst in with his silly 'da-da' of a fanfare employed to announce his safe return from Liverpool's docks.

The docks had killed him. His funeral had been enormous, and few men had sought work on that day, because he'd been a good, well-loved man. Eileen remembered a full church, flowers, and a box near the altar. She would never meet his like again, but Keith Greenhalgh was a fair copy. In fact, he was cleverer than her beloved Laz had been, and–

Nellie came in. 'Hello, love. All by yourself? She's a mess next door. When push comes to shove, I'll not be surprised if she stays here. Eileen? You all right, queen?'

'No, I'm not. I need help.'

'Right.' Nellie sat down near the fireplace. 'Is it him again?'

Eileen nodded. 'I'm frightened. Frightened of me.'

Nellie understood. 'I know. There's something about him. I saw it meself just before I took the swing at him. What needs doing, then?'

After a lengthy pause, Eileen made her reply. 'Dockers' Word. Make it real.'

'It is real.'

'Mam? I thought you were kidding.'

Nellie Kennedy folded her arms. 'You are my life, girl. I spoke to Nobby Costigan, and he rounded up a few of Laz's mates. The Word's out.'

Eileen's jaw dropped for a second or two. 'I don't want anybody dead. And I don't want Laz's pals in prison. I just need Tom to know it's real. Like a warning. No real violence. Their faces must be covered by something or other, and it'll have to be done in the dark. How much will it cost?'

'Nothing. It's for Laz.'

'Right. Can you deal with it?'

'Consider it done. They'll scare the living be-Jaysus out of him, as my old gran would have said. He'll be needing clean underpants and a body-guard, but you just forget about it. It'll be a cold day in hell before he lays hands on you again.'

Bertie ran in and started complaining loudly about Miss Pickavance and the five times table. Tables were for eating off, and what had five times to do with that? He was fed up and he wanted to come home. Mel collared him and prepared to drag him back to be reincarcerated at number one.

Phil and Rob arrived and helped their sister to return the miscreant to the posh prison where the food was good and a bit of homework was a small price to pay for spare ribs followed by trifle, followed by cheese and biscuits, followed by cocoa.

Nellie puffed out her cheeks. 'When was life easy, Eileen?'

'Before my body started screaming out for a selfish man who has the power to make my insides turn to un-set jelly.'

Nellie went to brew tea. Halfway through the exercise, she had a thought. 'Like I said, it's this bloody war we're waiting for, folk getting wed and all sorts.' She paused. 'Why don't we do turns?'

Turns? What was she talking about? A song and dance act? 'How do you mean, Mam?'

Nellie appeared in the doorway. 'Well, if Miss Morrison and your other ladies can put up with me, we can swap every couple of weeks, then Tom Doodah won't know whether he's coming or going.' She grinned impishly. 'And you can get to know Keith Greenhalgh. If we can get the transport, that is.'

'Mam, your blood's worth bottling.'

'I know. I'm great, aren't I?'

For October, the weather was good. A slight breeze shifted leaves, causing some to flutter downwards to the ground where they joined close relatives in crisp red and brown heaps. The sun had said goodbye, though a trail of salmon pink and blush red reminded any onlooker that tomorrow would be equally gentle. Time slipped by, and the sky darkened towards an inky blue.

Offices and shops, now long closed, stood like sentries ordered to attention. Like the rest of England, Liverpool waited in stillness for the unimaginable to begin.

At approximately eight o'clock, Dr Thomas Bingley left his Liverpool Road surgery. He rummaged in his pocket for keys as he walked round the corner to where his car was parked in a side street. Thoroughfares were no longer lit, while houses, too, were blacked out against the threat of bombardment. He stood for a while to allow his eyes to adjust. After a late evening of catching up with notes, he had to linger in order to allow the pupils to widen and absorb the meagre offerings of late dusk. The drive home would have to be careful, since shaded headlights were almost useless. Fortunately, most people stayed in their houses; only wardens and fire-watchers patrolled streets that would be completely black within minutes.

When he reached the car, he suddenly found himself lying face down on its bonnet, both arms pinned behind his back, severe pain invading his left shoulder. There were two of them. He could hear their heavy, unsynchronized breathing. The second man gripped his neck, the hold vice-like, yet restrained. These were powerful men, and they had him at their mercy. Mercy?

'Stay away from Eileen Watson,' one hissed. 'Go anywhere near her, and you'll need a sodding wheelchair for the rest of your life. You hearing me?'

'Yes.'

'Say again.'

'Yes.'

The other man spoke. 'Dockers' Word. You know about that? See, some people have the Freemasons and all that farting about with handshakes and pinafores, but we have the big boys. Some of us were there when he died. The last word on his lips was her name. That means something. Leave her alone. Dockers' Word. Understand?'

'Yes.'

They picked him up and pushed him down again. In that moment, his left shoulder dislocated, and he groaned. Unfazed, one held him down while the other snapped the ball back into its socket. 'If we have to do this again, you'll have a broken back. See, when you work on the docks, you learn all about dislocated shoulders and snapped spines. Oh, yes. We're clever enough, doc. All right?'

'Yes.'

'Stay down there and count to fifty. One shout, one scream, and you'll be wishing you'd never been born.'

Tom heard them as they ran round the corner. His shoulder hurt like hell, but he didn't count to fifty. Instead, he climbed into the car and wondered how the dickens he was going to get home. He managed to shift the gear stick into second, and he drove at snail's pace through Crosby. A black eye, now an injured shoulder; was she worth it? Was she?

The terrible truth was yes. She was worth it, and he was a fool.

Eight

Jay Collins came home to the gatehouse after five days. He was rested, lively, and a nuisance. Gill put about the legend that Ward D2 had been approaching the brink of collapse, since her dearly beloved had caused enough trouble to instigate disputes between visitors and staff, cleaners and orderlies, and patients and nurses. The food, he maintained, had been hogwash. Pigs at Neil and Jean's home farm were better fed, while he'd never had a decent cup of tea during the whole of his time in what he chose to term the torture chamber. He was not going back. If he had to become a pincushion, he would manage on his own, thanks. Oh, and he didn't like saccharine, so he'd stick to sugarless tea, very strong and with a drop of milk. No porridge. If he saw another dish of this-is-very-good-for-you-but-use-mostly-water, it would be out of the door quicker than dry sand off a shiny shovel.

Gill did her best to keep him in the house for a while until he got used to his insulin and the new diet, but he wasn't prepared to listen. He knew he couldn't drink beer, but that wouldn't stop him getting out and about. He was the estate handyman, for goodness' sake, and invasion was imminent. The fact that he could not serve in the armed forces had finally been accepted, but he remained determined to do his bit on the estate.

'I'm going out,' he called while Gill was upstairs. There were things to do.

Willows was holding its breath not against the Germans' coming, but against Liverpool's. The Scousers were on their way, and he had to make sure all hatches were battened down, all doors closed and locked, all windows in good working order with strong catches in place. Liverpool people were tough, so he needed to be several steps ahead.

Keith helped. He was there to assess his employee's health and to make sure that he fell off no ladders, but he pretended to be assisting rather than acting as monitor. It was not an easy task. Jay, a natural clown, carried on much as before. He was funny, enthusiastic, friendly and difficult to judge when it came to health. When he started tripping over his own feet by accident, Keith was at the ready with barley sugar. 'Eat it.'

'I can't. I'm diabetic.'

'That's why you need it. You've run out of sugar. The reason you're not walking properly and not listening to me is that you're hypoglycaemic.'

'Big word, that.'

'It is. So eat it.'

'Can't eat a word I don't know how to say. Hypo who?'

'Glycaemic. Eat the bloody barley sugar, or it's back to the bacon factory you've complained about for the last three hours.'

'D2?' Oh, he remembered that dump, all right. 'Give us that thing here, because I'll do just about anything to stay out of that ... what was it?'

'Hospital.' Jay was losing his words. When the sweet had been consumed, Keith delivered yet another lecture. 'In a minute, you'll feel great. Remember that, because I won't be with you all the time. When you start losing words and legs, eat sugar. Right?'

'Yes. I feel fine now. So the thing that can kill me, which is sugar, is the thing that saves my life?'

'That's it.'

'Mad.'

Jay spent the rest of the day telling everyone he met that sugar could finish him one way or another, though he seemed to be cheerful enough about the whole thing.

Keith went off to report to Gill. Any awkwardness had to be overcome, because he had probably imagined her fondness for him, and life needed to continue as normally as possible in spite of the expected influx of evacuees. His pulse quickened. Eileen would not be here this time, but she'd visit soon. He still wrote and she still replied, though a small degree of reserve lingered in her letters. He would find a way to see her soon. He had the Crosby address and phone number.

Gill was her usual self, bright, sensible and trying to feed up her visitor. Something happened to Lancashire women the moment that band of gold was on their third finger. They fed anything that moved, particularly creatures on two legs. The refusal of an offering could cause great offence, so he made his way through three slices of buttered fruit cake and two cups of tea. There was no particular affection in her face when their eyes met. Yes, he had clearly mistaken her behaviour the other day.

'So he's up ladders?' she asked. 'You've let a loony climb ladders?'

'Part of the job. I've left him with more barley sugars and instructions to eat one if he starts feeling weak or forgetful.'

'And he'll forget what you said when he gets a bit hypo. You finish your cake while I walk down to the Edge and make sure he's all right. No, stay there, Keith. We've all got to get used to this.'

Alone, he drained his cup and took the latest missive from Liverpool out of his pocket. She, too, was funny sometimes. And there was no mention of Dr Tom.

So I am going to live in the beautiful house of a headmistress, while my boys are now with Miss Pickavance, who has turned out to be quite a good teacher-cum-jailer. Bertie makes the odd dash for freedom, but he's always dragged back by the other two, who enjoy Hilda's cooking and listening to her wireless and gramophone.

Meanwhile, Kitty-next-door, who is supposed to be having the empty house in Willows Edge, keeps throwing all kinds of fits. In spite of lovely new teeth that actually fit after adjustment, plus a second-hand bargain dress and jacket from Paddy's Market, she doesn't want to leave the house at all.

She's never been further down town than the Liver Buildings, hasn't even been over the water on the ferry. She thinks Birkenhead is a foreign country, while London probably exists on the moon or Mars. She's also frightened of empty fields and quietness, I think, and she'll be scared to death of cows and the like. We're used to horses, because they're part of our life round here, but I don't think Kitty's ever wondered where milk and butter and cheese come from. The Co-op, I suppose.

Mam says Kitty won't come to Willows, but I hope she does because since her husband fell in the river and died she's been weird, and a new start might shock her out of her depression. Charlie Maguire was an alcoholic, and she's better off without him, but she doesn't know that yet. Her children will thrive well in the fresh air, too, so we're trying to knock a bit of sense into her – not easy! Aren't people daft?

That last sentence was from the previous Eileen, the one who wrote from the soles of her feet, no holds barred, a smile or a wry comment in every paragraph. Some decision had been made, and a problem she'd encountered had either reduced in size or been eliminated. She was, he suspected, a complex character, highly intelligent and probably self-educated. He couldn't wait to see her again, yet he had to wait.

I seem to have inherited a sewing machine, which happy accident means I can cobble together some bits and pieces for Mel. She keeps up well at the school, and she seldom complains, but I know she feels the difference between herself and some of the other girls. They have ponies, new bikes and nice houses, but they don't have my girl's looks and brains. Mel's old-fashioned, and she comes out with some stuff when I ask does she mind being poor. One of her answers was that a Rolls-Royce might drive a girl to Oxbridge, but only exam results could open the doors to a college. I don't mean she's cocky, but she does have a clever answer for everything.

It sounds as if my mother and Mrs Openshaw might clash. Mam has been one of the unofficial midwives and layers-out in Scottie Road for twenty-odd years, and she doesn't care whose business she jumps into. She gets all the gossip from the bag-wash when she goes down with our washing, then I think she adds bits on while she walks home. So if somebody's had a big baby, like a ten-pounder, it'll be twelve pounds by the time Mam comes through our door.

He smiled to himself as he pictured Nellie Kennedy pushing an old pram filled with washing through the side streets of Liverpool. She was a character, all right, and she had birthed another character, who had produced yet another. These were his kind of women, because they never gave up. 'Neither do I, Eileen,' he said to the three pages. She cared. No one would write all this without holding some kind of interest in the recipient.

Jay came in, face split from ear to ear with an east-to-west grin. 'I'm the one with diabetes, and she's the one who stood in a cowpat.' He looked over his shoulder as a shoeless Gill entered. 'See? So busy keeping an eye on me, she ends up covered in sh– in shame.'

Keith looked at the pair and wished, hoped, that Gill loved the father of her long-awaited baby. Jay was a jester, but he was a good man who deserved the best. Then Keith caught Gill staring again, damped-down longing in her eyes. Immediately, he jumped to his feet, uttered a quick goodbye and left the house. There was something in Gill's head, and it was not appropriate. Bugger. He ate quite frequently at the gatehouse, and he enjoyed greatly the company of the couple who lived there.

'She looks at me the way I look at Eileen,' he told one of the six willow trees. Had he explained to Miss Pickavance that these weepers liked people, that they thrived on conversation? If the willows did well, stock thrived, crops burgeoned and the orchards bore enormous fruits. 'What's the matter with her?' Pregnant at last, she should be celebrating with her man. Fronds rustled and brushed against him, caressing his face and neck. Eileen's children would play here. Their noise would feed the willows and, because her blood was in the boys' veins, she, too, would be providing nourishment.

If Gill felt for Keith what he felt for Eileen, she would be in pain. What could he do? He'd never been married, but estate management involved interaction with many people, and pregnant women were odd. They developed strange likes and dislikes, had mood swings, ate coal and orange peel and, sometimes, went a bit wild.

Was Gill off her rocker? If she was crackers, would she mend straight away after the child's birth? What if she started with that decline some women went into after confinement? Should he talk to her? He left the trees on which everyone's welfare supposedly depended, and entered the main house. Tomorrow, he would pick up from Trinity Street station two women, three boys, and assorted small pieces of luggage. The main items had already arrived, but the car would be packed. With Miss Pickavance in the passenger seat, he would need to squeeze into the rear of the car three boys in assorted sizes, and a well-built though not overweight grandmother.

The house looked cosy. Gill and Jean had brought in some of summer's lingering blooms to brighten and freshen the rooms. Beds had been made, furniture waxed, oil lamps filled, wicks trimmed. He lit fires in every room, opened windows slightly to encourage airing. Tonight, he would sleep here on a camp bed in the kitchen. Willows was too precious to be left while wood and coal burned in grates.

He led the horses from the paddock into their stables, stood in the yard and looked at the stars. There could be frost tonight, because the sky was clear and inky. Tomorrow, the rebirth of Willows would begin under the guidance of a new mistress, one who might take an interest in the welfare of this vast estate and its many inhabitants. She was a good woman. Old Mr Pickavance had not been bad, but his connection to the land of his forebears had been minimal. Yes, there was a war on, yet the ill wind had delivered the promise of a new beginning in which Willows might find itself again.

All Keith needed now was for Gill to settle down with her excellent, well-meaning if chronically sick husband, and for Eileen to visit. He closed the stable doors and went into the kitchen. With a fire in the large grate, it looked homely and welcoming. For many years, this house had been lonely, neglected and unloved. 'As have I,' he said just before noticing the PTO at the bottom of Eileen's third page.

Mam and I have been talking. If we can get transport, she and I will change places from time to time so that I might keep in closer touch with my sons. Mam is very fond of Mel, and they will miss each other if the war lasts. Perhaps you might help by giving some thought to how we can travel the thirty-odd miles to and fro.

Another thought. I beg you to bring Mam next week. Between the two of you, you might manage to get Kitty Maguire out of number four. She is promised a job in the main house with Jay's wife. She will clean while her kids are having lessons in what my mother calls the afternoon room. Kitty needs my mother. A fresh start would do no harm, either. With her husband dead and her small children running wild, she could easily lose her mind completely here.

Love and best wishes, Eileen.

Hope attacked his heart from two fronts, a pincer movement seeming to squeeze all air from his body. She would be here, and not just for the odd weekend or half-term. And she had written a word that was taken too lightly these days. *Love.* 'Don't love me like a brother or a friend,' he begged. He had never expected to meet again eyes like Annie's: honest, beautiful and unafraid.

'Of course I'll pick up your neighbour. By the hair, if necessary.' He made toast and cocoa. Sometimes, life tasted good.

Nellie Kennedy was having a day and a half. Saying goodbye to Rachel Street wasn't easy; saying goodbye to Kitty Maguire was proving a near impossibility, because the thin woman had fastened herself to Nellie's clothing. 'You can't leave me on me own, Nell. I'll not manage without you.'

'If you rip that sleeve, I'll give you a clout round the ear 'ole. Come with us. Get the kids, pack your bits, and–'

'I've never been away from here. I've never been on a train.'

'I'll be with you.' But they wouldn't all fit in the car at the other end. Someone would have to stay behind at the station in Bolton and wait for the first lot to be delivered to Willows. 'Next week you'll be joining us, Kitty.'

'I daren't.'

Oh, but she would. Nellie reclaimed ownership of the sleeve, then folded her arms. 'Three or four days,' she said. 'If we don't come Monday, we'll be here Tuesday. Kitty, I've things to do. I can't stand here like the bloody Venus de Milo, because I need to use me arms to get the last of our things wrapped up. You've got to pull yourself together, queen, or we'll all be in a mess. Keith Greenhalgh is meeting us, and we have to be on that train.'

'But your Eileen's at work. She can't look after me.'

Nellie looked at the sky as if seeking guidance. Saying ta-ra to Eileen and Mel this morning had been the hardest thing. 'From tomorrow, Eileen will be in Crosby. Miss Morrison's health's gone worse, so our Eileen's had to give up all her other jobs just to look after the old lady.' Eileen was to have a small wage and, with food, fuel and shelter already paid for, she'd survive as long as they didn't get bombed.

'I can't be on me own,' Kitty wailed.

'There's a whole street of people here. You won't be by yourself.'

'They're fed up with me. There's only you cares.'

Nellie was as fed up as everyone else, but kindness had prevented her from giving up on this poor, confused woman. If the odd behaviour went on, Kitty might well find herself in an institution, and her kids would become genuine evacuees like most of the children who had left their parents at the beginning of September. 'Kitty, you have to get a grip, but not on my best clothes. If you turn up at Willows Edge in this state, and if your children carry on running wild and dirty, nobody will help you. People help those who make an effort.'

'I can't.'

'You bloody can and you bloody will. There's a nice clean cottage waiting for you. There's a job. Look, I know what it is to be widowed, and I feel for you. There's no one else to blame now, is there? It's just you. Charlie was always pickled, and the behaviour of your young ones was his fault. But I'm telling you now, Kitty, Willows is your only hope. If you don't take that house, somebody else will. Now, I'm going.'

'But–'

'I'm going to save my grandsons. If you don't mind your kids dying, stop here. If you don't mind dying yourself and leaving them three little buggers as orphans, stop here. Your future, with a job and Miss Pickavance to teach your babies, is about forty miles away. Liverpool will be flattened. It's up to you.'

Kitty burst into tears and fled through the front door of her filthy house.

Nellie continued giving away bits of furniture, pots, pans and anything that might be taken over by a new tenant if she didn't allocate it now. She hung on to two beds and enough bits and pieces for Eileen and Mel. Tonight would be their last in this house. Remaining items would be disposed of tomorrow, and keys would be returned to the landlord's office.

It was the end of an era. Nothing would be the same after today. New addresses, new friends, new way of life for everyone. But Nellie was determined to walk on, because she could not, would not, remain here. She picked up a few packages, left the house and, after locking the door for the last time, posted her key through the door. Eileen had her own key, and she would get rid of both tomorrow.

Nellie crossed the road to number one. Three shiny-faced angels stood with Miss Pickavance, brown paper parcels clutched to their chests. The older two seemed composed, but poor little Bertie, who had managed to survive past his seventh birthday in spite of his mother's teasing, was white-faced and clearly frightened. Nellie placed her own packages on the ground before squatting down at his level. 'Shall I tell him now?' she asked.

Hilda Pickavance pretended to consider the question. 'Well, if you must. It was supposed to be a surprise when he gets there, but he seems a little sad.'

'Don't want to go,' Bertie said. 'Me friends are all here. I like Liverpool. I don't know why I have to go.'

Nellie blinked back a river. 'Your own horse, babe. A pony. It's called Pedro and it's a palomino. Like a pale gold colour with white mane and tail.'

The child blinked. 'Has it got big feet?'

'No. It's not like the one you pinched, love. This is a proper riding pony, but Neil and Jean Dyson's girls have grown a little bit tall for it. They live at the home farm, and the youngest's nearly ten. So Pedro's yours.'

'Mine? I don't have to share?'

'All yours.'

Bertie didn't understand not sharing. Even at school, the books were all one between two. At home, first up best dressed had often been the rule, but they were giving him a whole horse. 'I'd rather have me mam,' he admitted, 'but if I can't have her, a pony's nearly as good.'

Those words became Nellie's unspoken mantra as they rode the tram to Liverpool, a train to Manchester, another to Bolton. Keith Greenhalgh picked them up and drove them out of town and up to sweeping stretches of moorland. All three boys stared at what they saw as a void, since there were no shops, theatres, cinemas, trams or crowds.

Nellie sat tight-lipped, because there was a hole in her chest, a space in which she had held Eileen for thirty-three years, Mel for thirteen. Strangely, she kept seeing the Liver Birds, twins that sat and overlooked the waterfront. They had to stay. No Nazi missile could touch them, or the city would crumble. It was just a piece of local folklore, but– Oh, Eileen. Oh, Mel. Then she looked at Bertie and smiled. A pony was nearly as good...

At first, Eileen felt rather trapped, because Frances Morrison needed almost full-time care. But three immediate neighbours offered to help so that shopping could be done, and she was promised the odd day or evening off. The doctor was just round the corner, Miss Morrison's house had a telephone, and ... and yes, the doctor was just round the corner.

Miss Morrison was a kind and gentle woman whose breeding and education showed without being overpowering. A further surprise came Eileen's way when she discovered that the people of Crosby and Blundellsands were rather more than all fur coats and no knickers. They spoke well, but they had their feet planted, showed few airs, and were more or less like everyone else except they had better houses and good furniture.

The old lady was now confined to the ground floor. A nurse came in daily to check on her, but the hour-to-hour care was Eileen's province, and she was determined to make a good fist of it. Three pounds a week, with all necessities already found, meant she was comparatively wealthy. So she helped with the disposal of dining room furniture, and was on hand when the space was turned into a bedroom. Neighbours sold table, chairs, display cabinets and sideboard, while Eileen concentrated on comfort. Wireless and gramophone were moved into the newly established sleeping area, while a firm, low chair was placed near the fire.

The neighbours, impressed by Eileen's dedication to the cause, told her as discreetly as possible that should Miss Morrison lose the fight for life, alternative work and shelter would be arranged for her and Mel. It was in that moment that the woman from Scotland Road became certain that people were good for the most part. But the doctor was still round the corner.

On the day before the move, he arrived. After awarding Eileen the filthiest look in his repertoire, he marched into the ex-dining room to examine his patient. When he returned to the kitchen, where Eileen was preparing an apple pie, his tone was terse. He banged a bottle of medicine on the table. 'Keep her in a sitting position for the most part. Don't let her sleep flat, either, as pneumonia would not be a welcome visitor at this point. With the right care, she has a few years' wear in her yet.' He then told her that the bottle contained an expectorant designed to clear Miss Morrison's chest.

'Right,' said Eileen, picking up the medicine.

'One teaspoonful four times a day, don't miss it. When do you move in?'

'Tomorrow.'

'Then instruct the neighbour who will be here tonight. The medication must be taken. And thank you, by the way.'

'For what?'

'For the second attack. At least they knew what they were doing, since they popped my arm back into its socket. It hurt like hell.'

She found no immediate reply. Dockers were tough creatures, and they had clearly gone at least a mile too far. The idea had been to frighten him, not to give him pain, and guilt shot through her like an arrow from a longbow.

'Nothing to say for yourself, madam?'

'Nothing. You were warned.'

'And given a black eye by your delightful mother.'

'You don't know her. She stands by her family no matter what the cost to herself and to strangers. As for the other business, there's a special bond among the dockers of Liverpool, and I'm a docker's widow. They look after their own. I'm sorry you were hurt, and I mean that, but as I said just now, you were warned.'

The doctor's bag was placed none too gently on the table, where it disturbed a great deal of flour. Eileen looked down at the resulting mess and opened her mouth to speak, but he was quick. More arrows pierced her body, but this time they brought pleasure. Her response was automatic, and she cursed her own lack of strength.

He released her very suddenly, and she backed away to depend for support on the sink. 'Bloody hell,' she breathed.

The same expression with which he had greeted her returned to his features. Without a word, he retrieved his bag and used a cloth to wipe most of the flour from its base. For at least a minute, he stood in silence, eyes fixed on her in a cold, almost forbidding stare.

Eileen shivered. This was a man who was capable of overcoming her with very little effort. She was in danger of losing control, of losing her mother and her job. But Mel would be here sometimes and, when she wasn't, there was Miss Morrison. Eileen would have to learn to recognize the sound of his engine in order to ensure that she could be safely out of reach or with his patient whenever he came. Because she knew he could win. He knew he could win. And he knew that she knew... Silently, she told herself to shut up.

'I love you,' he said finally, though his eyes did nothing to back up the brief declaration.

She remained silent. He was the fly in ointment that had promised to be cool and soothing since she had fallen on her feet here, on the border between Crosby and Blundellsands. It wasn't love. It was unadorned, naked lust. Once indulged, it would require regular feeding until it burned itself out. Even then, the ashes would need to be very cold in order to prevent rebirth of the phoenix.

He read her mind. 'No, it's gone beyond the physical. While you pretend to seek a sensible land steward, you want me. You want to wake in my bed, not his. This isn't over. Even if it ends, it will never be over. You will remember me.'

Eileen found her voice again. 'I am easily as cunning as my mam. I can tear my clothes and scream rape.'

'It would kill her.' Tom nodded in the direction of the dining room. 'She's your lifeline. I'll be back.' He left the kitchen, called a goodbye to the lady of the house, opened the front door and went. The car started. Only then did Eileen dare to breathe. Her body screamed for him, but her mind was fixed squarely on the welfare of her daughter and on the old lady who needed company, help, food and kindness.

She finished her pie, stopping partway through to look at the shape of Tom's bag in scattered flour. She missed him. He was right; even if this ended, it would never be over. There was little she could do. With Laz, there had existed a potent mix of sex and another kind of love, the sort that brought respect and caring into the arena. But her feelings for Tom stopped when she considered anything other than physical joy. He was wrong for her; there were good men in the world, and she had encountered one of them recently.

She needed to go to church, wanted to confess her sins of thought, word and deed, must get a man of God to pray for her. Yet sometimes she looked up into the wide blue yonder and knew that this little earth was not alone, that space was unlimited, that Darwin was right. Was God there? Whilst Darwin and God did not need to be mutually exclusive, a saying from another man sat in Eileen's mind. Hadn't Marx concluded that religion was the opium of the people? Was Catholicism just another fairy tale in which the good survived and the wolf got chopped to bits by the woodcutter? 'Oh, don't start with the stupid deep thinking,' she chided herself quietly. 'You've pots to wash.'

After putting the dishes to soak in the bowl, she sat for a while, her mind wandering unhindered through the old neighbourhood, all those preparations for war and against the threat of invasion. Then there was the other business, the giggling, the groaning in dark alleys where couples grabbed their moments. 'I swore the disease would never get me,' she whispered.

Before the declaration, Eileen's adherence to the moral code hammered into her head by Mam and by school had been total. Then, on a sunny Sunday, things had changed for everyone. 'But not in my head,' she said quietly. 'This is not of my choosing, because it's animal, pure animal.' Yes, she understood the girls and boys who fumbled beneath the imposed cloak of darkness.

She moved to the sink and stared unseeing through the window. There would be quick marriages during leaves; there would be unwanted babies. Young mothers and their offspring might be cast out, orphanages could be filled, and she was no wiser than the youthful miscreants. She needed love, needed to be touched, needed sex. There. She had achieved diagnosis. Angry with herself, she took it out on crockery and cutlery. Eileen was vulnerable, and she hated that.

The apple pie finally found its way to the oven. Having a gas cooker was one of the pleasures of life in this house, as was the garden, where autumn had arrived to colour trees red, gold and brown. She could still feel his hands on her body. Daffodil and tulip bulbs needed planting, but the fortnightly gardener would see to all that. And her mouth felt bruised. A piece of ham had produced the basis for pea and ham soup, one of Miss Morrison's favourites. And the ham would do for sandwiches. She wanted no more babies, since four were enough for anyone, but she needed comfort, closeness, fulfilment, excitement. That was selfish. If she gave in, she would be indulging a need that would be better ignored.

It wasn't a case of if. It was when. Because she

understood with blinding certainty that the mating ritual would continue, and that she would inevitably be worn down, as she wanted him as badly as he wanted her. For the sake of her daughter, Eileen Watson would postpone the event for as long as possible. But it would happen. Wouldn't it? Or might someone else fill the void in her soul?

It was Saturday. Keith rounded up the three boys and stood them in a line at the bottom of the staircase. The youngest was in a fairly good mood, as he had a pony, but the other two were bored. There was nothing to do. The rest of the evacuees were not yet here and, even when they did arrive, there would be miles and miles of wind-whipped fields between Willows and the other farms. Home Farm was nearby, but the Dysons wouldn't be taking anyone after all, as their spare bedrooms had been commandeered by Land Army girls.

'There's nothing to do,' moaned Phil for the umpteenth time. 'No shops, one pub, no trams. It's like being dead.'

'How do you know?' Keith asked. 'You've not been dead. Yet.'

'Is that a threat?' the oldest of Eileen's boys asked.

'Call it a promise.' Keith folded his arms. 'This is the deal. Saturdays, as long as everything here is up and running, I take you to town. You can go to the Lido or the Odeon for a matinee while I shop and so forth. Any thieving, fighting or messing about, and I'll drop you at the police station myself.'

Bertie declined with thanks. He'd been here

only a day, and he was intending to move into the stables for a few hours. 'Pedro has to know who I am. So I'll sit with him and read comics.'

'Right.' Keith studied the other two. Like the young one, they were good-looking, and they gave the impression that butter wouldn't melt. But he had their measure, as Eileen was very open when it came to describing her sons. What had she written? *They look like little angels, but the devil lives in their shoes.* 'One foot, one boot or shoe out of step, lads, and it'll be the junior prison.'

They glanced at each other. Neither had the slightest intention of tolerating any more of this. They followed Keith out to the car. Today, they would find out the lie of the land. During the coming week, money would be acquired by fair means or foul. After that, Liverpool in all its glory would be waiting for them. They hadn't said anything to their younger brother. When it came to secrets, Bertie was as much use as a bucket with a large hole in its base.

'So how do you like your new home?' Keith asked as he drove down the lane.

'All right,' answered Rob.

'Big,' Philip added. Having been held prisoner for long enough in Rachel Street, he was not prepared to allow the situation to continue. He and Rob had mates at home, and someone would take them in. War? Apart from a few soldiers and sailors passing through, there'd been no sign of it. It was almost as if some conspiracy were going on, a plan to keep the Kennedy/Watson clan out of circulation for a year or two.

'Bertie likes the pony.' Keith began the descent

into Bolton. 'He's as happy as a sand boy. Perhaps I should look for a couple of horses for you?'

Philip was ready for this offer. 'We'd rather have bikes,' he said. 'Second-hand would do as long as they work.' Forty miles wasn't far. If he could get his bearings for the East Lancashire Road, a new route designed and built to connect Liverpool and Manchester, he and Rob could be as good as home. 'If we had bikes, we could visit the other farms.'

Keith, as yet not fully aware of the dogged determination of his passengers, took what they had said as a positive sign. They were preparing to settle, and that was good enough for him. 'Forget the picture house for today, then. Let's go on a bike hunt, get a bit of dinner, then you can have a walk round while I do my own shopping.'

In the rear of the car, two intelligent and calculating boys smiled at each other. The plan was working like a dream.

'Don't cry, Mam.' This was terrible. Until today, Eileen Watson hadn't been able to remember some details of her husband's death and the ensuing funeral, but it had all flooded back while he prepared to leave the home she had shared with him. 'Mam?'

'Leave me a minute. Go and give Freda Pilkington your gran's best frying pan and a couple of pillows. I promised. Go on now.'

Alone, Eileen sat halfway up the stairs. She remembered him singing *'and when they were only halfway up, they were neither up nor down'* while taking his children to their beds. He had been a good dad and a wonderful husband. His right hand was calloused from the repeated used of his docker's hook. A powerful man, he never hurt a fly.

In her mind, she opened the door. Three of them stood there, caps in hands, blood on their fingers. A trio of big, burly men stood and cried like babies while she sank to the floor, a very young Bertie clutched to her chest. The men's faces were clear at last, and she even recalled two of their names. After they left, she became a wooden doll. Time after time, her mother said, 'You stayed where you were put, so we had to remember to shift you.'

His mates sat the final vigil. They drank beer and used the coffin top as a resting place for their glasses and bottles. That was the right thing to do, because they were including him.

He was a big man, and his coffin filled the front room. She touched the wood. The lid was nailed down, because he was so badly injured. Warm wood. She could feel it now. Inside the warmth, he was probably cold. They walked behind him all the way to St Anthony's, where he had been baptized and educated. His mother was hysterical. She died three weeks later.

The church was standing room only. Hundreds of people, and the dockers wept again. She'd always remembered that bit, but now she saw the hole. They put her Laz in a great, yawning hole. Worms. Flowers. Philip, Rob and Mel crying, Bertie held in his grandmother's arms. Eileen hated the sun for daring to show its face. Trams ran, birds sang, children played nearby. It should all stop, but it didn't. Dinners to make, ships to load and unload, bets to be placed in the ready hands of Nobby Costigan. She wanted to scream, but the priest was here, purple vestments, black biretta, open prayer book.

'Mam? Mam?'

Without. In the house, in the street, in her heart, she was without him. The space inside her body and soul felt bigger than the grave in which her beloved man had been placed. 'Hello, love. Did you give Freda the pan?'

'Yes.'

'And the pillows?'

'And the pillows.'

Only now did Eileen realize that she was weeping.

'Have you remembered all of it, Mam?'

'I think so. This is where we lived, Mel. This is where I had my babies and where I was when he died.'

'You've let go,' Mel said. 'To let go, you had to remember all of it, not just the church bit. My dad was a lovely man, and you hid yourself away for safety's sake so that you could carry on looking after us. I suppose it was quite sensible in its way.'

'There's nothing sensible about making myself go a bit mad. Now, on your bike and go to Miss Morrison's. I'll give the keys in, and see you later.'

'Are you fit to be left?'

Eileen laughed. 'It's not me that's unfit; the real daftness is next door. I have to go and do three rounds with Kitty, because Mam and Keith are coming for her on Monday or Tuesday. I don't know whether she's fed the kids. They were as black as sweeps the last time I saw them, so I wouldn't be surprised if they got taken away from her. I mean, we've loads of poor people round here, but she's in a class of her own when it comes to filth. I bet she's sold all the funeral clothes. There's nothing for her here, nothing for any of us. But will she listen?'

'No,' they both chorused.

Mel kissed her mother, wheeled her bike into the street, and left her old life behind. With her usual positive attitude, she looked forward, never back. School would be nearer, Mam was going to be safe, while the rest of her family lived beyond the reach of danger.

Eileen pulled herself together. It was time to go. Without another glance at her home, she walked out, locked the door on her past and put both keys in her bag. This was going to be the hardest bit, because Kitty's decline had worsened since yesterday, when Mam had left for Bolton. Neighbours had been alerted so that the three young ones might be captured, fed, watered and cleaned, but Kitty was the biggest worry. If her mind had gone, Willows Edge would never cope, since they weren't used to her dirty ways and knew nothing of her history. There was also the probability that, in unfamiliar territory, the woman would panic even more.

But there was no one in the house. The smell was unbelievably bad, and the movements of rodents could be heard even now, in daylight. 'God help us,' Eileen whispered. 'But most of all, help poor Kitty.'

Nine

'Are you sure you want me to drop you off here? You might need help with her if she digs her heels in.' Keith stared at the front of a house whose windows had probably not been cleaned since the end of the Great War. The whole street was dark and dingy, but number four was spectacularly scruffy.

Nellie pondered for a few seconds. She studied the place in which she had lived and, after just three days away, found herself wondering how and why the slums were allowed to exist. 'Right, put it this way, Keith. Most round here have become immune to her house and the state of it. For you, it'd be a shock, and you might catch something. Go and visit our Eileen, because you didn't give her a definite time to expect you, and I'll see you back here about three. The neighbours'll help me round the kids up.' Nellie paused again. 'Go and see her, lad. She'll be as pleased as Punch when you get there.'

'Thanks.'

She touched his hand for a brief moment. 'Good luck, love. She likes you. Only she's been a bit distracted just lately what with one thing and another.'

Keith decided to dive in at the deep end. 'By a Dr Tom?'

Nellie's jaw dropped before she had the chance

to control it. 'How do you know about him?' That bloody doctor got everywhere, or so it seemed. 'He's married with twins, and his wife deserves a bloody sight better than him by all accounts.'

He shrugged. 'When she writes, I read the words she's left out. Anyway, as you say, he's married and I'm not.' He sighed. 'I know I've seen Eileen just once, and for a matter of minutes, but it was the same with Annie, and there's been no one in between. I'm one of those blokes – it either happens, or it doesn't. Usually, it doesn't. I can tell from her letters she's more than a pretty woman. So I fell headlong.'

She nodded sagely. 'Yes. With my Eileen, it happened, whatever *it* turns out to be.' She wasn't surprised. Apart from her beauty, Eileen had a lovely nature when she wasn't riled, and that nature shone in her eyes. 'Are you sure?'

He chuckled. 'Aye, and for the first time in over twenty years.'

'Go and get her, then. I've three mucky kids and a crazy mother to find, God and the angels help me.' She puffed out her cheeks and blew. 'Oh, I don't know whether I'm doing right. She's not all there in her head no more, and Willows Edge might want rid. She doesn't clean, doesn't control her kids, can't be bothered with anything. The last time she got excited was when she bought her new teeth. I mean, Charlie had been dead a week, and she was more bothered about her gob than she was about him and the funeral.'

'Are you sure you don't need me?'

'When you get back to pick us up, I might find a use for you. Three o'clock, then.' She laughed.

'If you're a few minutes late, I'll understand. Love can't be hurried.'

'Stop mocking me, Nellie Kennedy.'

As she stepped out of the car, she blew a perfect, if rather loud, raspberry.

Keith left Nellie and drove off. He stopped at a barber's on Scotland Road, had a second shave and a haircut, found a couple of little shops, bought a potted plant for Eileen and a little string of beads for Mel. He was a mere five or six miles from Crosby, but it would be a long drive, because he wanted to be with her *now*.

He travelled a route that ran parallel with the dock road, realizing how close Eileen's ex-home was to ships and warehouses. Crosby, while further along the coast, was still next to the Mersey. She could be hit. But she would not leave Mel, and refused absolutely to interfere with the girl's chances of a superior education. Had he been father to a similarly gifted child, he would probably have acted in the same way.

When he found St Michael's Road, he was pleased to see that it was a good half-mile from the river, though that was no distance at all to an off-course plane with a load to drop before flying home on a teaspoon of fuel. But he had to be positive. She had made her decision, and she would stick to it. These were lovely houses, the sort that lay within reach of doctors, lawyers and business folk with old money and decent incomes. They hadn't the potential grandeur of Willows, but they sat well beyond the pay packet of an ordinary working man.

He parked, stepped out of the car, then reached

in for plant, beads and a brown paper parcel from the back seat. Eileen wouldn't be offended, would she? She was too down to earth to take umbrage over a few small gifts. As instructed, he walked round to the back of the house and tapped on the kitchen door. Miss Morrison was ill, was downstairs, and she should not be disturbed by the front door bell.

When Eileen opened the door, he almost dropped her plant. 'God,' he muttered before he could check himself. 'You're more beautiful than I remembered.'

She just laughed. It was clear that she had grown used to such compliments, and she took all in her stride. 'Come in,' she said. 'Miss Morrison's having a nap, so I'll put the kettle on and we can sit and chat. It's good of you to bring Mam over. Oh, she said on the phone that Jay's diabetic. That's a shame. We all like him. He even made Miss Pickavance laugh.' This was a far better man than Tom Bingley. There would always be Tom Bingleys, but men like Keith were rare. She liked Keith, and liking was important. And she desired him, which was strange, because most women were one-at-a-time people, but she decided not to think about any of that. Keith Greenhalgh was marriage material, while Tom Bingley was a balloon on a stick, bound to burst at some stage.

Like a man in a happy dream, he watched while she moved round her domain. She was elegant, graceful, lovely – too lovely to have come from the slum he had seen earlier. The stork had left a princess in a hovel, and she had thrived in spite of that. Her dress was in a material he thought was named crêpe something-or-other, green, with a square neck and a single imitation teardrop pearl on a black cord at her throat. Her hair was up, and tempting tendrils caressed the nape of her neck. He imagined lifting those curls and kissing the hollow just below her hairline and above the cord that held the pearl. He wished he could afford a real pearl. Even a genuine one would be outshone by this wearer.

She turned suddenly. 'Scone?' she asked, trying hard not to laugh again. He was lovely. He reminded her of an overgrown teenage boy who was having trouble coping with the onslaught of puberty. 'Keith?' And he was better looking than she remembered. He was certainly more handsome than Dr Ants-in-his-Pants. In fact, he was not far short of bloody gorgeous.

Keith blinked. 'What?'

'Do you want a scone with strawberry jam?'

'Er ... yes. Please.'

'Right.'

She brought food and tea on a tray and sat opposite him. 'I've enjoyed your letters,' she told him.

'Me, too. I mean I enjoy yours.'

'Good. How are my boys? The same? Worse? Better?'

Meeting her eyes was difficult, just as it had been all those years ago with Annie. But if he lowered his gaze, he would be staring at her body, and that might be considered bold–

'Keith?'

'Oh, yes. They've had a job to stop Bertie sleeping with Pedro. He's learning to groom him, and I'm cobbling together bits and pieces of gear so that I can start teaching him to ride. I like him.'

Eileen smiled sweetly. 'Don't be fooled. He's just a younger version of the other two. How are they?' she asked again.

Keith swallowed a mouthful of scone; he must not speak with a full mouth. 'Erm ... a bit bored. We got them a bike each, because they're not interested in horses. I made a bargain with them. As long as they behave themselves and if I'm free, they'll get to the cinema every Saturday afternoon.'

'And my mother?'

'I shan't be taking her to the pictures. She's still all clever comments, but she gets on very well with Miss Pickavance, so she'll be all right. She's capturing Kitty and the wild ones down the road as we speak.'

'Good.'

The conversation dried. Keith passed the plant and the beads across the table.

'Lovely,' she said. 'You're a kind man.'

He reached for the parcel. 'I was... I mean after I'd seen about the bikes, I went... The boys were wandering about town and...' He gave up trying to talk like an intelligent person and thrust the package across the table. 'Cloth,' he managed. 'Bolton market. You can buy patterns and pin them on the cloth, then you cut round and make a dress.'

Eileen was having more trouble keeping her face straight. This man wasn't frightening or threatening, but he was adorable. He was carrying on an old-fashioned courtship with letters, poetry and gifts. Pleasing to look at, he possessed an innocence that was rare in modern humankind. He had loved Annie, and Annie had died. Now he thought he had found someone else who fitted his idea of perfection. She opened the parcel. Inside, several yards of cloth had been folded carefully.

'They were ends,' he said. 'Ends of rolls, so I just had to take what was there. That blue will suit you. And the green. They're definitely fents, but I looked for flaws and couldn't find any.'

'Lovely,' she said. 'And I make my own patterns. The gold colour will be nice for Mel.' He was rooting in his pockets. What on earth was he up to?

'Matching thread,' he announced, slamming at least a dozen reels on the table. Several rolled off, and they both got down on the floor to retrieve the escaping objects. For a brief second, they came face to face before Keith stood up in a hurry and banged his head on a corner of the table. He was becoming thoroughly annoyed with himself. Always a competent communicator, Keith Greenhalgh had suddenly been reduced to the mental age of three, give or take a year or two.

She was touching him. She was looking at his scalp to see if there was blood. Oh, hell, she was kissing his injury better. And she was lifting his face, and he wondered whether she was going to kiss him properly on the lips.

'You're not bleeding,' she informed him. 'I think you'll live.' And he made ten of Tom Wotsisname. Bingley.

'Good.' This single syllable emerged from the throat of a fourteen-year-old whose voice still sought its true level. Well, that was progress, because he'd been an infant just moments earlier. Her face was so dangerously near. 'I think I love you,' he said. Had he said it or had he thought it? She was smiling. He had said it, and he was a clown.

'I know you think you do,' she replied. 'And I think I may think the same given time. You're the best idiot I've come across in a while. I collect idiots. My mother was my first.'

He blinked.

'You know what I mean, Keith. We're good friends, you and I. That's the best basis for everything, isn't it?'

He wasn't sure about that. Both times, he had fallen without thinking, and friendship hadn't figured largely in the recipe during the early days. He'd wanted Annie, and now he wanted this one. But it was more than the bed stuff; it was sitting together in the evenings, having a meal, going to the pub, visiting friends, laughing, drinking tea and cursing the government. And it was looking at her, just looking and enjoying what he saw, living with perfection even when it wasn't perfect, when face cream covered skin, when hair was in curlers, when she was too tired to be pretty. So friendship was necessary, he supposed. 'I don't want to be just your friend,' he said carefully.

'What do you want, then?'

'To be with you.'

'That's friendship. Sharing things, being in the same house, talking and laughing – that's the cake before it gets iced. I worked out that people have to be joined at the head as well as by other parts. Laz was my best friend in the world. I missed me bezzie mate most of all, Keith. Fancying somebody isn't enough.'

'I know,' he replied. 'I was taking friendship for granted – it's in the letters. I already know you and like you. From that, it was a small step.'

'And you love me?'

He felt silly, stupid, inadequate. 'It was the same twenty years ago,' he said lamely. 'Since then, there's been nobody who mattered.'

This man would never hurt her. She would never fear turning away, because he wasn't going to pounce, threaten, mither... Tom did all that. Sometimes, he drove past the house several times in a day, and she often wondered where he was going and whether his journey was really necessary. Petrol was already in short supply and–

'Eileen?'

'What?'

'Is there someone else?' He could not betray Nellie by mentioning the doctor.

'No. I can't fasten myself to anyone because of my three heroes. Bertie's seven. It'll be about ten years before I can think about myself. Where we lived, there was no way of containing them. I won't inflict them on anybody, because they're hard work.'

'I agree that they're hard work. But they can be improved.'

Eileen noted the challenge in his eyes. 'You think you can tame them?'

'I can try.' He stood up. 'Is it all right if I borrow a little kiss?'

She folded her arms. 'And how do you pay back?'

'With a second one.'

Shakespeare's sonnets, dried flowers, his soul

on paper. A flight of geese, the birth of a foal, the mending of a wall; all these he had given to her. Keith Greenhalgh was a tall, broad man, yet he was not intimidating. And she responded to his embrace, just as she had with Tom. Was she becoming a nymphomaniac, a trainee whore? She raised her hands and placed them on the back of his neck, because she didn't want the kiss to end. Confused was not a strong enough adjective. This was a man she had known forever. 'You're adorable,' she said when the kiss ended. 'You owe me another one of those.'

Keith paid his dues. He forced his hands not to wander, and was careful not to push his body against hers. Etiquette had to be observed in most areas of life, and he was determined to be polite and controlled. His body had other ideas, but he would deny instinct and go slowly. She was too precious to be used for his own satisfaction.

The doorbell sounded, and Eileen broke away from her delightful visitor. 'Get that, will you? I'll make sure Miss Morrison's all right.'

Keith reclaimed his ability to breathe before going to answer the door. He carried with him a slight smile, because Eileen had treated him like a member of the household – you do this, while I do that.

In the ex-dining room, Eileen found her charge fast asleep. Her hearing was deteriorating along with her heart, so the bell hadn't disturbed her. Eileen smiled down on the old lady. When awake, this woman could talk all four legs off a table, but peace continued for now.

Not for long. Two people now occupied the

kitchen, and one of them was clearly out of order. 'Mam? What is it? Whatever's happened?'

'You tell her,' Nellie said to Keith.

He had to hurt her. He had to be the one to say the words. 'Eileen, your next-door neighbour won't be coming back to Willows with me and your mother, because–'

'Because she's dead,' Nellie said. He shouldn't have to do the telling, so she needed to be brave.

Eileen dropped into a chair. 'Kitty?'

Keith nodded.

'But the kids?' Eileen grasped her mother's hand. 'The kids, Mam?'

Nellie inhaled unsteadily. 'She suffocated the poor little buggers. I found them.' She began to rock backwards and forwards. 'The smell. The terrible smell. I know the house stinks anyway, but this was ... it was different. The police came. I had to answer questions, then they brought me here.'

'Kitty?'

'Was hanging in the back bedroom. All black, she was. The only white bits were her bloody teeth. How I got back downstairs I'll never know. Just sat on her doorstep and screamed and screamed, I did. The police said it was unusual for a woman to hang herself. They usually swallow poison.'

Keith moved his chair and sat with an arm round Nellie's shoulders. 'Come on, love. She wasn't right. I've heard you saying she wasn't right. Sweetheart, don't make yourself ill.' He turned to Eileen. 'Get Miss Morrison's doctor. Your mam wants calming down.'

So the rivals met. Tom, forced to attend a woman who had given him a black eye before causing him to be attacked by a pair of dockers, doled out tablets and suggested that Nellie should not travel back to Bolton today, as she needed rest and quiet after the shock. Eileen explained the situation to Miss Morrison, who insisted that Nellie should share Eileen's double bed, while the young man, whom she had not yet met, could use the small front bedroom, as her larger room was no longer furnished. 'Terrible,' the old lady said. 'The husband barely cold in the grave, and now those poor, poor children. Feed everyone, dear. I shall meet your mother and Mr Greenhalgh later.'

While Eileen put her mother to bed, the two men stood in the kitchen. 'So, you're the land agent.'

'Steward, yes. I've worked at Willows for about half my life. And you're the one whose daughter's a friend of Mel's.'

'Yes.'

Keith wanted to laugh. This situation put him in mind of childhood, when boys lined up to fight the king of the class. Anyone who beat the king took his invisible crown, and assumed the duty to defend it. This meant that a monarch fought every day on his way to school, at playtimes and at dinner time; even the homeward journey at the end of the day wasn't safe. Once battered to within an inch of his life, he passed on the onerous position to the next lunatic in line. Keith had never been king. In his book, a king was a fool, and Shakespeare had proved that in at least one of his plays.

'You have her boys?' Tom asked.

'Only on Saturdays. Nellie and Miss Pickavance

look after them during the week. The youngest is settling; he has his own pony.'

'Good, good.'

The doctor was clearly waiting for Eileen. He didn't want to leave her in the company of Keith, who was fully aware of what was going on. The medic was handsome, married, and probably self-absorbed. He didn't love or respect his wife, and he wanted Eileen Watson. 'I'm staying tonight,' Keith said. 'If Nellie's better, I'll drive her home tomorrow.'

Tom lowered his head thoughtfully. 'Look, I have work to do. Tell Eileen I'll make sure the Maguires get a decent funeral. There'll be no difficulty about declaring her of unsound mind, so she should be able to be buried with her husband. I helped then, too.'

Keith offered no reply. Tom Bingley was letting him know that he was already part of Eileen's life, that he would control events resulting from three murders and one suicide. He was important, educated, middle-class and financially comfortable. And married, though he chose not to mention that fact.

'I'll ... er... Tell Eileen I'll see her later,' Tom said.

Keith stayed exactly where he was while the doctor turned to leave. He knew with absolute certainty that Dr Bingley would leave his wife and family if Eileen said the word. He also knew that such a creature could never manage Philip and Rob Watson.

'Young man?' The voice came from the next room, and Keith tracked it to its source.

'Help me up, please. Good. Yes, another pillow. Now.' She smiled. 'I'm Frances Morrison, and you are Keith Greenhalgh, so we can put the niceties out of the way. Would you make me a cup of tea, dear? Eileen's with her mother. Oh, and a scone, please. Then you can tell me all about yourself. There are some pills marked two o'clock; she keeps them in the kitchen.' The smile broadened. 'This is the first time a man other than a doctor has entered my bedroom. Quite an adventure for me.'

'Right. Tea and a scone, plus pills. Anything else?'

The old woman stared right through him. 'She talks about you, enjoys your letters. You're right for her. For obvious reasons, my doctor isn't.' She lowered her voice. 'I'm not quite as deaf as I pretend to be. And I can walk further than people expect. The lady upstairs who found that poor family today has blacked his eye, I believe. She also set some of Eileen's dead husband's friends on him. He's lucky to be alive, because we have some tough people on the docks.' She looked him up and down. 'I have never been married, young man, but I know a good match when I see one. And I see one now.'

Keith laughed.

But Miss Morrison had moved on. 'They're the first of Hitler's Liverpool victims,' she said. 'The idea of going to live inland was too frightening, I suppose. Scotland Road has a quality too many of us ignore; it teems with all kinds of life, and humanity prevails. It's a support system. She couldn't leave her children, so she took them with her. Get my pills, there's a good chap.'

In the kitchen, he found Eileen preparing Miss Morrison's snack. 'Is your mam asleep?' he asked.

She nodded. 'The curtain between life and death's thin, isn't it? I should have stayed with Kitty.' Suddenly, she staggered away from the tray she was about to lift. 'She was already dead when Mel and I came here. I went in her house. The place was empty.' She threw herself into Keith's arms. 'But it wasn't empty. It had already happened, Keith. Thinking back, I never heard a sound from that place after Mam left for Willows.'

He pushed her into a chair before carrying the tray into Miss Morrison's room. 'Do you want this in bed, or shall we put you in the chair? Your pills are in the saucer.'

'I'll stay where I am. Go back to her at once.'

Keith carried his precious human burden into the front sitting room and closed the door. On a sofa, he held her until she ran out of tears before kissing her hands, her forehead, her eyes. 'You did nothing wrong, love. It was nobody's fault.' He wished he had the ability to take her pain and feel it for her, as he could not bear the sight of her suffering. She was a giving person, a woman who cared. 'Kitty can't suffer any more, Eileen. Her children are no longer poor and deprived. In heaven, they'll have shining faces.'

'They were babies. If you caught them and hung on long enough to wash them, they were beautiful. Little Molly was just three. Kitty wasn't well. There should be more help for people who get ill in their heads.' She paused. 'Kiss me on the mouth and let me know I'm alive.'

He followed her order, and she clung to him as if drowning. 'You're alive,' he told her. 'And while we're alive, we should stick together and trust each other when it comes to your boys. You and I can manage just about anything.'

'Yes.'

'Yes, what?'

'Yes, I believe you, we're a good team. But there's a war to be got through when it starts. And Mel will be home in a while.' She had to tell her daughter. Mam, who had discovered the bodies, should not be forced to relive yet again the scenes she had found in Rachel Street.

Eileen continued to cling to him, and Keith had an idea why. Sudden death often pushed people towards rash behaviour. Many a child was conceived in the aftermath of a funeral, because the bereaved hung on to each other in order to prove that life continued. 'I'll tell her if you like.'

'Why?'

'Because sometimes news as bad as this comes better from a stranger.'

'And she'll remember forever the first time you spoke to her. Meet her, by all means, but don't be the one who tells her about Kitty and the children.'

Keith knew in that moment that Eileen was considering him as a potential suitor. She had spoken about the war as if she intended to be in his life when the conflict ended; now she was indicating that Mel should have a positive picture of him. 'Can I be there when you tell her?'

'Yes. Yes, I want you there, but let me say the words.'

'All right.'

Through new tears, she smiled at him. 'You sent me poems.'

'Yes.'

'And letters full of word-pictures.'

'Yes.'

'That's friendship.'

'And more. Believe me, Eileen. It's a lot more.'

Hilda Pickavance replaced the receiver and walked into the large kitchen. As ever, Philip, Rob and Bertie were reasonably well behaved in her presence. She should have been a teacher, as she would have needed no primitive weapons in order to keep control and hold the interest of her charges; Hilda was a born educator, but no one had noticed. And now she was alone once more with Eileen's offspring, because their grandmother was being treated for shock.

As gently as possible, Hilda told the boys what had happened in the house next door to theirs.

'Why?' Bertie asked. 'Why has she deaded herself and her kids?'

Mental illness was hard enough to explain to an adult; with children, it was a near-impossible task. 'She was ill in her head,' she tried.

'A headache?' The youngest boy's eyes were rounded by astonishment. 'She deaded her kids–'

'Killed,' interrupted Rob.

'She killed Stephen and Lucy and Molly and herself because of a headache?'

'Not that sort of ill,' Philip snapped. 'She went crackers. The thought of coming to live out here drove her mad.' It was enough to drive anyone crazy, Philip believed. This dump was hell on earth, and Kitty Maguire had realized that. Sensibly, she had shuffled off before being landed with grass, cows, more grass, pigs, hens, goats, horses, more grass, walls, and a post office that sold paper, envelopes, stamps, matches, lamp oil and candles. Apart from all that there were hills with sheep on them. And a lot of grass.

'She was afraid,' Hilda said.

'She was right to be afraid,' Philip insisted. 'Because if me and our Rob have to live here much longer, we'll be out of our minds too.' He folded his arms defiantly. 'It's horrible here, Miss Pickavance. The only good thing is the food, but we can't sit eating all day, can we?'

Hilda pursed her lips and thought for a moment. 'We've found you a school. It's two miles away, and that's no distance on a bicycle.'

'Or a horse,' Bertie cried.

'It's a school for older children,' he was informed. 'You'll stay here with me. And when you do go to school, there'll be no stable for Pedro, so forget that idea. Now, look at me, all of you.' She waited until all the scuffling and whispering had ceased. 'You are silly, ungrateful and petulant boys. Not you, Bertie. You are safe here, all three of you. Have you any idea of what is about to happen in Liverpool, especially near the waterfront?'

'No,' the older pair chorused.

She continued. 'Since the reign of King John, Liverpool has been the gateway to the Atlantic. It's the biggest docks in the world. Weapons and ammunition will be brought there for distribution. Germany will be aware of that, and bombs will be dropped. Do you want to die?'

They shook their heads.

'I can tell you now, only London will be harder hit than Liverpool. You are here to stay alive. Now, go to your room, because I have things to do.'

When the boys had left, Hilda sat and gazed into the fire. She remembered that thin, almost toothless young woman who had lived across the street, three children clinging to her skirts, two girls, one boy, all dirty and with tangled, curly hair. The husband had come home from time to time, then his brief appearances stopped when he drowned in drink and the River Mersey. Kitty had finally got her teeth, and Dr Bingley had paid for them to be made more comfortable. Dead. All three children dead, the mother hanged in a back bedroom. Horrible.

She missed Nellie. There was something so solid and comforting about the woman, as if she knew everything there was to know about life. But poor Nellie was in shock so she, too, clearly had her limits. One good thing had come from this dreadful mess. Eileen and Keith were together for a little while. They were well suited. If anything decent were to come from this war, a marriage between those two would be a clear winner. It was a match made in heaven, though hell had to be visited first.

Mel took it badly. Keith watched two beautiful women trying to comfort each other and, after deciding there was little else he could do, took over the cooking. Eileen picked at her meal, Mel made no effort, and Nellie slept through it, though Miss Morrison was complimentary. 'Not just a pretty face, then, young man. How are they?'

Keith gave the best account he could manage.

'So no one's eating?'

'No.'

'Put it all in the larder. We can't waste good food while there's a war on. I need the pills marked five o'clock, and ask Eileen to come in when she's in a better state, poor girl.'

While washing dishes, Keith realized how easy it was when a person lived alone: one cup, one plate, a few items of cutlery. Even so, he'd give up his freedom in a flash if Eileen would have him. Perhaps she would have him. After the war, after her youngest had had a few more birthdays, after Mel had gone to Oxford, Cambridge or wherever. Mel was a gorgeous girl, but he wondered whether she would ever match her mother for beauty. He didn't doubt for one minute that no one could be as beautiful as Eileen. Could he possibly be prejudiced?

Mel went upstairs, Eileen sorted out Miss Morrison, and Keith found a book on the history of Crosby, amazed to discover that there was still a manor house in which the descendants of Blondell the Viking lived, that a person had to be a Catholic to have a cottage in Little Crosby, that any minerals found anywhere on any land reverted to the Blundell family. 'It's still feudal,' he muttered. 'The only completely Catholic village in England. All that's changed is the spelling, from Blondell to Blundell. Well, we live and learn.'

Eileen entered the kitchen. 'They want toast,'

she said. 'Miss Morrison's asleep, but Mam and Mel have ordered toast and tea.' She passed him the toasting fork. 'You hold that in front of the fire and I'll find you some bread to stick on the end of it. I wish...' She started to cut the loaf.

'Wish what?'

'That you were staying permanently. I feel safe with you here.'

For now, this had to be enough. She wanted him in her life, and he toasted her bread.

Eileen was a bad woman. She was sitting on the stairs holding a lighted candle and wearing no more than a thin nightie, and she knew he was just feet away. What the scouse with pickled beetroot was she thinking of? Was she nursing a vague idea that if she gave herself to Keith, Tom the Torment would disappear in a puff of smoke? No. She wasn't quite that daft. 'I'm an honest woman,' she told the banisters. She had kept herself to herself since the death of Laz, and–

His door opened. 'Eileen?' he whispered.

'What?'

'Are they all right?'

'Yes.'

He came to sit next to her.

'Hello, Julius,' she said. 'Or are you et tu Brute?'

'Keith will do, thanks. Are they asleep?' He hung on to his sheet. 'No pyjamas,' he whispered. 'I don't wear them anyway, but I would have brought some with me if I'd known. Are they asleep?' he repeated.

'Both doped,' she told him. 'Mam had a double dose. It said on the bottle two at night if required.' He was virtually naked, as was she. 'And Mel was crying, so I knocked her out, too.'

'The Crosby poisoner,' he breathed. 'And you're wide awake.'

'Yes.'

'Why?'

'You're the same. Why?'

Keith chuckled quietly. 'Only the guilty answer a question with a question.'

'I can't work out what's the matter with me,' she said. 'But it's as if I've known you all my life. A woman I cared about died today, and all I can think about is being with you.'

Yes, here she came, the girl he loved. The honesty that always shone in her eyes was pouring softly from lips he wanted to devour, but he continued to hold on to his sheet. Eileen was capable of naughtiness. This delightful trait, coupled with intelligence and humour, was all he wanted in a wife. 'I won't take advantage,' he declared.

'No, but I might.'

'You mustn't.'

She looked him full in the face. 'Never tell me what to do or what not to do. I'm contrary. You'll notice the same stubbornness in my sons, and in my daughter. So.' She touched his hand. 'You don't want me?'

'Don't talk daft.'

'You do want me?'

'Stupid question.'

'You're as bloody-minded as I am.'

'Yes. I don't want to face you tomorrow if you have regrets.'

Eileen stood up, climbed the top few stairs and

entered the room she was currently sharing with her mother, who snored. She wondered whether Keith snored. If she spent the night with him, she might find out. In the interests of research, a person needed to gain as much information as possible in order to compare and tabulate results. Who was she kidding? She had met her Waterloo and her second husband. The boys would do as they were bloody well told, and that would be an end to their shenanigans. 'I may be in love,' she told her sleeping mother. 'And if you wake, you'll know where I am.'

Mam didn't approve of sex outside marriage, but Eileen nursed the suspicion that an exception might be made in this case. Everyone liked Keith. Even Mel, who'd been terribly upset about the Maguire family, had voiced her approval. As for Tom Bingley, he could hang himself out to dry, because his luck was running out fast. Hang himself? She shouldn't have thought those words, because poor Kitty...

In the bathroom, Eileen cleaned her teeth for the second time tonight. She washed her face, combed her hair and walked into his room where she pressed herself ham-actress-fashion across his door. 'I must tell you something,' she said in a voice that wasn't a bad imitation of some Hollywood queen. 'I have stretch marks.' She blew out her candle.

A small night light burned on the mantelpiece, and the pair gazed at each other in the glow of its meagre flame. 'Are you sure?' he asked.

'You can look at them if you like.'

'Eileen!'

'What?'

'Are you sure about this?'

'Yes. There's something about you I can't ignore, as if we've met before. And I know you feel the same, so why wait? The worst that can happen is a baby, and we'd cope. Don't worry, I think I've already decided to make an honest man of you, Keith Greenhalgh. I'll still respect you tomorrow after I've had my wicked way.'

'Come here.'

So for once, Eileen did as she was bidden. She perched on the edge of the bed and on the hemline of sin while he looked at her sternly, as if he were her father. 'What's the matter?' she mouthed softly.

'Dr Bingley is the matter. And don't bother asking how I know, because I felt the change in the tone of your letters. Also, he made it perfectly plain today that he regards you as his property. Don't mess me about, Eileen Watson. You're beautiful, and you know how I feel about you. But the world is not your oyster. This is a difficult moment for me, and it can't be easy for you, because you know how beautiful and desirable you are, so rejection's something you won't expect. Yes, I love you; no, I won't share you.'

Eileen stared down at him. He was in even deeper shadow now, since she sat between him and the candlelight. She was angry, mostly with herself.

'You have to work out whether you want to be a rich man's mistress, or a working man's wife.' He sighed. 'He stood in that kitchen today and looked at me as if I were rubbish.'

She rose to her feet. 'You don't know me at all. There's been no one since Laz, because I respect myself too much. Tom's a pain in the neck, but I'm used to that kind of thing. But you?' She raised both hands in a gesture of despair. 'I decided, very foolishly, that you were probably right for me.'

'So go away and lose the probably.'

'Did you wonder about Tom when you kissed me?'

Keith considered that. 'No. I thought about this moment, all the time knowing that it shouldn't happen yet. Courtship takes time. Because of the way I am, love comes suddenly and not often. You're female.'

'You noticed.'

'Yes. Females calculate. If you watch the animal kingdom, the males have to work themselves silly. Their mates think long and hard, because they're the ones who get invaded and impregnated. Humans are the same. Do your thinking. If you need to sleep with him, get it over with, but don't try me for size first.' He paused and smiled. 'That wasn't intended to be vulgar.'

For a while, she didn't know what to say. He was sending her away, and she hadn't expected that, but, as a Liverpudlian woman, she needed the last word. 'I wasn't intending to give you a reference, or marks out of ten for performance. I came here because the probably had begun to disappear. Big mistake, eh?'

'Eileen?'

'What?'

'I love you. I love you too much to lose you by

that mistake.'

With that, she was forced to be satisfied. Back in her own room with a snoring mother for company, Eileen spent a sleepless night. How could she meet his eyes in the morning? Why had she placed herself in such an embarrassing position? But that was just pride. The fact was that Tom flaming Bingley was stamping on her life, and nothing this side of death seemed enough to put a stop to him. Keith, an old-fashioned type with Victorian values, was too sensitive for his own good. There was no probably. The probably had died while she'd read his letters, because their minds had met. Which fact didn't mean they would always agree, but the fights would be fun.

When morning came, she went down to prepare the coddled egg and milky tea that were her patient's usual breakfast. She carried in the tray, placed it on a bedside table, and found Tom Bingley on her heels. 'I'm here to see your mother,' he said. 'Good morning, Miss Morrison. How are you today?'

But the old woman was concentrating her attention on Eileen, who didn't seem right. Frances Morrison leapt from her bed with surprising alacrity just as her carer fell in a dead faint. 'Pick her up. Put her on my bed. See if her heart's good.'

'Just exhaustion,' he said after a brief examination. 'She probably didn't get enough sleep.' He listened to Eileen's heart. 'Yes, she'll be fine. I'll leave a tonic.' Had she been kept awake by Keith Greenhalgh?

Frances Morrison had seen and heard enough lately. She had to do something about this situation. 'Now, I don't want you to take offence, but in future I'd like to be attended by Dr Ryan. I think you know why.'

'What? No, I don't know why. Have I neglected you in some way?'

'No. You've been very attentive, especially since Mrs Watson came to live here. I'm not quite as deaf as I appear to be. Thank you for all you have done, but leave us now. She and I will care for each other, and Dr Ryan can look after both of us. Goodbye, Dr Bingley. I shall get Dr Ryan to look at Mrs Kennedy when she wakes from her drug-induced sleep.'

This conversation drifted into Eileen's ears as she neared consciousness. She opened one eye and looked at Tom. 'Hey, you,' she said.

'Yes?'

'Shut your mouth. There's a tram coming.'

Frances Morrison turned to face the window. She wanted to laugh, but she mustn't...

Ten

Nellie was complaining about musical beds. She had left her place of rest, and her daughter was now flat out on the same mattress because she hadn't slept a wink. 'Never mind,' she said finally. 'I'll go downstairs and get to know Miss Morrison, then you can go and live at Willows. We should get you out of here and away from you-know-who.'

But Eileen was having none of that. 'I'm not leaving Mel. We'll take turns, like we said. And I have to think about stuff. When it starts, I'm going to be there, do my bit for my country.'

'The bombs. There's a war on in case you've forgotten. I know people are calling it a dummy war, but it won't always be this quiet.'

Nellie dropped onto the dressing stool. 'And what good will you be to Mel dead? What good will you be to anyone?'

'Mam, you can say that about any mother or father. I'm joining the WVS and I'll do my knitting and stuff here. But when it all kicks off, I'll be at my post on Scotland Road. It's not just soldiers and sailors, you know. We all have to fight for our children. Don't start. I am going to help in this bloody war no matter what you think or say. It'll be for a couple of hours a week, and Mel can mind Miss Morrison. Go and look after that old lady. She sacked him.'

'Sacked who?'

'Dr Thomas Bingley. Tell Keith I want tea, toast, butter, marmalade and something to read. Probably.'

Nellie folded her arms. 'So you got rid of one, and you're ordering the other about as if he's already wed to you? Our Mel's the same. She changes when there's men about. Like you, she knows her power, doesn't she?'

'Probably,' Eileen repeated. The probably had to go. Keith had said last night that there couldn't be any probably, because she had to love him and only him. He had made a takeover bid, and she was sorely tempted, but the war needed to be over first, didn't it? Did it? At this rate, they wouldn't get to kick off till about 1950, by which time there'd be no sugar, no petrol, no fruit... She couldn't do without him for that long. Yes, she loved him. Probably. He made her tingle, anyway.

'Are you listening to me, soft girl? Did what I found yesterday mean nothing? You'll be as dead as Kitty if you start bloody WVS-ing.'

But Eileen had made up her mind. Everyone was in danger. The whole of society in several countries was being threatened by a jumped-up jackass with a toothbrush under his nose and eyes that seldom blinked. That, she had read somewhere, was a symptom of psychosis, so he was likely to be as mad as a frog in a bin. He was also unforgivably ugly, and she was going to help to save people from the craziness of a man who was rumoured to have lived for a while in Liverpool. 'Upper Stanhope Street,' she declared. 'I bet you never knew about that, eh?'

'You what?'

'Hitler lived there until 1913 with his brother Alois and sister-in-law Bridget. She was Irish.'

Nellie made the sign of the cross. 'God bless us and save us,' she muttered. 'We nursed the devil in our bosom, may the angels preserve our souls. That's terrible.'

Mam was funny. Reared by an illiterate but wise Irish mother, she was full of little sayings and prayers that sounded as if they were issuing from someone born in County Mayo. She'd start singing 'Faith of our Fathers' in a minute. 'Mam, I fainted. Food would be good.'

Nellie stalked out of the room and went downstairs. No sooner had she entered the kitchen than he started his mithering. How was Eileen, was she looking better, did Nellie think she'd be all right, should he take her to the hospital, did she need anything? He went on and on until Nellie told him to shut up, or she would remove his tongue by any means that came to hand. 'Are you engaged to her or something?' she asked, the tone trimmed with sarcasm.

'Probably.'

'What does probably mean, Keith?'

He shrugged. 'I don't know. Ask her.'

It had been a difficult time for poor Nellie. She remembered the Sunday on which war had been declared, remembered Kitty comforting her and telling her to bear up. But Kitty had been the one in true need of support. 'I should have sent her first,' she mumbled to herself.

'Eh?'

'Kitty,' she snapped. 'Look. I love the bones of that girl upstairs, but she's not the centre of the bloody universe.' She gave him a hard, penetrating look. 'But she's the centre of yours, isn't she?'

He averted his gaze. 'Yes.'

Nellie sat down, 'Well, I can tell you this for no money, I would be made up. I would, lad. But let's get on, shall we? You've to make her some toast and take it up. I've got to get sense out of that telephone thing and talk to Hilda. We may have to stay another couple of nights and sort out the funeral. In which case, you'll need to go and buy underclothes. I can manage with our Eileen's at a pinch, and it is a bloody pinch. So you do the queen's breakfast while I sort things out with Miss Morrison. Oh, and Madam Butterfly says she's joining the WVS and going into the bomb zone when it all kicks off.' She marched off muttering that if it wasn't one thing it was another, and some people should sleep at night instead of running after men and being too soft in the head to eat a decent breakfast.

When Keith finally got upstairs, Eileen was asleep. He placed the tray on a small table and sat with her. She had fainted due to lack of nourishment, yet he wasn't happy about waking her. 'Eileen? Come on, you have to eat.'

She opened one eye. 'Where've you been?'

'Getting a lecture from your mother.'

'About what?'

'Everything.'

'Right.' Having been a recipient of such diatribes for most of her life, she found his explanation acceptable. Between bites of toast, she delivered the opinion that Mam took some getting used to, and advised him to develop a degree of deafness. Miss Morrison found the affliction useful, and so would he when they got back to Willows. 'Miss Morrison sacked Tom Bingley because he was getting on my nerves, not hers. So she's heard him and me quarrelling, and that's because she pretends she can't hear. Just a suggestion.'

'It won't stop the doc chasing you,' Keith said.

'I know. I've had many a hopeful follower since Laz died, and I'll manage, thanks. All you need is a giant fly-swatter, because if you hit them in the fly it upsets them.'

She was better. She was feisty, slightly vulgar,

and almost back to normal. 'Come out with me,' he begged. 'Nellie's getting to know Miss M, and I need to–'

'I'm not leaving Mam. After what she went through yesterday, she needs me.'

The door swung inward. 'Get some sleep, then go out with him. Me and Frances is getting along great, ta very much. Anyway, Dr Wotsit's paid for the funeral, and they can all fit in with Charlie. But the bodies are down the hospital getting looked at. There have to be certificates before they get released. Me and Keith can't stay here long, because Hilda's stuck up Willows with them three.' She looked Keith up and down. 'If you're going to marry this one, I hope you know what you'll be taking on.'

'Yes,' he replied lamely.

The arms folded themselves yet again. 'So? Are you starting courting, then?'

'Probably,' they chorused.

Nellie looked at the ceiling, her lips moving in silent prayer. Young people these days were rubbish when it came to decision-making. Eileen should grab this one, because he was house-trained, handsome and willing to have a go with the Terrible Trio. He could even cook, for goodness' sake. 'Go out with him,' she snapped. 'And thank your lucky stars for the man, because he's a rare beast.'

'That's me told.' Eileen drained her cup and lay back on the pillows. 'Get lost, both of you. I'm having a day off.'

Nellie led her chosen son-in-law downstairs, where she delivered another lecture, this time on a subject entitled How to Win the Hand of Eileen Watson. There was a hefty sub-section pertaining to the boys, and a smaller essay on Mel, who liked clever people. 'Can you play chess?'

He nodded. Getting a word in would have been difficult, so he decided not to try.

'Cribbage and backgammon?'

Again, he inclined his head.

'Good, so you'll be in there with that one. The other three? Oh, bugger. But I think you're on the right road with Bertie. Phil and Rob were older when their dad died, so they took it bad and started running wild. With me and our Eileen having to work, we couldn't keep hold of them. She could do with marrying a prison guard, I suppose.'

'I'll manage. Don't forget, I was a sergeant major, and that's as good as any prison guard, Nellie. She'll marry me if I have to break her legs.'

'Don't do that, love. She's got great legs.'

'I noticed.'

'Nellie laughed. 'And she's a poser. Likes men looking at her, but she's never looked at them, not till lately. As for our Mel, she's got brains and street-wisdom, so she already knows how to get attention and how to manipulate idiots. She loves male company, but she'll flirt with you.'

'I've told you, I'll cope.'

'Make sure you do. Take madam to the pictures tonight. There's that *Gone with the Wind* one, always makes me think about somebody what's ate too many sprouts. Withering Heights, or whatever it is, Wizard of Oz, then Boris Wotsisface messing about in the Tower of London. Plenty to choose from. Take her in the back row for a cuddle, she likes a cuddle. And liquorice allsorts. See? Job done.'

Keith loved Nellie's philosophy. She saw a gap in the market, sucked on her dentures for a second or two, then filled the space. Eileen was aware of her desirability, seemed interested in him, so liquorice allsorts, a good film, a cuddle in the back row, a chance. Mel, on the other hand, was aware and educated, so she would need watching. Whatever, he seemed to have passed the unscheduled interview, and Nellie had appointed him keeper of the keys to some dungeon in which he would be expected to store her grandsons. By default, he was now guardian of Mel's chastity, and husband-in-waiting for Nellie's daughter, because Nellie had decided. Scarcely addressed was the rest of the equation, because Nell and Eileen came as a pair, and mother-in-law would definitely be nearby or in the household. If they ever achieved marriage, that was.

Strangely, he didn't mind any of it. His disposition was inclined towards the let-it-be school of thought, and matriarchy didn't frighten him. Nellie was a sensible woman underneath the aprons and behind the pot teeth. There was no harm in her, and he adored her daughter. It would all work out, he reassured himself.

They didn't go to the cinema. Instead, the pair sat in the rear seat of Hilda Pickavance's car, ate fish and chips, found a rug and cuddled up together under a full moon whose mirror shone in the Mersey behind a row of railings. Their thoughts were shared, though largely unexpressed at first. This angry stretch of water, governed by the Irish Sea and the silver body that currently hung in the sky, was peaceful tonight; scarcely a ripple, no sound, no need to be afraid, not yet. 'It will happen,' Keith said at last. 'Once the Krauts have airstrips in France...'

'Yes. Yes, it will.'

'Are you frightened, love?'

Eileen nodded. 'Only a fool could fail to be afraid. It's too quiet, too eerie. But you can feel it, can't you? Like when there's going to be a thunderstorm and you get a headache. Oh yes, they will come here. And they'll bomb us and burn us, so we'll bomb and burn them. Even if you leave the people out of it, look at all the wonderful buildings that'll be lost. Such a waste. War is stupid.'

'It is. I remember the last lot, and I wish I didn't.'

The kissing and whispering started, and by half past ten they had begun to explore one another in the exquisite discomfort of a confined space. Among chip papers, and surrounded by the heady perfumes of vinegar and cod, they became aware that the future was deciding for itself. 'I didn't need the liquorice allsorts,' he said. 'And what happened to probably?'

'It died in its sleep. Come on, we have to get back. Mam will be wondering where I am.' How on earth could she have imagined that she was attracted to Tom Bingley? This man had soul, kindness and a generosity of spirit that was rare in humankind. And he was a very desirable property.

'She'll think we've had sex.'

'Well, we nearly did.'

He burst out laughing. 'I'm old enough to be needing a bed for that sort of malarkey. Gone are my days for jumping off wardrobes wearing only a big smile.'

'Have you really done that?'

'No, but a man can dream. When we eventually do the deed, I'll probably have to recuperate for days in a darkened room with a wet cloth over my eyes, because I've never done it with a woman I love.'

'You said probably.'

'Did I?'

'Probably. Let's get back before the Germans come.'

They returned to what Eileen described as chaos on wheels. Miss Morrison, in what she referred to as her chariot, was at the kitchen table with Nellie, and she was normally in bed long before this time. She hadn't quite mastered the art of steering, and the whole ground floor bore scars from her twisting and turning, particularly in doorways.

Nellie had been weeping. She looked at her daughter and probable son-in-law, and made just a few remarks. 'Your buttons are wrong, girl. Keith, if you're going to mess about with bits of me daughter, put them away properly before bringing her home.' She covered her tear-stained face and shook her head slowly from side to side.

In spite of everything, Miss Morrison had to choke back a giggle. She hadn't had this much fun since being locked in the school cellar with a caretaker whose jokes had been rather risqué. But this was not an occasion for hilarity. There was trouble afoot, and no one should be laughing, because Nellie was terrified.

'We're courting,' Eileen said.

'I should think so too, with the bloody state of you. He looks like he's been dragged through a hedge backwards as well. It's like having a pair of blinking teenagers in the house, both ragged after billing and cooing all over the shop. Eileen, love, they've gone missing.'

Eileen looked down at her bosom.

'Not them, you soft mare. Your two eldest, my grandsons. They've buggered off with bread, boiled ham, cheese and two bikes. Oh, and a couple of bottles of dandelion and burdock. The only hope is that they've overloaded themselves and won't get far. And money. They've took a few bob.'

Eileen dropped into a chair. 'In the dark?'

Keith, hands in trouser pockets, was staring at the floor. He'd remembered something. 'They've become very interested in maps just lately,' he said. 'I should have known it was too good to be true. They didn't want a horse, they wanted a bike each. A few times, when there was a clear sky, I caught them staring at the evening sun. So they've worked out which way is west, and they're on their way to Scotland Road.'

'I'll kill them,' Eileen declared.

'You've to find them first,' sighed Nellie. 'Miss Pickavance is halfway out of her brainbox. Neil and Jean have taken her and Bertie down to Home Farm, but she can't stay there in case the two heroes return and there's nobody in to flay them within an inch of their lives. What next, eh?

We don't need a bloody war, because we've already got one. Poor Kitty, now this. Come on, Keith. We'd best get back to Willows.'

But he put his foot down hard. Driving any distance in a blackout was not a good idea. The boys would not be visible at night, and if they had any sense they would have found somewhere sheltered to sleep. And what was the point of going to inland Lancashire when the lads were on their way to Liverpool? 'Let the police look for them till morning then Eileen and I will go down the road and find the little devils. From now on, they will work with me and the farmers. Miss Pickavance should not have to put up with my ... my charges.'

'What if they get run over and killed?' Nellie screamed.

'They won't,' Eileen told her. 'The devil looks after his own.'

Miss Morrison nodded thoughtfully. 'I always found the complete removal of all privileges to be effective, but that was in a school environment. You are right in your decision to put them to work Find a farmer or a farmhand you trust, and hand them over. No puddings or treats until they have proved themselves. If they cooperate, open up a small bank account, but don't allow them access to money unless they have been spectacularly good. Reward decent behaviour and withhold all possibility of reward if they don't buck up.'

'Didn't you teach girls, though?' Nellie asked.

'Oh yes, indeed. Girls are more cunning and they refine their skills at an early age. Boys are difficult, but rather less aware of the action and reaction process. They tend not to think things through very well. So it isn't difficult to stay one step ahead. Oh, and if you find them in Liverpool, Mr Greenhalgh, bring them here. I should like to meet these fine young men. Eileen? Put me to bed, dear.'

Nellie and Keith were left alone. She looked him up and down. 'You and our Eileen, you didn't...?'

'No, we didn't. And forget about that till we've found Philip and Rob. I'm worried in case the police get them. From what I've heard, they've come pretty near to being sent away, and we don't want them in Borstal, do we?'

She sighed heavily. 'It won't happen. This country's full of runaways trying to find their way home from evacuation billets. But you've got to catch them, love.'

'I know. I promise you I'll get them back. Go to bed.'

But Nellie had no intention of going to bed. She was staying near the phone, and she would be here if the police rolled up with that pair of ragamuffins. Like many women, she displayed fear as if it were anger, and her only consolation was a picture of herself with her hands round Philip's throat. At eleven, he should have had more sense.

Mel wandered in, balled hands rubbing her eyes. 'What's going on?' she asked. 'It's like trying to sleep in the middle of a playground.'

Nellie explained, adding a brief remark about Eileen and Keith courting.

'Good,' Mel said. 'I like you, Mr Greenhalgh. I'll make some cocoa. And don't worry about that pair, since they're sure to be noticed. They couldn't escape from a plate of blancmange, because they've only one brain cell between them, and they've lent that to Bertie. The youngest has more sense than the two of them put together, but then so has a dead rat. Anyone else for cocoa?'

Midnight found Nellie, Mel, Eileen and Keith sipping hot cocoa at the kitchen table. Tales of the boys' exploits were bandied about, and Keith found himself suppressing laughter yet again. The humour was an unexpected bonus, and he relished it. The pair had brought home dogs, sacks of molasses, coal, rotted fruit from the back of Paddy's Market, and half a pig pinched from the yard of a butcher's shop. 'What did you do with that?' Keith asked.

'We ate it, of course,' Nellie answered. 'It was half a pig, it was dead, and it was in our house. It took some chopping up, but we managed.'

'Double standards.' Eileen touched his hand. 'It happens where there's poverty.'

'I know,' he answered. 'I come from a similar background. I haven't always lived in the glorious Lancashire countryside. Life's hard.'

'It's what you make it,' Mel announced with a toss of her head.

'Drink your cocoa,' barked her grandmother. 'And be grateful, Miss Clever Clogs.'

It was dark, it was cold, and they were both fed up, though Philip remained determined to see the mission through. 'What did it say on that last sign?' his brother asked.

'Lowton,' Philip snapped.

'Where's Lowton?'

'Near Leigh.'

'Where's Leigh?'

'Near Lowton. Now shut up, or I'll bloody strangle you. We have to find somewhere and wait till morning. That big road to Liverpool's only a mile or so from here.' There was a moon. The moon was the reason they were here, because they'd have needed to wait another whole month for light. Everywhere was blacked out, curtains closed, street lamps unlit, most people in bed. Rob wanted to turn round and go back, but Philip was adamant. Hell wasn't about burning; it was mile after mile of open space, *PLEASE CLOSE THE GATE,* ill-tempered bulls, chickens scratching, cows lowing to be milked, no shops, no picture house, no human life.

'She'll be out of her mind,' Rob said. 'Miss Pickavance, I mean.'

'But we won't.' Philip dragged the younger boy down the side of a house. 'We're going home. See? An Anderson. We'll sleep in that tonight, and tomorrow we'll be back where we belong.'

Rob wasn't sure where he belonged. All he knew was that he needed food, warmth, and familiar faces. Sitting in a chilled Anderson shelter with dampish blankets was not his idea of fun. Sometimes, they had a fire in their bedroom at Willows, and it was cosy. The food, too, was good, and he didn't mind digging up potatoes and carrots, because it was great to eat vegetables that had been grown on land belonging to the house.

Philip managed to light a small paraffin stove. 'Now you can stop moaning,' he said. 'And in a few hours we'll be back where we belong.'

Rob still wasn't sure where he belonged. He wanted Gran. Gran was a pain in the backside, but he missed her. He'd have preferred Mam, but she was in Blundellsands or somewhere posh with an old lady and Keith Greenhalgh and Gran and Mel, because Kitty-next-door had gone to hell for murder and suicide, and it was all very confusing for a nine-year-old lad who just wanted a mug of hot milk and a warm bed.

But when Philip was asleep, Rob discovered that he hadn't the courage to go off on his own, as Philip was older and knew where things were. And a two-hour stint on a bike hadn't been good for the legs, so Rob laid himself down and ached. There was hardly any pop left, and most of the food was in a bit of a mess, as it hadn't been wrapped properly and things were crumbly and rather mixed up.

Rob stared up at the corrugated container in which he was confined. At Willows, they had a double bed and a single bed, and they took turns. Bertie was funny; he didn't like sleeping alone. Thinking about his little brother curled up all by himself made Rob tearful. His limbs hurt, his back hurt, his arms ached, and there was a hole in his heart where the life to which he had started to become accustomed no longer sat. What could he do, though? Was there a police station nearby? Would the police take him to that prison for young offenders in Derbyshire? And what about Phil?

At last he fell asleep. When morning came, Phil woke him, and they sneaked back up the side of the house. After just a few minutes, they were sitting on the grass verge of the East Lancashire

Road eating crumbs of bread and Lancashire cheese. Although they were nearer to Manchester than to Liverpool, the end was in sight. Behind them, the sun had risen; ahead, their destination awaited their return, and although Rob prayed that they would soon be found, he followed his brother and hoped for the best. It would be an adventure, but surely they would be rescued soon?

'Come on,' Phil chided. He guessed that his companion's heart was no longer in this expedition. 'I don't want to eat any more of that muck. When we get to Scotland Road, we'll find plenty to eat.'

Plenty to eat? Mam had tried her best to make sure there'd been enough, but plenty had started first at Miss Pickavance's house on Rachel Street, and had continued at Willows. Rob scarcely dared to ask, yet he managed. 'Plenty? Who's going to give us plenty, Phil? We don't belong to anybody now.'

'Then we'll pinch it.'

'And end up at that school for bad lads?'

Phil threw down his bike and took hold of his companion's clothing in the neck area. 'Listen, soft girl, if you want to go back, bugger off and see if you can remember the way. I'm going home.'

Rob swallowed. 'Right.'

'Are you with me? Because I'm telling you now, I could get there a damned sight faster without you holding me back all the while.'

'I'm with you.' There was nowhere else to be. Rob wouldn't find his way to Willows in a month of Sundays, and they both knew it. So they carried on along a rough footpath that ran parallel with the new road. One way or another, Phil Watson would be home by lunchtime.

Things were changing at a rate of knots in the St Andrew's Road house. Tom, having been dismissed by Frances Morrison, was no longer able to visit the woman he wanted. Advised by his daughter that Eileen and the Greenhalgh fellow were enjoying each other's company, he was not in the best of moods. Then there was Marie. She was floating round with her feet about six inches off the ground, and she looked different. In fact, both females in the household looked different. Gloria's skin had improved, her figure had developed in a matter of weeks, and she suddenly owned visible cheekbones.

Marie's hair was softer, and it framed a face that seemed to be eliminating pockets of loose flesh at the jaw line. Her eyes appeared larger, waist smaller, legs better than ever. She sang a lot. He listened carefully when she was on the telephone, because she had a special voice for one caller. The business voice was employed for her WVS coven, but a certain person named Norman made her giggle and simper like a young girl. She imagined that she was in love. Tom knew Norman, since the chap had owned a few pharmacies, and he was about as interesting as drying paint, but Marie was clearly impressed by him. He was probably dependable to the point of predictability, and that would please Marie, who wanted life to be the same every day.

Tom no longer felt at home. In fact, he was completely isolated. Marie slept in the spare room, and was not always present at meal times. Never sure where she might be, he spent many evenings alone, and having once visited the hall in which the WVS met and discovered a locked door and no sound of life from within, he guessed that she was often with her new man friend. Peter and Gloria lived more or less upstairs, the former sometimes out playing badminton, the latter learning how to preen in front of a mirror. Life had gone crazy.

Driven by loneliness and boredom, he had eavesdropped not only on his wife but also on his daughter and Mel Watson. 'Stick them out,' Mel had ordered. 'You are going to be gorgeous, girl. Belt as tight as you can bear it, belly in, tits out. If they don't quite fill the bra, pinch a bit of cotton wool out of your dad's bag.'

'That's cheating.'

'It's survival. When you talk to one of the other lot, lower your head a bit and look at him through your eyelashes – no! Not like that; you have to be subtle. Yes, that's better. They mustn't know that you know what you're doing.'

'But I don't know what I'm doing,' poor Gloria had cried.

'You'll learn. And don't let them get close, always have witnesses. Remember, this is all rooted in survival of the species, so you're working on their weaknesses, which are also their strengths, because they have powerful bodies. To get into a girl's knickers, some would sell their souls. If you learn to manage them, you're a winner. Make them want you. It drives them mad, and they start being nice and giving you things.'

Tom smiled to himself. He had given Mel a

bike and money for clothes. She understood the game, had probably learned it from her mother. Part of him felt glad that Gloria was showing promise and that Mel had noticed the improvement. But the loss of innocence was sad. Even so, the father in Tom felt a degree of relief, because if Gloria followed Mel's rules she might keep herself safe, at least.

His marriage was burned out. He would not be the one to leave, since he had nowhere to go apart from the flat above the surgery, but it looked as if Marie might be about to break her word for the first time within his memory. Would she take his children? Of course she would. Perhaps Peter might opt to stay behind, but Gloria would definitely accompany her mother. This was the lowest point in his life so far. And while Eileen Watson existed, Tom Bingley could not look at another woman.

He drove past the house whenever he could, often going well out of his way in order to have a small chance of seeing that wretched female. The knowledge that he hovered on the brink of obsession did not sit comfortably in his mind, because he'd attended his fair share of lectures in psychology, but what could he do? He loved the bloody woman, lusted after her, had no outlet for his frustrations.

It was after midnight when Marie came home. 'Still up?' she said brightly.

'Apparently so. I'm downstairs and awake, so yes, I'm still up.'

Marie removed hat and coat. The man's sarcasm made her want to shake him, but he was too big for that. But she could shake him in a more permanent way any time she chose. She could leave him, yes, she could and would. 'I've a meeting in Manchester next week. Top brass coming up to teach backward northerners how to cope with the homeless. I shall probably be away overnight.'

'Right. I expect Boring Norman will be away at the same time?'

Marie was ill-equipped for her husband's games. Unlike him, she had not gone out looking for Norman, had not chosen him, had not even allowed him a kiss. 'Don't make the mistake of judging me by your standards. Norman is a good friend. He plays the piano while we make up parcels and fold slings and knit socks for soldiers. I have been to his house, as have some of the other ladies, and he has cooked for us.'

'How nice.' The use of the word 'ladies' was typical of Marie. She never got things quite right, always erring on the side of politeness, usually worrying about how things looked, and were they correct, and what would people think? 'What will the community make of you when I sue for divorce and name Norman as co-respondent?'

'I have absolutely no idea,' she replied quickly. 'But I would advise caution. Norman's brother's a barrister. A slander suit would do you no good at all.' She walked out.

He suddenly found her almost desirable, yet he remembered only too well the non-responsive creature with whom he had shared a bed for years. What was the point? She was not combustible, had been born without passion at any level. It had taken a declaration of war to enliven her and give her a sense of purpose. Tom shifted in his chair. A doctor had to be careful when it came to putting himself about, so recent experience was minimal, but it occurred to him, not for the first time, that their failure in the bedroom could be his fault.

It wasn't a comfortable thought. He was a medical man, so he knew more than most about the mechanics of sex. Foreplay? Marie didn't like it, so he'd stopped bothering with it. She'd been a depository, no more than that. Stimulated by other women, he had used her mercilessly, and he was perilously near to the edge of self-hatred. This couldn't go on.

Tom Bingley walked upstairs and into his wife's room. She sat on the edge of a narrow bed, her face tear-stained, hands folded in her lap. 'Please,' she begged. 'No more. Because of the children, I won't scream, but have mercy, I beg you.'

Wearing his doctor face, he sat next to her. 'It's all right, dear. I just want to talk. Do you mind talking?'

She shook her head.

'Did you ever feel anything, Marie? When I touched you, I mean.'

She thought about that. 'In the early days, before we married, there seemed to be a promise of something, but the only fruit it bore were the twins. The whole business is embarrassing and untidy.'

He agreed. 'God has a sense of humour, you see. He put all primary sexual organs in the same area as the unpleasant end of our digestive tract. Then some silly ass came down a mountain with rules carved in stone, which were also designed to make us uncomfortable. Popes scream to this day about chastity, yet half the priests are indulging in some sort of activity.' He paused. 'Could you consider trying again if I promise to stop when you say so?'

'It would always be stop.' Her spine was rigid. 'Yes, I'm afraid it would always be stop, Tom. It's something I was born without, I think.'

No one was born without needs and desires. 'You must have been born with the need for a partner and for children. Even nuns have it, though they dedicate themselves to denying that area of their lives. This Norman – you are fond of him, I can see that. Is it because you think he will never touch you? Do you desire him?'

With excruciating slowness, she turned to look at him. 'He's kind to me, Tom. I have been as dutiful as I could manage. I've been tolerant, useful, kind, and a fairly good mother. But I shall no longer do as I am told. Once upon a time, I did as I was ordered. Yes, Norman is a comfort. But nothing will come of it, because I know I'm frigid.'

'You did as you were told when you were a child?'

'Yes.'

Tom sat as still as stone. 'Did anything happen to you when you were little?'

'Can't remember.' She began to weep noiselessly.

Gently, he laid her on the bed and placed himself beside her. For the first time in many weeks, they were together. Tom and Marie Bingley, fully clothed and on a narrow bed, clung to one another and cried themselves to sleep.

Freda Pilkington, now the proud owner of two decent pillows and Nellie Kennedy's best frying pan, was pleased to allow Nellie to use her house. She went out for a stroll with her children and her husband, who was due to report to training camp in a few days. Freda and her toddlers had been allocated the Willows cottage that should have gone to Kitty Maguire. Since poor Kitty and her children were to be buried on the coming Tuesday, Freda had moved up the list.

Next week, a charabanc would pick up and carry to Willows several children from the Scotland Road area. They would travel by train to Trinity Street station in Bolton, then would be collected in the coach and allocated to farmers and villagers for the duration. But two who had already been taken into the safer zone had absented themselves, and Nellie, Eileen and Keith were on the case. Nellie fastened herself to Freda's window and waited. They would turn up in this, their own street, sooner or later.

Poor Mel had taken a precious day off school in order to mind Miss Morrison, and these two boys were in a chasm of trouble. No longer fearful for their safety, Nellie felt only anger. She looked across at the house in which she had lived with her daughter and grandchildren, then moved her eyes until they rested on Kitty's place. Behind dirty windows, it awaited fumigation, after which all trace of Kitty and the children would disappear from the planet. Those panes were reminiscent of blind eyes, because Kitty no longer stood there and watched the small slice of life with which she had been familiar.

Among all this sadness and in spite of the dread of war, Nellie's two older grandsons had taken off without a word to anyone. They seemed to care for no living soul, and they needed a firm hand. Yes, they had run wild since the death of their dad, but Nellie had worked five mornings and three evenings each week, while her daughter's jobs had spanned four full days, because rent and bills had to be paid, food and clothes cost money, and both women were widows. But this time there was a plan. Thanks to Miss Morrison, the pair of ruffians would soon be too scared to breathe normally. 'You'll get your comeuppance,' Nellie muttered. 'Then I'll nail both pairs of bloody feet to the floor.'

The door crashed inward, and Phil was thrown into the house. Behind him, a furious Keith entered. 'Don't you ever speak to your mother like that.'

Rob, his head bowed, followed Keith.

'Where's Eileen?' Nellie asked.

'She's giving the bikes to kids who'll appreciate them.' He picked up the older boy, stood him against a wall and pushed his face to within an inch of Phil's. 'In fact, don't talk to anyone until you've rinsed your mouth. What did Eileen do to deserve an odious little toad like you? You are grounded, boy. One wrong word, one dirty look out of you, and I'm the one you answer to. What you want doesn't matter. Your unhappiness is nothing, because you're just a small speck at the front of a big painting, and that painting's a world war. You got taken up yonder so that you won't get killed by a bomb. You get given a bike, and you run away on it. I can see Rob's heart wasn't in all this, so I am holding you fully responsible for the pain your mam and your gran have gone through. Nasty piece of work. Your father would be ashamed.'

Nellie guessed that this was probably the longest speech the quiet man had ever made. For Eileen, he would do anything, or so it would appear.

He spoke to Rob. 'When I first went up to Willows Edge, I hated it. Like you, I came from an overcrowded street where everyone was poor. It grows on you, Rob. Give it time, son.' He turned and winked at Nellie. They both knew that Rob would settle, because he liked growing his own food. Rob might become a happy soul, but Phil was more rigid. Phil had suffered when his father died, and it was showing now.

Eileen entered the scene. She stood with her back to the door, arms folded, lips tightened in her pale, tired face. 'Get the car, Keith,' she said. 'I'll stand guard.' She moved to allow Keith to leave.

Phil stayed where he had been put, arms folded, face expressionless. For the rest of their short stay in Freda's house, not a word was spoken. During this weighty, uncomfortable pause, the lad began to understand the enormity of what he had done. According to Keith, three police forces were out searching for the Watson boys. Bolton, Manchester and Liverpool were paying men to search not only for them, but also for other evacuees who had decided that the move from home didn't suit them. He was eleven. He should have known better. Fear of leaving home was for little boys, not for the likes of him.

Eileen and her mother sat and allowed the quiet to continue. Let him have the chance to reflect on his actions, because the day would get worse for him before it got better.

It got worse.

Phil, the bigger sinner, was locked in Miss Morrison's old bedroom, which contained one chair and a blanket. Rob, in his mother's room, found himself well furnished but lonely. Both boys, isolated completely, were given hours during which to contemplate what they had done. Mam and Gran were trying to save them, and the two ingrates had thrown everything back in the faces of those they loved.

A silent, grim-faced Keith served meals on trays, returning only to remove debris before locking doors in his wake. No one spoke to them. In two separate rooms, clouds of foreboding gathered and hung in the air like the threat of thunder. Something was happening downstairs. They heard little, saw nothing, sensed disaster. Rob, flat out under his mother's eiderdown, rested bones still weary from the endless ride; Phil wondered how old he needed to be to join the army and whether he would get his bicycle back.

The policeman came for them at about six o'clock. He had stripes on his arm, a face like a train crash, and very big feet in very shiny shoes. In the hall, he explained that courts were busy, so juvenile sessions were being convened out of hours in schools, other civic buildings, and occasionally the house of a magistrate. 'Be truthful, polite and brief,' the man advised. 'Your future hangs in the balance. Miss Morrison is a magistrate of long standing.'

Three justices sat at the kitchen table. The one in the middle introduced herself as Miss Morrison, owner of the house in which Philip and Rob had been incarcerated. A public gallery, consisting of Mam, Gran and Keith, was wedged just inside the back door. The witness box, a metal walking frame belonging to Miss Morrison, was situated between a gas cooker and the kitchen sink.

When the two offenders had been sworn in, a list of crimes was read out by the police sergeant. It seemed that Philip and Robin Watson were responsible for all the ills in the world, with the possible exception of diphtheria and a couple of wars. In a moment of reckless clarity, Phil demanded a lawyer. 'Silence,' called the magistrate in the middle. 'These are uncertain times, you are children, and your behaviour is beyond the pale.'

Phil wondered what a pail had to do with anything; it was just a posh bucket when all was said and done. They were now talking about suitable placement, and Derbyshire was mentioned again. Not only was the school for bad boys far away from family, it was far away from anything. He listened while the place was described. The words frying pan and fire paid a brief visit to his consciousness, because life in the Peaks sounded a sight worse than life in the house named Willows.

Mam was employing one of her hard stares, so both boys pleaded guilty. They were taken by the policeman into the hall while their future was decided. Phil, seated on the fourth stair, decided that he didn't want to go to Derbyshire. Being locked in here had been bad enough; the thought of real captivity was terrifying. 'We have to go back, Rob, and do as we're told. Otherwise, we'll finish up with a load of fifteen-year-olds who'll beat the you-know-what out of us.' He glanced at their minder. 'Glad you think it's funny. Hey! Put me down, put me down.'

'There you go.' The man deposited Phil near the front door. 'Ever had a hiding from a cop, lad?'

In the kitchen, Frances Morrison was managing to keep a straight face, though the mother and grandmother of the accused had taken a break from the strain of this, their acting debut. The policeman and two magistrates had been borrowed from St Helen's church drama group, while everyone's scripts had been provided by Keith, who was also remaining stony-faced. The pair of malcontents would be placed under his charge in more than one way, as he would be their stepfather as well as their warden, and he intended to play both roles with more dignity than was currently being displayed by his future wife and mother-in-law. 'Stop it,' he whispered.

Eileen grabbed his hand. How could she have imagined feelings for anyone other than him? 'We'll be all right in a minute. It's Mam. She can sense one of her turns coming on.'

'Turns? What turns?'

'Well, if she needs to laugh and can't, she gets hiccups.'

'Oh, bugger. Nellie?'

'What?' The first hiccup exploded.

'Go in the shed. Go on. This is too important for you and your turns. They'll know you're trying not to laugh. Get out now. Take Miss Morrison's shawl – try next door. Run any-bloody-where, but no hiccups in here, love.'

Nellie snorted, hiccuped and left.

Eileen's grip on his hand tightened. 'I love you,' she whispered. It was the truth. He was magnificent, and getting to know him would be great.

'You'd better. I'm taking on the Third Reich single-handed here. In recompense, I may decide to expect your hand, plus the rest of you, in marriage. Eventually. No, forget that. Bugger eventually, I'd rather have soon.'

The court reconvened with the policeman standing between the two accused.

A sentence of two years in a secure juvenile unit was handed down before the magistrates indulged in a whispering session. When all the muttering was over, the boys' sentences were suspended for eighteen months. Rob didn't fancy getting suspended, because it sounded rather like Kitty-next-door, but he became reassured when suspension was explained. If he or Philip put one foot wrong within the next year and a half, they would be thrown to the wolves for two whole years.

They were sent to share a single bed in the smallest of the bedrooms while Mr Greenhalgh slept on a downstairs sofa. One of the few good things about being poor was that folk got used to being squashed at night. Their door was not locked, because this was the first test; if they didn't run, they had a chance of staying out of jail.

Morning found them sitting side by side on the edge of the narrow bed. 'What we need is something to be interested in,' Rob declared. 'I think I like digging things up.'

'Tell the vicar in Egerton,' snapped Philip. 'He'll take you on in the graveyard.'

Rob drew himself to full seated height. 'That's not digging up,' he said. 'It's planting. Soon, I'll be setting spuds and carrots. Bertie has his pony and the rest of the horses, but what have you got?'

'Paint,' came the reply.

'What?'

'You heard. Don't go deaf as well as daft. They said I have to get attached to Mr Collins. He does all the painting and mending, and he's got something called sugar. That means he falls off ladders. I have to learn painting, mending, and picking him up off the floor. It's an important position, being deputy handyman. Gardening, too.' He sighed heavily. He had no experience of paint, mending, gardening or sugar. Unless the odd handful of stolen molasses counted as experience in sugar.

Mel entered the room. 'Breakfast is served,' she announced. Fully aware of the previous evenings charade, she asked about their sentence.

'We're suspended for two years,' Philip replied dolefully. 'Mr Greenhalgh is in charge of us. And we have a book each. We have to write in it every night about what we've done during the day.' He shrugged. 'I hope we get a place in that school, wherever it is. School's going to be a rest.'

Mel went downstairs to report to the chief magistrate. Miss Morrison had been a magistrate in real life, so she was the only kosher member of the previous evening's shenanigans. 'They're terrified,' Mel announced.

'Good.' The old woman attacked her coddled egg. She felt almost healthy, because life had become entertaining at last. There was a great deal to be said for distractions, as they took one's mind away from one's ailments. One's ailments would be set aside for the foreseeable future, because Scotland Road had arrived on the cusp between Crosby and Blundellsands, and Scotland Road was interesting.

'Do you need anything else, Miss Morrison?'

The woman in the bed grinned. 'Not immediately, dear. But make sure they visit me before they go. Did I tell you about the time when I was trapped in the cellar with a vulgar caretaker?'

'Yes.'

'Well, it's been rather like that all over again. Did they really put someone's undergarment up a flagpole?'

'Yes.'

'And a carthorse in the yard?'

'Oh yes.'

'The stolen police dog?'

'It was nearly a police dog; it was still in training. I don't know whether it passed its test after being exposed to the company of my family.'

Miss Morrison stared hard at Mel. 'You know, my dear, you should write all of it in a journal. I have some nice hard-backed notebooks left over from my school. One day, this should be published. Like all good comedies, it sits against a background of great tragedy and deprivation.'

Mel chuckled. 'It was never a tragedy, Miss Morrison. It was loud, colourful and sometimes hungry, but there's nothing tragic about the Scottie Roaders. Outside the undertaker's, there's a coffin with Hitler's name on it. The barber's thinking of changing the name of his shop to It'll Be All Right When It's Washed, because that's what mothers say to their sons when they get a haircut. They're clever. One day, they'll be remembered for what they really are.'

'Which is?'

'People, Miss Morrison. Special, but just people.'

PART TWO

1940

Eleven

Keith was a hungry man. Tender though never timid, he appeared to be making up for two loveless decades, since he seldom left his wife's side for weeks following the wedding. After promoting Jay Collins to deputy steward and land agent over the whole Willows estate, he docked his own wages and followed wherever Eileen led. Miss Frances Morrison now had a beautiful house, as he had painted every room. Her old first-floor bedroom belonged to Mr and Mrs Keith Greenhalgh, who took great care of their generous landlady.

Eileen's second husband was also very funny. Unlike Liverpudlians, he delivered few quick answers, preferring instead to simmer for a while before offering up a killer reply, usually after the subject under discussion had been long abandoned. Stony-faced and quiet-voiced, he could reduce a room to hysteria in seconds. He adored his Eileen, grew fond of Frances Morrison, and spent many hours in battle with Mel over a chessboard.

But his favourite pastime seemed to be kissing. When questioned about the frequency of the attacks, his stock reply was that every man needed a hobby, and it was her fault anyway, since she was far too beautiful for her own good. On one occasion, he wore a sticking plaster over his mouth, though it didn't last, because Eileen's giggling became contagious, and he laughed the plaster free. He submitted a written complaint to management, and her reply, delivered on the banks of her beloved river, was verbal. 'Does all this kissing not make you want the rest of it?'

'Yes.'

'So?' Eyebrows raised and hands on hips, she waited for his answer.

'I'm good at procrastination.'

'And I'm not.'

'I know that.' He gazed out over the river. 'Ever had a bank account?' he enquired.

'No. The few times I've been in a bank, it's been for Miss Morrison.'

'The kissing is my deposit. I collect my interest at bedtime.'

A few beats of time slipped by while Eileen contained her laughter and made her face stern. 'You are one devious and cruel swine, Keith Greenhalgh.'

He narrowed his eyes. 'True. Delicious though, isn't it?'

'I'm like a bloody pan left on a low light. Or a slow rice pudding in a lukewarm oven, do not disturb till Christmas.'

Keith awarded her his full attention. 'You're no pudding. You're a diamond-studded rainbow with a pot of gold at each end.'

She wagged a finger. 'Don't be coming over all poetry, Keith. I can't be poetical in the fresh air. Not here. Please don't start kissing in public places.'

'Wouldn't dream of it.' He looked at a beach donated to Crosby and Blundellsands by the Irish

Sea, aided and abetted by the Mersey. This was a place where children played each summer, where families sat and watched ships lazing their way towards busy little tugs. 'I see no ships today,' he said. Hospital vessels were a too-familiar sight these days, sad, grey things marked with a red cross. 'Hell will be packed with Germans, so we'd better put our names down for the other place,' he quipped.

'It won't be packed with Germans at all. Just Nazis, and some of them are English.' She pointed at the mix of sand and mud below. 'Used to come here with Mam and some of my friends when I was a kid. Stripped down to our knickers, we were all the same. Rich, poor, or in the middle, we all played together. Look at it, Keith. What a bloody mess. They won't land here. There's been nobody invading Liverpool since the Vikings, because they've all learned the hard way that the natives are fierce.'

Five barrage balloons loitered idly in still air, while on the beach rolls of barbed wire kept company with dragons' teeth: pyramids of concrete dug in to prevent any vessel from coming ashore. This was Liverpool, and Liverpool was Hitler's second target, so it had to be guarded. The BBC Home Service mentioned from time to time a raid on a 'northern port', and everyone knew that all weaponry and ammunition passed through these docks, that citizens were living in mortal danger, that they would endure till the last brick had fallen and the last man was dead. But for the sake of security, Liverpool was given no identity in bulletins. According to statements from the War

Office, spies were everywhere. A person could become paranoid with very little effort.

'Keith?'

'What?'

She swallowed. 'We have to go home.'

He looked at his father's watch, a battered piece that lived in a jacket pocket. 'She'll be all right for a few more minutes. Eh? What's up with you?'

'Home, Keith. Your home, so my home, too. Willows Edge, my love.'

'Erm ... why?'

'Don't kiss me.'

'I won't kiss you.'

'Promise you won't kiss me.'

'I promise I won't kiss you.'

'You're going to be a daddy.'

He kissed her.

Hilda Pickavance, owner and mistress of the Willows estate, was a political animal with an inquisitive mind and a tendency to be inwardly critical of all who walked the corridors of power. Far from evangelical and allied to no party, she watched and made written comment on the performances of representatives local and national. In quieter moments, which were relatively few, she looked at her older writings while adding what she could manage about events of the day. Most of her recent essays were on the subject of Eileen's boys, all three of whom had improved considerably during their year in the wilds.

Everything had changed, and not just because of the war. Down the road, amid the dark, satanic mills, poverty ruled. But the south had basked in glorious affluence until last year; it had hardly been fair.

The decade of duality was finally over. The 1930s, ten years during which Britain had prospered in the south and decayed in the north, had survived Wall Street because of one man, and that man was Neville Chamberlain. Swept aside to make room for Churchill, he was now a creature people remembered as naive. In the minds of the populace, he carried in his hand a crumpled paper signed by a liar, a monster, a nutcase. 'There was more to Chamberlain than that,' Hilda muttered to herself. 'Perhaps he ignored the north, but he saved the Exchequer.' He had built a wall around the islands, had traded carefully and wisely, had kept the country away from the brink of total perdition. 'The good is oft interred with their bones,' she quoted. Shakespeare was usually acutely and painfully correct, even in this day and age.

Jarrow had been horrible, but the fact remained that Victorian factories were already in decline, and manufactured goods were purchasable at lower prices from worldwide sources. A swathe of dire and infected deprivation had spread itself across northern counties, and life had been hell on earth. So they had marched and shown themselves, down at heel, clothes torn and tattered, heads high. 'We are the same as you,' that march had screamed. 'And you are taking not just the cream, but the whole pie. While you eat, our children perish.' Had anyone listened? Did anyone ever listen?

In the south, arterial roads were laid, houses with front and rear gardens were bought via mortgage by members of the middle class and, more recently, by ordinary working men. For less than a thousand pounds, such a house would have a garage. Factories that looked like exhibition buildings cropped up, and while many northern towns had unemployment of up to 60 per cent of the available workforce, the south was fully utilized except for 3 or 4 per cent who were too ill for work. Commuter rail systems were installed, and the south was very well, thank you.

And here came war. Ill-nourished and exhausted Jarrow marchers fought alongside healthy southerners, and the divide would still be there when the war ended. 'We need a women's party. We need to occupy the lobbies and the benches to show these silly little boys how to live creatively.'

The produce of another scribe lay alongside Hilda's in a drawer of the bureau. Mel Watson had the eyes of an eagle and the ears of an alley cat, and she pulled no punches. The list was enough. Although Mel collected and recorded detail, it was safer to look just at the headings. In July, Altcar searchlight post was eradicated, but they missed Fort Crosby. August saw the battering of Birkenhead on the Wirral, and the first outright fatality was a female domestic servant. Wallasey came next, followed by Liverpool's dock road and overhead railway.

West Derby received a shower of incendiaries, one of which hit a nursing home. Towards the end of August, just before the wedding of Eileen and Keith at St Anthony's on Scotland Road, West Derby was pounded by high explosives. From early September to its end, there were sixteen raids on the city, eleven on Birkenhead, nine on Wallasey and four on Crosby. Walton Jail was hit, resulting in the deaths of wardens and prisoners, and, days later, the Argyle Theatre in Birkenhead was demolished and cremated.

There was humour, too. A crazed German fighter pilot fixed his sights on a Liverpool bus. Flying perilously low, he peppered the vehicle with bullets while passengers squeezed under seats. The driver was not amused. He leaned on his horn and ploughed on like a dodgem at the fair until the German got fed up and beggared off. No one was hurt except for a few bruises resulting from the driver's actions, and the only victim of the airborne lunatic was a fireman's hat, which got blown off and dented during the episode.

Smiling grimly, Hilda put away the writings and sat on her bed. Several good things had happened, and the best was the marriage between Eileen and Keith. Even an old maid could not fail to be aware of the chemistry between them. Better still, they were the greatest of friends and happy companions, while all four children had begun to respect their stepfather, so the future seemed bright. Except, that was, for the small matter named war.

Someone tapped on the door. 'Come in,' she called.

It was Bertie. He was as black as an old pot, a creased forehead betraying him as a thinker, and there was straw in his hair, but that was all par for the course. 'Hello, Bertie.'

He announced that he now knew what a fetlock was before parking his less than clean person next to Miss Pickavance. 'Miss?'

'Yes?'

'You know like a half-brother what we're getting?'

'Or sister. Yes.'

Bertie delivered a loud, damp raspberry. 'We've got Mel, and she's enough. We don't want no more girls. Now, I'm not daft. I'm eight now, so I'm not a little 'un any more.'

'Of course you're not daft.'

'I know a half-brother doesn't mean one arm, one leg, one eye, one ear, one–'

'Yes, yes. I'm sure you're aware of all that.'

'So what does it mean, then?'

Hilda opened her mouth, closed it again. She was a good teacher. She had been offered a place on a twelve month course created to bring more educators into the profession during and after wartime. 'Well, your father was Lazzer. Lawrence was his real name, though. Splendid man.'

'Yup.'

'And Eileen's your mother.'

'Yup.'

'Bertie, say yes.'

'Yup. All right. I mean yes.'

'So your half-brother or sister will be from the same mother, but a different father, and that will be Keith, who is now your stepfather.'

Bertie took a deep breath. 'But dads don't do nothing about a baby. It's the mam what screams and swears and pushes the new one out of her bum. I know, cos I've heard it in our street. And what does "tell him to tie a knot in it" mean? That was what Mrs Pilkington yelled after she throwed him out in the street. He had to sit on the doorstep while she shouted swear words and that. Nearly crying, he was. I sat with him and he said I was a grand lad. Held me hand, he did. I felt sorry for him. Mams can be very fierce people.'

Hilda sighed heavily. Teaching was often a rocky road. 'Hens lay eggs,' she said, wondering immediately why she'd said it. What on God's good earth had she been thinking of?

'And mams lay eggs?' the child asked. 'Do they? I never seen one.'

'Er ... in a way, yes, they do lay eggs.'

'But you don't boil 'em or fry 'em.'

She smothered a grin. 'No. Without a strong microscope, you wouldn't even see them, because they're very tiny.'

'Oh.'

She wished she'd never allowed this to start. She was standing on a slippery roof, no ladder, no rope to tie to a chimney, no idea of what to do to save herself... 'Ask your grandmother. She should know more than I do, because she's been a mother.'

'I did ask her. She sent me to you. She said you'd know all about it, on account of you're the teacher, like.'

Oh, God. Nellie's devilment was on the loose again. Biology. Hilda jumped headlong into a chaos of which she had never before been a victim. 'The cockerel has to cover the hen and make the other half of the chick. If the hen's been covered, the egg's not for boiling, but for hatching.'

'Cover? What with? A blanket?'

She swallowed. 'With himself.'

Bertie pulled a piece of straw from his hair and chewed on it thoughtfully. A penny dropped. 'Is it to do with all that kiss and chasing about and stuff? With people, I mean. Cos I can tell you now my mam's fedded up with it. She's happy about the baby, but she keeps hitting Keith with towels and all sorts. Only it's a game, see? She's laughing, and you can tell she's happy. Does that end up with him being a cover like the cockerel? And was my dad my cover?'

She wouldn't laugh. 'Broadly speaking, yes, that's the truth of it.'

'Oh, right.' Bertie studied his soggy straw. Then, with that seamlessness known only to the young and precious, he moved on. 'Why doesn't it hurt when Pedro gets his shoes nailed on? I wouldn't want nothing hammered onto my feet.'

Hilda, unaware until this point that she had been holding her breath, allowed her chest to relax. She loved these terrible boys. Bertie was as bright as his sister, though academia was not for him. Robin read hungrily, pouncing on anything connected to the art of arable farming. As for Philip – oh, what a victory. 'Bertie, get a bath, please. We'll talk about horseshoes and farriers tomorrow. You smell very horsey.'

'Better than our Rob,' the child replied. 'He stinks of ferti ... ferti ... of all kinds of muck, says he's going into Brussels sprouts next year. Can you imagine anything as daft as that?' He stalked off, dignity diminished by mud, straw, and a large hole in the seat of his trousers.

A sheepish Nellie put in an appearance. 'Did you tell him, then?'

'Of course.'

'Bloody hell, Hilda.'

'Quite.'

'Our Eileen would have told him, but she's too ... too head-on. It would have been drawings of willies and women's personals, and–'

'Stop it.' Hilda held up a hand. It occurred to her that she would miss this dear woman, but someone had to stay with Mel and Miss Morrison. 'Nellie?'

'What, love?'

'I want to show you something. And I want you to keep it secret for the time being. I mean that. You mustn't say a single word.'

'I promise, I do. I promise on both me bunions.'

'Oh, I shall miss you, Nellie. And I shall stamp on both your bunions if you let me down. We need to tread softly for a while.'

Nellie bit back a remark about always treading softly near people's bunions. 'I'll be here some weekends and school holidays. There's somebody with the WVS says she'll look after the old lady for us. Don't be sad about me going. Eileen and Keith will take at least one of the lads.'

Hilda, halfway across the bedroom, stopped in her tracks. 'Of course they must go to their mother if they wish, but that's a very small house, and...'

'And you love your boys, eh, Hilda?' In less than a year, Hilda, Neil, Jay and Keith had tamed even the oldest. Philip, a natural handyman, had proved particularly good at painting and decorating. He had also developed a strong affection for Jay Collins, who was not always careful with his diabetes. 'He's happy, our Phil. Isn't he?'

'Oh, yes.' The mistress of the house pulled something out from beneath her dressing table. 'More than happy, Nellie. A lot more.'

Nellie took the pad. It boasted page after page of sketches, some in pencil, others in charcoal, one in black ink. Jay Collins, eyes closed, sat on the ground and leaned for support against the scarred wall of a barn. With his cap worn sideways and his ankles crossed, he slept through his lunch break, an empty butty tin on the cobbles beside him. Nellie could almost hear his snores. Every flaw on the stone-built barn was recorded; even the frayed edge of Jay's cap was in its place.

Trees seemed to grow and sway, horses wanted to leap from the pages, people were practically walking off the paper. 'You're a clever girl, Hilda.'

'They're not mine, Nellie. I didn't do them.'

'No? Aw, look at this – Gill and Jay's Maisie asleep in her pram.'

'Phil did them.'

'Eh?'

'They're Phil's.'

Nellie pushed the pad away because she didn't want to mar perfection with tears. 'He's a good drawer,' Eileen had said frequently, and clever Nellie had agreed, offering the opinion that Phil was a full chest of drawers, as he often concealed goods, usually stolen, about his person. Mel was the family genius; Phil was a lazy sod who did as little as possible. 'It's been waiting to come out, hasn't it, Hilda?'

'Yes.' She went on to explain that Philip, while tidying the attic, had found Uncle Adam's pads, pens, chalks and paints. 'He dug out easel, canvases and paints. You should see what he can do with a palette knife, Nellie. But that's all under his bed – he doesn't know I know he took it. He thinks he's lost this sketch block, so I plan to "find" it and ask him who owns it.' She paused. 'Nellie?'

'What?'

'Don't cry. This lot has to go to Manchester. Phil deserves a place in a good school of art. First, he has to know that I know. It has to be me. I am unbiased, since I'm not family.'

A stunned Nellie dried disobedient eyes. So. Eileen had produced a lawyer bound for Cambridge, an artist, a farmer and a soon-to-be expert on horses. What was she carrying now? A brain surgeon? 'I wish I could be here,' she moaned. 'But Eileen has to come back with her husband, bless them. She'll be safer at Willows Edge. And I'll be there for our Mel. Doesn't everything happen at once?' She scuttered off to her own room where she could weep privately. Her Philip was a Leonardo da Vinnie. Something like that, anyway.

It was a slow and tedious process, and it was clear that Marianne Bingley was occasionally having her patience tested, but she was too stubborn to abandon the project. Coming to after a session was unnerving, because little shards of deliberately buried memories lingered for a while just beyond reach of her consciousness, so she never got the whole picture. Yet she was, for the most part, calm and unafraid, so some good was coming out of the treatment.

Sally Barnes of Rodney Street was a pioneer. A

psychologist, she employed hypnosis, and was considered by most medics to be a quack, but Tom believed in her, as she had achieved marked success with those who could afford her fees. She trod softly. Marie needed softly. And it was worth a try, surely? Divorce was messy and expensive. Divorce hurt people, many of whom were children who might well grow up with no belief in love, in endurance, in effort.

Tom watched his wife as she emerged from the consulting rooms. The change in her was remarkable, not to say miraculous. This was a woman lighter of step and of heart, a prettier person, one who was ordered now to sleep with her husband, but never to touch him. He, too, had to keep his distance. Marriage to a victim of abuse would never be easy, but he was doing his bloody best.

After settling in the front passenger seat, she informed him that she had signed an agreement, and Tom could now speak to Sally Barnes.

'You're sure, Marie? She'll be telling me what she's discovered about you.'

'Of course. Also, it's your turn to be a guinea pig. Remember? The treatment's for both of us. I've signed so that she can discuss my progress, but you need help, too.' She smiled at him. 'Don't be a coward.'

He stared through the windscreen for a few moments, the past year running across his mind like a quickened movie. Eileen had rejected him. That beautiful urchin had decided that Dr Tom Bingley was not a nice man. Uncertainty had crept in then, had been underscored with double black lines when she had married the chap from

Bolton. 'Marie?'

'Yes?'

'Please tell me I'm not a bad man.'

Whatever Sally Barnes did while Marie was under hypnosis seemed to be working, because she suddenly needed to comfort her husband, but she couldn't, since contact was forbidden. 'You aren't a bad man. Now, get in there and find out what's what and who's who, and when the war will be over.'

He laughed. 'She's not a blooming fortune-teller.'

'Isn't she? Oh goodness, I've been coming to the wrong place for months.'

The dull wife had humour. He remembered the timid rabbit, the 'rape' victim, the aprons, a well-set table, gravy in a little silver-plated boat. These days, cutlery was piled in a shallow box on the sideboard, fight among yourselves, not enough napkins today because she's done no washing. No longer apologetic about dried egg and meat-free dishes, she giggled and laughed during tasteless meals, and their twins were happier, too. Gloria was becoming seriously beautiful. Peter continued a star, while their father delivered his collection of near-risqué jokes along with mashed potatoes and home-grown carrots. 'It would be easy to fall in love with you, Marie Bingley, but it's forbidden. We must not touch. She is a cruel and heartless woman.'

'Yes.'

'What does yes mean, madam?'

'How the hell should I know? I'm always under the spell of Mesmer when she gets stuff out of me and plants ideas. Ask her. I just know I'm different, that's all. I've changed. Sometimes, I don't know me.' Norman didn't matter any more. Marie wanted her marriage to work.

She was different, all right. Tom leapt from the car and ran up the stone steps of a rather grand Georgian terrace.

He was talking quite normally, asking questions, making comments about his wife; then, suddenly, he woke up. 'What happened?' he asked. 'What have you done to me, Sally?'

Sally Barnes laughed. 'You now know all you need to know about that wonderful, sweet woman you married. It's been deposited in your mind and in hers, and it may surface, may not. From now, we go onward, not backwards.'

'What use is that?' he blustered. 'I need to know her past and the reasons for her problems. Was she abused?'

'Yes.'

'By whom?'

The woman lifted her shoulders and raised both hands, palms upward. 'Tom, I don't believe in shock therapy. If I did, I'd have handed Marie over to some mouthy psychiatrist, and she'd be lying on a trolley with electrodes on her head. The Marie I found, the inner Marie, remembers everything. She's a fine woman with a good brain, so just leave it. There are people all over this country whose brains are fit only for serving on toast after too many electro-convulsive sessions, and no one knows how much is too much, so I kept her away from bloody psychiatry. You both know all there is to know. The question you ask about her abuser needs no reply from me, because the answer's taken root in your head. Shocks may come, though they won't be electric. Find yourselves.'

'But I don't remember–'

'You will if and when you need to. As will she. I do not use invasive treatments, and it is my belief that you will thrive. No sexual contact. Not just yet.'

Tom narrowed his eyes. 'And I'm paying you?'

'Handsomely, and I love you. But not enough to take my knickers off.'

'Bugger.'

'Buggery? Only if desperate, and don't get caught.'

As he left the room, Tom realized that he felt lighter, happier. This had been the case with Marie for months, so there was wisdom in the hypno-psychologist. He sat in the car and studied his wife. The blue coat suited her.

'Well?'

'Exactly. She put me under, my dear. While I was not of this world, she probably told me all about you and all about my failings. When I emerged from the trance, I remembered nothing.'

Marie tutted. 'So, if and when we do remember, we are to contact her, Tom, in case we're traumatized. We should make sure we remember in the early hours of a cold morning, then we'll get our money's worth. And we should be extraordinarily traumatized. We might wear strange clothes and scream in the streets.' A barrier had been taken down, and she no longer spent time thinking of Norman; instead, she thought of Tom.

'The neighbours would die of shock.'

She grinned impishly. 'It would make a change for them. Most have been no further than Southport, and hell could be illuminating.'

Where had she hidden for so many years? Marie had been one of those plain women who, when approaching middle age, reaped the benefit of having been ordinary in youth. She had good skin, pretty eyes and a generous mouth. And he suddenly knew that it was his fault, if fault could ever be the right word. He'd made no effort to coax and coach her, had failed to enliven a girl whose sense of humour seemed to have died. Until now. It wasn't too late. Madam up-the-stairs Mesmer knew what she was doing, and he saw straight through her. Sex was off the menu. It was off the list so that they would disobey like naughty children. Was Marie ready? Was he ready to be rejected?

'Let's go home, Tom.'

He started the car. 'I love you,' he said.

'And I love you, though I have to confess to having wanted to kill you.'

'That's normal.'

Her head shot sideways and she stared at him. 'Rubbish.'

'Females of all species get bogged off with being imposed upon.'

'Sexually?' she asked.

'And darning.'

Marie went back to studying the comings and goings on Liverpool's Harley Street. The corners of her mouth twitched while she composed in her mind a picture of a cow with a darning mushroom and an oversized needle. All species? 'You're incurable, doc.'

'Yes. Let's try to get fish and chips on the way home, eh? I can't go another six rounds with your vegetable pie. It's gross.'

'Darn your own socks, then.'

'Bloody hell, Marie–'

'Take me home. Now.'

He took her home.

The next morning found a stark naked doctor sitting on the cushioned seat of a wicker chair near a bedroom window whose curtains and blackouts remained closed. Feeling slightly punch-drunk, he gazed at the form in the bed, a woman with whom he had lived for many years, a woman to whom he had made love just once. The experience had been ... intense.

She hadn't told him to stop, hadn't cried or sighed sadly, but she had fallen asleep very quickly afterwards. And why was he sitting here like a child after a spelling test? Was he waiting for marks out of ten? Did he need a reference, a badge of office to sport on a lapel, *I finally managed it?* Had he managed it? Apart from one shallow scratch on a shoulder, he had emerged unmarked, so the token bite-back of the tigress hadn't been employed. Nor had the Vaseline... It was progress, surely? *Dear God, let it be progress, and don't allow me to hurt her ever again.* That had to become the eleventh commandment: *thou shalt not damage thy wife.*

She turned over, and he found himself biting the knuckles of a closed right fist. He was perverse, and he knew it, because he'd started desiring her as soon as she had stopped wanting to stay married to him. After failing to catch Eileen Watson, he'd commenced a search for treatment so that Marie might be resurrected for his sake. He was a selfish man.

Marie shot into a sitting position. 'Tom? Where are you?'

'I'm here. Switch on that lamp.'

She complied. 'We shouldn't have. She said... We'll be in trouble.'

'So?' Her hair was tousled, and he found himself thinking of children on Blackpool beach, sand pies, tumbling locks of curly hair, shoes buried somewhere with Dad's glasses and the *Daily Express*. 'You could have told me to stop. I told you to tell me to stop.'

'She'll kill us. We weren't supposed to... We had to wait until... Don't you dare laugh. Laugh, and I'll dam your mouth shut. As the leading light in the WVS, I am a dab hand with needle and wool, so be careful.'

She sounded happy. He wanted her to be happy. 'You'd have to catch me first. Calm down. She told us not to have sex so that we would. Remember Peter when he was a terrible two? You forbade him to eat his vegetables, so he ate them. Then he ate Gloria's, yours and some of mine. Simple reverse psychology. You see, the level at which Sally works on us is forever the child. In all of us, that two-year-old thrives and keeps banging its head on the wall of life. It's petulant, disobedient and bloody-minded. She dug us out, Marie.'

'Did she?'

He nodded. 'Did I hurt you?'

'No.'

Instinct forced him not to pursue this line of

questioning. 'We have half an hour before reveille. Move over, I'm coming aboard.'

She whispered her worry about screaming and disturbing the twins, and he told her that she could scream into his mouth, and that he would swallow her noise. 'Why would you scream?'

'Because something's happening. Inside me.'

Tom Bingley would never know why he wept in this acutely erotic moment. Perhaps it was the sense of loss, of time wasted, of the pain she had suffered. Guilt settled like a rock in his stomach, and he was unequal to the task of serving her properly. He was useless, stupid, and filled with self-loathing.

'I can hear her,' Marie whispered. 'She told me while I was under what to do if this happened. She's right. What she tells us comes back when we need it. Clever woman. Don't cry. I'll be gentle.'

Tom blinked the saline from his eyes. Reverse psychology, now role reversal. Sally Barnes was worth every penny. And he was the one who screamed.

Mel fixed her gaze on Gloria Bingley. This same Gloria Bingley had been, until recently, a dumpy girl with sepia skin, dull hair and no discernible physical assets. Then she had blossomed. A small part of Mel was envious, because people with darker features were more clearly defined, while blondes lacked edges, since hair drifted into skin without showing a join. Gloria was going to be a stunner. She was also picking up on the academic front, because improved looks gave her confidence in several areas of life. 'What's wrong now?' Mel asked.

'It's embarrassing,' Gloria pronounced. 'Isn't it enough to have a brother who calls me Titty-Fal-Lal since I developed? Now I've also got parents who've gone from stalemate to at-it-like-rabbits. My mother's an out-and-out trollop, and my dad's a sex maniac. This is no way for an impressionable girl to live. I've been reading a bit of psychology, and the books say we should be nurtured mentally and physically. Well, all the nurturing's going on upstairs and we don't get a look-in. Just as well, since I'd hate to watch them at play.'

Mel delivered a raspberry. 'At least you have a decent brother. All I have are three criminals in the brother department. Mind, I have to say, however begrudgingly, that the hellions have improved. Then there's Mam, Gran and Keith the Kisser. My mother's just married the man of her dreams, and it's a full-blown nightmare. Miss Morrison seems to think it's hilarious, but I've always suspected a bawdy side to her – something to do with a caretaker in a cellar centuries ago – don't ask. Mam's pregnant already, and they've been married all of five minutes. I could finish up with twenty siblings.'

Gloria hadn't thought about that side of things. 'Buggery,' she spat.

'Illegal, but buggers don't produce brats, so that's something in their favour.'

'I don't want any mucky-bummed infants parked in the hall. I keep my bike there when it's cold or raining. Then there's the coat stand. Yuk. Mel, what can I do?'

Mel shrugged. 'If they were dogs, the vet would

see to them. But as things stand, all we have is a rumour that Hitler plans to have undesirables neutered. Your mother and father aren't Jewish, Romany or mentally retarded, so–'

'My mother can't count.'

'Gloria, cling to that thought. If we lose the war, the invaders will have your mother spayed.' She sighed heavily. 'What's come over them? Is the government putting something in the water so that we'll have another generation to fight for us in twenty years?'

Gloria shrugged. 'Dad says we're programmed to cull ourselves. If we don't kill each other, we have plagues instead. Bubonic, Teutonic–'

'*Titanic*, but that was just a few people on a ship. Oh, Gloria. What have we done to deserve this?'

They burst out laughing simultaneously, because they realized that they were talking like parents. Delinquents in their families were from the older generation, and the only sense in two houses, one on St Michael's Road, the other on St Andrew's, was the property of two teenage girls and Peter Bingley who, being a mere boy, was not really up to scratch.

After tapping on the back door, said mere boy put in an appearance. 'Sorry,' he mumbled. 'But I had to get out. They're drunk in charge of a gramophone. One more run of Ravel's *Bolero* and I would have had to turn them in to the law.'

'See?' Gloria threw up her hands. 'Even this ghastly person can't cope. Now, if you and he were at it, that would be different.'

Peter punched his sister's arm. 'Shut up, Fal-

Lal. Mel knows I like her.'

'We shall marry after Cambridge,' Mel said with mock seriousness. 'And stop making him blush. He's too pretty to have a stained face. So. We're a quorum, the meeting is convened, and there's nothing we can do. Any other business?'

Gloria insisted that Mel had no real problem, because Eileen and Keith would soon be replaced by her grandmother, who was hardly likely to start running around with a man. 'We're stuck with it,' she grumbled.

'Would you rather they split up?' Mel asked. 'Because people do separate, you know.'

'Separate?' shouted Gloria. 'Separate? We'd need a fireman's hose to keep our two apart. Where did we go wrong? We brought them up as best we could, didn't we, bro?'

Peter shook his head. 'I blame it on saccharine and Pasha. Mum was far better on real sugar, and Dad hates those Turkish cigarettes. But I think we should try to–'

The earthquake happened then. Although the siren had sounded, no one had bothered to go to the Anderson. People were becoming too blasé, too careless. Heinkels were suddenly overhead, that sick phut-phut sound of accompanying fighters making a backbeat for the bombers' continuous drone. The three youngsters dived under the kitchen table. And they heard it, picked out easily the bomb that bore their names. It whistled happily, the pitch changing as it neared the target. 'Mam!' Mel screamed. 'Get under something.' She held on to Gloria's hand. It occurred to her that she hadn't finished her geography homework, that she might never finish it...

It landed eventually. The blast rippled through the house, and Peter threw himself on top of the two girls. Dad had told him about blast victims. They were lifted out unscathed, not a mark, not a drop of blood. But inside, major organs had been battered and broken through being shaken about, and Peter didn't want that to happen to Fal-Lal or the beautiful one. All air was sucked from the room. With it travelled pots, pans and cutlery, every item following shards of glass from the over-sink window. When air returned, it brought with it dust, bits of plaster and debris that made breathing a near impossibility.

Peter crawled out, stood up, and dragged the two girls to the door. He doused all lights before depositing both in the garden. For a moment, he listened to the disappearing aircraft and watched a blood-red sky. Liverpool was burning. In fact, it was nearer, so it was probably Bootle. Nearer still, a newly released missile was doing its job. It had hit a house in the next avenue, was burning fiercely, and people were screaming. The bomb meant for St Michael's Road had left a huge crater in the playing fields behind Miss Morrison's house.

A believer in Christ, Peter bit back a prayer and replaced it with a curse. 'God damn you for all eternity,' he whispered. 'May you rot in pieces.' He ran into the house. Miss Morrison, dusty but unhurt, demanded a cup of tea. He explained that she might have to wait, because the kitchen needed checking for safety, especially where town gas was concerned.

Upstairs, Eileen and Keith emerged from a huge Victorian wardrobe that looked hearty enough to survive Armageddon. 'Mel?' Eileen asked Peter as he entered the room.

'Outside.' Peter sat on the floor, his legs suddenly frail. 'We were in the kitchen and it caught the back-blast from a bomb in the field. The girls are all right, though they might be getting a bit cold. Kitchen's a mess, and a bungalow at the other side of the playing field took a direct hit. I've turned the gas off at the mains just in case, and Miss Morrison wants a cup of tea.'

Keith muttered about a paraffin stove in the shed before going to check on the girls.

'Are you sure my Mel's all right, Peter?'

'I put them in the fresh air. There was dust and stuff all over the place. I was all right. I was fine till now. There was no air, so I put Mel and Gloria on the path. Go and see them, Mrs Watson – I mean Greenhalgh.'

'I'll send Keith to help you down the stairs. You're in shock, love.'

Alone, the fourteen-year-old crawled out to the staircase and finally allowed his tears to break free. He was at a strange place in life, neither man nor boy, a slave to hormonal invasion, insanely in love with Mel, not old enough for that, not young enough to be satisfied with a googly or a six at the crease. And his parents going all doolally wasn't making life any easier. He knew what they were up to; the whole of St Andrew's Road probably knew and, while Peter was glad that the separate rooms thing was over, he wondered why they had to keep reminding him that the only fun he could have was solitary, untidy and slightly embarrassing?

'Peter?'

Through silly, girlish tears, he saw her looming over him. Although a couple of stairs lower, she was standing, and he felt small, mostly because he was sobbing. 'Mel. There's grit in my eyes.'

'Yes.' She squeezed in next to him and gave him a cuddle. 'You may have saved our lives.'

'Doubt it.' Sometimes, she seemed almost glacial, but this was not one of those times. She cradled his head; he could hear her heartbeat behind the rise and fall of her breasts. 'Mel...'

'I know. We're too young, beautiful boy. Just make your way to Cambridge. You'll be right up there, top of my list after I've invented the ten-day week.'

'The what?'

'Ignore. It's a joke between me and Mam. If we told anyone we have feelings for each other, we'd be laughed out of court. My mother would throw an apoplectic fit, and yours would need morphine. Keith and your dad might well be pistols at dawn on the beach or in Sniggery Woods, and the war would become a side issue. Even Gloria doesn't know how I feel about you. I wasn't sure myself until recently, because you got on my nerves something shocking till I stopped being thirteen.'

Peter swallowed painfully. It was an audible gulp, and he wished he could bite it back, because it imitated some dire digestive ailment, and he needed to be perfect. 'Can't we be together sometimes?' he managed. He had to know, had to find out about... And he loved her – he did!

Mel grinned. 'Of course we can; there's a war

on, so there's rationing enough without cutting out all the fun. As a racy girl in the sixth form told me, we can have the overture, two movements and an interval, but no intercourse.' She was being a clever clogs again, but that was fine, since she was talking to another clever clogs. 'And no telling Gloria, or I shall remove all privileges with a very sharp knife.'

She was just like her mother, unusual, funny, occasionally inscrutable and chilly, always beautiful. She was so ... so adult, so clever. He didn't know what to say to her. Just now, he was a small boy aching into the soft comfort of a female form. Top of the class at school, he was retarded while on the stairs with a princess who had half promised to become his companion in naughtiness and joy. 'Thanks,' he achieved finally.

'What for?'

'For being you, Mel.'

Eileen found them like that. 'Has he stopped trembling?'

'Yes.' Mel ruffled his hair and sat him up. 'My hero,' she said. 'Covered in dust, but still a hero.'

The three went downstairs. One thing was clear to Eileen; she and Keith could not go back to Willows Edge until the kitchen had been made safe for Miss Morrison and her carers. Help was promised already. A local builder, who had arrived to check damage in several houses, intended to return and pump concrete under the floor. The gas supply was intact, as were water pipes and drains. Miss Morrison had her cup of tea, so all was well with the world for now.

No. All was nearly well. Eileen studied her

daughter. Something was going on between her and Peter Bingley. Could Nellie manage this? Mel was clever, the lad was clever, and they were both fourteen. Gifted kids matured early and got into all kinds of scrapes. Mel must remain untouched, because she had a dream that could not include children, not for some considerable time.

The all-clear sounded, and the Bingleys set off for home. Eileen dragged her daughter into the hallway. 'No,' she said, a finger wagging an inch from Mel's nose. 'Don't start. Not with him, not with anybody. With a promising future, you don't want to be throwing yourself away, do you? You could have a baby.' Eileen remembered her own youth. Raging hormones plagued everyone, not just this younger and slightly more outspoken generation. And Mel, like Eileen, was bold and direct.

'Not if I don't get pregnant. Actually, fifteen or sixteen is the ideal age from a physical point of view. Society made it wrong, so too many of us have trouble delivering later in life. But I shall not let you down.'

'Promise me, sweetheart.'

'Honestly, I won't let you down. More to the point, I've no intention of letting me down.' She chuckled. 'He is delicious, though, isn't he?'

'Mel, I–'

'You're the motherly one, come in number five. Gloria and Peter are going through a terrible time, because their parents have revived their relationship. They're living in a den of iniquity. We've all heard of Jack the Ripper, now we've got Keith the Kisser. Three impressionable young people living in unwholesome atmospheres.' Mel giggled.

Eileen smiled in spite of herself. 'There's nothing unwholesome as long as there's a marriage certificate and a wedding ring.'

'And you've never been tempted?'

In her head, Eileen heard the voice of Tom Bingley. *Even if it ends, it will never be over.* And *I'll lick the butter from your fingers.* 'Yes, I've been tempted. I always swore I'd tell all of you the truth unless a lie might do some good.' But the whole truth in this instance? Could she speak about Peter's father? No. 'Yes,' she repeated slowly. 'I've carried the devil with me, and listened to Satan's whispered promises. But I never gave in.'

Mel sat on the bottom stair. 'You should write, Mam. While you're pregnant, do some writing.'

Eileen shrugged. Writing? 'How can I write when I'm worried about everything and everybody?'

'Write about being worried about everything and everybody. After the war, as long as we win, people will want to know about what it all meant to real folk. There'll be medals and speeches, fireworks and flag-waving, pompous figures strutting up and down the Mall. What about cooking for your children, clothing families when everything's rationed, watching your city burn? What about Kitty? And our two loonies making a break for Liverpool? Mam? Why are you smiling?'

'Not sure.' But she was sure. That nice little woman from St Andrew's Road had her husband back. Dr Tom Bingley had finally learned to count his blessings. The smile faded. 'Mel, you're so young. I need to lay this on with a trowel. Stay safe.'

'I shall. Get back to Keith the Cuddle before he fades away for lack of nourishment.'

Head shaking, Eileen walked out of the hall. Her first-born had spoken in short sentences before walking properly, had fed herself early, had raced through junior school like the Flying Scotsman, and now seemed to have fitted herself with a forty-horsepower engine. Mel was speeding through life at a terrifying rate, and nothing could be done to halt her, nor would she be slowed. There was always a price to pay when a special child was involved.

Keith found her. 'Are you all right, darling? Miss Morrison's on her second cup of tea, this time topped up with a dash of Scotch.'

Eileen sat down on the living room sofa. 'Mel's fourteen going on forty, Keith. The trouble with having a daughter like my Amelia Anne is that she leaves you behind. Don't get me wrong, babe, because I had sexual urges at her age, but I wasn't so old in the head. She's after Tom Bingley's son.'

'Tonight's brown-eyed blond?'

'That's the chap. They were sitting on the stairs together and ... oh, God.'

'Don't cry, love.'

Eileen dashed the wetness from her cheeks. 'This is going to sound so daft you'll want me locked up.'

'Only if I have visiting privileges.'

She pondered for a while, took time to shunt her thoughts into some kind of order. After that, she needed to find the words. 'A premonition,' she said finally. 'It's daft, I know. But I looked at them; she had an arm round him and his face was on her chest. They were both covered in muck, but so very beautiful. It was like something done by Michelangelo. And while the sensible side of my mind was horrified, some part of me felt not happy, but all right. As if I could see them sitting like that forever, as if they belong together.'

'You're right, you need to see a doctor. Did you have your cod liver oil and malt?'

Eileen tutted. The trouble with men was that they had the imagination of dead reptiles. A woman looked at the sky and saw eternity; a man saw blue and wondered where the nearest pub might be. 'Vive la bloody difference,' she muttered.

'Eh?'

'Nothing. Just a saying of our Mel's. Drink your tea, we've things to do.'

There was more wrong with Frances Morrison's house than had met the eye of a builder speculating in the dark after the bombing was over. Several homes had been disturbed, while the old couple in the bungalow had both perished. Work continued during daylight hours, and all available men toiled to stabilize the buildings. Liverpool already had many homeless families, so labourers battled to hang on to as many homes as possible.

A system developed almost of its own accord. While fuel lines and water pipes were checked and restored where necessary, neighbours who were unaffected did the cooking. It finally reached the stage where no one knew whose crockery was whose, so items were piled up until someone ran out of plates or cups and came to reclaim her property. The someone would arrive, find her displaced items, and stop for a chat.

All of this suited Frances Morrison down to the ground. Eileen became make-up artist, dresser and manicurist, while the old woman bucked up no end during this supposedly dark time. She had visitors almost daily. Some had exciting tales to tell, and she lapped them up like a thirsty cat with a bowl of milk. One neighbour spoke about her son who, at sixteen, was already a volunteer fire-fighter. The rules regarding age had been bent, and that young man was happy to stand with two others and hold on to a massive hose through which many pounds of pressure flowed. 'If they let go, it would kill their comrades.'

A nurse with a badly affected house told tales of women giving birth while buildings collapsed all round them, of people so badly injured that only morphine would do, of the packing of open wounds, of death and tears and fury. She had a fair share of funny stories as well. A man who lost a leg in the Great War lost it all over again. 'Not a mark on him, but his house was flattened, and he ordered his rescuers to get back in there and find his missing limb. Needless to say, they didn't.'

If it hadn't been real before, if the red skies at midnight had not managed to convey the message, news from living, breathing people brought it home. One woman could never stay long, because she had to keep a close eye on her husband, who was yet another victim. 'Pulling dead children out of debris is one thing, Miss Morrison. But pulling out a piece of a child finished him.' The poor man had lost his mind. So keen had he been to find the rest of the infant that he had dug himself into a pile of smouldering debris which had almost become his grave. There was a possibility that he might never regain his senses.

The knitting began then. When it came to knitting, Miss Frances Morrison displayed all the dexterity of a small iceberg approaching a miniature *Titanic*. But Eileen encouraged her before retrieving socks clearly made for giants, dwarfs, or people with deformed feet. Eileen unravelled the disasters, washed the wool to remove the kinks, knitted it again and passed usable items back to the WVS. Convinced that she was contributing to the war effort, the old woman continued with her labours. She was doing no good, but she was occupied, and she did no harm.

Christmas approached. The pregnant Mrs Greenhalgh could only watch and wait while the house was restored to some semblance of order. She had never spent Christmas away from her mother and the boys, and she became anxious.

Keith also watched and hoped. He rolled up his sleeves and worked alongside plumbers and builders, did some carpentry and rubbish-shifting, cooked, made endless cups of tea. But he wanted to send his wife home. He wanted her safe and unafraid, but she flatly refused to travel without him. 'When I go, I go with you. And when Mam comes here after Christmas, I want this place straight. She's not young.'

Another fly committed suicide in the ointment. The WVS member who had promised to stay with Miss Morrison over Christmas suddenly left the area. A single woman, she moved to the other side of Liverpool to be with her sister, and Eileen refused to countenance the abandonment of her landlady. 'Yes, the neighbours would see to her, but I'm not leaving things casual. She's good to us, and she needs watching.'

'We can take her with us, love.'

'No.' That chin came up. Like her daughter, Eileen had a determined little chin. 'She's unfit to travel. We'll have to stay for Christmas. So will Mel.'

'But your mother–'

'Is tougher and younger than Miss Morrison.' Eileen folded her arms. 'It can't be helped. We'll take their presents over in the New Year.'

But Hitler had other ideas. In December 1940, his Luftwaffe delivered gifts aplenty to the city of Liverpool. And there was no gathering in the city centre at New Year.

Twelve

Weather and more urgent commitments slowed the work on St Michael's Road. Most small builders spent time after a raid shoring up the salvageable, demolishing the dangerous, boarding up broken windows with sheets of wood, and dealing with immediate daily emergencies first. Frances Morrison was lucky, since Keith had managed to replace the kitchen glazing, but other work remained unfinished, and it was now December. Frost was not the builders' friend, so the chances of replacing wall ties and completing work on foundations, gables and rainwater goods were remote. Stability had been achieved by shoring up houses with struts, but such measures were supposedly temporary.

Miss Morrison found the whole business rather exciting. 'It's like being down the mines,' she commented on one of her rare expeditions into the garden. 'They're all props and struts, you know. What an adventure.' For a woman with a weak heart, Frances Morrison certainly took war with Germany in her stride. Keith had built a sturdy shelter around the old woman's bed, and she lived happily in her cage, deliberately oblivious of danger, because she had her heart's desire. She loved people, her house was full of them, and she growled amiably through the bars at anyone who approached her territory.

While Miss Morrison took her afternoon nap, Eileen's beloved and mischievous mother was shouting down the telephone. She was in a state. Mam in a state was not to be taken lightly, but at least she wasn't here in person. Nellie Kennedy's voice grated at the best of times and now, magnified by microphone, it was enough to shift paint off the walls. 'I should be with me daughter at Christmas. It's not right for us to be separated like this when we've always been–'

'Mam?'

'What?'

'I'm in Liverpool, and you're at Willows.'

'I know that, you soft mare. There's no need for

you to tell me where I am. I seen meself in a mirror not five minutes back. I think it was me, anyway. Unless some bugger's pinched me blue pinny and me best hairnet.'

'Stop shouting, you are not in Australia.' Eileen held the receiver away from her ear. Nellie, aware of the distance between herself and her beloved daughter, was screaming across forty miles. 'Talk normally, Mam. There's no need to yell, but thanks for shifting the wax in my ear. I think you've blown it all the way across to the other side of my head.'

Nellie lowered her tone. 'But you have to come for your dinner, Eileen. It's Christmas, love. Christmas has always been important.'

Eileen blinked moisture from her eyes. It was true. Poverty had never diminished Mam's joy when the festive season arrived. But this was different. It was a new war, a war unlike its predecessor, because a thousand tons of ironmongery and explosives seemed to drop from the skies with monotonous frequency. 'There's a massive fight on, Mam. Very few families will be completely together for Christmas dinner. We've nobody at the front or on a ship or in a plane, so be grateful. I can't just leave Miss Morrison. The neighbours are good, but there's no one who can stay with her twenty-four hours a day. I want this place declared safe before you come.'

'Safe? Safe? You've been bloody bombed.' The tone of this statement was accusatory.

'Yes, we have. Adolf asked for permission, and we agreed to be a target, cos he wanted the practice. I'll phone you later.' She turned to her husband once the connection to Nellie was severed. 'We're not leaving her.' She waved a hand in the direction of Frances Morrison's ground-floor bedroom. 'I want this place in better shape before we do the permanent swap with Mam. And Miss Morrison can't travel, so that's an end to it.'

'It is indeed. Don't cry. You know I have to kiss you when you cry. And you know I have trouble stopping kissing when I start.'

Eileen had the same difficulty, because her husband was a fabulous kisser. But she wouldn't tell him that, since he already knew. 'Are you a sex maniac?' she asked pleasantly.

'Erm ... not yet. I have to do the written test and a series of practicals. But I'm working my way up to it.'

She wagged a finger at him. 'Just make sure I'm the practicals. Or you'll wake up a little bit dead.'

Nellie placed the receiver in its cradle. Her Eileen was in trouble. She was living in a propped-up house, she was pregnant, and she was afraid. Keith was with her, thank God, but what if the Germans came back to Crosby? There was a fort nearby, and there were searchlights waiting to be bombed. 'Bugger,' she spat. 'Staying in a place held together with faith, hope and putty. And pregnant on top of all that.'

'Nellie?'

She turned. 'Ah. Hilda. They won't be coming for Christmas.' Hilda Pickavance was a clever woman but, in the opinion of Nellie Kennedy, she sometimes lacked a bit of courage. 'I'll never understand you leaving our Phil to find his sketchbook and never saying nothing to him. This has been going on for weeks now. What are you scared of? He's not going to bite your head off, is he?'

Hilda wasn't scared; she was cautious. 'He wasn't ready,' she answered. 'I didn't want to disturb him in case he stopped sketching.' Phil was a reserved, wild thing. If anyone tried to get too close, he put up shutters and displayed a *CLOSED* sign. More important, his talent was developing at a rate that wanted neither help nor interference. 'I am waiting for him to talk to me.'

'And I'm waiting for me daughter, though she won't be coming.'

Hilda, lost in her own thoughts, frowned and nodded pensively. 'When I loosened the pages, I hoped he would believe the one I stole had fallen out accidentally, but he's been looking for it. That sketch was the only one in ink. Fine detail is his forte.'

Nellie sat down. Hilda had taken the sketch to Bolton for framing. It was meant to be Eileen's Christmas present, and the artist had no idea about any of it. As far as he was concerned, he had mislaid the ink drawing, and no one knew about his hobby. 'Where is it?' she asked.

'Wrapped and at the back of my wardrobe,' was Hilda's reply.

'We have to get it to Crosby.'

Hilda tutted. 'How? We've no car. Keith and Eileen have it.'

'I don't know how, do I? Borrow a couple of bloody donkeys or some roller skates. We've still got trains and buses.'

'They don't always run to timetable.'

'Hilda, for God's sake–'

'No!' shouted the usually soft-spoken woman. 'For Eileen's sake, we must stay away. Hasn't she enough trouble without worrying about her mother turning up out of the blue? And Phil needs to be told before we start to give away his work.'

'That was supposed to be your job. When it comes to painters and the like, I don't know me *Laughing Cavalier* from me *Whistler's Mother*. Find our Phil, Hilda. Find him now. He has to be told that we've had his drawing framed. Go on. I'm off out for an hour. See you later.' Nellie leapt to her feet, pulled on a coat and rammed a woollen hat almost all the way down to her eyebrows. Hilda Pickavance could manage on her own. Hilda Pickavance should have managed on her own weeks ago, and Nellie was off to visit her friend.

Carrying a small torch, Nellie made her way down Willows Lane until she reached the Edge. Her decision to make an ally of Elsie Openshaw had been made some months earlier. It had been a case of irresistible force and immovable object; as a team, they were monumental. Elsie was happiest when Nellie was at Willows, and she was currently sad because Eileen was due to return soon with Keith, while Nellie would be needed in Crosby.

'Open up, queen – it's only me.' The door was pulled inward by Elsie. 'I think God forgot to light the fire tonight,' Nellie continued. 'I'm froze right through to the bone. He might be having a few days off with it being near Christmas.'

Elsie opened the door to her pristine shop and greatly improved living quarters. 'Whatever are you doing out and about at this time? Get yoursen up to my fire. I'll make you a cuppa and get you a slice of parkin.'

Nellie removed her outer garments and watched the large woman as she bustled about. Elsie was clumsy and prone to accidents, but she was cleaner, and she had new teeth that actually fitted. Some people imagined that she had suffered a 180-point turn in the personality department, but the truth was simpler. She smiled because she had comfortable teeth. A sliver of pain pierced Nellie's heart. *Oh, Kitty, we could have done so much for you and the babies.* Like Kitty, Elsie smiled in a bid to display new mouth furniture. And in order to match the smiles she needed to be pleasant, so she was pleasant. Well, for most of the time.

'There you go, Nellie. Cup of tea and a nice chunk of cake. Right. To what do I owe the pleasure of your company, missus?'

Nellie shrugged. 'I'm not sure.' She knew the secret now, understood how to keep Elsie onside. The woman was a gossip, so no one ever confided in her. Little by little, Elsie Openshaw had become Nellie Kennedy's confidante. While helping the woman to clean up house and shop, the visitor had let drop small, unimportant pieces of information about herself, her family and the new owner of the Willows estate. 'Don't say a word,' had always been the final request and, true to her one and only friend, Elsie had kept her mouth shut.

'You've not walked all the way down from yon for nothing in pitch black, Nellie Kennedy. I can tell with your face, any road. With a frown as deep as that, you favour the Town Hall clock just before it strikes midnight.'

'You'll miss me,' Nellie said. 'When I go back to look after Miss Morrison, I mean.'

'Course I'll miss you. I missed bloody toothache when I had them all pulled.'

Nellie chewed thoughtfully. Elsie's baking was rather hit and miss; the parkin was a definite miss. 'I could ask Miss Morrison,' she said. 'We'd both be working, because, on paper, we could each be responsible for her twelve hours a day.'

'You what?'

'After Christmas, come with me to Crosby. I reckon our Eileen'll be stopping here with Keith and the lads, so I'll be in Liverpool for the duration.'

'What about me house and me post office?'

'Somebody will see to all that.'

Elsie considered her options. She could stay here and be safe, but lonely. Or she might be able to spend a few months or years in Nellie's company. Yet Liverpool was a mess. The chances of being bombed here, in Willows Edge, were negligible, while the house in which Nellie and her granddaughter would be living had already been shaken right down to its footings. 'Eh, I don't know what to say, lass.'

'Say nothing,' Nellie advised. 'The old lady hasn't been consulted yet, though I do know she loves company. It's my belief she would have keeled over months ago if she'd been left on her own. Anyway, I'm going to take the lads over to see their mam tomorrow. With luck and a good following wind, we should make it there and back in a day.'

Those words would haunt her for years.

A very rigid version of Philip Watson perched on the end of his bed. Glowing cheeks were the only reaction to Hilda's opening remarks, because he didn't know how to feel or what to say. He'd never been any good at anything, had he? Reports from school declared him to be a bold, stubborn boy with no desire to learn, while the cops in the Scotland Road area were seldom surprised by his attempts to pervert the course of justice. 'They're just scribbles,' he murmured eventually. 'I'm not one of them soft girls who go in for art and stuff.'

Hilda was prepared for that one. 'All the greats are men, Philip. Michelangelo, da Vinci, Botticelli–'

'And Watson?' At last, he grinned. 'Naw. It's just something I do when I'm not helping out with Mr Collins. I've no bike, I don't ride horses, so I have to do something.' He was glad that the school was full. Like many evacuees, the Watson boys were not in full-time education, since Miss Pickavance had been judged good enough to fill the gap. She had their work sent down from the school, and sent it back to be checked from time to time by the head teacher. 'See, Miss Pickavance, our Bertie's got Pedro, and our Rob's up to his eyes in the rotation of crops, so I had to find something to do.' He stared hard at his hostess. 'You took it, didn't you? You took the pad and pretended you hadn't.'

Hilda nodded.

'Why?' he asked.

She took a deep breath. 'I showed your work to

a lecturer from Manchester College of Art. He lives in Bolton, he wants to see more, and he wants to see you.'

Phil concentrated on his breathing for a few seconds. 'And the ink drawing?'

Hilda laughed. 'Everyone's favourite. It's framed for your mother. Young man, you are incredibly talented. You can make your living through your art. Not yet, not while the war is on, but later. Your eye for detail is amazing.'

'Why didn't you say something before?' he asked after another lengthy pause.

So Hilda explained about waiting until he was ready, about her fear of embarrassing him. There was a new quiet in him, a need for privacy. 'I felt I had to leave you to it, but now I am absolutely convinced that you are gifted beyond the norm. And you can't own a gift, Philip. It's lent to you for your lifetime, but you have to pass on the results to the rest of us. Writers, composers of music, actors and painters – these people share what they have, what they know. Many artists died young and in poverty, because they worked full time on their talent and others reaped the benefit.'

'So it's a curse as well as a gift.'

This was another Watson moment. Hilda should have become used to such events, because each of Eileen's boys had hidden depths. Mel's were on display, but she was female and unafraid. Boys were so vulnerable and terrified of criticism that they hid their light under any passing bushel. *It's a curse as well as a gift*. That a street urchin should have such perception was amazing. 'I am so proud to know you, Phil, to have been a witness and a friend to you and your brothers. Robin loves the land and knows more than many grown men when it comes to arable farming. Little Bertie's a natural horseman, while you, dear boy, are an artist.'

Phil blushed. 'Have you any ink? I used it all.'

'You have ink. I bought it as one of your Christmas gifts. Do you need it now?'

'Not really. I can do the Mr Collins asleep sketch any time.'

'Shall I get it for you to copy? It's upstairs.'

He shook his head. 'I'll just do it from memory.' Tapping his forehead, he grinned broadly. 'I keep them all in here,' he explained. 'Let's face it, there's plenty of room. And I can do it better this time. Thanks.'

'For what?'

'For pretending not to notice when I pinched all your uncle's stuff out of the roof. If that hadn't been there, I might never have found out how much I like drawing and painting.' He would be a man; he would do what needed doing this very moment. After jumping to his feet, he crossed the room and kissed Miss Pickavance clumsily on the cheek. 'Thanks,' he mumbled again. 'Without you and this place, I might never have found out about myself.' He left the room at speed.

'And Hitler,' she whispered. Had the war not happened, Phil Watson might well have followed his peers to the docks. Even the illest of winds carried some good news. Well, she had done her duty, and it had been a pleasure. The wildest and naughtiest Rachel Street boy had turned out to be the best. 'Never judge a book by its cover,

Hilda,' she told herself. 'And never judge a boy by his sins. I wish those two policemen could see his work. As Nellie might say, that would wipe their eyes good and proper.'

With the exception of rickshaws and bicycles, Nellie and her two older grandsons had used almost every form of land transport known to man. They travelled by horse and cart, a train, two buses, one tram and a filthy delivery van. They were now staring at part of their beloved city. Smoke and dust filled the air. Steam struggled through heaps of brick and slate that had, until now, been family homes. Underneath all this, there would be bodies.

'Bloody hell,' Nellie breathed. Distance and countryside quiet had made the war almost unreal, because the fortunate residents on the Willows estate heard and saw nothing at all. 'We don't know we're born,' she whispered. In an effort to keep the boys cheerful, she chivvied them along. 'Come on, lads. I can't wait to see your mam's face when you give her that drawing, Phil.'

Phil stood as if frozen.

'What are you doing?' Nellie asked.

'Remembering.' His tone was sombre. When he got home – yes, it was home – he would commit to paper what he saw today. Slates slipping and shunting to the edge of a roof; behind them, a hole through which a feeble flame struggled in its search for oxygen. On the pavement, two ragged little boys chewing on bread, their movements automatic, expressions fixed, souls depleted. Everywhere, bricks and roof tiles and shattered glass. Two shocked children breaking bread in a scarred city. What had they lost? Were they brothers? Where was their mother? Somebody would come for them soon, surely? Phil committed their faces to memory. The sky was dirty. Perhaps the sun shone behind layers of bitter smoke. 'Gran?'

'What, love?'

'I'm glad Bertie didn't come. This would have given him nightmares for weeks. Is Rob all right?'

'He will be.' She shouldn't have come. She was a stupid woman–

'Mrs Kennedy?'

It was him. It was the doc, the one she had clobbered, the bloke whose arm had been wrenched from its socket by a couple of old dockers. He was offering them a lift to Crosby. Rob was looking a bit green round the gills, while Phil was simply staring, taking it all in. This wasn't right.

'It's a long walk,' Tom told her. 'Get in. My wife will have my lunch waiting.'

'Thanks,' Rob yelled. He had seen enough. 'Come on, Gran. I don't fancy walking seven miles.'

The boys sat in the rear seat, Eileen's Christmas gift clutched to the artist's chest. This meant that Nellie had to place herself next to the driver, the very man who had awakened Eileen's lonely body, who had probably pushed the girl into the arms of Keith Greenhalgh. Mind, the marriage was a good one, so Dr Tom Bingley had merely hastened the inevitable. She studied him. He was as black as a chimney back, and something akin to the colour of blood stained his hands.

'Where've you been?'

'To hell,' was his quiet reply. 'I couldn't just sit there in Crosby when I could hear what was going on. I've been among the dead, the barely alive, the young and the old. You shouldn't have come back here.'

'But it's Christmas.'

'Yes. The Germans know it's Christmas, too, Mrs Kennedy. They imagine us sitting round our hearths with the children's stockings hung and waiting, so they bomb us. The young among us look to the sky for reindeer and a sleigh. Instead, they get Heinkels and tons of shrapnel. I did what I could. We all did what we could. But the people, including the walking wounded, are so unbelievably brave. I dressed the hands of a man who had prised off two fingernails in order to dig out his family, and he felt no pain.'

'Did he get the family out?'

'Oh, yes. Except for his wife.' He swallowed. 'If that happened to Marie, I don't know what I'd do, Mrs Kennedy.'

So the rumour was true, then. It had come from Gloria, had been filtered through Mel, then via Eileen. But this was no game of Chinese whispers. He was back with his wife. 'Good lad,' she said softly.

'Is she ... all right? Eileen, I mean. Is she happy?' he asked.

'She is. And expecting.'

'Good.' He stopped at a level crossing. 'Sometimes, we don't know what we have until we throw it away. Marie needed help, as did I. Tell Eileen I was asking after her.' He pulled away when the crossing barriers were lifted, drove up Liverpool Road, then stopped suddenly outside his surgery. 'Stay here for a minute or two, boys. Mrs Kennedy, come and give me a hand.'

She waited while he unlocked the door, then followed him into his surgery. 'What?' she demanded. 'Are we here for a repeat performance? I can hit your jaw for a change if you like.' She smiled at him. 'Pulling your leg,' she said.

He told her about the town hall, municipal offices, a food warehouse, shops, an hotel, houses, the docks. 'There are five railway arches down. People were sheltering, and it could take days to get the bodies out. Fires are being dealt with by people who work all day, only to come out again to man trucks and hoses at night. You shouldn't be here. Last night was the worst so far, and I suspect we'll be getting repeat performances. I think they got West Derby again, and Waterloo Grain House was fire-bombed and destroyed.'

'I didn't know,' she whispered.

'You're supposed not to know, because what the populace knows, the enemy knows. They are among us, Nellie. And that's not paranoia; it's a fact.'

She dropped into a chair. 'If we'd stayed at Willows–'

'Stop it,' he ordered. 'I won't have you making yourself ill because of this one mistake. What I am saying is that you must take the boys back. Stay here tonight. Keith Greenhalgh and I will put our heads together with regard to petrol. I have an allowance, and I use a bicycle when I can, so I should be able to spare a gallon. And I have patients who might donate some.' He looked her up and down. 'But God help you when she opens that door. She has a feisty side, as I'm sure you know.'

Nellie smiled ruefully. 'Her dad was a quiet man, so she got her temper from me. Keith manages her.' Keith loved Eileen, and Keith was capable of loving only one hundred per cent, but the doctor didn't need to know that. Between Eileen and Keith there was a chemistry so powerful that it seemed to colour the air around them. Those long, long kisses they stole when they thought no one was looking, soundless word-shapes mouthed across a room, his hand in her hair, her head on his chest while they listened to the wireless. Tom Bingley had wanted Eileen; Keith Greenhalgh adored her.

'I promise I'll take you back tomorrow,' Tom said.

'Thanks. And...'

'And what?'

'Sorry I hit you and put the Word out on you.'

This woman had done the right thing. Eileen had been his for the taking, and it would all have been so wrong. 'Come on, madam. Those boys probably need feeding, and you've a virago to face.' He wished he had to face... No, he couldn't wish, mustn't start that all over again!

They stepped outside. While he locked the outer door, Nellie had a quick look round. Everything was standing, no gaps between houses, no dying flames. The Crosby bombs had fallen nearer to the river, and just two houses had been wiped out. She would be living here soon, but she would rather be here now and know that Eileen was safe at Willows. Mel needed looking after, as did Frances Morrison. 'My daughter won't let me come back till the house is all right,' she complained.

Tom laughed. 'It won't fall down, believe me. It'll be months or years before it's finished properly. Stick to your guns. I'll take you back to Willows, because all your things are there and the boys need a lift, too. But choose a date and tell her you're coming back. She and her baby need to be away from here. The house is stable enough, I promise you. While it looks odd, it's been passed as habitable by the corporation and the fire chief.'

'All right.' Nellie sat in the car and turned to her grandsons. 'Your mam will kick off,' she advised them.

'We know,' said Phil. 'And we're not bothered.'

The back door flew inward and Elsie Openshaw stepped in. 'I've fetched you two bottles of Guinness,' she cried. 'Good for you and for the babby. How is our Maisie?' She entered the living room. It was a tip, and Nellie, who sometimes helped Gill, had buggered off to Liverpool with two of her grandsons. The third boy was helping Collie Crawford, because Collie looked after Pedro, and Bertie liked to show his gratitude. When she got back from Crosby or wherever, Nellie would clean up Gill's mess. Elsie, who was averse to housework anyway, had to open up the shop in half an hour, but she had promised to call in here while Nellie was absent.

Gill Collins wasn't coping. Like many who wait endless years for an imagined child, Gill found the reality of motherhood disturbing. Several days each month saw her hurtling to Willows Edge or to the main house in search of advice when the baby vomited, when she seemed too hot, too cold, too fretful. And Jay got on his wife's nerves.

Elsie placed the bottles of stout in a small space on the cluttered table. She hadn't been a good mother, and she didn't want to watch Gill failing at this very important job. Oh, well. At least the nappies had been washed, because a dozen or so were hanging as stiff as boards in the freezing cold outside. 'Shall I fetch your washing in, love?'

'What?'

'While you're feeding her, shall I get the nappies in and put them to dry in here? There's no breeze. They'll be frozen solid by teatime.'

'Oh.'

Elsie waited. 'Right. I'll fetch them in and they can thaw out near the fire. Then I'll make you a bit of tea and toast, eh?'

Gill shifted the infant to her other breast. 'If you like.'

The old Elsie revived and bridled. Jay was a grand lad. He was on the daft side, very good at acting the rubber pig, but he had a big heart and he loved his wife and child. 'You want to pull yourself together, missus. Yon man of yours is ill–'

'So was yours,' Gill snapped. 'But you still mithered him till he keeled over. Don't be lecturing me, Elsie Openshaw. You've only gone nice since Nellie came and helped you out in the shop. So think on before you start telling the rest of us how to fettle.'

Elsie had learned from Nellie how to hold her

tongue. And this girl wasn't well. She'd settled down during the pregnancy, but once the baby became a reality Gill started losing her grip. The gatehouse deteriorated into a mess, while Jay, who had special dietary requirements, was abandoned to manage for himself. That might have worked had he not been such a clown, but his diabetes was fast becoming unstable, because he let himself run too low on sugar before noticing that he felt odd. With Phil Watson away, Jay had no help, and he could let himself go all the way to coma if this wasn't sorted.

While Elsie went to bring in nappies, Gill stared into nothingness. She remembered, just about, imagining herself in love with Keith Greenhalgh. She'd even been upset when he'd married the Liverpool glamour girl, but now she knew the truth. The fact was that she wanted to be married to somebody sensible, and Keith had happened to fit the brief. Jay had been fun at the beginning, but she'd grown up, while he had remained a child. She had two children. One was at her breast, while the other was outside somewhere clowning about up a ladder or on a roof. 'I can't worry about both of you, Maisie. There isn't enough of me to go round, you see. And that was why I thought I wanted Uncle Keith. He's dependable.'

Elsie came in and began to place ice-stiffened washing on a couple of clothes horses. The nappies would thaw out faster near the fire. 'Shall I come back after I've closed the shop? I can cook something and tidy up a bit in case Nellie doesn't get home in time.'

'I'm sorry, Elsie.'

'Nay, lass. Put your name down for a good skrike. Tears and temper are good as long as you let them out.'

'He's driving me mad. Remember when he got tanked up on Guinness and came home a bloody fighter pilot? I half drowned him, but I managed to keep going. Even then, before Maisie, I was wishing I'd wed somebody with a bit of gumption, a gradely chap who didn't go round acting like somebody let out for a day from the loony bin.' She placed the child in a pram and fastened her blouse. 'I've a baby to wean. When she starts crawling, I'll have to watch her. And I have to watch him, him, him.' Her voice rose with every repetition. 'I can't do it. I can't listen to his stupid jokes any more, can't watch him playing the fool all the while. He's a father, and he should act like one.'

Elsie pushed a pile of newspapers from a chair and sat at the littered table. 'Does he know you feel like this?'

Gill shook her head. 'He'd stop looking after himself altogether, and he'd die, then that would be my fault. I am so bloody tired, Elsie.'

'I know, love. Look, I can leave the shop shut and stay with you if you like.'

Gill shook her head. 'I'm best by myself, thanks all the same. God knows where he's got to. It's all the worry. Cleaning up's beyond me, and I even forget to cook. Sometimes, I can't remember what happened yesterday, because life's always the same, like a muddy ball of Plasticine when all the colours have got mixed up together. There's no order any more. He comes home, the singing, dancing joke of a husband, and I don't hear him these days, hardly see him till he picks Maisie up.' She couldn't let him hold his own daughter. What if he had a hypo? What if he jiggled the child until she vomited? What if he dropped her on her head?

Elsie left the poor young mother with a cup of tea and a couple of biscuits. Feeding a kiddy took a fair lump out of a woman, and Gill needed help. The post office could look after itself for once, because this problem needed a solution. One of the Land Army girls hadn't taken kindly to field work, but Elsie had a use for her.

At Willows Home Farm, the large woman stopped and reclaimed her breath while preparing to knock on Jean Dyson's back door. The Land Army girl in question lived in Jean's house, so the farmer's wife had to be consulted. Jean opened the door. 'I thought I heard somebody out here. Get inside before you freeze to the ground. We'd do better if it snowed. Apart from anything else, snow would confuse the Germans, and we'd be that bit warmer, too.'

Elsie sat down in the kitchen and accepted a welcome cup of scalding tea. Words tumbled from her tongue in no particular order, but Jean was good at jigsaws, and she managed to piece together the message after just one repeat. 'Gill can have her for a few hours a day, and welcome. She's one of the older ones from a family of eight, so she should be all right with the baby and a bit of tidying up. No good at all on the land, Elsie. It's like sending a fox to mind the chickens.'

Elsie managed a smile. 'Nellie says the girl's nesh.'

'Nesh? What the hell's that?'
'Mardy. Soft. A moaning Minnie.'
'She's all of the above. I just hope she does better for Gill than she has for us.'
So it was sorted. Until Neil Dyson walked in with an unconscious man in his arms.

'You've no idea,' Nellie moaned. 'When she was fourteen, she fell hook, line and gobstopper for the milkman's lad. I gave her down the banks for it – I never stopped shouting at her for about four hours. So she moved out. She didn't go far; she went living with her friend four doors away. For the best part of three weeks, she never spoke to me. Her dad was dead, bless him, so there was just me left to manage Madam. Anyway, she came home because she decided the milkman's lad was a few sarnies short of a picnic, but she carried on sulking.'
Tom tried not to laugh. Nellie Kennedy was afraid of her own daughter. He had parked the car a few houses away from Miss Morrison's, because Nellie's panic had started about halfway up Manor Road. There was some heavy breathing in the rear of the car, too, since both lads were tired and hungry. Eventually, Phil declared that he'd had enough of this malarkey, so he and his brother were off, thanks, and they were grateful for the lift.
Nellie watched them as they walked to the house. 'The big one's a Leonardo de... Italian bloke, I think. Or a Botticell-something-or-other,' she announced proudly.
'Botticelli.'

'Yes, him and all. I'd best go, eh?'

'You'll be all right. She loves you.'

Nellie opened her door. 'I know that. She loves me enough to kill me.'

'Good luck,' he called.

'Hmmph.'

Tom chuckled to himself when Eileen appeared in the street. She grabbed her mother and dragged her through the front gate just as the doctor's car shot past at speed. He couldn't have coped with Eileen Watson as a lover; she was too hot to handle. But God, she was beautiful.

Inside, one angry woman stood at each end of the kitchen table. Between them, Keith occupied a chair at one of the two longer sides, a newspaper spread before him. While they argued for several minutes, he turned pages and pretended not to be there. The boys, having discovered a tin of jam tarts, had gone off to eat these treats while examining bomb holes in the playing field. Miss Morrison parked herself in the hall, wheelchair wedged between front door and coat stand. She liked a good row. Nellie and her daughter were brilliant at rows, since they were loud enough to be heard quite clearly. This one was heating up nicely.

'You shouldn't have brought the boys away from Willows. There's dead bodies and all sorts down there in Liverpool.'

'I didn't know that, did I? If nobody tells us nothing, we don't know nothing, do we?'

Frances Morrison decided not to stand up and argue the case against double negatives. She hadn't counted them anyway, so Nellie's nobodies and nothings might have worked out positive...

Language could be quite mathematical if one thought about it. But she couldn't care less at the moment, because Keith was stepping into hot water, and Keith was quite effective when it came to the management of his wife. It was rather unfortunate, really, because he often put a full stop before a sentence had ended.

'Eileen?' Keith looked first at his father's watch, then at his beautiful partner. 'Right, that's six minutes, and I'm chucking in the towel. Stop it. My newspaper's curling at the edges, so give over. We all know what's going to happen, because it's like a bloody pantomime. You tear strips off your mother, she bounces back and calls you all the names under the sun. She cries, you cry, and all that energy's been wasted, cos we all end up supping tea anyway.'

'But she's fetched two of my lads into a burning city, and–'

'Stop it,' he repeated. 'I'm not having behaviour like this in a house belonging to a woman with a weak heart.'

He had forgotten, just for a moment or two, that he was living in a matriarchy. Lancashire women were strong and bolshie; those who clung to the banks of the Mersey were particularly robust.

'Spoilsport,' called Miss Morrison, thereby proving to the only male in the house that even she was his superior, and she was supposed to be polite, since she came from the posher end of the conurbation and had a bad heart. They always bloody won in the end, didn't they? Though he usually got some sense out of Eileen when they were alone. And horizontal. Oh, God, he mustn't start laughing. His sweet angel would probably beat him about the head with a wet dishcloth if he kicked off laughing. And the cast iron frying pan was still standing on the hob.

Nellie turned and leaned on the sink, but her shoulders betrayed the fact that she was trying not to chuckle. Eileen stared hard at the man she worshipped. There was amusement in his eyes, and he had not been given permission to be amused. 'No interest for you this quarter, young man; I don't care about the size of your deposits.' His smile melted her heart, and she left the house in order to retrieve her sons before they took a nosedive into a bomb crater.

While marching across the playing field, she wore a daft smile. She was putty in his hands, and she would deal with him later. Or would she? 'Come on,' she called. 'All the explosives have gone, so there's nothing to laugh at.'

Inside the house, a delicate truce clung desperately to life. When Frances Morrison had been wheeled back to her room, and her lunch had been delivered, five people sat round the kitchen table. At its centre sat a package wrapped in red crêpe paper done up with a festive if rather squashed green ribbon. Phil's cheeks burned brightly.

'For me?' Eileen asked.

Rob nodded. 'He drawn it,' he said, a thumb jerking in the direction of his older brother. 'But Miss Pickavance put it in a frame and wrapped it up, like.'

'Shut up,' cried Nellie. 'Don't spoil the surprise.'

Eileen opened her gift slowly, her gaze fixed on Phil. He had made whatever this was just for her.

The lad had changed. She remembered his scribbles and how he had guarded them, head down, arm shielding the work from prying eyes. Her children were growing up, and the war had stolen precious months, because they could not be together as a family all the time. Phil was twelve, and his head was almost level with Keith's shoulder. Soon he would be a man, and if she was going to be there to see him grow she would have to leave Mel, who was up to something–

'Oh,' she breathed. 'Oh, Phil. That is wonderful. It's Jay. Look, Keith; it's him to a T.'

Phil continued to blush. 'It's called *Man at Work.*'

Eileen shook her head in near-disbelief. He'd always been able to draw, but this was the work of a trained artist. 'Ink?' she asked.

'Yeah. I found it in the roof.'

Keith looked at the drawing. 'You've even got that sideways twitch on his nose – he always goes sideways when he snores. The barn, the yard – I feel as if I'm there. That dandelion seems to be growing while I look at it.'

Nellie broke the spell. She could always be depended on when it came to emotional moments. 'He's another Van Cough,' she announced, 'what cut his ear off and posted it to some poor bugger instead of a birthday card.' She knew the words were wrong, but this was her way of making up with her daughter.

Eileen ignored her mother. 'Has Miss P looked at this?'

Phil nodded. 'Yes, she's looked at them all. I've done some watercolours, too. And I've tried with oils.'

'And what did she say, Phil?'

'I have to see somebody about it. Manchester College of Art. She wants to put me in some exhibition gallery after the war.' He pondered for a moment. 'I've got more in my head now; things I saw today. Because I want to tell the truth in pictures. Like a diary, but sketched.'

'Bombed houses.' Nellie folded her arms. 'He wants to draw the mess in town. You're right, they shouldn't have come here.'

'That's what I said till my dearly beloved shut me up. Phil, this is magic, son. There's something about my kids. Every one of them's talented. But this? Well, I don't know what to say.'

Keith cleared his throat. 'That'll make a nice change.' He stood up, reached out his right hand and shook Phil's. 'You're a star, lad. If you've shut your mother up, you're a walking miracle, and I thank God you're here. And ... well, wherever he is, your dad'll be proud of you. I'm proud, and I'm only your stepdad.'

Nellie took the boys and the sketch through to the ground-floor bedroom. From the kitchen, Eileen and Keith heard the old lady as she exclaimed over the quality of Phil's work. 'Life's full of surprises,' said Eileen, her eye on the kitchen clock. 'Where is she?'

'Mel? With Gloria, I expect. School holidays – they'll be trying clothes on.'

But Eileen didn't agree. There was a glow in the cheeks of her fourteen-year-old daughter, a twinkle in her eyes. 'I reckon she's with Peter in Rachel Street, Miss Pickavance's house. She has a key. They'll be up to no good.'

Thirteen

'Jeanie!' Neil Dyson staggered into Home Farm's kitchen, the unconscious Jay Collins a dead weight in his arms. 'He gets heavier with every step, I swear to God. Blankets.' He placed Jay on the sofa before taking a few deep gulps of oxygen into lungs that had been working overtime for the best part of a mile. 'Come on, Elsie. There's nothing new on this earth, nothing you haven't seen before. Strip him. His clothes are wet through and frozen. We've no chance of warming him up till we get these things off him. Towel him dry once he's bare – there's some nice rough towels on the pulley. We need to keep his blood on the move.'

Elsie thrust her cup into Neil's hands. 'Get yourself outside that tea. You look nearly as bad as he does.' She glanced at Jay. He was frighteningly still and, she suspected, near to coma. She grabbed towels from the line above the fireplace, put them on the fireguard to warm, then began to peel off the poor young chap's clothing. There was hardly anything of him. She'd noticed that young ones with diabetes tended to be on the thin side. He needed building up and looking after, but would Gill Collins listen? Would she buggery. It was like trying to talk to a heap of coal in the dark. 'Come on, lad. Buck up, eh?' she whispered to the motionless Jay. 'You've got to fettle a bit better than this, son.'

Exhausted, Neil dropped into a chair. 'Jean, run up to Willows and ask Miss Pickavance to tell the operator we need an ambulance fast. Hypogly-wotsit and hypothermia. Or diabetic, unconscious and very cold's easier. Go on, love. I'd go myself, but I'm puffed after lugging him up from Four Oaks. I had him in a barrow, but the wheel shaft broke and I had to carry him. Soft bugger must have keeled over and fallen in the horse trough. Ice on the water wasn't thick enough, so the mad article could have drowned in six inches of wet. I pumped the stuff out of him, and he's breathing, but not for much longer if we don't get help.'

Jean screamed for her daughters. 'Stella? Pat? Bring every sheet, blanket and eiderdown you can manage. Fill some hot water bottles.' She grabbed hat and coat before running to the big house. Of course, it wasn't the big house any more, was it? The big house had been pulled down years back and– Why was she thinking about this kind of stuff? Jay Collins lay near-dead, and here she was trying to remember the original sandstone building that had all but fallen down years ago.

And she had bread in the oven, and the kitchen copper was boiling water so that she could do the extra sheets for Land Army girls' beds. Wasting wood or coal was a sin, especially now. *Oh, Gill, why couldn't you have looked after him just a bit better? You know he's no idea when it comes to counting points against insulin.* 'Jay,' she muttered, 'you'd best pull round, because we don't want to bury you before we've given you a bloody good telling off, you mad bag of bones.' Fighter pilot? The air force needed Jay like it needed squadrons of blind monkeys. He was lovable, though...

Why couldn't his wife love him? He needed taking in hand, but who had the time these days? Every farmer was up to his ear holes trying to make a hundred acres do the work of a thousand. 'You'll pull round, too, Gill Collins, if I have to break every bone in your miserable body. No time to play the wild card, not with a war on. Nervous bloody breakdowns are a luxury we can't afford till later. Post-natal depression – huh!'

Back at Home Farm, Elsie and Neil were trying to rub some life into the patient's chilled limbs. Stella and Patty warmed blankets and quilts at the fire, and Elsie piled items on top of Jay until he was almost buried beneath layers of various fabrics. Metal shelves from the oven were wrapped in towels and placed underneath the bundle Jay had become. 'Faint pulses in both feet,' announced Elsie. 'Thank goodness for that.'

'Why?' Neil stared at her quizzically before returning to his task.

'They lose limbs. Diabetics, I mean. He's lucky, because even at this temperature the blood's getting through. But he's still blinking cold, Neil. And I daren't give him any sugar in case it chokes him. Oh, I wish they'd hurry up with that ambulance. I know we're a few miles out, but this fellow needs help now. I mean, what more can we do for him?'

'Is it possible to warm him up too quickly?' Neil asked. 'Can we do any damage this way?'

'I don't know.'

That was a change, thought Neil. Usually, Elsie knew everything. He went to change his own damp clothes.

Miss Pickavance arrived with Jean. 'I've made a bottle of hot sugar water,' the older woman said. 'Just to wet his lips. If any of it does get into his mouth, it will do no harm as long as we don't overdo it and choke him.' She knelt on the floor and, with the tip of a finger, began to moisten his lips. He stank of pear drops, and that meant too much insulin, not enough food. 'Come on, Jay,' she whispered. 'Don't let us down. In a few weeks, you'll be ratting with Mrs Hourigan's Jack Russells. Remember? Everyone calls them 'ourigan's 'orribles? We can't have the rat-kill without you. The barns will need clearing, and we've fencing to mend. We can't have anything without you to keep us all smiling. You have to get through this, my friend.'

'She's upset,' mouthed Elsie to Jean. 'Thinks the world of him.'

Neil returned, still pulling a dry jersey over his head. Miss Pickavance was especially fond of Jay, because he never failed to amuse her. And she always calmed him down and made him talk about sensible things like lead for flashings, painting everything green in line with War Office orders, the best wood for replacement fencing. He was almost the son she'd never had.

'Does Gill know?' the lady of the manor asked.

'No,' Neil replied.

'She's not with us,' opined Elsie. 'She's gone AWOL in her head. Well, it needs saying, Neil. No point pussyfooting about. She can't look after herself at the moment, Miss P. And she loses patience with all his clowning. I came here to ask if I could borrow that Land Army girl, the one who hasn't took to the job in the fields. I thought she might be put to better use helping with the baby and seeing that Jay eats properly.'

'That sounds like a good idea,' said Hilda Pickavance. 'From what I've heard, the girl's no use where she is. However, back to the point. Jay's wife needs to be told.'

Nobody moved. Then Neil spoke up. 'She won't go with him in the ambulance because she refuses to leave the baby with anyone. And she'll not take her to the hospital; she thinks Maisie'll catch something. We'll tell her. After he's gone to the hospital. To be honest, I don't think she'll notice he's gone; she's been shutting him out of her mind for months.'

'He drives her mad,' Elsie commented. 'That's the top and bottom of it. She got sensible and he stayed daft.'

'That's as may be,' Neil replied. 'Me and my Jeanie have got on one another's nerves for many a year, but we don't turn our backs on each other. Gill's not well herself. She's been like a cat on hot bricks ever since that baby was born. I just feel that news like this could tip her further over the edge. She doesn't say much, so we've no idea what's going on in her head.'

Elsie voiced her agreement that Gill wouldn't notice Jay's absence. 'He's got to have warmed up a bit by now. Give him another drop of that sugar water, Miss Pickavance. Get us your balaclava, Neil. Even his head's cold.'

The ambulance people arrived and started all over again with Jay. By the time they had finished with him, he resembled a clean version of something that had been pulled from a pyramid and lifted out of a fancy coffin. 'Will he be all right?' Hilda Pickavance asked repeatedly. The men and their nurse assured her that Jay would receive the best treatment available, and invited her to accompany her son to the infirmary.

'He's not my son,' she replied, regret colouring her tone. 'And I have an evacuee at home, so I must go. I have to fetch him from the vet's, where he's been helping out.'

'Right-o.' They lifted the patient and his stretcher towards the door.

'I'll go with him,' sighed Neil resignedly. 'I don't know how or when I'll get back, but I'll try to phone you, Miss Pickavance. Jean, you or Elsie can go over to the gatehouse and tell Gill. She has to be informed. God knows what she might do if he just went missing.'

The door closed behind the patient, his companions and Hilda, who was on her way to pick up Bertie from the vet's surgery.

Elsie and Jean looked at each other. 'We get some great jobs,' Elsie said. 'We'll both go. That way, we can share the blame and the grief. And I might stay the night with her. I put a note on my door earlier, but Miss P has Nellie's key if anyone needs anything. Nellie's not back, is she? God knows how she'll carry on over there. People say Liverpool's took a few batterings.'

'I don't know. It's as if the whole world's falling to bits, Elsie.'

Once again, they donned their outer clothing before stepping into the unforgiving frost of late

December. In three days, it would be Christmas Eve. And poor Jay Collins might not wake to enjoy it.

Tom Bingley knocked gingerly on the back door of Miss Morrison's house. Having been dismissed by the owner and given a black eye by her latest visitor, he was not expecting the warmest of welcomes, though Nellie Kennedy seemed to understand him better now. Nor was he in a good mood. The proposed encounter promised not to be too happy, because his boy was missing, and he knew who had led him astray. At four o'clock on the afternoon of 21 December 1940 it was already dark. The sirens had sounded, so the Germans were probably planning an early visit, and, although Liverpool was seven miles south, planes could be heard and fires were visible in the distance. Eileen opened the door. 'Tom? Where is she?'

'My question exactly,' was his reply. 'And where's my son? Legend led us to believe that he was playing chess with a boy from school, but the boy from school is visiting grandparents with his mother. We checked.' Peter was a decent boy, and this piece of gross dishonesty would be the fault of Eileen Watson's daughter. She had her mother's looks and her mother's wiles; she could probably ruin his son's life before it had even started. 'This is not at all like Peter. We have had no behavioural problems with him until very recently.'

'Oh.' She widened the door. 'Come in. My husband's just making a pot of tea.' She must not appear worried. She must not allow herself to think the worst of her daughter. 'Peter isn't here,' she said. 'We've not seen him today.'

'And your daughter?'

Eileen swallowed. The situation could not be concealed, especially now. It was dark, and the Luftwaffe was getting frisky. 'We thought she was with Gloria. She said something about wrapping gifts and swapping clothes.' The enemy didn't usually arrive two nights in a row. 'Germany isn't playing fair,' she said in a weak attempt to lighten the atmosphere. 'No warning, not even a post-card.'

He frowned. The woman was prettier than ever. Pregnancy clearly suited her. 'She is not with Gloria. Marie is almost out of her mind. It was bad enough when the bombs fell here and the wardens wouldn't let us come round the corner to see if our twins had survived. But this is worse, because neither you nor I know where our children are. One thing is certain: they are together.'

'Sit down, Tom,' said Keith. 'Eileen, tell him what you know.'

Eileen perched on the edge of a ladder-back chair. 'They're fourteen going on forty,' she said. 'Mel has a key to Miss Pickavance's house in Rachel Street. She goes down from time to time in daylight, and she writes and tells Miss Pickavance what she sees. Oh, and she keeps the house as clean as she can. It was a promise.' Her voice died. 'Dear God,' she whispered as a thud reached her ears. Often, the wind blew the sound of falling bombs all the way up the coast. 'I thought I heard a couple earlier on, but that one was a definite.'

'My son may die because of your daughter.'

'I could say the same in reverse,' she said.

'Oh, stop this.' Keith slammed the teapot onto its stand. 'We all know what happened. You fell for Eileen and went a bit crazy; now history seems to be repeating itself in the young ones. You know the strength of such feelings, and you must realize, as a doctor, that young people fall in love at the drop of a hairpin, never mind a hat.'

Tom glared at the man who had once been a rival. His glance roved across to Eileen, and he nodded knowingly. 'You and your daughter cast spells without knowing what you are doing.' Eileen was lovely, but she was not a gentlewoman; Marie was infinitely superior to this divine, delectable creature. 'Your daughter is the one with the key to that house. If they are in Rachel Street, there can be no doubt that she has told Peter about the key. Any sexual activity will have been at her instigation.'

Before Keith could react, Eileen had jumped up and raked her nails down Dr Tom Bingley's cheek. She remembered. *Even if it ends, it will never be over.* She hated him. 'You monster!' she screamed. 'I'll kill you, I will, I will. Mel's a good girl, too sensible to ruin her future for your precious little mother's boy of a son. As for him, he's far too effeminate to be of interest to my daughter. Put him in a frock, and you'd have twin girls.'

Keith lifted his wife and placed her none too gently on the draining board among pans and various utensils. 'Stay,' he snapped in the manner of one addressing a dog in training.

She stayed.

Keith mopped at his wife's handiwork with

cotton wool and diluted Dettol. 'You'll live,' he pronounced. 'Sorry. She gets a bit worked up, I'm afraid, especially when she's worried.'

Nellie entered the arena. 'Who did that to him? They're bombing Liverpool – can you hear it? Where's our Mel? Are the blackouts all up? Our Phil's drawing a picture of our Rob. He says it's the first time Rob's sat still for five minutes. What's the matter? Have I missed something? Were you shouting, Eileen? Why are you sitting on the sink? Did you scratch him?'

'Shut up,' called Eileen and Keith in unison.

But Nellie wasn't as easy as her daughter. Keith was running out of draining boards on which he might park his difficult women, and he was busy disinfecting the victim of one of them, so he allowed Nellie the floor. 'Sorry,' he said to the doctor. 'They aren't easy to handle, but they're worth the bother. In fact, they can be quite entertaining occasionally.' Nellie was ranting at Eileen, thereby allowing Keith a private moment with Tom. 'We'll go to Liverpool,' he said quietly. 'You and me. But first, these two Amazons have to be safe.' He put away the first aid box.

'I was down there last night, Keith. It's a bloody nightmare.'

Keith turned to his pair of malcontents. 'Right. Under the table; I'm putting the cage on.'

'I'm not going in no cage,' Nellie announced.

Eileen hopped down from her perch and ordered her mother to do as she was told. When both women were safe, Keith fetched Phil and Rob from upstairs; they were to spend the evening, and possibly the night, in the back garden

Anderson shelter. 'No messing,' he told them. 'Remember, you're bound over and you could go to that place in Derbyshire if you don't shape. In fact, I'll drive you there myself if necessary. With a whip.'

Outside at last, the two men breathed a sigh of relief, though it didn't last long, because Eileen shot out of the door.

'I'll padlock that cage,' Keith threatened.

'Don't get killed,' she begged, her voice trembling with fear.

'I won't.'

'How do you know?'

'Get back in there. I love you so much, I'll crawl home whatever happens. Go on. I've a daughter to find, and he has a son to crucify.' He kissed her. An embarrassed Tom Bingley climbed into his car. The kiss was like something choreographed by an over-enthusiastic Hollywood director. It was lengthy and passionate. But Tom wasn't jealous. He had a wife in full working order, and Keith was welcome to his lively little bride. Wasn't he? 'Is it always like that?' he asked when Keith was sitting beside him.

'No,' Keith answered. 'Sometimes it's as boring as the next house. And sometimes Eileen's in a bad mood. That wasn't a bad mood; it was the orchestra tuning up. And when Nellie's in a temper, I live in the shed. As for Eileen, she's perfect for me. I was a dyed-in-the-wool bachelor who needed livening up a bit. She's given me plenty to live for, and I'm going to be a dad. What more could a man want?'

Tom began the journey down Liverpool Road.

Anyone with a vehicle and sense would have been driving in the opposite direction, but the need to find offspring had blurred the edges of reason. 'Into the valley of death,' he said wryly. 'And if they're not in that house, they'll be the proverbial needle and the haystack might well be burning.'

They had eventually decided on law. Anyone overhearing their discussions would think they were listening to eighteen-year-olds. Peter Bingley wanted to become a barrister, and he would 'prat about in a daft wig and a teacher's gown', according to the girl who, in ten years, would be Mel Bingley. She was more interested in the coalface, in people and in the preparation of briefs, but both she and Peter were attracted to criminal law rather than the pedantic and predictable side of legal work. The knowledge that she would do the real job while he 'pratted' about was a great source of amusement for both. 'You do the acting, and I'll write your scripts,' she reminded him on a regular basis. 'I'll be the brains, and you can be the muscle.'

A small fire flickered in Miss Pickavance's grate. On the hearthrug, two beautiful children lay, clothes piled on nearby chairs, bodies calmer and appeased after their carefully constructed games. The decision not to indulge in the full act had been taken, and each had pledged to steer clear of such dangerous behaviour until they were much older. Every cell might scream for fulfilment, but such noises would not be heeded, because the future mattered. But Peter was suddenly quiet. He valued Mel, admired her. But... But what? He was confused. *I love her, I do, I do–*

A siren sounded. This was a din they dared not ignore. Like a perfectly oiled machine, they responded immediately, clothes first, then a preplanned pattern of behaviour. Peter doused the fire with water while Mel removed evidence of their feast: greaseproof paper, a pop bottle and a few slices of mousetrap cheese. 'Cheddar?' she said to herself. 'More like soap.'

'I think we made a mistake.' Peter straightened the rug. 'It was rash to think the Germans would take the night off. They seem to be becoming obsessed with the idea of wiping Liverpool off the face of the earth.'

Both stood still in the middle of the room. It was nowhere near four o'clock and the first wave was already on its way; a dull drone was just about audible above the sound of running feet. People were clearly rushing towards shelters.

'We'll be all right,' Mel said reassuringly. 'You know we'll be fine.' With the certainty possessed by all young animals, Mel and Peter remained firm in the knowledge that they could not die. Other people would lose their lives, but the youthful, the beautiful and the gifted were untouchable. And they'd already had their bomb in Miss Morrison's house.

Shielded by love and faith, they walked round the outside of the house, opened the rear gate and took their bikes from the yard. Incendiaries floated gracefully through the evening air, landing almost soundlessly on roofs. By some strange, almost osmotic process, these quiet killers disappeared under slates to start deadly fires. The only hope for anyone in a fire-bombed house lay with fire-watchers, ordinary folk who worked during the day and patrolled a sector at night. Flares and fire-bombs were useful tools for the Luftwaffe, because they turned night to day and made the destruction of Liverpool much easier.

'We won't make it back to Crosby,' Peter said as they crossed the main road. 'Let's find a shelter. If we follow all those people, they'll lead us to safety.'

'No, I have to get home. Mam will be worried sick, and she'll kill me.'

'Mel, if we don't take shelter–'

And it happened. The house in which they had so recently lain was sliced off the end of the terrace. Peter threw his companion against a wall and covered her body with his. The noise was deafening. Some instinct informed him that the recessed porch of a shop doorway was nearby, so he edged his way to the right inch by inch, Mel clasped tightly against him. Debris landed on him, and he felt a series of sharp pains in his back. The air was thick and hot. His throat almost screamed for water.

'Don't touch my back,' he whispered loudly into her ear. 'I have glass in it. Pretty large pieces, I think. So we must stay calm, then I shall bleed more slowly. Well, I think so, anyway. Please don't worry. And we mustn't pull the glass out. My dad would tell us not to pull the glass out.'

Reality crashed into Mel's brain. They weren't magic. No angel protected them just because they were young and beautiful and clever. Like everyone else, they were flesh, blood and bone; they were vulnerable. 'Peter, don't die. Cambridge. Chambers at one of the Inns, me nearby in the city robbing the rich so I can buy their innocence. Professional liars, you and I are going to be.' She didn't know what to do. The bomb that had taken Miss Pickavance's house had been followed by others, and the very building in which she and Peter sheltered could be the next victim. 'Peter?'

'Yes. I'm fine, don't worry.' He wasn't fine. He wasn't yet a paid liar, so he should be telling her the truth. 'Use the whistle,' he said. 'I need attention. Bleeding. I feel a bit faint.' And confused, though he didn't admit that. He loved her, but... God, he was cold.

Mel took the whistle from her pocket and blew hard. 'Sorry,' she said. 'That must have hurt your ears.'

Tom heard it. Travelling at snail's pace with windows open, he applied his brake. 'Get out, Keith. Look along the road and in doorways. They could be anywhere here, or behind the Rotunda theatre. I'm going into Rachel Street.'

'Number one, the house is,' said his companion before leaving the vehicle. 'I'll blow my whistle if I find them, Tom. Good luck.'

But Tom could not turn into Rachel Street, because the first house was spread across cobbles and two pavements. He began to tremble. His heart kicked into overdrive, and in spite of the cold, sweat beaded his forehead. His boy. His lovely, clever son who wanted to play cricket for his county, who was top of his class in five subjects...

Bombs continued to fall nearer to the docks, their real targets. Number one Rachel Street was no longer here. There was a crater, there was rubble and, in the dim light provided by other fires, he saw furniture clinging to what was left of the upper storey. A pale dressing gown, hardly touched by the explosion, fluttered on a door. The side wall of the house had crumbled completely. His boy was under that lot. The girl, a clone of her mother, had enticed Peter to his death. But the boy could be alive even now. Pockets were often created among tumbling masonry, which meant that people could be trapped almost unhurt. But then there was the blast syndrome, and– Oh, poor Marie. She would never recover from this.

Another whistle sounded. On grit-laden air, Keith's voice floated down Scotland Road. 'They're here. Tom, Peter's here.'

For the rest of his days, Tom Bingley would fail to remember the next couple of minutes, but he must have turned the car round and driven no more than fifty yards. Peter was on his knees, the girl crouched beside him. Blood soaked through the boy's clothes and stained the hands of Mel's stepfather.

'You,' snapped Tom. 'You Watson girl, get in the back of the car, young lady. My son will be on his face, and we shall bend his knees so that he will fit. Take his head in your lap and keep him as still as possible. Pray he does well, because you will answer to me, miss.'

But Mel heard none of his threat. Miracles did happen. She and Peter were special, were meant to live, because the people who had responded to the blast were Peter's father and her stepfather. She sat in the car and received the precious boy's head and shoulders on her lap. His father folded Peter's legs and closed the door. 'You'd better drive,' he said to Keith. 'My limbs are not dependable.'

It was a difficult journey, since the need to reach safety quickly fought with the desire to cause no further damage to the patient It was pitch dark, and the car's hooded headlights offered few clues about where road ended and pavement began. But Tom, who had learned the route off by heart, knew when they had arrived. 'Stop here,' he said. 'His best hope is in my office where I have some equipment. The hospitals will be too busy.'

At the surgery, Tom regained sufficient strength to carry the unconscious Peter through to his consulting room. 'Sweep every bloody thing off this desk,' he snapped at Keith. 'Then phone my wife and yours. No. Wait while I think.' He placed his son face down on the patients' trolley before hurriedly covering his desk with trays and instruments. 'Take my car. Take her with you.' He nodded in Mel's direction.

'I'm going nowhere,' she said.

'Tell your wife, then pick up Marie.' Tom faced Mel. 'You have to go to show Keith where my house is. If you insist, I suppose you may return here.'

They left. *Please let the research be right. O negative is thought to be the universal donor, and I need to believe that. Did a German discover it? Clever bastards, the Krauts.* He rifled madly through papers on the floor, found the document, scanned it. Yes. For almost two years, O negative had been keeping people alive until their own group had been located. He had to trust that.

Tom cut away his son's clothing and discovered that no major vessel had been ruptured, though there was considerable damage. Peter needed a transfusion, because a great deal of glass was embedded in his flesh, and an incalculable amount of blood had been lost. Trauma and bleeding were the probable causes of the boy's failure to wake. First, the shards needed to be removed. This was the most terrifying moment of Tom's life so far.

Slowly and carefully, he picked out the larger pieces, thanking God that Peter remained unconscious during this process. Having removed all visible foreign bodies and smaller glass fragments, the doctor stopped and watched the bleeding. It was not too bad, though there had probably been a sizeable loss of blood since the bombing.

Determined to succeed, he placed a hypodermic in his own left arm, another in his son's. With O rhesus negative dripping down a tube into Peter, Tom continued to inspect the wounds. He had to concentrate. Passive blood donors often felt faint, and he was playing two parts, donor and surgeon, so his blood would leave him more quickly due to a faster heartbeat.

One-handed now, he lifted the glass away from his son's prone form and placed it on a corner of the desk. He checked Peter's bleeding again, then sat and waited, left arm held aloft so that the transfusion would be effective. One of the wounds remained feisty, and he stuffed it with wadding. Marie would soon be here. Marie would help in the saving of this precious life. Not for the first time of late, he thanked God for his wife's existence.

When he knew he had reached his limit on the blood-letting front, Tom removed the needle from his arm and placed a plaster on the small wound. This valued boy would live. 'But don't wake up yet, son.' He couldn't get the suture right, couldn't hold the needle steady. He had done the right thing, because Peter had needed blood, and Tom was almost sure his red stuff could keep anyone going. 'I gave too much,' he said to himself before sinking to the floor.

The door flew open. Keith, Eileen, Marie and Mel entered the room.

'Oh, my poor darlings.' Marie rushed to her two boys. The senior one was on the floor. 'How much?' she asked. 'How much have you given him? And aren't you O? But he's A like me.'

'It's all right. The antigens won't fight – Rh neg, and it'll keep him going. I showed you how to suture, didn't I? About a pint and a half, I think I gave, and it left me too quickly. I was working on him.'

She checked her son's pulse. 'You saved him, Tom. Thank goodness you found them, Mr Greenhalgh. Eileen?'

'Yes?'

'Hot, sweet tea for the upstanding and floor-sitting. Keith, is it?'

'Aye, that's me.'

'Blood group?'

'A positive.'

'Good. Will you give? No bad illnesses, hepatitis, TB, blood disorders?'

'No.'

'Will you give?' she repeated. 'Because I will be stitching his wounds, so I need to remain intact.'

'Of course I'll give. I already donate regularly for the war effort.'

'Sit on the windowsill and keep your arm up as high as you can. Another pint will suffice. Now. Sutures.'

Like a well-oiled machine, Marie Bingley set up the crude transfusion system, plucked packing and debris out of her son's wounds, washed them, stitched her baby back together, checked the flow of Keith's blood, shone a light in his eyes to make sure all was well. 'Drink your tea,' she ordered. 'You need it.'

Tom was picking up. He glared at Mel. 'It was all your doing,' he accused her vehemently. 'Had it not been for you, this would never have happened.'

Marie tutted. 'Oh, do shut up, dear. He's been after her for months, and well you know it. Fourteen is like twenty these days. But no babies, Mel. I'll say the same to this fellow when he comes to. There. He's all stitched up like an old darned sock.' Only then did she react. When the last stitch was in, she sat in her husband's chair and wept like a child.

Eileen joined in. She wasn't one for allowing anyone to weep without company. She looked at Marie Bingley with respect, because the quiet little woman had proved her worth tonight. Eileen liked her. More than that, she knew she had a friend, as the woman was trying to smile at her.

Mel stepped forward and hovered over Tom,

who was sitting up and drinking tea. 'I'm sorry. I don't know what else to say to you. We're young, but we love each other. We're probably older in our heads than most people our age.'

'I shall send him to boarding school,' he barked.

She shrugged. 'Send him where you like, because he'll come straight back.'

'She's right, I will.'

'You said that without moving your lips, Dr Bingley.' Mel squatted down and stared into the eyes of her beloved Peter. 'Thank goodness you're back, you dirty stop-out. You've a road map on your back. Very colourful. Keep still, because my dad's blood's going in, so don't waste it.'

Keith grinned. This was the first time he'd been called Dad by any of Eileen's children.

'Where does the map go, Mel?'

'All the way to Cambridge.'

Peter turned his head and looked at his father. 'We're like a pair of gloves, Dad. She's the left-hander, because she'll be the one voting Labour. She's still not forgiven Churchill for bombing the French fleet in Oran.' After this lengthy piece of oratory, he passed out again.

Marie pulled herself together before separating Keith from the recipient of his blood. 'Thank you so much. Now he's fit to travel to hospital. We aren't going to bother the ambulance service; from the sound of the symphony down the road, they'll be up to their eyes. I shall drive. Eileen, if you and Keith would walk home when he gets steady, we'd be grateful. Mel can come with us. It's plain now that these two will not be separated.'

Throughout this speech, Tom's eyes stared

directly into Mel's, and she gazed back at him without fear or embarrassment. He was a doctor, a clever man, a member of polite society. Yet she scarcely blinked, because that unswerving arrogance granted to the young and gifted was alive and well in her soul. He was a man; he was an adult. Yet she was his superior, though she didn't know why or how. Perhaps she would learn in the future; perhaps she would come to realize that the females of the species were born old, while males sometimes remained forever children. Tom Bingley was vulnerable, and he wore his heart on his sleeve. Mel kept hers hidden…

'What do you mean?' Gill cast an eye over the two invaders. They seemed very worked up and out of sorts, and that would be Jay the Joker's fault. A great charmer of women, he could persuade the fairer sex to believe just about anything. She would put their minds at rest immediately. 'He's at work. He isn't in hospital, he's fixing a sink somewhere and putting shelves up in a pantry. Four Oaks, I think. Anyway, Maisie wants changing and she needs a feed, so I've no time for his larking about. He needs to grow up.'

Elsie looked at Jean; Jean looked at Elsie. They would probably have got more sense out of the baby had she been capable of speech. 'Gill?' Elsie walked up to the young mother. 'Look at me. He fell in the trough at Four Oaks and came out soaked to the skin in ice-cold water. He's got hypothermia, and that's the top and bottom of it.'

Gill shook her head. 'No. He gets hypo-something or other, but it's not thermia. It's to do with sugar if he doesn't eat right.'

'Well, he's got that on top of the other.'

Gill expressed the opinion that Phil Watson was a good minder, and he wouldn't allow anything like that to happen to her husband. 'He's a grand lad, is that. More sense in his little finger than Jay has in his head. He wouldn't let anything go wrong, because it's his job to make sure Jay's in one piece.'

'Phil's in Liverpool,' Elsie said. 'Visiting his mam. He, Nellie and Rob set off this morning. Seems they haven't got back yet.'

Gill Collins blinked, picked up her child and changed the nappy. She wondered what Elsie and Jean were talking about. He was out. He went out every day and came back every day. No matter what, he always came back and made a thorough nuisance of himself. The clock ticked and hiccuped. It was old and slightly unpredictable. Jay was young and very unpredictable, and this clock had been his dad's. 'He was eccentric,' she said to no one in particular.

'Eh?' Elsie placed a hand on Gill's arm. 'He's still eccentric,' she said.

Gill shook her head. 'No. He's dead.'

'Who's dead? Heck, yon lad's not dead, love.' Jean smiled reassuringly. 'He's in hospital with hypothermia and trouble with his sugar too, I shouldn't wonder.'

Gill tutted. 'He's in Tonge Cemetery with a nice headstone. Italian marble, it is.'

Jean, thoroughly confused, did what all Lancashire women do when their environment deteriorates – she put the kettle on. When she thought about Fighter Pilot Night, she knew how silly and confusing men were capable of becoming. And when Jay was included in the recipe, there was no chance of anybody's remaining on an even keel.

Gill continued. 'After his wife buggered off, he lived over the brush with a woman from Fallowfield. He combed his hair across the big bald spot on his head, so he grew it dead long on one side. Every time the bloody wind blew, he looked like he should have had a frock on, because his hair streamed behind him – it was very, very silly. The clock's nearly as daft.'

Jean and Elsie busied themselves with cups, saucers, milk and teapot. There seemed to have been a marked deterioration in the mental health of their hostess. According to Gill, Jay had been fixing a sink, but now he was dead and buried. Elsie suddenly stopped what she was doing. She stared ahead at nothing in particular before addressing their neglectful host once more. 'Gill?'

'What?'

'Who are you talking about?'

'Jay's dad, of course. He gave us that clock, and it's nearly as doolally as he was. He's been dead a while now. No loss. Her from Fallowfield buggered off with the window cleaner, and that was that. We got the clock and that rocking chair, end of story.'

Elsie was growing tired. She lowered herself into a chair and took a long, hard look at Gill. The girl wasn't mad; she was simply overloaded. The chattering was a distraction; she probably talked to the child and to herself most of the time. Yes, it was all getting Gill down. One baby might not seem much, but for a woman who had expected to be barren, it was clearly one too many. Gill's dedication to Maisie, all the watchfulness, all the feeding and holding and worrying, came from guilt. *I was the same,* Elsie said silently. *My kiddies were more burden than joy. She wanted Maisie till Maisie became a reality.* But what could be done to help?

Jean Dyson drank her tea before excusing herself. She had daughters and hungry Land Girls to feed. Her husband was at the infirmary with Jay, and the chances of his finding transport home today were remote, so she would have to do his early morning jobs as well as her own. But, as she reminded herself inwardly, Willows folk stood by Willows folk, and Neil was doing what needed to be done, as must she.

Elsie stayed where she was. If she waited until Nellie came back, they could unite and tackle this lot together. But it was Jean who returned unexpectedly, slightly out of breath and with a message. She had met Miss Pickavance, and Nellie was not expected back tonight because Liverpool was being bombed again, a close friend of Mel's had been hurt, and Miss P's house in the city no longer existed. 'She was going on about how she should have saved more photographs and her mother's knitting. So as if we haven't got enough with this one here, there's another fretting in the big house. I swear, Elsie, the world is going to the dogs. And I've a meal to cook.' She left the scene and ran home.

Elsie realized that without Nellie she was just half of something useful. Nellie would have found a way of making Gill Collins listen, whereas Elsie

Openshaw didn't know how to kick off. All those years of banishment were still telling on her; although she was now treated much the same as anyone else, her communication skills remained slightly corroded, despite the fact that Nellie had dragged her back into the realms of humanity. But Nellie wasn't here. God alone knew when Nellie would be here.

'Gill?'

'What?'

'We're not joking, you know. Jay is back in hospital.'

The younger woman glanced at the clock. 'He'll be home in a minute. Somebody would have told me if he'd been in the hospital.'

Elsie hung on to her temper. 'We did tell you. Jean told you and I told you. You don't listen, love. You don't hear what people are saying to you.'

'It's just a joke,' Gill insisted. 'Like being a fighter pilot was a joke. He's always pulling my leg. One of these days, he'll pull it so hard that the foot on the end of it will kick the teeth out of his stupid gob.'

It was hopeless. It was also time for tea, especially for a woman who was breastfeeding. Elsie set to and made poached eggs on toast. While the two women were eating, Elsie noticed Gill's eyes wandering from time to time to glance at the clock. 'It gains, then it loses. That clock's as much use as a rubber knife, but will he buy a new one? No. There's an alarm clock upstairs, and I have to go all the way up there to make sure of the time.'

Elsie knew that the young woman was waiting

for her husband. He got on her nerves, but he was part of the scenery, and he seemed to have disappeared.

Gill stared at Mr Collins Senior's clock again. If the old fool's son was pretending to be in hospital ... if he was pretending to be in hospital, he would end up in hospital, because his insulin was here in the pantry. 'Elsie?'

'What, love?'

'It's not a joke, is it?'

Elsie shook her head. 'Nay, I wouldn't have shut King George's post office for a joke. And Neil Dyson wouldn't have abandoned Home Farm for a joke. He's stuck down yon at the Royal Infirmary, and he'll likely not get back till tomorrow. That means Jean and the Land Girls have all to do in the morning and no man to help.'

'Oh.'

'You can't get to the infirmary now, Gill. But you can take the torch and go up to Miss P's house, ask to use the phone, and the hospital will tell you how he's going on.'

Gill stood up and blinked a few times. 'What about Maisie?'

'I'll mind her.'

'Oh.' The young mother still didn't move. 'You were no good with your own kids, were you?'

Again, Elsie sat on her old self. 'I've changed, Gill. We all have to change, you included. She'll be all right with me. I promise.'

Thus it came about that Gill Collins left her baby for the first time. More significantly, after expressing milk so that Elsie could feed her, Gill allowed Maisie to be nourished by another while she was driven to the hospital by an acquaintance of Miss Pickavance. She needed to see the idiot she had married. He was a pest; he was also her husband and Maisie's dad.

Tom and Marie had done a good job on their son. The hospital doctor looked Peter over, declared him to be disgustingly healthy and, after handing over medicine and some dressings for the wounds, invited him to leave the premises after resting for a further hour. Throughout his brief time in Outpatients, Peter communicated with his mother and with Mel, but not with his father. Tom, acutely aware that his son was deliberately ignoring him, made his way to the gents. When he came out, the girl was waiting for him in the corridor. 'Ah,' he blustered. 'So this is where you pick up your men friends.'

Mel folded her arms, lolled against a wall and simply stared at him.

'What do you want?' he asked.

'A bit of honesty would do, doc. Peter knows about you and my mother.'

He swallowed.

'Beautiful, isn't she? Of course, she married someone else.'

'And your point is?'

Mel subdued her fears. 'We're young. But you're not, and maturity doesn't bring sense with it, or you wouldn't have been running after my mother. So that's you explained, eh? We're too young? What was your excuse? Retarded? Daft? Special and with rules of your own?' Her heart was doing a fair imitation of a jungle drum. She should not talk like this to an adult. As daughter of Eileen and a pupil of Merchant Taylors', she had been educated in respect. But, as a product of Merchants, she had an advanced sense of language and a large vocabulary.

He tried to conceal a smile. Always, always, Eileen Watson, now Greenhalgh, would own a huge piece of his heart, and here she came again. The tilt of the head, determined chin, pert little nose, mouth good enough to eat– He cleared his throat. Like her mother, she could wrap any man round her little finger. 'Look at it another way, Mel. Love's an illness. Especially at the beginning when hormones collide and confusion reigns. Throughout life, we meet people we desire. Fourteen's a bit young to be considering permanence.' He could still taste the kisses he had stolen from Eileen...

She favoured him with a dazzling smile. He liked her; he wouldn't kick her out of bed. Like her mother, Mel was acutely aware of the effect she had on men. 'We're old in our heads, Dr Bingley. And look at me – strong as a horse, stubborn as a mule and feisty as a polo pony on its day off. New blood. A bit of working-class backbone to inject into the equation. You don't want to be all Blundellsands and Crosby, do you? Get a bit of spirit in your genes.'

Tom glanced at the ceiling as if seeking inspiration. 'No one of fourteen can possibly know who he or she will marry.'

'Then you've no worries, have you?'

She was quick, he had to give her that much. 'You are old enough to bear a child.'

'But not daft enough.'
'Catholic?'
'Debatable. There will be no contraception, because there will be no fornication. Is that plain enough?'
She was her mother all over again, and Peter was going to be a lucky tyke. 'Those feelings overwhelm. The urge to connect completely may become too strong.' No way would he be able to resist this one. But he wouldn't get the chance, and he was happy now with just Marie. Wasn't he?
'We'll manage. Now. Are you going to behave yourself, or shall I set my gran on you? She's wonderfully fierce.'
Tom loved Marie. He had dragged her out of a pit created in childhood, had learned how to conduct himself in order to make the relationship work, and he no longer regretted the marriage. But his peripheral vision still held images of this child's mother, and he was glad that she was going away in the New Year. Mel, however, would be hanging around. 'You leave me no option, Amelia. Your grandmother has already given me grief, so I shall just have to do my best to accept my very young son's fiancée. I still find the whole thing ridiculous, though.'
As they walked back to the small room in which Peter was resting, Mel slipped her arm through Tom's. 'Please don't fight me,' she begged.
'Because I'd never win?'
'Something like that, yes.'
After she had withdrawn her hand, Tom's arm tingled for seconds.

In another hospital just under forty miles away, a second young man lay. He would not be going home after an hour's rest, because his core temperature remained below average, while diabetes added to the problem. Warm saline and a heated bed did their slow work while specialists tested his blood.

A door swung inwards. 'Blood's as flat as a pancake,' the sister shouted.

Neil and Gill were sent away while flat-as-a-pancake was dealt with.

'Do they mean dead?' asked Gill.

Neil shook his head. 'Nay, he's just out of sugar, that's all.'

'Oh.' She chewed her lip. 'So what will they do?'

'They'll fill him with the stuff.'

'It's rationed.'

The farmer failed to prevent a smile. 'They're not going to pour a two-pound bag of Co-op's best granulated down him, love. It'll be like water and it won't be much. They'll drip it into his blood.'

Gill sat very still and stared into the future. It shouldn't be like this. She had the child she'd always craved, a decent home if she could be bothered to clean it properly, a husband exempt from the forces but with a job, and lovely people around her. 'Neil?'

'What?'

'You know how he gets on my nerves?'

He nodded.

'How can I cope? And have I had a nervous breakdown?'

Difficult questions. He had to think hard before answering, because this woman would probably hang on every word. Of late, she had scarcely listened to anyone, but she was certainly concentrating now. 'I don't know about nervous breakdowns, Gill, because I'm not a doctor. But I do remember Jeanie after she had our Patty. Every time I spoke to her she bit my head off. I used to read in the shippon with my cows. Then one day she was right again. We've always argued, but we don't let the sun go down on a quarrel.' He didn't need to tell Gill about his and Jean's wonderful sex life. That didn't continue in every marriage, so Gill needed to find her own way home for part of the route.

'So I could be out of flunter because of Maisie?'

'Oh yes. Definitely.'

So that was the answer to some of it. 'And what about him in there?' she asked.

Neil shook his head. 'You have to look at it this way, Gill. Part of it could be his illness. He was diabetic for a long time before it was noticed. Again, I have to say I'm not a doctor, but I've heard Elsie Openshaw say that diabetics get moods. You've a choice. You can stay with him or leave him.' He refused to add the fact that Jay was fighting for his life just yards away.

'Where would I go?'

'No idea.'

A lonely tear found its way down Gill's cheek. 'He makes me that mad, I could kill him.'

He had to do it. Shock sometimes worked where kindness failed. 'You may not need to.'

Her head shot round to face him. 'What did you say?'

'He's not out of the woods, sweetheart.'

Gill shot out of her chair like a bullet from a gun. She wasn't having this. If young Phil Watson hadn't gone to Liverpool, her daft swine would have been all right. She stopped in her tracks and walked back to Neil. 'Why did you carry him all the way to Home Farm? Why didn't you take him into Four Oaks and get him dry there? Happen he wouldn't have caught his death of cold if you'd–'

'It was locked, Gill. There's been a bit of light-fingering going on, and after Jay had finished they locked up before going back to work. Home Farm was the nearest.'

'Oh. Sorry.' She fled once more.

Back in Jay's room, she surveyed the people surrounding the bed. 'Is he all right? He'd better be, or you'll have me to answer to if he turns his toes up.'

'Gill?'

'What?'

'Shut up.'

But she was riled. 'He's got a little daughter, not even weaned yet. It's not his fault he fell in the trough. If you got his diabetes right, he wouldn't be lying in ice-cold water, would he?'

'Gill?'

'He's only thirty-four. That's no age to–' She stopped and blinked several times. None of this lot knew her name, but someone kept saying it.

'I am not dying before I have a cup of tea.'

'For God's sake,' cried the ward sister. 'Nurse, will you fetch this person a cup of tea?' She spoke to the person's wife. 'We had to hang on with nil by mouth until we checked his kidneys, but we've had him on a drip. All I can say to you, love, is I hope you take him home soon, because he's driving us round the bend.'

'He does that,' Gill replied. 'There's no cure.'

At last, she was alone with him. He looked so small in the bed, so thin. 'Get yourself right,' she ordered. 'And shape up, will you? Be a clown just on Fridays down at the pub.'

'Yes, miss.'

'Stop doing stuff when you're tired.'

'Yes, miss.'

It was hopeless, and she knew it. But she also knew she wanted him alive. And she would learn to love him again if it killed her...

Fourteen

'Wake up, you dozy, wonderful woman.' Keith stroked her face with a forefinger. She felt like a peach, smooth and soft but downy. Her hair gave off the aroma of spring flowers, and if he wasn't careful he'd end up on a dusty, forgotten bookshelf with the rest of the romantic poets, because he was certainly becoming daft enough.

This gorgeous woman had caused many changes in him. She had made him younger, happier, less careful, more inclined to read Keats, Wordsworth and even a bit of Shelley. The worries of the previous evening had left her tired, so he would cheer her up a bit in a minute. Well, he would try. One of her best qualities was her inclination towards natural happiness. 'Come on, Chuckabutty.

Wake up and talk to this rather pleasant young – youngish – man.'

Eileen yawned and opened one eye. 'On a scale of one to ten, how safe am I?' He was hovering, elbow bent, head resting on a hand. The devil was visiting those beautiful eyes again, and his left eyebrow was slightly raised. When that item relocated itself, people should lock up their daughters and root round for chastity belts. 'Man the bloody lifeboats,' she sighed. 'Get women and children off this ship.' He was working his way up to something, and it was breakfast time. 'Well?' she asked once more. 'How safe am I in your company, sir?'

Keith considered the question. They were in bed. They were in bed together. He was stark naked, as usual, while she was wrapped in a hideous dressing gown that looked as if it had been cobbled together by a visually challenged person whose only available fabrics were army surplus items. 'If I can get you out of that horse blanket, you'll be about as safe as a rabbit with the business end of a gun up its nose. Well? Are you going to carry on lying there all enigmatic and silent? I can do enigmatic and silent, but I won't be still. In fact, I may come over rather vigorous.'

Eileen delivered a long, damp raspberry in his direction. The house was full of people. One was her mother, two were her sons, the fourth was her daughter, while the householder would be expecting eggs, toast and milky tea in about fifteen minutes. Eileen had things to do, and last night had been horrible. Poor Peter. If he got Mel in trouble, the lad would be doubly poor, that was a certainty. 'Does it have to be now? Only

I've other clients in need of attention.'

He nodded gravely. 'Has to be now. Part of my course work, as I seem to remember explaining on several occasions. I told you about the practicals, didn't I? There's the oral exam you can help me with– Ouch. That hurt, madam. I shall park you on the draining board again if you're not careful. Right, I'll settle for a kiss and a bit of mechanical engineering.'

'Mechanical excuse me?'

'It does no harm,' he said seriously, 'just to check from time to time whether all your parts are in working order. We don't want rust eating away at your bodywork. It's a classy chassis, is that. Also, if you keep sleeping under that bloody tarpaulin, I shan't be able to check your oil levels or your transmission. What if your independent front suspension goes? And how are you at double-declutching? I have a full set of tools here, including dipstick and socket set, so let's have you up on the ramp.'

'Have I got independent suspension?'

'So far, yes. The rest of the motor car industry's been a bit slow, but you're a comfortable vehicle. I've no complaints. Do any of your other passengers voice concerns after a ride? We could compile a questionnaire and pass it round.'

Eileen enjoyed the close company of a vulgar man. This one was cleverer than her Lazzer had been, though Lazzer's good points were certainly worth remembering with affection and gratitude. 'You are not nice,' she told Keith. 'This tarpaulin belonged to Miss Morrison's father, and she values it. It keeps me warm when you pinch all the eiderdown in the middle of the night. If this carries on, I shall have to wear a vest in bed.' She had never worn a vest since childhood, and she'd no intention of starting now.

'I'll keep you warm. Come here.'

But she wasn't going to cooperate, especially with a quorum plus full committee in the house, and her mother was as good as a three-line whip. She leapt from the bed, grabbed her clothes, made a dash for the bathroom, and locked herself in. Laughing almost uncontrollably, she leaned against the door for support. Was she laughing, or was this hysteria?

He was amazing. So controlled and dead-pan serious, so dependable and strong, he was as mad as a March hare in the bedroom. She laughed again. As mad as a hare with a gun up its nose. He was scratching at the door. Last night had been difficult: young Peter with all that glass in his back, Tom and Marie so upset, Mel determined, almost impudent, and probably sexually active. Eileen was exhausted. Even so, she wanted to hug her idiot husband. The trouble was, he'd turn a hug into a three-ring circus, and breakfast was required.

'I told you it were grim up north,' Keith stage-whispered from the landing. He was only trying to keep her happy, she guessed, but there was a door between them. Sometimes – and this was one of those times – she wondered how life would have been had she never met him. Would she have consoled herself by having an affair with Marie's husband? Would she have given in?

'Go away,' she hissed. 'You are interfering with

the balance of my components.'

'Chance would be a fine thing. Let me in.'

'No. And I hope you're wearing something.'

'I'm not.'

She panicked, opened the door, and he pushed his way into the small room. Triumph written all over his face, he winked at her.

'You lying toad,' she accused. He was wearing a shirt and trousers.

He washed her, dried her, dressed her, talking all the time, speaking soft words of love, lust and silliness. There was something strangely erotic about being dressed by a man. She could tell by his quickened breathing that he felt the same. 'Do I need an oil change?' she whispered.

'No.' That special, satanic glint showed again in his eyes. 'But I'll replenish your fuel tank later. Talking of fuel, Dr Bingley's taking them back to Willows. If we get rid of Mel and wait till Miss Morrison takes her nap this afternoon we'll be able to...'

'Mel,' she said sadly. 'Oh, Mel.'

'It will be all right. She's got too much sense to muck up her life. Come on. Breakfast for the mob.'

'Keith?'

'What?'

'I love you so much it hurts.'

'Don't worry.' He grinned broadly. 'I'll charge your battery when I get the chance. Soon have you running smoothly.' He left the room. At the top of the stairs, he stood for a while and smiled to himself. He had managed to capture a wild creature, and she would never eat out of his hand. She suffered no morning sickness, no fools and no nonsense. She carried on whatever the circumstances, loved her children, loved life, loved him. He was a fortunate man.

The bathroom door opened. 'Are you lurking?' Eileen asked sweetly.

'It's part of the course.'

'Really?'

'Oh, yes. After I pass the sex maniac degree, I may do a masters in dirty old man. All I need is a mac or an army greatcoat.'

Eileen shook her head and wagged a finger. She had eggs and toast to prepare. But he wouldn't leave her alone. She found herself drawn into yet another of his kisses, one that went on so long that it left her breathless. When she regained her composure, she fixed him with a stare that was meant to be steely. 'Did you pass kissing?'

'Oh, yes. Flying colours, A-plus, and a mention in dispatches.'

'Who did you kiss?'

'The teacher, of course. I want first class honours. He didn't seem to mind.'

'Fair enough. Come on, let's start the day.'

When Keith entered the kitchen, he stopped dead in the doorway. It was an unfortunate moment, because his wife was draped over one shoulder in a fireman's lift. It would now be clear to Dr Tom Bingley that Keith Greenhalgh had a habit of lifting women and parking them all over the place, so he followed through by dumping her once again on the draining board. 'Good girl,' he said. 'Stay, and I'll fetch you a biscuit.' Wearing an air of false nonchalance, he bid Tom good morning and wondered aloud where the dog food was.

But Tom knew he was witnessing something special. These two were deeply in love, and his heart hurt. Eileen was fun. Marie, God love her, was an amazing and capable woman, but she would never be– He shouldn't stare at Eileen, mustn't look at her. Just once. If he could have her just once, he would go to the grave faithful except for that just once.

'Mam?' Mel joined the pantomime. 'This drawing of our Phil's – I've never seen anything better.' She showed it to Tom. 'Look, Dr Bingley. Look what my naughty brother did. He wants to draw what's left of Liverpool, but he has to get back to Willows to look after Jay. This is Jay in the picture.' While addressing him, she looked him full in the face.

Tom took the work and looked at it.

'Mam?'

'What, love?'

'With all that happened last night, Gran didn't get the chance to talk to you properly. The hospital kept Jay in. He was poorly because of the cold and low sugar. Gran and the boys have to get back today. Miss Pickavance has been fretting again on the phone to Gran this morning, because on top of Jay being ill she knows her precious little house has been flattened. She's worried that Gran won't get back. I think she believes Liverpool's going to be eradicated.'

Nellie came in. 'Big word for early morning, Mel. Liverpool is here to stay.' She had fed Miss Morrison. 'Just as well I was here,' she said. 'All the larking about upstairs. That poor woman could have been waiting till a week on Thursday. Anyway, she'll be better off with me here come the New Year. I don't go messing before breakfast. It's like having a couple of daft kids in the house. Hmmph.' There. That was the doctor told yet again. If he still had intentions regarding Eileen, he might as well know that she and Keith were blissfully happy. 'Like a couple of elephants in clogs,' Nellie added for good measure.

Tom studied Phil's picture. Well, he pretended to study it, but his inner eye was focused on Eileen and Keith messing about before breakfast. His shoulder ached as he recalled the two dockers and their roughness. Marie would never mess about before breakfast. And Nellie had almost broken his skull. His wife was livelier than she had been, but still dignified. He loved her; he did, but... Keith Greenhalgh was a lucky devil.

'Have you come for us?' Nellie asked. 'Because we're ready when you are, doc. Though my grandsons haven't had much sleep, bless them.'

He told her he had acquired the petrol, and the car was waiting outside. Phil and Rob came downstairs. Eileen was glad of her seat on the draining board, because the kitchen was becoming rather crowded. Her eyes filled up, since she would not be with Mam and her three boys for Christmas. 'Don't forget to take the presents,' she said, her voice cracking slightly. 'This house has been declared safe, so we'll swap soon.' She placed a hand on her belly. Keith's child had to be guarded, but so did Mam. And this problem with Mel ... oh, what a mess. Could she leave Crosby? Could she leave the Mel problem to her mother?

Tom stepped up to the table and addressed Phil. 'Right,' he said. 'I know you want to record Liverpool and all her sorrows. Would photographs be any use to you? I have a rather good Swiss camera, and I can go down sometimes during the day and get some pictures for you – architectural damage, people – whatever you want. I develop my own in a darkroom, so it's no problem if I throw in a few extra negatives.'

The boy's jaw dropped. 'Would you do that? Really?'

'Yes. I don't mind going out of my way for a special young man.'

Again, Eileen caught her breath. Tom was right; she did have special children. They were all willing to work towards a goal, and the change in the boys was remarkable. What would Keith's son or daughter be? 'Thanks, Tom,' she said. 'He needs and deserves help.'

Tom went to sit in his car. He'd already taken a load of earache from Gloria, who was decidedly uncomfortable about the situation between Mel and her brother. She had screamed about becoming a wallflower, about her parents' betrayal of her, about losing her best friend. She wouldn't listen to reason, refused to believe that Tom and Marie hadn't known about the situation. For once, Tom would be grateful for the company of Nellie Kennedy. *Marie, I do love you, but this one, this Eileen, is ... unique.*

It seemed that Eileen Watson, daughter of the slums, had produced remarkable children. Mel was academically brilliant, the oldest boy seemed in danger of becoming a great artist, while the middle one of the three was said to be preparing to dedicate his life to the soil. Her youngest sounded fun, too. Aged only eight, he couldn't make his mind up between veterinary science and horsemanship. And in her belly, Eileen now carried an unknown little one to be released within months on an unsuspecting world. Sometimes, class and environment didn't count; he knew several wealthy and well-placed families whose children were as thick as planks. Even extra tuition didn't work for many of them.

Mel sailed through everything, sometimes after a minimal amount of studying. Gloria was coming on, as the improvement in her appearance seemed to have given her a boost in other areas, but she would never have a brain as quick as her ex-friend's. God. There was all that to be dealt with when he got back: Gloria wasn't speaking to her brother, and had declared her intention never to speak to Mel as long as she lived; Marie was upset and confused, while Tom didn't know where to start.

Eileen had everything, he supposed. For a start, she had love, and it looked real. Her sex drive was strong, she would be living beyond the reach of bombs, and her offspring were bright. Oh, she was creeping back into his heart, wasn't she? And he would see her, by heck he would. Photographs for Phil. They might suffer ill treatment in the post, and he could get the petrol from time to time, so the photos could become an excuse. He was not supposed to think about her. He was going to dedicate his life to Marie and the twins.

But it would never be over. Even though it had ended, it would never be over.

She was on the path, was kissing her mother and her boys. Her eyes didn't redden when she wept. No matter what she wore, she shone, and he was going crazy again. Madness was a luxury he could ill afford.

Fifteen

'He still loves you.' Keith was brushing her hair. Eileen enjoyed having her hair brushed, and had been known to express the opinion that it was nearly as good as sex and a lot less complicated.

'Tom wants me. You love me. I know the difference. Anyway, he's reconciled with his wife, though how she tolerates his selfishness I shall never know.' Eileen glanced at the alarm clock. 'It's almost tablet time, and we'd probably shock our patient to death if we turned up in the nude. One verbally offensive experience in a cellar with a caretaker was not enough to prepare her for naked people.'

'But we are beautiful naked people,' he said.

She reminded him that beauty existed in the eye of the beholder. A door slammed. 'Mel's back,' Eileen announced. Like lightning, they threw on clothes, unlocked the bedroom door and moved to the landing. They could hear Mel weeping in her room.

'I'll do snack and medicines, and I'll sit with

Miss M for a while,' Keith volunteered. 'You have other fish to fry from the sound of things.'

Eileen closed Mel's door behind her and approached her weeping child. She *was* a child. At fourteen, she was nowhere near old enough to be experimenting with sex. This was all ridiculous, yet no laughing matter. 'Mel? Sweetheart? Come on, look at me.'

The girl lifted her head. 'Gloria hates me; her mother pretends to like me, but she hates me, too. And as for the doctor, he looks at me as if I'm a meal waiting to be devoured once he's poured the gravy on.'

Eileen told her daughter that no one hated her. 'You're too like me, you know, too honest for your own good. Tom Bingley likes pretty things, and you are a pretty thing. He's no threat. Marie's a good woman, but she's frightened. If you get pregnant, both your mothers will be destroyed. As for Gloria, the idea of you sharing secrets with her brother is uncomfortable. She was your confidante, and you were hers. She doesn't want her brother knowing anything private.'

'But I wouldn't.'

'I know that, you know that, but she doesn't. This is all happening because you and Peter have stepped beyond your time. You're the ones out of order, Mel. At fourteen and a half, you should still be playing rounders and hopscotch. He ought to be hanging round with a few lads his own age, football, cricket, skimming pebbles on the river. Now. Tell me what you've done with him. You can't shock me, because I've had two husbands, four children, and a mind broader than the Mersey.'

Mel faltered while she described as best she could what had gone on between her and Peter Bingley. Thrown into the cold light of day, the words were meaningless at best, silly and childish at their worst. There was no pleasure in mere speech, no way of bringing to life an experience that had been joyful. It all sounded so stupid, yet Eileen didn't mock.

'I've been there, Mel. Admittedly, I was older than you are, but I do know what's going on. Believe me, sweetie, one of these days the messing about you describe won't be enough. You'll think once won't matter. You'll convince yourself that there are times when pregnancy is impossible. My Bertie shouldn't have happened, but he did. The little lad who stole a carthorse can't possibly have done that, because his existence was a supposed impossibility.'

Mel swallowed and dried her eyes. 'What am I expected to do now, Mam?'

'Stay away from him.'

'Mother!'

'I know, I know. Some men I've had to avoid because I desired them. When I met Keith, I knew he was right. At the same time, another man appealed to my baser nature, so I stopped seeing that man. He happens to be married.'

'You saw him this morning.'

Thrown for a moment, Eileen paused.

'Peter heard something. It was Dr Bingley, wasn't it?'

'Yes.'

'And you wanted to–'

'Yes. But no longer. Keith is right for me. And I'm thirty-four, Mel, so I have three decades under my belt. You are wading in treacherous waters. Have a baby, and it's all over. Your ambitions will curl and dry up like a pile of dead leaves. By the time you reach my age, your child could be your age or older. Say you had him or her at fifteen – you'd be only thirty and mother to a hormonal kiddy. Just stop it. I don't want to upset you, but you know I'm making sense.'

So they sat holding hands, Mel sobbing from time to time, Eileen simply being where she was needed. She would be needed downstairs shortly for Miss Morrison's bed bath, but Mel was important. The girl had to see sense; for once, the younger should heed the experience of the older. Eileen sighed. The trouble with life was that parents limped through and watched their progeny making mistakes. The parents had made the same mistakes, but the young refused to listen. They had to learn via their own errors. Mel was too pretty; in her day, Eileen had been the prettiest girl in school, so she knew about having her head turned, having the boys look and whisper and wonder who would be first to get under the clothing.

'I can't not see him,' Mel said at last.

'Then I can't put a burden like this on my mother's shoulders. She's not young enough to make you keep your knickers on. I can't have her breaking down from worrying over you. Which means I must stay, Keith will lose his job because he won't leave me, so he'll have to carry on as a labourer with Liverpool builders. And your grandmother will have to stay permanently at

Willows, all so that you and Peter Bingley might be stopped. I shall stop you. I am telling you now, Mel, if I have to tie you up, I will. If I have to break Peter's legs, I bloody will. I am not having you throw away Cambridge just for a stupid carry-on with a boy.'

'I love him.'

'And what is love, Mel? Rolling about on a floor till the bombs come? Being lumbered with a child when you're just a kid yourself? Watching Peter going off to Cambridge while you stay at home and boil nappies?'

'So now you hate me too.'

Eileen shrugged. 'Not at all. I love you, and I know what the word means. I love you enough to make appointments with the head teachers of both schools. I love you enough to ensure your safety. Whatever it takes, Mel. Whatever it takes.' She kissed her daughter and left the room.

The bombing of Liverpool, though toned down by distance, had kept the boys awake and terrified until after five in the morning. For the first time, the city had endured over twelve hours of intermittent bombardment. Crosby was untouched, but the night had still been frightening for Phil and Rob, who were used now to the quiet of the countryside. Gone was the recklessness that had sent them back to Scotland Road on second-hand bicycles; it had been replaced by the healthy determination to survive and thrive. Although Phil wanted to record the damage, he no longer wanted to live or die among it.

By the time Tom had driven just a few hundred

yards, both boys were fast asleep in the back seat.

Nellie glanced sideways at the handsome, well-dressed driver. He still had strong feelings for Eileen, but the girl shouldn't be around for much longer, which was just as well, because this chap was a selfish and decided creature who was capable of just about anything to achieve his own way. Nellie needed to persuade her daughter to do the swap no matter what Mel was up to. Nellie could deal with Mel. And this fellow would deal with his son, or the dockers would be back. But she wouldn't talk about that now, since the boys might wake, and it wasn't their business.

'What did the Germans get last night?' she asked. 'Apart from the street we lived in. I know they hit that, because my friend's house is gone, and our Mel and your Peter were up to no good inside it.' She lowered her tone at the end of the sentence.

'Quite.' He told her what he knew. The docks had been thoroughly battered yet again, while people in shelters had inhaled the scent of their Christmas dinners being cremated in a nearby covered meat market. A chemical factory in Hanover Street had provided a giant firework display, and an electric power station had been disabled. 'The fire service saved St George's Hall, thank goodness. It was heavily fire-bombed. When places like that disappear, people lose heart.'

Nellie delivered her firmly held belief that nothing at all would quench the wrath of Liverpudlians. 'We don't need nothing,' she told him. 'As long as we have a bite to eat and a cup of tea, we'll fight. That's nothing to do with buildings.'

She looked at him again. It was plain that this fellow was no proper Scouser. 'You've no idea, have you? We're different down there. The Liver Bird would be missed, like, but we can put up with most things. Strong, you see. Not all fur coats and no knickers. My Eileen's as tough as old boots. She may look like one of Cinderella's glass slippers, but she's tanned leather underneath. Keith can manage her, but he's just about the only man who can. She's difficult when she wants to be, so he puts her in her place.'

'On the draining board?'

'Sometimes, yes. Or in a cage under the table. She'll never best him, you know. But if anything happened to her, he'd kill.'

He heard the warning, and took heart from it, because it possibly meant that he was in with a chance. Not yet, of course; not while she as carrying a child. Almost seamlessly, he picked up where he had left off. The best-loved Catholic church in Liverpool, Our Lady and St Nicholas, had been gutted. In Anfield, seventy-four had perished in a direct hit on a shelter, while two infirmaries and a school had been bombed. 'Countless houses. Relentless,' he concluded. 'They are bloody determined, because they know we have weaponry on the docks.'

'How do they know?' she asked. 'It's not the only city with docks.'

'Spies. English people who support the Nazis.'

Nellie wasn't having that. 'Load of rubbish,' she said. 'There's no spies down in real Liverpool. Though in my experience, all men will do anything to get what they want, even if they don't have a use for it and don't deserve it. Germans who fly planes and drop bombs are men. They don't need spies, because they can see everything from up there in the sky once they've set fire to a few things. Well, I say men should all be locked up, let women take over for a while. We make things like babies, homes and dinners. Men destroy our work.'

Tom changed the subject, asked how she liked the countryside and would she stay there after the war.

'I well might. You get used to the quiet after a few months; you even get used to cows, pigs and all that. The air's so fresh it cuts into your chest, and the people are much the same as anywhere, really. Once you get used to them talking funny, it's all right. I tell you what, though. I said we'd make Liverpool and back in a day, and I'll never forget my stupid stubbornness. We might not have got home at all except for you.'

He choked on a chuckle, turned it into a cough. Nellie had a true Scouse accent. If something wasn't fair, it wasn't *fur.* If a woman got a new fur coat, it was a *fair* coat. Words that ended in ck came out so guttural that they sounded German, vowels were broadened to destruction, and an interpreter would have been useful at times. And here she sat complaining about inner Lancashire's flattened tones. He wondered how the people of Willows fared when trying to make out what she was saying. She was a character. She had thumped him, but he couldn't help admiring her.

'I was needed,' she continued. 'The odd job man's gone odder than ever, in hospital with

diabetes and hypo-thermals.'
'Hypothermia.'
'Yes, that's what I said. So poor Elsie's been stuck with his wife what's had a baby and gone all peculiar. Started talking to herself, you know.'
'Whose wife?'
'Jay. The one in Phil's drawing. Odd job man. See, he starts smelling of acid tone and–'
'Acetone.'
Nellie grinned. This one hadn't yet picked up on the fact that she twisted words deliberately. 'Yeah, that as well. So our Phil shoves a barley sugar in his mouth and tells him to sit down while his level climbs up again. But our Phil wasn't there. And I promised, said I'd be back last night, because we've no idea up at Willows, you see. I mean, we've got Land Army, and you can't slaughter a pig without a papal blessing and three forms filled in – oh, and you have to grow loads of vegetables – but war? We see nothing up there. So I said I'd be back, but I wasn't, because we don't think. I mean we know it's happening, but it's not real when you're as safe as we are. I let them down. I kept Phil away, too.'
'Not your fault.'
She sniffed. 'Well, if I'd never come, our Phil would never have come. And if our Phil had never come, Jay wouldn't have ended up face down in a horse trough with icy water in it. He's got delicate constitutionals with all this sugar and everything. I mean, he was daft to start with, but he's gone worse.'
Life was always more complicated once Nellie Kennedy entered the arena. She had a quick

mind, an explosive temper, and an advanced sense of humour, but she was not particularly well organized in the verbal department. Yet he sensed that had she been on the receiving end of an education, she might have been dangerous, especially in the field of politics or unions. 'So he's in hospital?'

'Yes. So that meant the post office was closed.'

He was losing the thread again. 'Oh, I see.' He didn't see at all.

'Because Elsie stayed at the gatehouse and waited to see if Gill got back from hospital last night. She's not been herself. Gill, I mean, not Elsie. She had to mind the baby, did Elsie, and she's not fond of kids. And the lamp oil man was coming to make a delivery to the post office. So Freda Pilkington what lived in Rachel Street had to accept the lamp oil for Elsie and put it in the shed. She took Kitty's place, you see. Kitty what killed her kiddies and hanged herself upstairs. You remember her? All teeth, she was, God rest her.'

'Yes.' He had never forgotten poor Kitty with her smelly house, empty eyes, dead husband and no hope. 'So the house meant for Kitty and her children went to Freda.'

'Pilkington, yes. Her man's in the army, and she's a decent soul, so we brought her here. Right, stop now and have a look.'

He stopped.

'That's our Eileen's house. Well, it's Keith's, but this is where they'll be living. There's Freda's, then the one with the post box is Elsie's. She's my friend. These cottages are all Home Farm tied. People what live in them work at Home Farm or

Willows – that's the house. Then there's Four Oaks, Cedars, Pear Tree and Holly farms. They pay rent to Miss Pickavance, cos they're what's called tenanted holdings. It was her house down Scottie Road what my granddaughter and your son was messing about in. She lived at number one, then she inherited all this lot.'

'Fascinating.' Tom felt as if he had entered some parallel universe where things were nearly the same, but not quite. Apart from his companion's disjointed meanderings, these rolling hills were beautiful, while people who lived on the Mersey plain led the flatter life, no movement in the land, no dry stone walls, no dales. But he could not countenance a life without the river, so he probably was a true Liverpudlian. 'So what do you do all day?' he asked.

'Every-bloody-thing. See, Miss Pickavance has to be Miss Millichamp.'

'Yes?' It was happening again.

'Miss Millichamp had a hacadamy in Liverpool what Hilda went to when she was a kiddy. Now, this here Miss Millichamp never caned nobody. She just got so saddened over bad behaviour that the kiddies were upset. So Hilda – Miss Pickavance – pretends to be Miss Millichamp and she teaches school for the ones from Liverpool that wouldn't fit into real school. She does that in the morning in the afternoon room. I help. Because them hard-faced little buggers from Scottie need a thump sometimes, and she won't give 'em one, so I do it.'

He turned into Willows Lane. 'You're a professional thumper, then.'

'Yeah. And I supervise cleaners in the house, help Elsie in the post office, do a bit for her because she's too fat to clean right. I bake, do washing, light fires, clean windows – you name it, I do it.'

He asked whether Eileen would be expected to do the same after the change-about, and Nellie answered in the affirmative. Her Eileen didn't go to bits when pregnant. In fact, she could probably scrub a floor half an hour after giving birth, because she came from good stock. 'Strong bones, you see. It's the Irish in us.'

So this was where Eileen would be living with her much-loved husband. There would be no electricity, no gas, no decent plumbing. Lamplight would suit her, as would the shimmering flames from logs on an open fire. There was, no doubt, a thriving black market in meat, there were fresh vegetables, plenty of eggs and an abundance of untainted air. She would thrive here. Yet he hoped she would not become ruddy-cheeked, because her porcelain skin and delicate features were perfect as they were. This was supposed to have stopped. Hypnotherapy was helpful, but not a complete answer. Anyway, the fellow she had married was strong, so was it worth dying just for one chance with Eileen? Did he know the answer to that question?

At the house named Willows, he was introduced to Miss Hilda Pickavance, whom he recognized from Kitty's funeral, a Jean from Home Farm, a Gill from the gatehouse, a babe in arms called Maisie, also from the gatehouse, several evacuees, and Elsie Openshaw from the post office. She looked far too large for one of those diminutive houses, and she had a great deal to say for herself. The cacophony was deafening. Nellie threw out the evacuees, told Elsie to shut up, sat down and asked for a cup of tea for herself and her chauffeur. 'The lads are still asleep in the car,' she said. 'Right, doc. You tell 'em what's happening to Liverpool.'

So he was forced to repeat all that he had related to Nellie at the start of their journey. Apart from little Maisie, everyone in the room was quiet. Unimpressed by tales of arson and bombardment, she continued to coo. Her belly was full, so all was well with the world.

'And you're going back to all that, Nellie?' Elsie asked.

'I don't know,' Nellie replied. 'I mean Crosby's safe enough. But there's a bit of family business going on, and Eileen might want to tackle it herself. Only there's Keith's job and his house, you know–'

'Safe,' pronounced Miss Pickavance. 'If they have to remain in Crosby, so be it.'

Nellie glared at Tom. None of this would have mattered had he been able to keep his son in order. But she had to admit, however grudgingly, that Mel had probably taken after her mother, who liked and desired close male company. Peter Bingley wasn't the only spoilt brat in the mix. Nellie had spoilt Eileen, and Eileen had been too easy with Mel. Tom Bingley might be a weak man, but the Kennedy/Watson clan was far from perfect.

'I were looking for'ard to that,' Elsie complained. 'Goin' t' Crosby, seein' 'ow t' other 'alf lives.'

Nellie straightened her spine. 'For'ard? For'ard? Ah mun tell thee now, Elsie, tha were terrified when I asked thee.'

Elsie started to laugh. Nellie's attempt at Boltonese wasn't half bad. In fact, she was picking up a gradely way of talking if she'd shape a bit better and concentrate. 'Tha's passed th' exam,' she roared. Her body shook like a giant jelly. It was clear that she had no ongoing relationship with corsetry. Perhaps she wore it on special occasions, and this occasion was far from special, since rolls of blubber collided all over her very ample body.

Tom thought of Marie and smiled. She had her corsets made by a lady named Mrs Wray, the corsetière extraordinaire of Crosby, Liverpool. Now that Marie was more relaxed, she had made her husband laugh about corsets. 'No woman can taste true happiness unless she experiences the intense joy of those few moments after her release from whalebone. Freed flesh itches, and scratching is ecstasy.' Yes, Marie was coming along nicely, and he wished with all his heart that he had never met Eileen Watson.

A young boy entered through the back door. Behind him, a polite, blond-headed pony put his head into the house. 'Stay,' ordered the boy. 'Good boy. I'll get you a carrot.'

Tom grinned. At least Eileen's youngest hadn't placed the animal on a draining board. 'Are you Bertie?'

'Yes, I am. Did you bring Gran back?'

'I did. She has your presents, but you can't open them before Christmas Day. So you're the horseman.'

Bertie fed his best friend. 'Or a vet if I'm clever enough.' He turned and looked at Tom. 'Are the Germans knocking Liverpool down?'

'Some of it, yes. We will rebuild it, son. Nothing will ever make our city lie down completely. Just you remember to say your prayers. That's all we can do for now.'

Bertie nodded thoughtfully. 'Gran said on the phone you go down sometimes and rescue people. She says you're a very brave man who couldn't go to war because of two left feet and a duff ear.'

Tom found himself laughing. 'I'm a bit old for war, Bertie. So I do what I can.' He felt strangely pleased because Nellie had praised him; like a schoolboy who had been given a star for getting his homework right. Hell's bells, he was a doctor, a diagnostician, a saver of human life. Yet he blushed because a loudmouth with a punch like a heavyweight boxer had expressed approval of him. 'I'd better go,' he said. 'Patients to see, things to do.' He accepted gratefully gifts of four chickens, two dozen eggs, two pounds of butter, some cream and an assortment of vegetables. These items were to be split between his household and Frances Morrison's for Christmas. When the sleepy boys had been evicted from his car, he waved to the gathered crowd. It was a crowd because Elsie was there, he supposed. He liked her; she was a good laugh.

As he drove away, he looked again at the idyll spread all round him. Even in the dead of winter, the moors were spectacular. Frost lingered to decorate fields and skeletal trees. This was a Christmas card begging to be photographed. He should have brought the camera to make cards for next year. He could have taken shots of the house she'd be living in soon. If she came back here, that was. He could not imagine her walking away from Mel at the moment.

Outside her house in Willows Edge, he stopped the car. These cottages were beautifully built, though probably not much bigger than those in Rachel Street. But they were pretty because they were constructed of stone, had gardens, paths, gates and solid front doors. Yes, this was a long way from slum territory. He had to forget her. He'd scarcely given her a thought throughout the adventure he had shared with his newly resurrected wife. 'I'm an animal,' he said aloud. Sometimes, he felt thoroughly ashamed of himself. This was one of those times.

Mel watched Gloria and her mother leaving their house and heading for the village. After hanging around in the cold for twenty minutes, she was not in the best of moods, and her teeth were chattering madly. But she had to see Peter, needed to warn him of her mother's intentions regarding their schools. Dr Bingley was in Bolton with Gran and the boys, so Peter was finally alone when his mother and sister left to do the shopping. Mel was still walking up the path when he opened the front door. 'Come in,' he said. 'They'll be back in about an hour.' He led her through to the dining room, bent to give her a kiss.

But she pulled away from him without understanding her action. 'How's your back?' she asked. Did she love this boy? Did she?

'Sore. Too sore for fun. And I can't live like this, Mel. Gloria in excelsis and I have never had a great deal in common, but hatred's hard to take, especially at Christmas.' He paused and tapped his fingers on the table. 'We have to teach them all a lesson.'

So she informed him of her mother's intention to visit the head teachers of Merchants Girls' and Boys' schools. 'You don't know what my family's capable of, Peter. And my mother will do just about anything to keep us apart. She may look all sweetness and light, but she's powerful. Quiet, yet lethal. I suppose it's because we're poor. If I throw my chance away, it will break her heart. She wants all her children to have the best possible chance in life.'

Peter, too, had news to divulge. His sister had already blackened Mel's name with just about every girl in their years. 'She's been phoning everyone except the school cat. You'll be lonely when term starts,' he said. 'She's told everyone we're doing it, that we were caught doing it by my dad and your stepfather in a house off Scotland Road. You have no idea how angry she is.'

At one time Mel could not have imagined Gloria in a temper, but she had felt the edge of it very recently, and that edge was honed to perfect sharpness. Isolation, unpleasant though it might be, did not frighten her. But if anything affected her work, she would surely become distraught. There might be whisperings, even 'accidental' collisions in corridors, elbows in her ribs. 'That's that, then,' she said. 'We have to finish.'

'No.'

'There's no other answer.'

'Really?' He outlined the plan. They would collect clothes, money and a little food. A friend in Rainford had been taken by his parents to a ski resort in Switzerland. The family would not return to their house until the day before school was due to reopen, and there was always a spare key behind the shed in a pot near the raspberry canes. 'A short ride up the East Lancashire Road, and we'll be there.'

'I can't do that to my mother, Peter.'

'Look what she's willing to do to us,' was his swift response.

Another valid point fell from Mel's lips. 'You've got stitches.'

'Yes, and if they weren't in my back I'd snip the buggers out myself. You can do it.'

'I wouldn't dare.'

'Then you don't love me.'

She heard the petulance, caught a brief glimpse of the child in him, dismissed the thought instantly. She was still capable of being infantile and silly, and he was the same age. 'I am not taking your stitches out. Your dad will do it in a few days.'

His jaw dropped slightly. 'What? You are condemning me to Christmas in this house with Gloria the glorious, with a sulking mother and a father who wishes he could touch you the way I did? As for you, how will you feel in the company of a mother who's willing to betray you to top brass? Well?'

'My mother's ... different. She's dead straight, that's all. I can do something about the damage your sister's causing, and my parents will make sure I get a good Christmas. My mother's said her piece, and she won't drone on. Gran's the droner. My mother's quiet most of the time.' And Eileen was happy. It was important to Mel that her mother was happy. 'I'm not running away with you. I'm not putting Mam through that pain.' A feeling akin to relief flooded her veins. She probably didn't love him at all.

They argued back and forth for the better part of the allocated hour, at which time he asked her to leave. And she refused.

'What?' he almost screamed. 'They'll be back.' Panic invaded his chest. He needed to talk to Mel, needed time away from here so that he could express himself and his fears to the one person he trusted.

'Exactly.'

'And?'

'And I'm going to be a lawyer.' She definitely didn't love him. It was all sex, and sex was a powerful thing. 'It's over. You and I are no longer an item.'

'What?'

The front door opened. Mel rose gracefully from the table, abandoned her erstwhile boyfriend and walked into the hall. 'Gloria Bingley,' she said plainly. 'I am going to see Dr Ryan to ask for an internal examination, which will prove me a virgin and you the biggest fair-weather friend since Judas. You have not only betrayed me; you have also told a massive untruth which is a slander. My name is blackened at school, and I shall see you in court. Or perhaps you would like to settle out of court once I prove my intactness?' She was glad she'd read that law book of Miss Morrison's just out of interest. 'Ask your father to let the moths out of his wallet and give me my start at Cambridge. And your brother can go to hell. He's a spoilt, whining brat I'd sooner lie down with the rag-and-bone man.'

Gloria burst into tears and ran upstairs. She should have realized that Clever-Clogs Watson would get the better of her, because the girl never lost an argument. In the debating society, she'd even carried a motion on communism being a good thing for Britain.

Marie stared sadly at Mel. 'Please, Mel.'

'Please what, Mrs Bingley? I think it's time I pleased myself as far as your family's concerned. You're married to a dirty old man...' She shouldn't have said that. 'And your son's a weak, spineless waste of space. Gloria broadcast an enormous lie about me and her brother, so can you blame me for asking my doctor to give me written proof of my status?' She would be the barrister, she decided in that moment. There were few females called to the bar, but she would improve that number by one. Arguing was second nature to her.

'Mel, you are cruel. Please stop,' Marie begged again.

But the girl remained in the saddle of a very high horse. 'Once. Once I allowed him to touch me, because he's handsome and ... and desirable. But it was just touching.' The back door slammed. 'There he goes. Your little boy has left the house, Mrs Bingley. Perhaps he needs a playpen.'

Marie placed her shopping on the floor. 'Slander works both ways, you know. Would you like it ifTom took you to court for describing him as a dirty old man?'

Mel tutted. 'Prove I said it.'

'There were ear-witnesses.'

Mel shook her head. 'Family. My witnesses are a couple of dozen girls who have been informed by your daughter that I am misbehaving with your son. No contest. And, being a family doctor, your husband has to remain squeaky clean. Remember the no smoke without fire saying?'

A few seconds of deadlock followed. 'Wait here, then.' Marie turned on her heel and walked into the office. Alone in the hall, Mel could hear Gloria sobbing in her room. *I didn't know myself till now. When it comes to making stuff happen, I am in my element. Parliament? High Court? Certainly not Mrs Peter Bingley, that's for sure.*

Marie returned with a cheque and pushed it into Mel's hand.

'Ah. Thirty pieces of silver.' Without looking at the scrap of paper, Mel tore it into tiny flakes that floated like snow down to the parquet floor.

'That was three hundred pounds!' Marie gasped. 'You asked for money.'

'Three hundred pieces of silver, then. I'm not purchasable, even at that price.'

'But you said–'

'I say a lot of things, Mrs Bingley. Now, I am off to see my doctor. You will tell her upstairs to telephone all those she has misinformed. Let her say it was a dare or something of that nature. As for your son – well, I can only wish you the best of luck. If he comes anywhere near me, have your sutures ready.' She walked out of the house.

Her legs didn't match any more. Stumbling like a recovering alcoholic who was having a slight relapse, Mel staggered to the end of the road. She had to make a better job of this walking business, because he would be waiting round the corner. Yes, there he was. Peter Bingley was beautiful. He was the sort of creature who might have given Michelangelo's David a run for his money. Not that statues could run, of course. Why was she having daft thoughts at a time like this when her reputation was in tatters?

She stopped and stared at him. He was across the road, frozen like a rabbit caught in headlights. 'Stay away from me, Bingley,' she roared at the top of her voice. Curtains fluttered. Two old ladies on opposite sides of the road ambled to their gates, shawls clutched as protection against the bitter cold. 'Go home,' Mel shrieked. 'Go home to your disgusting sister.' He ran, and she found herself smiling.

But when she reached her own lodgings, Mel was no longer proud of herself. Gloria was a friend of long standing. She was upset because Mel had not confided in her about Peter, and although her behaviour had been bad, she was probably deeply hurt. It must all be put right. But first, there was an appointment with Dr Ryan.

Tom brought in the food from Home Farm. He made two trips from car to house, because a couple of chickens and all the vegetables took some shifting. 'Nearly as big as turkeys, those things,' he said. 'Where's Keith? Where's Mel? And how's your Miss Morrison?'

'As excited as a child because she won't be alone at Christmas. She's a love. We sit and talk to her every day, but she tires.' Eileen gave him a cup of tea and a bit of date and walnut cake. 'To answer your question, Keith's gone to buy me a collar and lead. That's what he said, anyway, but really he'll be looking for my Christmas present. And Mel's gone to see Dr Ryan to prove she's a virgin.'

'What?' He almost choked. Cakes seemed dry these days, probably due to all the rationing. How lucky were the people who lived out of town... 'To prove she's a virgin?'

Eileen bit her lip. But it all had to be said. 'Gloria has been busy on the phone. She's told the whole class that Mel and Peter have had full sex. It was a nasty lie to tell, Tom.'

'What?' He leapt to his feet. Gloria was a sweet girl who wouldn't damage a fly. He couldn't believe his ears. 'Gloria? My Gloria?'

Eileen nodded. 'Yes, the very same. Sit down and hear me out, Tom. You know I have a temper?'

'Of course.' He sat. 'I explained away the evidence of your most recent assault as something that happened during the retrieval of our children. A falling brick if I remember correctly.'

'Well, my daughter has a temper, too. She's gone through your household today like a hot knife cutting butter. Peter is damned to hell, while Marie took the full blast, including the information that my headstrong girl thinks of you as a dirty old man. She regrets saying that, though she has told me on at least one occasion that you look at her in a certain way.'

'She reminds me of someone.'

'Yes.' There would be no nonsense. If she glimpsed the fringe of trouble, he would be out of this house in a trice. 'My daughter will be derided at school because of Gloria. So Mel made a scene, demanded compensation, bullied your wife into writing a cheque. Madam tore it up and stormed out. She then made another un-pretty scene outside. It involved Peter and she has ended her relationship with him.'

Tom remembered life pre-Eileen. It had been boring, but peaceful. 'Three generations of angry women; there's your mother, then you, then Mel. She got more than your beauty. I'm convinced that the brain came from your mother, via you.'

She told him the rest of it. At first Mel wanted to get a solicitor and apply for permission to print in the Crosby newspaper a statement saying that the gossip was malicious and untrue. But a calmer period had ensued, and Mel was missing Gloria already. 'So I don't know what to do,' Eileen concluded. 'You know what they're like at this age – up one minute, down the next.'

Gloria hadn't been like that, but he didn't say anything. His daughter had been good, perhaps too good. Of the two, Peter was the more unpredictable, and Tom had wondered of late about the boy's true nature. He was a better than average sportsman and a successful scholar, but there was a gentleness that went a little too far for Tom's comfort. He dismissed the idea yet again from his mind. Some heterosexuals were gentle, some homosexuals vicious. And some doctors were confused, because Peter had proved his sexuality by messing about with Mel.

'Tom?'

'What?'

'He has to stay away from her.'

The visitor sipped his cooling tea. 'How far did they go?'

'About as far as you and I did on one unfortunate occasion.'

He smiled.

'What's funny?' she asked.

'Nothing.' He could not tell her that the smile was a demonstration of relief about Peter. 'I suppose we all react differently when we realize that our children are almost adult. One minute it's a high chair and Farley's rusks, and the next they're experimenting with the opposite sex.'

'We have to get the two girls back together, Tom. Gloria's a steadying, sensible influence, and Mel keeps her optimistic. And I don't want Marie hurt. I mean, look at the man she married – isn't he trouble enough?' It was her turn to smile.

Mel came in, stopped in her tracks when she saw Tom, recovered quickly, and slammed an envelope on the kitchen table. 'Virgo intacta,' she said. 'And will you tell that daft daughter of yours that she's the nearest thing I have to a sister? I'm lumbered with three brothers, and she's stuck with Peter. I can't manage without her.' She stalked out.

'Going to be a barrister now,' Eileen said.

Tom picked up his trilby. 'It's enough to make you pity the criminal fraternity,' he said sadly before leaving the house.

Alone in the kitchen, Eileen found herself chuckling. He was perfectly correct. Mel would go onward and upward as long as nothing stood in her way. If anything did threaten to impede her progress, she would talk it out of existence. Hilda Pickavance, God bless her, had put away a sum that would support Mel through university. The bank book was to be Mel's Christmas gift from that lovely woman. If only the damage Gloria had done could be put right... 'What the–?' Keith had just entered the house. 'What's that?'

'I told you I'd get you a collar and lead.'

She stared hard at him. Once again, he was acting as daft as a brush. 'But ... there's a dog fastened to all that tack.'

'Is there? I never noticed.'

'And what's our landlady going to say?'

Keith grinned. 'She's in on the act.'

A diminutive black and white animal wagged a sad string of tail. 'What make is it?' Eileen asked.

'It's a spoodle, so it might not shed.'

She refused to ask.

'I made up the spoodle bit. Cross between a spaniel and a poodle, and she was cross, too, that woman. Her poodle passed its exams for dog shows and the spaniel got at her.'

Eileen could resist no longer. She picked up the pup and held it close to her chest. Keith was complaining about the bloody dog getting the best seat in the house, but his wife scarcely listened. 'Your mummy was got at, babe,' she said. 'I know how she must have felt, because I'm got at all the time.' The little animal was a bundle of soft and silky curls. 'I never had a dog, Keith.'

'I know.'

'Always wanted one.'

'I know.'

'Will it be all right with our baby? Will it kill your chickens?'

'Yes and no. He's from a farm in Lydiate, and he's been handled by children since he was five days old. His mother's very intelligent – all giant poodles are – and his dad's a spaniel. Spaniels are daft, clever, soft-hearted and loving. He'll be fine for both my babies – you and the passenger. As for chickens – he's been pecked to buggery and nothing died.'

'I love you.'

'I know.'

'And if you say "I know" again, I'll hit you.'

'I know. What's for tea, love?'

Sixteen

'Right.' Sister Pearson intended to teach Jay Collins a sharp lesson very soon. The man would not listen; therefore, he would not learn. He was refusing some of his food, kept complaining loudly about anything and everything, and was currently making a song and dance about yet another sub-standard cup of tea. Did he not understand that even a cuppa was part of the intake that would balance injected insulin? How would she get through to him? This primed and prepared audience might help. She sighed heavily. Anything was worth a try, she supposed.

She folded her arms and tapped an irritated foot on the floor. 'This delightful patient, ladies, is beyond the pale. He's been driving me perpendicular, the cleaners round the U-bend, and even the doctors are having to see a doctor.' She glared at Jay. 'Listen, you. There is nothing wrong with that cup of tea. It's the same as everyone else's, and nobody has complained.'

Jay arranged his features to express deep hurt. 'One look at you, and they daren't bloody complain. This tastes like somebody's peed in it.' He slammed the green cup into its green saucer. 'Disgusting.'

'Oh, I see. So you're used to the taste of urine, are you?'

'I work on farms. We see, smell and taste all sorts. Can't be helped, cos muck gets everywhere. Wouldn't suit you. You've got that ants in the pants illness, haven't you? Always scrubbing your hands – no wonder they're red. Stick a bit of Vaseline on them. You want to slow down, you do.'

Sylvia Pearson addressed her small entourage of cadets, first years, a second year and, bringing up the rear, a man with a bucket. She didn't know who he was, but she felt marginally better with a man in tow. If all else failed, he could threaten to hit the impatient patient with said bucket. 'This is all deliberate and for attention,' she advised the group. 'A sure sign of a bored man. He is on the mend after a mere twenty-four hours. Remember, some men are children, and they're naughty when well.'

'Yes, sister,' chorused her minions. The man with the bucket scratched his ear. He had work to do, but he'd been swept up by this crowd somewhere between beds eight and seven. He'd gone with the flow, because the flow had happened to be going in his direction, but he felt a right fool standing here with his second best bucket while the mickey got taken out of the bloke in bed three. This woman certainly went on a fair bit. She was opening her mouth to let the next lot of words see the light of day. He wished she'd hurry up, because it was nearly time for his tea break, and somebody's mam had sent in a chocolate cake. There'd be very little chocolate and no eggs in it, but it looked a bit like a cake.

'Why, oh why did you have to get a chronic illness?' the sister asked. 'A broken leg, traction, a bit of dysentery – all those things are soon sorted out. But no. You have to develop something that needs surveillance, and you don't look after yourself. You'll be doing the hokey-cokey here for years, in, out, in out. And you've been told how to manage. You're even one of the first in this country to test the home hypodermic.'

Jay grinned cheekily. 'Isn't she lovely when she's angry? Did anyone ever tell you, Sis, that behind the evil frown there's a gorgeous, sensuous woman? The staff, patients and visitors here say you park your broomstick in the bike sheds, but they're not being fair. And it's Christmas. You should get treated better at Christmas.' He was going home. If he had to steal clothes, drug staff, and walk ten miles north, he would be with Gill and Maisie by Christmas Day. In fact, he might seriously consider murder if it would get him away from Bolton Royal Infirmary.

Sister Pearson turned to her group of students. 'Monitor this one while you can,' she advised.

'He's not the first to cause this kind of bother. On paediatrics, you'll find similar behaviour in the under tens. The man is emotionally retarded.'

Jay continued unimpressed. 'So a Christmas kiss is out of the question, then? Or a quick fumble in the linen store?'

She needed to laugh, but she wouldn't. He would be missed. The man was a nuisance and a troublemaker, but her ward would be as dead as a path lab without him. He was attractive too, and she was sorry about the diabetes. If he carried on in denial, he would age very suddenly, lose his looks, his sparkle, a limb, a kidney, his life. 'Mr Collins, if you don't take your illness seriously, Maisie will walk up the aisle without you. In fact, she might even start school with just a mother at home. You don't want to die, not yet.'

She was being serious, Jay decided. Her tone was softer, and she cared enough to warn him. He felt warned.

Sister Pearson was getting a bit bored with the bucket man. He was like a spectator at some tennis match, head moving from side to side whenever she or Jay spoke. 'What do you want?' she asked finally. 'I wasn't aware that you were a member of my staff.'

'Hospital maintenance,' said Bucket Man. 'I'm on a job when I can get to it.'

'Oh?' She looked him up and down. 'Why, precisely, are you here?'

'Precisely, Sister, it's him.' The bucket was waved in the direction of the patient. 'He wants me to take the air out of his pipes. Says he's an emergency.'

Everyone burst out laughing. Even the poor little cadets in their gingham uniforms had a good giggle.

But Jay didn't laugh. He fixed Sylvia Pearson with a steely stare. 'There is nothing more painful than trapped wind. I can't sleep because of it. He's come to bleed my pipes.'

The sister wiped her eyes. 'Radiator?' she asked.

Jay nodded. 'Can't sleep for the gurgling. Why? What did you think I meant?'

She turned and sailed away, a flotilla of minions behind her. Jay chuckled and thanked Joe for coming up from maintenance. But oh, he was fed up. If he stopped causing traffic jams, arguments and heart attacks, there'd be nothing at all to laugh at. He was in a cream room with a green floor. The bedspreads were green, curtains green, face of the man opposite green. 'Grab your kidney bowl,' Jay screamed. The walls were two shades of cream, upper pale, lower a shade darker.

All lockers were cream with green tops. The man across the way continued to vomit. Jay pressed his bell. When a nurse appeared, he waved her in the direction of bed four, stomach ulcer, kidney bowl, face like an oversized bunion. Jay had heard of being browned off, but he was definitely greened and creamed off. It was time to go home, surely? He was warm, dry and conscious, so why was he here? They were usually glad to kick folk out at Christmas.

He had to think about himself. There was a right way, and a wrong way. The right way could be tedious, but it might stop the hokey-cokey. It would be necessary to stay at home for a while and trust Phil Watson to do all the jobs in the book. Then he would have to start walking, watching himself carefully and being at the ready with sweets. The next step needed to be checking on Phil, walking a bit further and staying out for a bit longer every day. Finally, he could do a few jobs. But he was never going to feel young and free again. As a married man and a father, perhaps he had no right to feel free.

The sister was back. Joe with the bucket did a disappearing act; he'd seen and heard enough of Sister Pearson for one day. 'Mr Collins?'

'Yes, Sis?'

'Your wife's here to take you home. I've given her my condolences, and she seemed to understand perfectly. Normally, we'd keep an eye on you for a few more days, but it's your baby's first Christmas.'

Jay leapt from the bed and kissed the sister's hand. 'A miracle,' he cried. 'I was spark out here a matter of hours ago, and you warmed my cockles, sweetheart. If I wasn't married, I'd propose.'

'And I might scare you to death by saying yes.'

'Promises.' Gill was walking towards him. Apart from on their wedding day, she had never looked so lovely. He had a wife, he had a daughter, he had a life. These were special, and he must start taking care of all three. 'Why didn't you tell me I was going home?' he asked the sister.

'Because I wanted to see your face when she came for you. And what I did earlier was staged just for you. Well, except for the man with the bucket. Stop the daftness and stay well. Please, I beg you. Diabetics can have wonderful lives. You just have to be careful, that's all. No beer.'

'I'll try.'

'Denial is normal in the young, so this is the day you grow up, love. Now, you have to take it all on board, and you will need monitoring. Good luck.'

He took the suitcase from Gill, noticing when he hugged her how tense she was. On closer inspection, her face looked drawn, her eyes sad and dark. He had done this. All his larking about and getting sick had taken its toll on the relatively new mother. What sort of man was he? 'I'm sorry,' he said.

'We've got a girl,' was her reply.

'Yes, our Maisie.'

'No, Land Army. Betty. She's done the house lovely.'

'I'm glad, sweetheart. I'm glad.' He claimed his own place in the ward by drawing curtains round his bed. Green curtains, of course. While he dressed, he fixed his mind on the poor girl who was his unfortunate wife. As he skimmed the surface of recent years, he wondered how the hell she'd put up with him. *Why do I do it? Is it to ward off sadness? Doctors say diabetes can make you depressed, so maybe my body was telling me I was ill, and I fought it by acting the rubber pig.*

Right, he was dressed. Right, he was lucky – bloody lucky. His Gill would always have gone to the ends of the earth to help a person in trouble, while he'd spun round making more grief for her. It had to stop. His pancreas didn't work properly, so he needed insulin. Food had to be measured to match the insulin, and any work needed to be done slowly, carefully, and in the company of sugar and young Phil.

It didn't mean there'd be no fun; but she mustn't get tired. She could start giving Maisie National Dried for a kick-off, because breast-feeding took a lot out of her, especially with a greedy little monkey like Maisie. At almost seven months, the baby was as strong as a carthorse, so she must shape up and wean. Jay would become a good husband. Well, nearly good.

The dog was a natural born lunatic. Shy for the first hour after his arrival at St Michael's Road, Spoodle soon changed his ways and went through the house like a fine-toothed comb in search of lice. He got into small places, demonstrated an uncontrollable urge to eat coal, chew newspapers, slippers and shoes, and finally settled for the company of Mel, who was fun, because she owned a small, soft rubber ball and he could pick it up with needle-sharp puppy teeth.

Exhausted after chasing Eileen's Christmas present all over the house, Keith placed himself next to her on the sofa. 'That Spoodle,' he moaned. 'I'm losing the will to live.'

'I knew we wouldn't last,' she said mournfully. 'It's all over, isn't it? He's chosen Mel over me.'

He drew her close and buried his face in her hair. 'He's moving back to Willows with us, Eileen. Spoodle's going to be a country dog, lots of walks, coming to work with me, playing with the boys.'

'But Mel will miss him.'

He didn't say anything. As stepfather, he had to

edge his way carefully into the established family. The boys still called him Keith, but Mel had started to use 'Dad', and that pleased him no end. Mel, however, was used to bending her mother to her will. She couldn't manage it with the bigger and more important aspects of life, but she was certainly capable of keeping the dog. But he refused to put his foot down heavily or too soon. Step-parent was the right title, because stepping softly was essential. If he marched in roaring like a lion, he'd get a press similar to Cinderella's ugly relations, so he kept his counsel.

'She loves him, Keith.'

'Yes, she does. Wait till he empties his little tummy and bladder all over her bedroom rug. When he does, you'll have your dog back.'

Eileen snuggled into her man and closed her eyes. He was definitely the most comfortable seat in the place that had become their living area. Miss Morrison was fast asleep in the next room. She would wake as if in response to an alarm clock when cocoa time arrived. For meals and tablets she was always alert, but for the remainder of the day she talked and slept. As time went on, she talked less frequently and slept more. Dr Ryan said it was natural in a woman of such an age, but Eileen still managed to worry about the old lady.

As predicted by Keith, Mel stalked in with a curly-coated puppy held at arm's length. 'He's sprung a leak,' she complained. 'He drips all the time.'

'They do,' Keith answered. 'So would you if you drank a lot and had a bladder the size of a walnut. He needs to go out every few minutes to get an idea of what's expected of him. To do that, he must live down here. I'll put paper near the door for during the night and, when he's older, he'll have a dog flap in my kitchen at Willows.' There, it was said. Without crashing through any barriers, Keith had made his point. Spoodle was Eileen's, and he would continue to be Eileen's.

Mel gathered up mop, bucket and disinfectant. Muttering darkly about the marking of territory, she made for the door. 'He doesn't do stairs,' she said.

'Centre of gravity's different from ours,' Keith told her. 'They master that skill within weeks, so keep your bedroom door shut. Once he starts, he'll eat anything and everything.'

The girl walked out.

Eileen expressed the opinion that Miss Morrison would miss Spoodle. He had chewed the sleeve of her best bed jacket, but she was delighted with him. 'I think he makes her feel happy because he's an idiot.' The couple stared into the fire, dozed and waited for the tinkling of Miss Morrison's bell. The dog, wedged between them, enjoyed the slumber of the truly innocent. Chewed paper and coal-marked carpets meant nothing to him. He was a perfect dog in a perfect world.

The perfect world was interrupted by a knocking at the back door. Keith went to answer while Eileen lifted her little doggy-baby into her arms. He was gorgeous, and he knew he was gorgeous. He buried his nose in her breast and snored lightly.

'Eileen?'

It was Tom. 'Hello. Where's Keith?'

'Making tea.' He bent to stroke the pup, allowed his fingers to stray slightly off course, and noted her sharp intake of breath. Acting as if nothing of note had happened, Tom took a seat nearer to the fire. 'Just a short walk, and I'm freezing.'

'Yes.' She hated her body, despised it because of its reaction. It occurred to her in that moment that women, like men, were capable of wanting more than one partner. The fable about monogamy could never be real. A woman was expected to marry and live happily ever after, her devotion to her husband special and exclusive. She would never betray Keith, but she now knew that she had to be stronger than ever, because Dr Thomas Bingley enlivened her, filled her with desire and wanted her. Being wanted was stimulating. But it was his sin, not hers.

'How's Mel?' he asked.

She shrugged. 'Well, she hasn't broken any windows, but she was as angry as I've ever seen her. She loves your daughter like a sister.'

'Love can be quite a nuisance, Eileen.'

'I've never found it so.'

'Really?'

She shook her head.

'Lucky you.' He laughed at the puppy. Spoodle was trying to climb up to his owner's shoulder, and he kept sliding down. 'He seems to be practising for the piste.' His eyes travelled up to meet hers. 'Though they're hardly nursery slopes, are they? Not for a tiny dog like that one.'

And she was blushing, damn it all. 'Stop it.'

'You want me,' he mouthed soundlessly.

'I wanted a big house of my own, but I won't

get one.'

Keith entered with a tea tray and jam tarts. 'Plum jam, sorry,' he said. 'We couldn't get anything more exotic.'

But Tom was still staring at Eileen. 'You don't know, do you? She hasn't told you.'

She continued to blush. He must not say anything untoward in front of Keith, or Keith would flatten him. Accepting a cup of tea from her husband, she managed to drag her eyes away from Tom. Tea, puppies and jam tarts were ingredients that didn't make a good recipe, so Keith removed the pup from the mix. He had made a secure run in the garden. It was designed to be Spoodle's bathroom, and he needed to shiver in it for a few moments.

Alone again with his beautiful prey, Tom continued. 'When she dies, this house is yours.'

'What?' Eileen almost dropped her cup.

'She has no one else. If you hadn't come along, it would have gone to an animal shelter. So you have your wish. You shall go to the ball, Cinders.'

Keith came back. 'Darling,' she said. 'Tom says Miss Morrison has left the house to me in her will. I feel uncomfortable. She's only known me for a couple of years–'

'No family,' Tom interjected. 'Sometimes, these old dears feel happy if they can find someone decent to inherit. She has no family, so why not you? She thinks the world of Mel, and she knows the money would be spent wisely.'

Keith clattered his cup. 'Is there a reason for your visit?' He didn't want the man sitting here discussing Eileen's future. Doctors, he decided, were intrusive people who fiddled about with detail. They wanted to know what they didn't need to know. He had met Tom Bingley's type before.

'The girls.' Tom placed his cup on a side table. 'We have to get them together in a supervised situation, but not at our house. Peter has gone into mourning in a back bedroom, so it would be better here.'

'They don't need supervision,' Keith almost snapped. 'They're intelligent girls with a sensitive problem to discuss. Let them get on with it.'

Eileen noticed the dark anger in Tom's eyes. He clearly didn't like being taken to task by someone he regarded as his inferior. 'Send or bring Gloria here,' she suggested. 'I shall be here all day tomorrow, and I can supervise if war breaks out. They need their dignity, you know. They aren't small children. What happened between...' She paused for a second. 'What happened between your son and our daughter is a delicate subject. No adult should intrude while it's being discussed.'

Tom noted the 'our' and the pause. 'Right, I shall take myself off. It might be as well if Mel rings and asks Gloria to come. They're both bereft, but we can only hope for the best. No, no need to stand up. I'll see myself out.'

Keith remained on his feet. 'I'm going for the puppy before he freezes to death.' His tone was as cold as the weather. He didn't like Tom Bingley. With steely determination, he left them together for a third time. Eileen would see the man off if he tried anything. He stood outside the back door for a few minutes. In the sitting room, he had felt the thickened atmosphere, had caught

Tom Bingley almost leering at her. 'Touch her, and I'll kill you,' he muttered.

'How's Marie?' Eileen asked the visitor.

'Fine. Abused as a child, but she's coming to terms. Our relationship's as good as it's ever going to be.'

She noticed. She noticed the arrogance, the mandatory inclusion of himself in his reply. His wife was in working order and was serving his needs. He offered no information about Marie, who was there to keep house, rear children and, above all, to satisfy his lust. 'Still with the WVS?'

'Of course. She likes to do her bit.'

'We knit.' Eileen shook her head. 'Miss Morrison's knitting is imaginative, so I pull it to bits and make socks with heels.'

'It's good that you allow her to feel useful.' He smiled and left the scene.

At the back door, he came face to face with Keith. 'Good night,' he said. 'That's a nice puppy.'

'Yes. Eileen's always wanted a dog.' When the door was closed behind the intruder, Keith locked it. Bingley would hear the key turning. It was childish, but he couldn't resist. The man was locked out, unwanted, unnecessary. And Eileen was waiting for her dog. He walked back into their living room. 'I agree with you. The man is crazy with desire, and I suppose I can understand that, because so am I. Do you think he's capable of something nasty, like…'

'Rape? No, never. He loves himself far too much to allow that kind of trouble to affect him. And I'll never hurt you, so I wouldn't go to him willingly.' She felt guilty, as if she had already betrayed a wonderful man. She hadn't. Her body had gone one way, but her heart and soul remained on track.

'If he touches you, I'll kill him.'

'We're going home, darling. He won't be there. And while I have to agree that he's attractive, I have my man. Good Lord, haven't I enough with you pouncing and kissing all the time?'

'Would you like me to stop?'

'No. It's the best kind of problem to have. I'm coming to love my place next to the sink, and I like the way you...' She searched for the word. Dominate was wrong. 'The way you manage me. It's exciting.'

'No complaints, then?'

'You know you're an excellent lover.'

'Takes one to know one.'

'Thank you.'

The mutual admiration society spent the next few minutes discussing Miss Morrison's will. They wondered how Tom Bingley knew, because the old lady would never have used him as a witness to the document. His attempt to pursue Eileen in this house had not gone down well, and she had even changed her doctor to underline her displeasure.

'I'm not going to tell her I know,' Eileen decided. 'So if she changes her mind, she doesn't need to feel bad. What I never had, I'll never miss. Yes, it would be lovely to have a second home over here, but I'd rather she lived a lot longer. She worked hard for years in that school of hers. I read somewhere that we'll soon have television. She'd love that.'

Spoodle had discovered the fire. It was warm, bright and cheerful. He tried very hard to sit like a proper dog, two legs at the front, two at the back, skimpy little tail supposedly acting as a rudder. His attempt to achieve a level of dignity failed parlously. The tired pup found he had too many feet, and that they were unnecessarily large. They also preferred to line up, a front paw, a back one, then two more in similar order. With a tail that was as much use as a piece of thin string, he fell over sideways, rolled, scrambled to his silly feet and tried again.

Eileen was hysterical; even Keith found tears streaming down his face. This was better than a Charlie Chaplin movie. Like Charlie, Spoodle could not walk in a straight line, was unable to sit in a normal fashion, and didn't do stairs. Like Charlie, he was going to be eternally forgivable.

The young dog eyed them lugubriously. He scratched an ear to prove his nonchalance, then repeated his trick. Determined to demonstrate to humanity that all he did was carefully planned, he spread himself out on the rug, all four legs stretched, nose in his front paws. Within seconds, he was snoring gently.

Eileen mopped her face. 'The dog's a fool,' she said.

'Yes. Dry me as well, please. He's a clown, Eileen. I think he'll fit in with us very well. Very well indeed.'

Hilda was preparing notes for a history lesson to be given in the New Year. But she couldn't concentrate on the task. Something was wrong, but she had no real idea what, and she felt seriously silly. Phil, Rob and Bertie were all upstairs and safe. The oldest boy was probably continuing the angry, sweeping charcoal drawing he had begun earlier. So fierce were his strokes that he'd gone through half a box already. Charcoal snapped easily, but so did Phil's heart. No. There could have been nothing easy about seeing broken shops, crushed homes and haunted people. Scotland Road. Would good old Scottie ever be the same again?

She cast an eye over the plague and the Fire of London before placing the papers in a bureau. It was no use. She couldn't focus on rats, fleas and Pudding Lane. Perhaps she'd feel better if she joined Nellie in the kitchen.

Nellie was a bit glum. She was sitting at the huge table with a newspaper and a mug of cocoa. Elsie had branched out into firelighters, wooden kindling and news agency. A van came through once a week, so they got a daily and a local paper, both on the same day. Some thinned out women's magazines completed Nellie's collection of literature, and she buried herself nightly in lurid tales of love, reports of crimes local and national, and a weekly account of the war's progress. Sometimes, the two women listened to the wireless in the evenings, but neither felt up to it tonight.

Nellie looked up from her *Recipes in Wartime* pamphlet. 'You still prowling about, love? What's up? Another cup of cocoa, eh? Have you seen my magazines? There's only about twelve pages. War? Hmmph.'

Hilda Pickavance refused cocoa. 'I feel strange.'

'Are you ill?'

'No, nothing like that. It's the light outside – the sky. It's not right.'

Nellie jumped up. 'Then we must put it right. Come on.'

They both donned hats, coats, scarves and gloves before stepping out into this last cold evening before Christmas Eve. Tomorrow would be all cooking and baking, so they needed to be early in their beds. 'Did you hear a thud a few minutes ago?' Hilda asked.

'I don't think so. I was raking ashes and damping down for the night in the kitchen. What sort of thud?'

'A thud, that's all. Like when a tree gets cut down.'

But Nellie hadn't heard a thing. 'It's red,' she announced when she looked up. 'But not for shepherd's delight, not this late.'

They moved round the house and found the true source of colour. 'Bloody hell,' Nellie groaned. 'It's Liverpool, isn't it?'

'Wrong direction, Nellie. That's Manchester. And the fires nearer to us are in Bolton.'

They stood very still on Hilda's high ground and watched a war that had never encroached before. They had seen few planes, had heard no bombs, no sirens. Down there, in a major city and in a huge town, people were dying. 'I feel sick,' Nellie said. 'It's so real for the poor buggers down there.'

'There's something else,' Hilda whispered. 'Something nearer.' She didn't know what she meant. Hilda Pickavance didn't believe in sixth sense or any of that nonsense, but her spine tingled and small hairs on her arms were standing to attention. It was the cold, she decided. She had gooseflesh, and it had probably arrived due to a mix of terror and frost.

Nellie stared hard at fires and at a reddened sky. So that was war. She'd been moaning because her magazines were on the thin side, but people not too far away were being maimed and killed. 'Hilda?'

'Yes?'

'What's the point of war? Why does it have to happen?'

Hilda did her best to explain about Poland, European Jews, the right to defend one's country, the evils of extreme politics at both ends of the spectrum–

Another stick of bombs hit Manchester. As they landed, they threw up clouds of debris, some of which could well be human flesh and bone. 'I hate bloody Germans,' Nellie spat.

'Bitte?'

Both women turned and saw his outline.

He smiled tentatively. 'Plane in field,' he said. 'No man, no woman die. I stop engine and jump. I am come to stay – prison camp, I care not. For me is finish and Reich has another plane gone. Mine friend, he has done same somewhere else. We are no Nazi.'

'He's a bloody German,' Nellie roared.

With the help of a torch, Hilda gazed into a perfect face, well chiselled and handsome. 'Yes, Nellie. He's surrendering. We must take him inside. He has every right to surrender, and we have a duty to treat him well. He is a prisoner of war and a visitor to our country.'

'Are you sure? I can't understand a word. We might be killed in our beds. He could be one of them spies.' She raised her voice as if she were addressing a very deaf person. 'Have you got a gun?'

'*Nein*. And this is not number, is meaning no.'

'You are in England now. Talk English when you do your words and numbers.'

Hilda forbade herself to smile. This young man's English was easy to understand, while Nellie's was variable at best.

They helped him inside, because he had a damaged ankle. 'You know what I must do now?' Hilda asked when he was seated by the fire.

He nodded. '*Danke*. I fly no more. I was fighter pilot.'

She spoke to Nellie. 'Deal with that damper, please. He's frozen to the bone.' She left to use the phone.

Nellie refreshed the fire, made him a cup of tea with three sugars, eased the boot off the painful foot and cut away the sock. 'This will hurt less than pulling,' she yelled at the top of her voice. 'It's not broke.' She picked up a dead match and snapped it. 'Not broke,' she repeated, her head shaking vigorously. While binding his ankle, she suddenly found herself weeping. Nellie wasn't a regular weeper, so she knew she must be unusually upset, though she couldn't think why. Yes, she could. He looked about three years older than Phil. This baby had flown planes to protect German bombers.

The young man touched her hair. 'Thank you,

good Frau. The tears of an Englander will clean me. War is bad. Many, many Germans are not wanting this, but we dare not say because of him.' He placed a finger under his nose to act as moustache, and performed a travesty of the Nazi salute. 'He is crazy.'

It wasn't the boy's fault. The culprit was only the uniform, not the person inside it. No soldier, sailor or airman could be blamed for the sick politics of his country. 'Your plane didn't blow up. I didn't hear you.'

'Fighter,' he said. 'Small plane. I cut engine and jumped. Plane is in field. No explosion, but tell people stay away from it.'

She dried her eyes. 'Where's your parachute?'

'In a...' He sought the right word. 'Where cows go at night.'

'In a cowshed? You've parked a load of silk where it can get covered in shit?'

He smiled again. 'I know what shit is meaning. No shit. Is on ... shelf with chugs.'

'Chugs?'

He made a pouring movement with his right hand. 'Chugs.'

'Jugs, love. They're jugs.' She took his hand. 'Don't tell nobody else,' she begged, her words separated by seconds. 'I can get two wedding dresses out of that – three if the brides are thin.' She bit her lip. 'What happens to you now, son?'

'Questions by Englander army police, prison to end of war.'

'Bloody shame.'

'No. They will find me work, and I will be careful. Other prisoners must not know I choose to surrender. My name Heinrich. This in English is Henry. My friend who jump near city of Chester, he is Günter. His plane did explode, but away from buildings. I am hope he is safe. I am hope he find good people like you. So. I am Heinrich Hoffmann, and friend is Günter Friedmann. We are having rear gunners, and they jump when we tell them plane is not work properly. They are not like us; they both believing in Hitler. So. Your name?'

'Nellie Kennedy, and she's Hilda Pickavance.'

When Hilda returned, she discovered the hardy perennial named Helen Kennedy holding hands with the enemy. 'Excuse me,' she said before leaving the room once more.

'She come, she go,' Henry remarked.

She came again with Phil in tow. 'Draw that,' she ordered. 'And when this bloody mess is over, your work will teach people that we were not at odds with the German people. We are fighting the Reich, as is this prisoner of war. The man chose to be here, Phil.'

Phil scanned the scene and committed it to memory. 'I will,' he said before marching up to the so-called enemy. 'Welcome to England. I'm Phil.'

'Heinrich – Henry in your language. I was in Luftwaffe and I choose to be prisoner in England. My grandfather has small part Jewish blood from his grandfather. If SS find him, he may die in camp.'

They didn't even knock when they came for Heinrich. The rear door flew inward and revealed two redcaps with rifles ready to fire, and an unarmed civilian policeman.

'On your knees,' shouted one of the military policemen.

Nellie released the hand of her new-found friend and marched up to the real invaders. A loaded rifle was pressed against her stomach, but the ferocity of her stare forced the bearer to lower his weapon. 'I should bloody well think so,' she roared. 'This is a private house on British soil. The German lad here crashed his plane on purpose so he could surrender. Harm one hair, and I'll spread you so far across the newspapers that you'll look like jam.'

'Only doing our job, ma'am.'

'And he's only surrendering. You'll find his mate somewhere outside Chester – he's dumped his plane, too. Their gunners baled out, but they are Nazis. These two pilots should have a bloody medal, never mind flaming guns pointing at them. You want to watch yourselves, you do. Jessie Turnbull's husband from the Edge went AWOL and finished up in the loony bin. He wasn't fit to fight, but did you care? Tried to kill himself. His mam lives down yonder, and so does his wife. Yous lot want talking about.'

Leaning on Phil, Heinrich hopped across the room. He held out his hands to be cuffed. 'God save your King,' he said.

'Are you taking the wee-wee?' the taller redcap asked.

Hilda decided to be in charge. 'No, he is not. His grandfather is part Jewish, and although this young pilot's Jewish blood is greatly diluted, he can't in conscience take part in the war. The top brass had a meeting, or so I'm told, and decided to allow some part-Jews to be Germans. He'll have been forced to swear an oath. For him, that oath was a lie. I am proud to know him. Our own royal family are part German.'

'You what?' The civilian policeman was scratching his head.

In Hilda's unspoken opinion, some people didn't deserve an education. 'When you have done with your questions, you may return him here if you wish. I will vouch for him, and for his friend, should you find him.'

Heinrich nodded. 'Günter Friedmann near Chester. He does what I do.'

When they had left, Hilda and Nellie sat close to the fire. For over ten minutes, neither spoke. Then Nellie, who had been thinking hard, aired her opinion. 'He's just another evacuee, isn't he?'

'Yes, dear. That's exactly what he is. They had better be good to him, that's all I can say. He was just a boy, Nellie. Their children are killing our children, and vice versa.'

'Merry blooming Christmas, eh, Hilda?'

'I think we deserve a small brandy, Nell.'

'Don't bother. Just bring the bottle and a couple of straws. I don't know about you, but I'd rather be unconscious after all that.'

Mam had gone all evangelical. Was that the right word? She'd delivered a sermon down the phone this morning, and its title had been 'Germans Are Not All Bad'. She'd met a German with a face like an angel, he'd ditched his plane on purpose in the middle of a field, and there were several yards of parachute silk, did Eileen want it? Oh, and happy Christmas Eve.

Eileen chuckled and shook her head in mock despair. She remembered lecturing her mother on this very subject, and Nellie Kennedy's opinion had changed completely. Mam got worse, she really did. She'd been going on about writing to Mr Churchill regarding the attitude displayed by members of the military police. The words still echoed. 'Police? Bloody police? They couldn't direct traffic, couldn't organize a kiddy's birthday party. Have you got Mr Churchill's address?'

'We gave up corresponding for the duration, Mam,' had been Eileen's reply. 'He's in a bunker somewhere down London way. Oh, and he's a bit busy these days.'

Spoodle yapped. Twenty-four hours in this house, and he'd already worked out how to get the two-legged to open the back door. His method of egress seemed unique. Having failed thus far to find his centre of gravity, he had fallen off the step a few times and landed on his head. So he shuffled round, allowing his fat little bottom to hit the ground first. Eileen could not believe the cleverness of so young a creature. Seven weeks old, and he knew already when to turn his back on a cruel world.

He waddled off into his pen, did his duty, returned to the back door. Coming back in was not dignified. He scrabbled and struggled until the woman lifted him in. But he would manage it soon; he was nothing if not dogged in his determination. It was all right here, warm, plenty of grub, nice naps on the old lady's bed. He panted a smile at Eileen and went off in search of trouble.

Right. It was now or never. Keith had gone to help builders who were still propping up a few houses down the road. Mel was upstairs writing about all the bombs that had fallen in the river last night. Keith had heard it from one of the carpenters; last night had been Manchester's turn for the bigger, nastier bombs. Now, Eileen would go and do what she had always done for her children – her best. She removed her apron and smoothed the front of her best green suit. The blouse, made from remnants bought by Keith from Bolton Market, was a triumph in pale cream. Her face was on, her shoes were polished; she was ready. The skirt's waistband was a bit tight, but she'd manage.

She went upstairs to inform Mel that she was in temporary charge of Miss Morrison. 'Sit and talk to her. I'll be back in time for tablets. Take Spoodle in with you. She likes Spoodle.'

'Where are you going, Mam?'

'Last minute shopping,' was the delivered lie.

'Have we any food points left? Or any coupons?'

'A few.'

'Right.' Mel jumped up and stated her intention to find the dog. 'You should have called him Colander instead of Spoodle. And don't lie, Mam. You'd never go shopping in those clothes. You're going to see Gloria.'

'Get yourself downstairs,' Eileen said. 'You're in charge, and I'm off.'

Outside at last, Eileen straightened her hat and strode determinedly towards her goal. There were things that could be sorted out only by a woman, but this time she was going to hire back-up. She needed Marie. His car wasn't there. 'Thank goodness for the sick,' Eileen muttered as she opened the gate.

Marie answered the door. 'Hello, Eileen.' At least they were now on first name terms. They often met in shops, and Eileen delivered her knitting to the WVS on a regular basis, so they were in contact quite frequently.

'Is Gloria in?'

'Upstairs.' Marie widened the doorway to allow her visitor to enter. 'Perhaps you and I should talk first. What a mess this is, and at the so-called festive season, too. Come through, I've made you a small Christmas cake. Don't ask about ingredients, or I might end up in jail.'

They got through the niceties in seconds – the lovely cake, the weather, rationing, bombs, the propping up of houses. Marie took a sip of tea. 'She's as miserable as sin up there in her room.'

'Snap.'

'And Peter's no better. Our girls were such good friends, Eileen. I even had a dream that Gloria would pull up her socks and go to university with Mel. They're so suited, and they could look after each other. Then Peter put a spanner in the works. Oh, I do hope he's not going to be like–' She cut herself off abruptly.

'Like his father?' Eileen finished on behalf of her hostess.

Marie nodded sadly. After a brief silence, she decided to fill Eileen in about all that had happened in recent months. She had learned about her own past and was now aware of all the facts.

An uncle, long dead, had stolen her childhood. Marriage had not suited her, and Tom had been a brute. 'He wanted you. It was written all over his face that first day – remember? We had Madeira cake?'

Eileen lowered her head for a moment. Denial would be completely inappropriate; this was an intelligent woman who deserved truth. 'Sorry about your childhood, Marie. And yes. He nearly got me, but I value myself too highly because of my family, mostly my kids. He is a very attractive and desirable man. My opinion is that he's never been technically unfaithful to you, because he wouldn't risk his standing in the community. Selfish, isn't he?'

Marie's smile was almost radiant. She had found pleasure. She was now using him just as he had used her. 'I do love him,' she admitted. 'But sometimes I don't like him one bit.' She hid her blushing cheeks with both hands. 'Now I've learned the mechanics of everything, I enjoy him.' These words were blurred slightly by her fingers. 'And I think he's aware that I'm inwardly critical of his performances. There's a chance I might start awarding marks out of ten.'

Eileen made a remark about a shoe and a foot, and both women had to stifle their laughter when Marie became rather anatomical and almost vulgar. She had never before enjoyed the kind of bawdy chat so treasured by females when free of their partners. Men were supposed to be the ones with crude minds, while women were expected to be gentle, careful and sweet.

'...so she booked him in at the vet's.' Eileen was

nearing the end of a ridiculous Scotland Road fable about a man whose body was unusual. 'Their name comes up, and they go in the surgery. Finally, soft lad sees all the pictures of dogs and cats on the walls, and realizes he's not in the doctor's. And she says to him, "Look, either that goes or I go. There isn't room for three in our bed."'

'So what happened?' Marie asked.

Eileen shrugged. 'Some say the vet did the job, some say the wife did it with pinking shears – well, she didn't want his wotsit to fray, did she? I've heard he emigrated to Australia, that he joined a freak show, that they got divorced.'

Marie threw her pinafore over her head and howled. Women could do this talking thing. They didn't need to be propped up in the corner of a taproom, pint of ale in one hand, cigarette in the other. All she and Eileen required was tea and the comfort gained from opening up minds and hearts at a dining table.

Eileen was enjoying herself. She'd seldom had a close personal friend, because, like ugly people, the unusually pretty were to be avoided. Today, she had come to plead for her daughter, and she had gained something for herself. 'You've come on a lot, Marie Bingley. From mouse to lioness is quite a stride.'

'I have an admirer, too,' Marie whispered. 'He's pleasant, older than God, on the plump side and with beautiful pianist's hands, but he's very, very boring. Tom is never that. In fact, he's probably the most exciting creature I've ever known, because I'm never sure. I don't know where he's been, what he's done, who he imagines I am while we're making love. Since I finished the treatment, I manage not to mind, because I can be selfish. It's my turn now.'

'Not before time.'

'Are you sure? Am I not being terrible?'

Eileen shrugged. 'No. Like I said, the shoe's on a different foot.'

'Don't start that again. You know where that shoe took us a few minutes ago. If I laugh any more, I'll need to rearrange some underwear.'

'Oh, I know what you mean. I once laughed so hard my waters broke. And I wasn't even pregnant at the time.'

Gloria walked in to gales of laughter. She stood in the doorway, folded her arms and glared at not one but two out-of-order mothers who didn't care in the least about her tragic life. Her very, very best friend had let her down in the worst sense. Her brother, her twin brother, was an oinker, a pig who had tried to have sex with said very, very best friend. And people thought it was funny?

Marie mopped her eyes. 'Sorry, darling. I know you're miserable, but we were just letting our hair down a little. We're feeling the strain, you see.'

'Sorry about that.'

Eileen stood up. 'Right. Coat on, please. You're coming with me. You have to meet Spoodle, who's gorgeous, and I'm sure my daughter, also gorgeous but sulking, would love to see you.'

'Then why didn't she come here?'

The visitor marshalled her thoughts. 'She's looking after Miss Morrison and trying to train Spoodle. I came here to fetch you because you have more sense than Mel does. She might be brainy, but she can be daft.'

Both women held their breath while Gloria chewed thoughtfully on a fingernail. 'Then you go and change places with her; tell her to come here.'

The mothers looked at each other. 'Gloria, you will go with Mrs ... Mrs Greenhalgh. She didn't need to come here, you know. She could have left us with a completely rotten Christmas. As things are, your brother's here, and you don't want him listening while you try to mend a broken fence.'

The girl started to fiddle with her hair. It was a habit repeated whenever she was perturbed. 'I did a bad thing.'

'I know,' chorused Marie and Eileen. 'Miss Clever Clogs will have an answer to that,' continued Mel's mother. 'God knows she's got one for everything else. I'm sick to death of getting educated by my own daughter. She's into silly ancient laws now, Marie. Anyone in Chester can kill anyone from Wales as long as they do it with an arrow at midnight on a Sunday – something like that. Can you imagine shooting straight in pitch black? And why stop at the Welsh, for God's sake?'

A strange noise emerged from the youngest member of the meeting. Gloria was trying not to laugh. She turned hurriedly and quit the scene.

Marie put a finger to her lips. Like most people, she knew all the sounds belonging to her house, and could identify and explain the slightest creak. Her shoulders relaxed. 'Getting her coat,' she mouthed.

'Now for chapter two,' came Eileen's quiet reply.

'Onward Christian solders. I'll put your cake in a box.'

Betty was a boon. She was as quiet as the grave, had been in service since leaving school, and seemed able to do the job of a gallon while furnished with just a pint. When asked about her excellent cooking, she replied by saying that she made it up as she went along. Except for Mr Collins's meals. Mr Collins's allocated points were pinned to the wall next to the oven, and they became known as Betty's Bible.

Furthermore, she cared about 'her' family, even going so far as to travel to Bolton to collect tins of National Dried for Maisie, who had been drinking her mother dry. She took complete charge of the binding of Gill's breasts with bandages and, when Gill was tempted to remove these supports, it was Betty who stepped in. Yes, the breasts were hard and sore, but Maisie was fine on powdered milk, and that was going to be an end to it. 'Time you stopped feeling like a cow wanting milking. I've done this for my mother several times. You'll get through it.'

This was when Gill discovered that quietly spoken words delivered by a taciturn person were more effective than shouted orders. Betty, a plump and rather unattractive female with a Midlands accent, meant business. Aware of her unappealing exterior, she empowered herself in domestic circumstances. Her whys and wherefores were of no importance; she was a godsend and a treasure.

Hilda Pickavance arrived. She had come to check on the progress of 'her boy' and was perplexed by his absence.

'Where is he?' she asked when the niceties were done.

'Upstairs,' Gill replied. 'He's doing a jigsaw, brand new, and getting his knickers in a twist because he says half the pieces are missing. Supposed to be relaxing. I think that word's missing from his dictionary. He can't rest. And he has to slow down for weeks.'

Hilda went upstairs to have a word or several with him. He was seated at a small table under a window. 'Hello,' he said. 'Come here, please. Sky, bit of cloud on it, two blobs off-set, and two holes, also off-set.'

Thus the lady of the manor continued her war work. She knitted khaki scarves, which were easier than socks, was involved with the welfare of the Willows community and its evacuees, and did jigsaws with a diabetic young man.

The German boys were being questioned in Manchester. If they satisfied the authorities, they would be moved to Yorkshire. It seemed that several young men had ditched their planes, and they were said to be working happily and with minimal policing in farms all over England's largest county. One or two of them were becoming friendly with the locals, and there were even tales of budding romance. Heinrich and Günter, too, were Hilda's war work. Heinrich had arrived uninvited, had stayed for a short while as a dependant, and had left as a friend. It was a confusing life.

She smiled to herself. Never mind. It was Christmas. And she had found Jay's delinquent piece of sky.

Spoodle became the bridge between the two girls. Gloria fell in love the moment she saw him, and she begged to use the phone long before sitting down to talk to Mel. She told her mother she wanted a spoodle, and that she could get the phone number of the poodle owner from Keith. So that was that. Instinct told Gloria that she could get what she wanted if she struck now.

They climbed the stairs and sat side by side on Mel's bed. The visitor opened the batting. 'I'm sorry, Mel.'

'So am I.'

'How can I mend what I did?'

Mel expressed the opinion that the mending might be fun. They could start a trend, but they needed to be careful of slander. 'Then, when enough lies have been told, we do a gullibility chart.'

Gloria pondered before answering. 'There's him.'

'Who?'

'My brother, of course. Pete the perfect. He'll be bragging about the things you actually did.' She paused. 'What did you actually do?'

Honesty was the only viable policy. 'Everything but the deed.'

'Everything?'

'I think so, though there may be stuff I don't know about.'

Gloria's cheeks blazed like a lighthouse in the dark. 'He'll brag about that.'

Mel shook her head thoughtfully. 'He won't. Because I carry a certain knowledge, a confidence he would hate me to disclose. Don't ask, Gloria, because I did make a promise.'

Mel closed her eyes for a few seconds, and he was crying like a baby wanting the breast. 'I don't know. I don't know what I am,' he sobbed. 'I love you, Mel, but there's something...' He raised his head. 'Sometimes I think I like boys.' Mel had cried with him for what had seemed like hours. *No matter what, Peter. No matter what, I'll be here for you.*

She opened her eyes and smiled at Gloria, who was in the here and now. 'It's enough for you to be sure I know something that could almost run him out of town. I can't and won't say anything more to you, but I am going to speak to Peter. This mess wants cleaning up before we go back to school.'

Gloria agreed. 'But don't forget to sew up my brother's mouth.'

'I won't forget.'

'Mel?'

'What?'

'Was it ... nice?'

'Yes.' And no more was said. They fell back into friendship as if there had been no rift, and spent the rest of the day at Gloria's house bullying Tom and Marie until Tom finally crumbled. 'Get in the bloody car,' he snapped. 'I phoned. There's one left. It's female and will need to be neutered.' When his daughter opened her mouth to tell him to make haste before someone else bought the animal, he held up a hand. 'I've reserved the dog for two hours. And you can pick up after it, madam. I see enough of the mucky side of life without cleaning up after half a poodle.'

'A half-poodle,' his daughter said. 'That is the correct term. It's a whole dog.'

'I'm sure it is,' he mumbled between clenched teeth.

Thus it came to pass that Gloria Bingley acquired Pandora, sister to Spoodle. The girls removed the S, I, E and L from spaniel, and added Dora, who had been one of Gloria's grandmothers. Pandora was reborn, and with her came the one item left after the opening of the box. In legend, Pandora hung on to hope. In reality, this puppy and her brother cemented a friendship that would last a lifetime.

My dear Miss Pickavance,

I think I'd rather like to be a journalist. Interviewing people is great; I seem to have the knack of getting them to talk. It's important, because so many will become nothing more than statistics once the war ends. The recording of individual statements will make people from Civil Defence real.

Hilda glanced out at the near-dawn of Christmas Day. It was bone-chillingly cold, and stars still twinkled, so there would be no cloud cover for a while. If the evacuees wanted snow, it would not arrive until afternoon, she believed. The Bolton area was famous for heavy falls and drifts, and the Liverpool children were looking forward to a white-out.

For a few precious minutes, Hilda was enjoying solitude in the company of Mel's letters. The girl wrote weekly, and was producing an intelligent young person's view of a city at war. Together with her brother's paintings, perhaps a package might be formed? 'Stop it,' she ordered herself sharply. 'Let them walk first, and allow them to choose their own pace when running begins.'

Her name is Barbara Scott, though she prefers Babs. A casualty nurse, she has seen at close quarters some horrible things. One man arrived in an ambulance, most of him on a stretcher, the right lower leg a separate item poking out of a bucket. He's doing well, thank goodness. The thing that upset Babs most was a blinded child whose whole family died. Babs's sister is going to try to adopt the little blind girl.

Sometimes Hilda wished she could be there. But, as she was constantly reminded by Nellie, she had probably saved the lives of over twenty people by bringing them here, and she was managing to educate most of them. A chuckle rose unbidden from her throat. The thefts at Four Oaks had caused some tension, because Liverpool had invaded and was, by default, the whipping boy. The thief, when finally caught through a booby trap, had been a Willows youth. Scousers were no angels, but they were mainly decent. Let Willows put that in its pipe and smoke it.

Shock is a real illness. Some patients don't start to shake until hours or even days after their experiences. They come in as black as coal; the only white bits are their eyes. Hundreds arrive at once and, in spite of sets of rules, the whole hospital is reduced to chaos, people spilling into wards and corridors and offices. They found a drunk in the women's toilets. He was quite happy, but locked in for – well, goodness knows how long he was there. They had to break the door down. He was sitting guard over twelve bottles of single malt singing 'Danny Boy' and asking had anyone seen his Mary. His Mary is in Anfield Cemetery, but he wasn't ready to accept, God love him.

Mel's interviews made everything frighteningly real, because she focused on individuals and their anecdotes, helped them talk, shared their burdens, offered sympathy and, above all, listened. Yes, journalism was a possibility. This was last week's letter.

The ARP currently has half a million members nationwide, but Churchill wants that number doubled. We may have won the Battle of Britain, but we are still very unsafe. America is our greatest hope; why won't they come? Yes, I know some are here already, as are many from Canada, Australia, New Zealand and other Commonwealth countries, but we need America to become official. The unofficial Americans tend to be Air Force – they love planes and are technologically advanced, but their President is afraid of unpopularity.

Bob Garnet is ARP. He treated me to a cup of tea in a little hut and said I was a bit young to hear his stories. So I told him I am a Merchants girl working on a project, which is true in a sense. He said they all have an area to patrol, and that they know the people who live in the houses, so they can tell at a glance who's missing or in a shelter. They dig and dig and bring out bits of people, trying to guess who's who and what's what. Sometimes organs end up in buckets and guesswork comes into play, but, as Bob said, there's a war on.

It's the children. He can't carry a dead child without weeping, and he does it openly now, because he's not the only one. The next worst thing, he says, is the smell of burning flesh. Well, you told me to be open and honest, didn't you? Bob's stomach is no longer strong, and his wife worries. They live in a place called Old Roan, somewhere on the way to Aintree.

Sighing, Hilda rose and walked to the window. Two typically angry robins were locked in mid-flight deadly combat. So much for the air force, she said inwardly. Cows had begun lowing in the Home Farm sheds. Cows didn't have Christmas, unless one counted a few in Bethlehem's famous stable. Their udders were full, and milking was required. This was just another ordinary day.

Bernie O'Hara got in the wrong queue. He was supposed to be volunteering as a messenger boy, but he found himself with a heavy helmet, leaden boots and a fireman's uniform. He explained that he wasn't quite fourteen, but he was told that these are desperate times, and he must get on with it. So he got on with it.

On his first watch, the bells 'went down.' That's what they say when the ringing starts. Poor Bernie found himself on a fire engine rattling its way to Millers Bridge. His description to me was, 'The whole world was on fire, and the flames were really tall. I could see Heinkels in the sky.'

They rolled out hoses and fastened them to hydrants. A real fireman took the hose and made Bernie stand behind him. 'Hold on,' he ordered, 'or we all die. There's forty to sixty pounds of pressure coming through here in a minute. If we let go, it becomes a giant serpent and kills us all.'

That was just the first battle for Bernie, an ordinary schoolboy. The heat was terrific. They had to cool down other buildings, because brick crumbles at a certain temperature, and some places caught fire just because they overheated. His face was burning. He couldn't touch it, because he had the hose. So he shuffled a bit, and some of the water came back at him. His uniform was steaming. It was wet through, but the flames heated it. Burning timber flew at him, crackling as it travelled. 'I know hell now,' he told me. At fourteen, at my age, he has already seen hell.

The rest of the message was amusing. Hilda found herself chuckling again, because Mel's palette changed in the blink of an eye, and she used just primary colours when describing her nearest and dearest.

You could cut the atmosphere here with a blunt knife. They are so in love, and they play all sorts of games. Keith pretends to be dominant, but he's about as threatening as a high tide at Southport, which, in turn, is as rare as hen's teeth. When he gets fed up with her misbehaviour, he sits her on the draining board and orders her to stay. They kiss all the time. She says kissing is his main hobby. He is a lovely man and I have started to call him Dad. That pleases him. He says he's getting her a collar and lead tomorrow for Christmas, and a voucher for ten lessons at dog training school. I don't think we'll be having Christmas – it will be more like Kissmas.

Hilda chuckled; she'd been told about Spoodle

via the telephone.

Miss Morrison does some pretend sleeping but she's really listening to the sounds of love's young dream. Her level of deafness alters daily; if there's something interesting going on, she hears it. I spend time with her every day. People her age are like living history books, so valuable. She says she's staying alive until Hitler's dead and disposed of and she's seen television. Nothing would surprise me where Miss Morrison's concerned. Sometimes I wonder what really went on with that caretaker in the cellar!

Hilda placed the pages with all the others in a drawer. It was Christmas, and there was much to do. Her protégés, spread as they were around farms and cottages, would each receive a stocking from her. This house would be packed to the gills, since Jay, Gill and Maisie were expected, as were Neil, Jean and their daughters. The Land Army girls had all managed to get home for a few days, and that was a relief, or lunchers would have spilled onto the stairs. So it was to be a meal for twelve, though Nellie insisted that she had it all in hand. Thank goodness they lived in the country and kept poultry.

Elsie was expected for afternoon tea, as were Freda Pilkington and her offspring, but the lunch guests would have left by then. As she combed her hair, Hilda Pickavance found herself smiling at the ageing figure in the glass. She was no longer lonely; she had a family at last.

'Well, this is a good start, I must say.' Keith joined

the weeping Mel on the sofa. 'Happy Christmas. It's all going very well so far. Your mother's in the bath, says she's staying there till New Year because I bought her some bubbles. Miss Morrison's had her breakfast courtesy of me, but she said her toast was overdone, and now you're carrying on all sad. Come on. Tell your stepdad what's up.'

Mel pushed documents into his hand. 'It's too much,' she wailed.

Keith looked at the bank book and covering letter, explaining that too much was fine in his opinion. 'Your mam and I got you clothes – good ones, but second-hand. So this too-much present evens things out a bit.'

'I could buy three houses with that, Dad.'

'I wouldn't bother, love. Some soft bugger keeps knocking them down or setting light to them.' Dad. This gorgeous girl was his daughter. 'Miss Pickavance loves you, baby. That money will see you through university, because brains are all very well, but they need food, shelter and transport. You're safe now.'

She grinned. 'Unless I get bombed.'

Like her mother, Mel was a rainbow when she cried and smiled simultaneously. 'Get a crowbar, sweetheart, and prise your mam out of that bathroom.'

But no such measure was required, because chaos erupted. Not one but two spoodles shot through the room like bullets from a gun. 'Did I imagine that?' Mel asked. 'Two nutters merged into one?'

He nodded. 'A ball with eight legs. It rolled that-a-way.'

They sat and listened as the two pups bounded upstairs. They could go up, but they couldn't come down. 'That'll shift your mam,' predicted Keith as Gloria walked in.

'Happy Christmas,' the visitor said grimly. 'My dad wants a divorce from Pandora, says two daft women in the house are enough, and he and Peter are now outnumbered. They're crying.'

'Tom and Peter?' Keith asked innocently.

'Spoodle and Pandora.' Mel dried her eyes. 'They can't get down,' she advised her best friend.

'We know,' was Gloria's reply. 'We found that out at three o'clock this morning. She's eaten a doormat and a draught excluder. Yours has started on a leg of the kitchen table.'

'We know,' they chorused.

'You little buggers,' came a voice from on high. 'Keith? They've got my towel.'

'You know what?' Keith rose to his feet. 'I'm beginning to sympathize with that poodle woman. We are paying for the spaniel's bad behaviour.'

All three walked upstairs. Eileen, stark naked and laughing, was pulling a large towel to which were attached two pups. She looked at the three new arrivals. 'You took your time.'

Dumbstruck, Keith noticed the swelling. That was his and hers, a daughter or son in a beautiful container. While the girls retrieved the towel, he simply gazed into his wife's eyes. He could not remember happiness as intense as this.

Eileen covered herself. 'Drown them,' she ordered before retreating to her bedroom. Keith followed, locking the door behind him. She was seated on the bed, a huge pair of scissors in one hand. 'Why do you have a murder weapon in your bedside cupboard?' she asked.

'To cut through all the red tape,' he answered.

'What?'

'Your tarpaulin.'

'You wouldn't dare.'

'Happy Christmas.' He gave her a white silk gown with matching nightdress. 'Used to be a German parachute, so if you ever need to jump, you just pull the cord and–'

It was her turn to cut off his words with a kiss. She dragged him back into bed and encouraged nature to take its course. Sometimes, a woman needed to dictate the pace.

Frances Morrison was waiting for them. 'Thank you for the lovely bedjacket. And the girls asked me to tell you that they've taken the spoodles to torment Dr Bingley. Oh, will you make me some toast, Eileen? Your husband should work at a crematorium.'

When they were alone, she patted her bed, and he sat next to her. 'Does she know, Keith?'

He nodded. 'Big-Mouth Bingley told her. She was shocked, but you know how she is. Whatever happens, she puts everything to one side and gets on with what needs doing.'

'I just wanted her to have something of her own – a house, a place.'

'Yes.'

'Make her take it when I'm gone. No selling up and giving the money to charity. She's a lovely woman.'

'I know.'

She gripped his hand with more power than should have been allotted to a woman so advanced in years. 'Look after them all, or I shall haunt you.'

They gave her the new toast and another cup of milky tea. Then they left her. 'It's time to prepare Christmas dinner,' Eileen told her.

Alone in her room, content in a house filled with love, Frances drifted on a bright, white cloud of memories. A school bell, the sounds of girls at play, a handsome, vulgar man in a cellar, sweet temptation, one stolen kiss in an office populated by filing cabinets, desks and daffodils. He knew she loved spring flowers. She could not marry a janitor; she should have married him.

Never mind. Onward, onward. Forty-three of her girls had gone on via Merchants to Oxbridge. Educate a boy, and you educate one man; educate a girl, and you enlighten generations. Too tired to call for company, Miss Frances Morrison took a road along which we are all destined to tread. Her last thought was for Spoodle. He could have two bedjackets now.

Marie, in the midst of chaos, snatched at the receiver. 'Eileen? What? When? Yes, of course I will.' She paused, a finger pressed against the free ear. 'Peter's avoiding us like the plague, so don't worry about him. Yes, yes. I am so sorry, my dear.'

Two girls and two puppies were running about. Peter was upstairs, stoic in his silence. Tom sat in his little office, an Irish coffee on the desk, an old crossword puzzle spread before him.

'Where's Pandora?' Gloria shouted.

Marie shut herself in the downstairs cloakroom. What the hell did it matter if the sprouts were soggy? The old lady was dead. Were the parsnips in the oven? Did she care? The running and shouting continued. This was her life; she had to live it.

When she reached the office door again, she paused to watch her husband betraying himself. In his arms, he cradled a happy pup. The newcomer he had dismissed as unclean and germ-ridden was licking his face. 'Who's my beauty-girl, then?' He used a silly, talking-to-a-baby voice. 'Who's had a permanent wave that went wrong? To hell with the spaniel, I'm your daddy. Yes, I am. Yes, I am.' He looked up. 'Marie?'

She entered and closed the door. 'We have to ask Mel to stay for dinner, Tom. Miss Morrison died.'

He closed his eyes. That wonderful, aggressive, determined suffragette had gone. 'She was born in 1850,' he said, his voice unsteady. 'February next, she would have hit ninety-one. Her brain was as sharp as the best carving knife, and she never missed a trick.' But she had missed the end of this bloody war, and she hadn't lived to see television. 'How are Keith and Eileen?'

Marie shook her head. 'Not good. They're not having Christmas, so they want us to keep Mel for a few hours. Peter won't come down if she's here.'

He stood up. 'Leave it with me, love. Time somebody sorted this lot out. You do your parsnips, I'll deal with Peter.'

He paused on the landing and stood in the oriel bay. From here he could see Miss Morrison's house – Mrs Greenhalgh's now. All curtains were closed. Dr Ryan's bike leaned against a gatepost, and the undertaker's car was parked nearby. A light had gone out today. That remarkable old woman had fought for women's franchise, and for an end to segregation in America. That hadn't happened yet, but she'd tried, had even travelled to the southern states. The slave trade was partly Britain's fault, and Liverpool had thrived on it. Frances Morrison had battled for a school of her own, for freedom, for the betterment of women.

'Dad?'

'Hello, son.'

Peter stood beside his father. 'Why are you crying?'

'A patient died. Miss Morrison. Mel doesn't know, and she's having Christmas with us, because her parents are busy.' He dried his eyes. 'You will go downstairs and be a man. Yes, men cry too. Go. Give your sister and her friend a decent day. Stop feeling bloody sorry for yourself.'

Tom sat in the bay window long after his son had gone downstairs. Puppies ran, two girls laughed and shouted, while the scent of food rose up the stairwell and almost made him gag. 'Silent Night' was playing on the wireless. Wasn't that a German carol? Wasn't it 'Stille Nacht'? And did it matter? He remained where he was through 'Silent Night' and part of Handel's *Messiah*.

For unto us a child is born, unto us a son is given. 'And from us is taken a pearl,' he mouthed before descending the stairs. He lied to Mel, said they'd begged her mother to allow her to stay with Gloria for a few hours. He carved the bird, told jokes, put food in two tiny bowls for two tiny dogs. The pups ate, looked for more, gave up and passed out near the fire. And the parsnips were slightly underdone.

PART THREE

1941

Seventeen

The second Great Fire of London had happened just three days before New Year. There had been no festive celebrations in Liverpool, but the Luftwaffe had lit up London in the worst way possible. Few in the north knew much about it, but, as ever, Mel Watson could be relied upon to winkle out the truth from any and every available source. As ever, she wrote down all she had learned and posted it to Hilda Pickavance.

Published now in a Liverpool newspaper, Mel and Gloria were two of several teenage pairs across the region who contributed to a small but humorous monthly column entitled 'A Young Person's Guide to Survival'. They offered advice on such subjects as the borrowing and lending of clothes, the making over of dresses, and the drawing of straight lines up the backs of mothers' legs in order to imitate fully fashioned stockings. Hilda chuckled as she read the latest contribution from Mel and her friend.

Keep your hand steady. Mothers are not impressed by zigzag legs, and punishments can vary from no sweets for a month to the terrible job of cleaning out the back garden Anderson.

Mel and Gloria wrote hilarious anecdotes about their families, their friends, and Spoodle and

Pandora, the Deadly Duo.

If you are afflicted by a dog, get the priest in and the house blessed. So far, we have lost items of underwear, a scarf and some Latin homework. Nobody told us that dogs eat stair carpet and table legs. As for the homework, why did the teacher laugh? IT WAS TRUE!

Hilda put away her first Great Fire of London lesson for the second time. The first fire had been a good thing to an extent, as it had eradicated plague by cleansing the city of rats and their disease-bearing parasites. But the present deliberate attempt to wipe out the City of London was appalling. Mel and Gloria were getting to know journalists, and journalists gossiped. Although positive propaganda was allowed, the people of Britain were, for the most part, shielded from the absolute truth. It was about morale. No matter what, as few as possible were allowed the full story. 'I suppose if we do get invaded, the first we'll know of it is the sound of jackboots pounding in our streets.' Hilda placed Mel's newspaper clippings in a folder and took out the latest letter.

My dear Miss Pickavance,

I have to thank you again for my bank account. I know I keep doing it, but you are my saviour, and I can now concentrate on exams. You are wonderfully kind and generous!

The most awful thing happened in London on 29 December, and it has taken me a while to collect information. The event almost defies description, and I doubt we shall ever get the full truth, but an American journalist who is trying to shame his country into helping us witnessed it and sent copies to newspapers everywhere, and I managed to read some of the piece.

'You would,' said Hilda to an empty room. Mel's inquisitiveness would surely land her in trouble sooner or later.

Wave after wave of bombers came over, and each bomb weighed more than five hundred pounds. An incredible fifty tons hit London, and they took out the main telephone exchange, damaged Waterloo, Cannon Street and London Bridge stations, hit shelters and people in the streets. At Moorgate, heat buckled railway lines. A breeze fanned the flames, and then the breeze became a gale. Buildings, some of them five storeys high, crumbled and collapsed, killing fire-fighters and citizens trapped by flames, heat and falling masonry. The true target, St Paul's, was completely surrounded by fire. Nelson, Wellington and Christopher Wren rest in the vault. Ordinary folk turned up at the cathedral to pray and to help. The dome, which is just lead resting on wooden joists, did catch fire, but amateur fire-fighters managed to extinguish the flames. It has been described as a firestorm, as the second Great Fire of London, and as the hurricane from hell.

A Victorian warehouse containing hundreds of thousands of valuable books was consumed. St Bride's, designed by Wren, is no more. Fleet Street is flattened, and many homes and places of work are gone. There was no singing in the underground on this occasion. People prayed to die rather than to survive injured, because many are already maimed and disfigured for life as a result of these bombardments. But this was a terrible night, the worst so far. London can't take much more. Firefighters are dying. Our capital will die, too, if this sort of bombardment is repeated. We have no alternative but to fight back in the same cowardly way, hit Germany and run, hit and run. Terrible.

Countless incendiaries were delivered so that targets would be visible, and it is rumoured that a third wave of bombers was ready to take off from France, but weather stopped it and Hitler was furious. We have lost banks and businesses by the score. They didn't get St Paul's. Churchill issued a direct order that St Paul's must be saved.

Hilda sat on her bed and wept. London belonged to everyone. Buildings designed and erected over hundreds of years had been razed to the ground in a matter of hours. Gone was Britain's strength as a near-impregnable island, because death arrived airborne these days. Roosevelt's contribution had been to make both sides promise to play nicely, and not aim for people in the streets, but this was Hitler's way. He walked into countries after the Luftwaffe had pounded them into submission; now he was attempting the same with England. He was gunning for innocent citizens. 'So yes, Mel, we have to do the same,' she whispered sadly. Heinrich and Günter, due to start working on Yorkshire farms, were proof positive that Germans were not all bad. But bombs did not discriminate, and Churchill would be hopping mad.

To be fair, the Americans had helped financially, but oh, how Britain needed their forces now. Hitler would resort to any tactic, however cruel and wild, in his insane search for domination. Nellie's 'Why?', asked on the night when Heinrich had descended from the sky, was unanswerable, because the explanations about Poland and saving one's country failed to address the basic question. There could be no sensible excuse for behaviour such as this. Germany had to be stopped for the sake of its populace, since the Fatherland was in the hands of lunatics.

Mum and Dad are almost ready to depart. It will be interesting to have Mrs Openshaw here, as she is quite a character, and she will be company for Gran. Fortunately, there's plenty of room in this place.

Sadness still sits in the house, because we all remember how lovely and funny Miss Morrison was. I claimed her little bell, the one she used to ring when she needed us or wanted company. I mean to treasure it for the rest of my life, since she was so precious.

Mam owns the property now, though probate has to be settled, and she was threatening to charge Gran and Mrs Openshaw rent. It was another joke, of course, one of the many we are forced to endure. I believe that Mrs Pilkington, originally from Rachel Street, is getting her mother over to Willows Edge to look after the children while Mrs Pilkington runs the post office for Mrs Openshaw.

I really do miss our landlady. Mum, Dad and I cleared the room out and Dad put the bed etc. upstairs in the old lady's original bedroom. We got some second-hand pieces and are now the proud owners of a formal dining room, though the chairs don't match each other. The sideboard was of poor wood and very plain, but it serves its purpose by housing Miss Morrison's lovely china. We have kept her easy chair by the fireplace with her favourite shawl draped over the back. Sometimes, I sit in it and talk to her in my head.

There was no Christmas. I spent the day with my friend Gloria and her family, and did not find out until I got home that Miss Morrison had died on Christ's birthday. We console ourselves with the knowledge that she was happy in our company and that she lived a long and useful life. My mother cried a lot. It was the first time she had helped lay someone out.

The funeral was amazing. Two of her 'girls' spoke at the service in St Michael's C of E church, and it was standing room only. They weren't girls; they were grandmothers, and it took them the best part of half an hour to read out the accomplishments of Miss Frances Morrison. Although the church was packed, you could have heard a pin drop. My mother spoke, too. I was very proud of her – she even made people laugh about the countless cups of milky tea, the coddled eggs and just-right toast, not too pale, not too dark. Knitting was mentioned, as was the old lady's tendency to be as deaf as she needed to be according to prevailing circumstances.

Right at the front, a very old man sat in a wheelchair. I spoke to him afterwards as he waited in the porch for his great-nephew to take him home. He was the famous vulgar caretaker. I told him that she had loved him, and he fixed me with the palest blue eyes I have ever seen. In a rusty, dusty voice, he said that she had been the only one for him, but he was from the wrong class. For once, I was lost for words. She never exactly told me that she loved him, but I could see it in her eyes every time she spoke about him. Why do people waste love, Miss Pickavance?

So we approach March, and Mam is more than six months pregnant. My stepfather's war work in Crosby has been with builders, and he has come to love our city while trying to keep it safe. Our house here is finally stable and free of what Miss Morrison termed pit props. I think Dad pulled a few strings.

Mam and he need to get away. I pray nothing else will happen to keep them here; I also pray for a sister. Can you imagine how life would be if we got yet another boy? Dad is diplomatic, says I'll need a bridesmaid in a few years, so he wants a girl. I know what he really wants – he wants the birth to be easy and his beloved wife safe and well. The sex of the child is not significant, because he loves Mam so much. So there are one-woman men. One is married to my mother, and another sat in a wheelchair in a church porch in freezing cold. Wasted love? How cruel life is sometimes.

Please, I beg you, look after my mother when she comes back to Willows. She has been well through the pregnancy, and I know Dad loves her to bits, but Gran has always been with her for births in the past, and she will be here looking after me. I begin to feel quite a nuisance. This will be our fifth baby, and I want her and my mother to be safe.

Thank you yet again, Miss Pickavance.

Hoping to see you soon.

Mel x

There were snowdrops outside, and they were fading fast. Hilda counted twenty-seven under her window, and she could see clumps of grey-white, drooping flowers spread round the edges of the lawn. Even in wartime, these preludes to spring caused hope to burgeon in the saddest of hearts.

Here and there, premature green swords thrust their first inch above soil. These gladiatorial announcements were a proud statement from daffodils, narcissi and cheerfulness. 'We're coming,' they said. Jay had planted them just about everywhere, including under the grass, so the first mowing could not take place until spring flowers had died off completely.

The boys were safe and behaving well. Rob, buried in his Christmas books about farming, muttered from time to time about turnips not being as easy as people thought, about the impossibility of resting land while there was a flipping war on, about spuds being good for the soil. He had gathered enemies and friends in the animal kingdom, and Bertie was his close ally when it came to ploughing. Those horses were brilliant when tractor fuel ran low. Bertie, too, was amazing, because he talked to the beasts and managed to urge them on till a job was done. But beetles, mice and crows were the enemy, and Rob fought them like a trooper.

Ah, here he came. After tapping on the door, he pushed his smiling face into Hilda's room. 'Well, I worked it out,' he announced. 'It was simple, really. The animals have to be closer to the farmhouse because they need tending. I'd never looked at it that way. Crops have to be further away.'

'So will you be arable or mixed, young man?'

'Mixed. I'm getting used to the animals. Bertie helps. He's turned out to be a good lad, has our Bertie.'

'You all have. So has he given up the idea of being a vet?'

'Too much blood. Me and Bertie want to stay together and rent a farm. He can run a livery while I do the rest. Anyway, Gran says are you coming down, because the food's going cold.'

'I'm coming.' So was Phil. He was walking across the lawn with Mr Marchant, his teacher. Mr Marchant had been known to say that Phil should be the teacher, so great was his talent. Snowdrops were not the only good news. Three boys who had led the wild life were gaining sense and knowledge. As for Mel, the world was her lobster, as Nellie often said with that cynical gleam in her eyes. Nellie was a walking dictionary. She knew all the right words, but preferred her own, and the gleam was the challenge.

'You coming, then?' Rob asked.

'Soon, yes.'

He left the room, muttering this time about soil suitable for carrots, the differences between early and main crop, and the difficulties attached to thin planting.

'I'll miss you, Nellie,' Hilda whispered. That lovely, voluntary Mrs Malaprop would return to Liverpool, and thereby leave a large hole in Hilda's life. Nellie Kennedy was a one-off, a light in the darkness, a true friend. But life, as people often said these days, had to go on...

Women would trek miles in search of supplies. A whiff of orange peel, a glimpse of a banana, a rumour regarding tinned salmon, and they were off like the proverbial bats out of hell. A treasure-huntress was easy to spot; the head was always down, the march brisk, the owner-occupier of the body totally out of reach when it came to conversation or even a brief greeting.

Her purposefulness attracted followers who tried to latch on without being noticed. They noticed each other, of course, though it was quite commonplace for the leader of this route march to remain completely unaware that she was exercising a whole regiment. Unfairness set in when the shop hove into view. It was easily identifiable, as there was usually a queue outside. The ranks put a spurt on and overtook their not-really-commanding officer, often leaving her to bring up the absolute rear.

When the shop door slammed and the CLOSED sign appeared, shoulders drooped and a corporate sigh was offered up by the whole congregation. Somewhere towards the back, a little woman would be on the rampage, spitting, swearing and clobbering people with an empty shopping basket. It was all par for the course, and no one took much notice. This did not happen in Crosby, of course. Crosby was too dignified. Underhand behaviour might elicit a quiet sigh of disgust, animal faeces on a gate and, occasionally, the odd unsigned letter that pulled no punches, but there were no wrestling matches in the streets.

It was after one of these fruitless treks that Eileen was stopped in the main shopping area of Crosby village. Her newly arrived companion was Dr Tom Bingley, who was developing a habit of popping up all over the place, and he was bearing gifts in the form of two tins of salmon and two oranges. 'For you,' he said.

She took out her purse to pay.

'No, Eileen. I get these things from grateful patients.' Even when pregnant, she shone. Clear eyes, glossy hair with escaping tendrils, perfect skin, slender fingers... Oh, he shouldn't look, shouldn't be so bloody stupid.

'Do you?' She remembered telling his wife that he would do nothing to damage his precious reputation, yet just a year or so earlier, he had threatened to embrace Eileen in public and cause a divorce. She didn't trust him. He was warming up again, was working on a last desperate plan before she left Crosby for Willows. He was actually panicking. 'Then I don't want them. The patients mean your family to have them.'

'But the baby–'

'Is my problem, mine and Keith's. Leave me alone.'

'I can never do that.' His voice was low and quite chilling. 'No matter where you go, it–'

'Will never be over,' she finished for him. 'I am six months pregnant with the child of a man I would die for. He loves me so well and so thoroughly that I have no need, time or energy for anyone else. I am off the market, Tom. Not just rationed and in short supply – I am completely out of stock.' It was true. Any residual desire for this man had dissipated completely. Did he care at all for his family? Was he aware that his son... No, she must not think of it. As the sole keeper of her daughter's big secret, she needed to tread softly.

'I love you, and you know it.'

He touched her hand, and she felt nothing apart from skin on skin. Well, almost nothing...

'You love Marie, and she knows it.'

'And you know I'd leave her for you. It makes no sense to me, either, so I just accept it.'

'And I'm pregnant.'

'And I noticed. You carry beautifully.'

'My baby wants no new visitors calling in.'

Tom hid a smile with his free hand. She called a spade a bloody shovel, didn't she? What was it about her? Why her? If he put his mind to it, he could surely find a quiet little woman with hidden depths and raging hormones. But he already had that in his newly improved wife. Whenever he thought deeply about Eileen, which he did frequently, he realized that what he loved was her playfulness, her outright silliness. He wanted to park her with cups on a draining board, carry her around like a sack of King Edwards, mess about before breakfast, chase her on the beach.

'Tom, I have to get home.'

'I'll drive you.'

'You've already driven me mad. Go away.'

'I'll miss you.' Even a glimpse of her in the street was pleasure. The thought of Crosby without her was unbearable. Taking photographs to Willows for Phil was not going to be enough, because he could not travel every week just to see Madam. He had already posted three packets. And Phil was living at a different address; he would probably stay there, as there was no room at Keith's place in Willows Edge. 'Your husband knows how I feel about you.'

'Yes.'

'Is he angry?'

She shook her head. 'He knows there's no

danger of me betraying him.'

'Yet you're tempted.'

'No. I am not. He is enough for me, Tom. We have a very strong bond, and only death could separate us. I was happy with Laz, but this is perfect. So stay out of it, because you are wasting your own time and mine. Oh, and don't think about killing him, because if anything happens I'll get the police on to you before you've breathed in. Now get out of my way, because I am going home.'

'You're furious.'

She made no reply, turned and strode away. With her fingers crossed, she walked over to the opposite pavement and prayed that he would not make a scene. There was madness in him, and not a little desperation. She knew how powerful and confusing love could be, knew the strength of his feelings for her. It hadn't been like that between her and Keith. Keith had tumbled clumsily into love, but she had eased her way towards him. She had chosen a good man, and had waited months to marry him.

The fool was kerb-crawling up Manor Road.

'Do you have half an hour to spare, miss? Want to earn a few bob? My place isn't too far away, and I've got some sugar.'

'What are you after?' she asked.

'Just your body.'

'That's all right, then.' Eileen climbed in next to her husband. 'This baby is huge,' she complained. 'I think she's going to turn up with a full suite of furniture and a gas mask.'

Keith's mind was still focused on Bingley. 'I watched you with him,' he said. 'He isn't giving up, is he?'

'No. He's behind us.'

Keith sighed and looked in his rear-view mirror. He understood the desperate mind of Tom Bingley, but had their positions been reversed Keith would have walked away. Perhaps in his twenties he might have resorted to unusual methods, but he had grown up. Tom Bingley hadn't; he was still a lad chasing pots of gold at the ends of rainbows. Dr Bingley's childishness reminded Keith of Jay...

'We'll be gone from here soon, Keith. And I look like the side of a house, so I doubt he'll pursue me.' *You carry beautifully,* he had said.

Keith stopped the car and waited until Tom had overtaken him. The fact that he was still in the picture while Eileen was temporarily misshapen carried ominous implications. It was becoming clear that the doctor's interest went beyond the merely physical; he had fallen hook, line and waders for Eileen and was bent on reeling her in. 'He loves you, and I can't blame him.'

She shook her head. 'He wants me.'

'While you're pregnant? While you're huge with our baby? Sweetheart, he's crazy about you, and he's out of control. He may think he's clever, and he may actually be clever, but he's as capable as the next man of losing his page in the book. If he slips off the edge of reason, forty miles is no distance for a madman. I'm going to talk to his wife.'

'No.'

'But Eileen–'

'No,' she repeated. 'She's been through enough. If anyone talks to her, it will be me. She's been a frightened, lonely girl for as long as she can remember. Men are not her favourite people, so leave her alone.' Eileen took her husband's hand. 'Do you mind if we baptize this one Francesca Helen? We'd use the Helen, but the fancy first name would be for Miss Morrison.'

It was ideal, and he told her so. Her mother was Helen, while his had been Ellen. 'But we don't want another Nellie,' he insisted. 'One's enough.'

She agreed. The thought of another Nellie Kennedy caroming her way through life was exhausting. In truth, Eileen was exhausted anyway. Had she walked too far in pursuit of salmon? Had she... 'Keith, we need to get home. Something's wrong with me.'

'What?'

'I don't feel well.'

Immediately, he set the car in motion. Should he drive quickly or slowly? Neither seemed right, so he went along at thirty. But he didn't take her home; instead, he drove to Dr Ryan's surgery. 'Stay there,' he ordered before dashing into the building. If Tom bloody Bingley's mithering had damaged Eileen, the man would be dead in an hour or two. She had to be all right. She mattered more than any baby.

Pandemonium followed. A man who had been waiting to see the doctor about an ingrowing toenail forgot his discomfort and helped Keith carry Eileen through to the surgery, where she was placed on an examination trolley. Keith stayed at the top end and held his wife's hand while Dr Ryan dealt with the lower department. 'The plug's out,' she announced.

'What plug?' the patient demanded.

Dr Ryan smiled at her. 'This is pregnancy number five, and you don't know about plugs?'

'Only in sinks and baths,' Eileen's replied. 'Can't you shove it back in?'

'Same principle as sinks and baths, but no, I can't just shove it back A plug of mucus wedges in the neck of the womb to protect the pregnancy. If it comes out, premature labour is a distinct possibility. Now, listen to me, Eileen. You aren't going to like this, but you sure as hell are going to follow my instructions. You will not walk at all. You will take wheat germ and vitamin C. The vitamin C will be in bottles of orange juice – like the ones we give to children, government issue.'

'Bugger,' said Eileen quietly. 'What about going to the lav?'

'Bedpan.'

'Shit.'

'Exactly,' said the seasoned medic. 'Keith has to nurse you. You are about twenty-seven weeks. The closer we can get to forty, the better. For meals, you may sit up. Apart from that, you lie flat with your feet raised higher than your head.'

'How exciting. And how nice for a man who still thinks I'm a goddess. He'll have to wipe my backside.'

The doctor continued seamlessly. 'A nurse will come twice a day. You may develop pressure sores on your heels and on your rear, so Keith and the nurse will rub the areas with surgical spirit several times a day. If you get sores, stop the spirit and ask the nurse for cream. Do not attempt to hold back faeces in order to avoid embarrassment. If you try to time bowel movements to coincide with the nurse's visits, you will harm the baby. The orange juice will keep you regular.'

Eileen closed her eyes. In her opinion, if men had to go through this kind of rubbish, on top of big bellies, exhaustion and pain, the human race would die out in decades. 'And when my legs seize up?'

'They will be massaged and exercised gently on a daily basis.'

'Whoopee.'

'Don't get excited,' advised Elizabeth Ryan, sarcasm tinting the words. 'We are going to save this baby. Mel needs a sister, and your lovely husband will enjoy being a daddy. So shut up and get on with it.'

The patient opened one eye. 'It could be a boy.'

'It's a girl,' the doctor replied. 'Don't ask how I know, I just do.' She spoke to Keith. 'Take no nonsense from her. If anything happens, call me night or day. If I'm not here, someone else will come to you. The main thing is to keep her still.'

'She has a low boredom threshold, doc.'

'I think we all know that. Oh, and the move to Bolton is not possible. I know it's not ideal, but she must stay here in Crosby, in bed, until she has delivered safely.'

For Eileen, this last piece of information proved too much, and she burst into tears. 'I'll never get away from him,' she sobbed. 'And I'll be a sitting – well, a lying-down duck when you're at work and Mel's at school. He won't leave me alone. You saw him today. He was standing there again, telling me how much he loves me. I'm too tired for all that rubbish.'

Keith stroked his beloved's hair and spoke to their doctor. 'Bingley,' he snapped.

'I know. Miss Morrison told me.'

'He's just kept her standing on Moor Lane for about ten minutes. Eileen, I will not leave you except for shopping. I may even get someone to stay with you while I'm out for a short time. He can't be allowed to win, love. We mustn't be defeated by a man as low as that one. For my war work, I'll join the ARP and be a warden in the evenings while Mel's with you.' He was terrified. He wanted to wrap her in cotton wool and lie with her until the baby was born. He also wanted to kick the living daylights out of a certain doctor who was hurting Eileen.

'Leave Bingley to me,' ordered Elizabeth Ryan.

Eileen's tears dried. 'What can you do? What can anyone do?'

Elizabeth's face was grim. At this moment, she was not a doctor; she was a woman fighting for one of her own sex. The woman wanted to kick seven shades of shit out of Tom, but the doctor had to be in charge.

'What can you do?' Eileen asked again.

'I can lose him his job.' She picked up the phone and gave the operator a number.

'Marie? Yes, yes, I'm fine. You? Good. That little makeshift ambulance the WVS has, does it have a stretcher? Oh, great. Mrs Greenhalgh is in danger of going into premature labour. I need your ambulance here and two or three big men round at Miss Morrison's house. Yes. Yes. I want the furniture bringing downstairs again, and the cage round the bed. Thank you. That's brilliant.'

Keith and Eileen breathed again. For a moment, they had expected Dr Ryan to tell Marie that her husband was out of order.

'Don't ask me any more questions about my ... colleague. Sorry about your dining room, but you'll have to store it upstairs.' She glared at the supine patient. 'You are staying downstairs because I don't trust you. On the ground floor, you'll be easier to watch.'

Eileen muttered something about handcuffs and the ill-treatment of innocent women. 'Miss Morrison was a suffragette,' she finished.

'Shut up,' Keith and the doctor ordered simultaneously.

Eileen shut up. There was a distinct absence of sympathy in the world these days. But she would save Keith's baby, by heck, she would. He wanted a child, and he would have to work hard to look after her, so he deserved the best child ever.

After listening to the patient's distended abdomen, Dr Ryan perched on the edge of Eileen's temporary bed. 'Right,' she began.

'What now? Haven't you done enough?'

'Well, there's just one more thing.'

'Fire away. And I want a new wireless, one less crackly than the antique we have. And it comes in the cage with me.'

The medic took Eileen's hand in hers. 'It's doubly important that you do everything I've told you, Eileen. There are two heartbeats.'

The patient blinked stupidly. 'Two?' She forced herself to relax before addressing her beloved. 'You never do anything by halves, do you? Two puddings, two biscuits, two caramels, two babies.

No wonder I look nine months gone already.' She grinned broadly. 'I don't half love you, sweetheart. But you should come with a hazard warning, like dynamite.'

He dropped into a chair. 'I didn't know, did I? I didn't capture two of the buggers and tell them to find an egg each.'

Elizabeth Ryan laughed. 'They could be identical. If they are, that's just one little tadpole and one tiny egg. If fault's the right word, it could be Eileen's body that went for a walk on the wild side. I'm still putting my bet on the bigger one being a girl.' She liked these people. They were honest, positive and funny. 'Eileen, do you have any savings? Sorry to ask, but...'

'We have money,' Keith said.

'Then I want you to allow a Mr Barr into your cage. He is *the* man, a consultant, so his fee will be three or four times mine. I'd like him to keep an eye on you and to be there for the birth in Parkside. It's run by Augustinian nuns, so it isn't expensive. You may need a Caesarean section.'

The chin came up. Even lying down, Eileen managed to demonstrate determination. 'There's enough bars in that bloody cage without bringing another Barr in. But whatever it takes, Dr Ryan, we save both of these kiddies. Now, where's that bloody ambulance?'

Nellie was going spare. Her one and only, her precious daughter, was having twins and she'd lost her plug. Nellie, who had been unaware of the existence of uterine plugs, was crying at Hilda Pickavance's kitchen table. 'Stands to reason. Pull the plug out of a sink and everything drains away. There's no chain with a womb plug, no saying "whoops" and shoving it back in and saving what you can. And she's no good at lying down and keeping still. I'm scared, Hilda. She needs me. And I'm stuck here with the three bloody musketeers.'

'Then go to her, but go alone. I fear Mrs Openshaw might be a little too much for Eileen given current circumstances.'

Nellie dried her eyes. 'A big too much, you mean. Oh, I don't know what to do. If it's not one thing, it's another. Life settles down, so you get Germans dropping in for tea, an unexploded bomb being exploded down the road, a genius artist in the family, Jay and his diabetes – what next? Creatures from another planet, a plague of frogs?'

Hilda was tired of telling her friend that Willows would not fall down without her. The schoolchildren had settled well, so Nellie's brand of punishment was seldom required, and Eileen's three tearaways had turned out brilliantly. But Nellie, whose attitude often embraced a healthy level of cynicism, continued to eye her grandsons with suspicion. They had been thieves, vagabonds and a threat to sanity, and she was waiting for them to kick off again. Leopards didn't change their spots, and vagabonds usually reverted to type.

'Nellie?'

'What?'

'Jay and Neil are nearby. It's my belief that the boys are so well settled that you needn't worry. But if you insist on getting in a state, just remember that we have people here who will help.

Go to her, I beg you. Phil, Rob and Bertie are evacuees, and most evacuees don't have family with them. She needs you. Let me phone Keith. If he sets out now, you'll be back in Crosby just before dark. Go on. Pack your things.'

'But–'

'I mean it, Nellie. If anything happens to Eileen or her babies, you'll never forgive yourself. I couldn't live with you if you couldn't live with yourself. Go.'

Nellie went upstairs to pack her bag. While she was gone, Hilda phoned Keith. He was so grateful that he almost wept. If anyone could keep his Eileen under control, it was Nellie. He had petrol, a neighbour would stay with Eileen, and he would be at Willows in just over an hour.

He replaced the receiver and went into the once more ex-dining room. 'Your mother's coming,' he advised the patient. 'I'm going for her. Mrs Anderson or Mrs Wrigley will sit with you.'

Eileen eyed him balefully. 'One condition.'

'All right.'

'Mam can be the keeper of the royal bedpan.'

Keith opened the cage door and stood over her. 'When I said there's nothing I wouldn't do for you, I meant it. But yes, Nellie can be chief bum-wiper. I'm going now to get a babysitter. Don't move. Oh, and I'm doing the rest of the looking-after bit. Your mother will have enough chores.'

She blinked rapidly, because she'd cried enough for now. This was a man who cared deeply. Every day he did or said something precious; every day he proved himself. 'I love you,' she whispered. 'You're beyond wonderful.'

'I know.' He sighed in an exaggerated fashion. 'And so modest with it. Mr Perfect, that's me.'

'Bugger off.'

He kissed her forehead and buggered off.

Elizabeth Ryan was often described as a woman not to be trifled with. She was straight all the way up and all the way down, no discernible waist, no bustline, no hips. During the war, she rode a bicycle whenever possible, because fuel was scarce and because she wanted to stay fit for her favourite pastime, which was golf. In spite of her slender frame, she had donated to the world two attractive, clever children and enough tournament trophies to crowd a mantelpiece. Like the Watson/Kennedy/Greenhalgh women, she was determined, strong and feisty; she was also quietly angry.

When Bingley's receptionist left, Elizabeth walked into his empty waiting room and tapped on the surgery door. 'Come.'

She went in. 'A word or several,' she said.

Tom looked up. God, what a sight this was. She looked like something that had miraculously survived six months on a desert island, starved body, skin like thin paper, a shadow of moustache threatening the upper lip. 'Liz,' he said, rising to his feet.

'Oh, sit down. You'll need that chair in a minute, Tom. I have a whole kipper full of bones to pick with you. Eileen Greenhalgh. Do I need to say more?'

He felt the heat in his face. 'What about her?'

'Sensible woman, pretty as a picture, decent

husband.' She leaned forward and lowered her tone. 'While you were declaring undying love for her on Moor Lane, she was almost in labour.'

Tom's jaw dropped. 'She should have told me.'

'She didn't know. I examined her and found the dislocated operculum. I surely don't need to remind you of the implications. She now has to be flat for weeks on end, her husband can't return to his proper job, and she is terrified. Of you.'

He closed his mouth with an audible click. 'God,' he groaned.

'Now, listen to me, you fool. There are two babies. One is large and reasonably well developed, the other is smaller. Both deserve a chance. By making her stand there while you carried on like a love-sick teenager, you may have cost them their lives. Even the bigger twin needs to stay where she is. The smaller one might not survive anyway – we all know twins do battle before birth, and the weaker one may not make it into the world. All that aside, my patient is taking legal advice, because you have plagued her for well over a year. Should you disobey a court injunction, you would lose everything – your practice, your family, perhaps your liberty and, of course, your precious position in local society. Stay away from her. You know me, Tom. No threat I make is empty.'

He swallowed noisily. 'I was just ... talking to her. There's nothing going on. There never has been anything–'

'Only because she has your measure.' She leaned even closer. 'Miss Morrison knew the lot – Dockers' Word, Mrs Kennedy's attack on you. And we all know why those things happened.

Eileen doesn't want you. She wants to go back to Keith's home and live the country life.'

He gave up. 'I know.'

'Then why, Tom?' Her anger melted. The man was vulnerable.

He steepled his fingers and placed his chin on the apex. 'It's ridiculous. I just met her and loved her, fought like hell for my marriage, tried to stay away, told myself it was just sex. But it isn't. And it isn't going away, Liz.'

'Willpower?'

'Where she's concerned, I have none.'

'Then we have a problem.'

They sat in silence for several minutes, at the end of which Tom Bingley conceded defeat. He would not see her again, would not telephone the house, would distance himself from the whole family. The daughters of the two houses were best friends, and Marie had grown close to Eileen, but Tom needed not interfere with any of that.

Liz studied him while he spoke. He was edgy, uncertain and terribly unhappy. She was one of his doctors, and she wasn't liking what she saw. She asked about sleep pattern and, as she feared, he displayed symptoms of both anxiety and clinical depression. Because he was a medic, he knew the implications, and the expression in his eyes screamed for help. 'You're no candidate for electro-convulsive or insulin coma therapy, Tom. Emotionally, you were quite well organized till Eileen came along. The woman in Rodney Street – do you think she could help?'

He shrugged. 'I'm too tired to try. Eileen has taken me over body and soul.'

'I can't move her to that village, and you know why. I'm putting her with Barr, and she'll deliver in Parkside if she doesn't miscarry. What the hell am I supposed to do? Prescribe bromide for you?'

Again, he raised his shoulders.

'Are you still intimate with Marie?'

'Sometimes, yes.'

'Bloody hell, man. You spent a fortune–'

'I spent a fortune to prove I was desirable even to Marie. It's always been about me, me, me.'

'You hate you.'

'Yes.'

'That's depression.'

'Yes.'

'Have you self-medicated? What's your poison?'

'Anything I can get my hands on in the evenings when I'm at home. Spirits, wine, beer if there's nothing else. The drinking's not yet out of control, but I'm afraid it may become so. And all because of a little woman from Scotland Road.'

Elizabeth Ryan was at a loss. Here sat a patient with full insight into his condition and its implications. He was intelligent, capable, and a darned good physician. And he had fallen in love. This was not a sin, but she had long recognized that it could become an illness. For most people, the disease righted itself, couples settled down, remained close and were cured. Or they parted, recovered and looked elsewhere. But the unrequited version was potentially deadly. 'I have a theory that testosterone kills off brain cells,' she muttered, almost to herself. 'Women suffer less. I don't know why, but there it is.'

'Oh, God.' He made a pillow with his arms and placed his head on it.

Liz had to make a decision. 'Tom, I can't certify you, because you're sane. You will have to volunteer. I'm naming it nervous exhaustion. We all know you've been dashing down to town to help after running two or three surgery sessions a day.'

His head shot up. 'We've lawyers down there who work full office hours before going out to act as firemen. Why am I different?'

'You just are. I'm going to talk to Marie. There is help. Naturally, I will not mention Eileen Greenhalgh to your wife. But you must go away from here, my friend. Please, allow me to help.'

Tom nodded his agreement. Unless something happened, he might go right under and be unfit for work. Liz Ryan, while not a gentle deliverer of bad news, always knew her onions. He was unbelievably tired, and she saw that. He wasn't eating properly, was getting very little sleep, and alcoholism lay in his path. But there might be a fork in the road. He couldn't yet see it, but someone else might spot it and get him to change direction.

'Tom?'

He looked up and, just for a moment, caught a glimpse of the reason why her handsome husband was so devoted to her. She cared, and her eyes were pretty. 'What?'

'You'll be all right. I promise you. *Nil desperandum.*'

'That's what Eileen calls the coal man. But she altered it slightly to Neil Desperado. He fancies her as well.'

'Is Neil his name?'

He shook his head. 'No. See what I mean? She makes it up as she goes along and she carries every colour of the rainbow in her palette. My head's full of her. When I wake at five in the morning, she's there. When I try to fall asleep at night, she's sitting on a draining board with three cups and a pan. Just a game she plays. With him.'

'He's a good man.'

'I know. This is obsession.'

Outside, Elizabeth dried her eyes. Detachment was vital in a doctor, but she was temporarily defeated. Tom Bingley was not a bad person; he was just a man who had suffered an accident. He was one of those who had fallen in love a little late in life. He had married, children had been born, and the love of his life had fallen into his path when he was over the age of forty. There could be no quick cure; he was already teetering on the edge. Such a bloody shame. Not for the first time in her career, she felt powerless. Broken bodies showed and could often be dealt with. But fractured hearts and souls were beyond her reach. He had to go away.

While Dr Ryan was dealing with one Bingley, Mel had her hands full with another of that clan. In truth, the reverse was nearer the mark, because Peter had handfuls of her. He had pushed her against a massive oak in Coronation Park, and his upper limbs were on the move. She was the only one. He had done his best to stay away thanks to the damage attempted by his sister, but that was all mended and forgotten now, so might they get together again? Secretly, of course. He wanted to prove that he wasn't homosexual, but Mel had sense enough to know that she could not be part of that process.

'Mel?'

'No.' The syllable emerged loudly and angrily. 'I can't live that kind of life. Mam's pregnant and not at her best, because it's a big baby and she's tired.' While Peter was weak, selfish and terrified.

'But Mel–'

'No.' She pushed him away and battered him with her school satchel. When her arm grew tired, she spoke to him in a quieter tone. 'Even if our relationship survived until we got to twenty, I couldn't exist like that. When my mother's back to normal, it'll still be impossible. There's no future for us. I may be a couple of months short of fifteen, but I've sense enough to know it couldn't work. I'd try to change you. I'd worry every time you left the house. In the end, I'd probably murder you, because you worry about no one but yourself.'

He sat on a park bench, and she joined him. 'Look, Pete. I feel really honoured that you talked to me, that you turned to me. But it wasn't love, and we both know that. It was mechanics. It was something everyone has to go through.'

'You said you'd always be there,' he said petulantly. 'Me a barrister, you a solicitor, one of the Inns, a house somewhere nice like Wimbledon.'

She turned to face him. 'Look. I've read about it, and it's against the law. The person who marries you will be a shield. But I will always, always be your friend.'

'That's why it has to be you. I can love you. We could be normal, have children, holidays, a good life. I know I can do that with you, and only you.'

Mel wanted to tell him that she wanted much, much more, that a life conducted behind closed doors was not for her. 'I know a little bit about homosexuality,' she told him quietly. 'Miss Pickavance's uncle was the same, and he kept on the move all the time, always aware that he could be arrested at any point. I can't be your lace curtain, wouldn't want to be.'

He stared at the ground. 'What's going to happen to me? It's so ... lonely. You're the only one I could tell.'

Mel feared for him. She'd come across the poem written in France by Oscar Wilde after his release from Reading Gaol. Hard labour, hour after hour on a treadmill, just because he was different. 'The only thing you can do, Peter, is to remain a bachelor, because no woman will be right. We're not just wives and daughters and mothers; we're people. When I went through that silly phase I thought I'd pay any price, because you're so beautiful. Then I got angry when you tried to throw me out of the house – remember? I wiped the floor with your lovely mother. Women aren't here just for men. That's all finished. Why did you grab me just now? I'm not what you want.'

He didn't weep, but his voice was unsteady as he tried to explain his feelings not only to her, but also to himself. He didn't want to be like this, hadn't asked to be born an outcast. Concentration was becoming difficult, and he was afraid of falling behind at school. 'The law exists to strangle people into submission,' he declared. 'I'm not sure I want to be a part of that.'

She'd been reading about the subject, of course. 'Greeks did it. Tribes who've scarcely been touched by civilization do it. Lions, porpoises – all kinds of animals behave in a homosexual manner even when opportunities with the opposite sex exist. You have to fight from within. You get to the top of your profession, Peter, then find a way of attacking the law. You walk on the Wilde side – the Oscar Wilde side – but not on a treadmill.'

'I'm scared, Mel.'

She understood that. 'I'll be there,' she promised. 'I will never desert you. We're friends.'

He muttered something about being better off dead, so she clouted him again with her heavy, book-filled bag. 'Selfish, selfish, selfish,' she said with every blow. 'Think about your family. Start talking suicide, and I start talking to your father. You bloody well stay alive. There are other people like you, women as well as men. We have to find them when we're older. We have to start a secret society, only it can't be secret, because we'll need to advertise. A movement. Yes, there has to be a movement. OWLS. Oscar Wilde Liberation Society.'

'He can't be liberated, because he's dead.'

'Just a bit, yes. True genius never dies. Don't simply give up. It's cowardly, and it would kill your parents. And if they found out that I knew why you'd done it, they'd kill me too. Gloria would have my guts for garters, so don't dare let me down, Peter.'

'I won't.'

They walked home, separating when they reached the junction of their two roads. She prepared to carry on in the same direction while he turned off into St Andrew's Road. For some unfathomable reason, this parting of their ways had significance. Mel stood for a few seconds and watched his progress. She was no longer his guardian, no longer his shelter. Any slight hope that had lingered in him was now removed. And she was the remover.

Eighteen

'Gran!' Mel closed the back door, threw down her satchel and wrapped both arms round her much-loved maternal grandmother. 'Are Mam and Dad off to Willows? Where's Mrs Openshaw? Oh, it's lovely to see you.' The greeting was followed by a big kiss on Nellie's cheek. 'I thought you'd never get here. Are the three musketeers all right? And Miss Pickavance? What about Mr Collins and the diabetes?'

'Later. Let's take a pew first, love.' Nellie Kennedy disentangled herself and led her granddaughter to the kitchen table. They sat down, and Nellie gave Mel the full story about Eileen. She had learned over many years that only the truth, the whole truth and nothing approaching decoration would satisfy Mel. 'So that's why I'm here, love. Your dad picked me up just before two o'clock, so I've not been here long myself. He got one of the neighbours to sit with her while he was out, because he's treating her like some rare plant. Anyway, it's this here plug thing, like I said. All she can do is lie there like cheese on toast, only paler and not best pleased. When I got here this afternoon, she was moaning and cursing fit to bust, and she'd been in bed just over three hours. Three hours, Mel. She's what my mam would have called mortallious troublesome.'

'Still thirteen weeks to go, Gran? That's a long time for anyone to be stuck in bed.'

'Your dad's been talking about strapping her down at night. He says she's a wriggler in her sleep. Anyway, it's a double bed, so he's going in with her to try to keep her still. He'll have to sleep during the day while I watch her. We'll need eyes in the backs of our heads, because she's always been a fidget.'

Mel folded her arms and stared hard at the head of her family. 'No we won't. She'll carry on complaining about this that these and those, but she won't lose her baby.' Mel's mother had her share of faults, but she believed implicitly in the rights of the unborn.

Nellie had forgotten to mention the other bit of the tale. 'It's babies, not baby. She's having a couple of them. Whether it's a matching pair or two separates, we don't know. She never had a minute's trouble carrying or birthing the four of you, so this must be on account of its being twins.' She didn't mention Dr Tom Bingley and his part in today's drama, though Keith had furnished her with the facts during the journey from Willows.

Mel groaned. 'It could be two more boys, Gran. Doesn't bear thinking about.'

'Yes, but we want them alive whatever they are. Keith's a lovely, special man, Mel. She loves the bones of him. If I'd picked him for her myself, I couldn't be better pleased. They're his children, Mel. In his forties and expecting twins, he'll be setting a lot of store by this pregnancy.'

Mel pondered for a few seconds. Gran was right, because Mam was happier than she'd been in years. It was as if she suddenly had all she wanted. Keith was a wonderful man, and these twins were his first hope of true fatherhood. 'Is Miss Morrison's davenport still in there with Mam?'

'It is.'

'Right. I'll do my homework at the davenport, and that'll give you both a break. If she puts an eyelid wrong, I'll clout her with the big frying pan.'

'And that'll show her how much you love her, eh?'

They were both laughing when the doorbell sounded. Nellie admitted a short man with a Victorian moustache, a large doctor's bag and wire-rimmed spectacles. He introduced himself as Mr Barr, specialist attached to Mrs Greenhalgh. 'We're all attached to her,' was Nellie's reply. 'You'll find her very lovable, but without much patience when it comes to lying there and doing nothing. She's behind that second door along.'

He disappeared for the better part of half an hour. While he, Eileen and Keith were closeted in

Miss Morrison's reassembled downstairs bedroom, Mel and Nellie started the task of turning five ounces of minced meat into a cottage pie for four plus dog. This involved many potatoes, a bit of leftover cabbage and a pinch of imagination. 'It'll have a bubble and squeak roof, this cottage,' Mel said.

'Shut up and keep peeling. There's folk in London, Liverpool and all over the place who'll never eat cottage pie again, because they're dead.' Nellie paused. 'That feller's a long time in there, isn't he?'

Mel said nothing; she'd been ordered to shut up and peel.

They heard the front door opening and closing before Keith joined them. Both fixed their eyes on him, and he was smiling, a very waggy-tailed Spoodle in his arms.

'Well?' Mel breathed.

Keith placed the dog on the floor and crossed his fingers as he joined them at the table. 'According to that chap, who seems to know his job, she's not in too bad a state. He's seen it all before. It's not uncommon for women to lose that oper-whatever plug thing days or even weeks before the kick-off, but with this being twins Eileen will have to stay in bed. The flat on her back business is a precaution for now, though she should be able to sit up for a few hours soon. We've got all his phone numbers, and he will deliver the babies himself. Because they're ... what did he say? Disparate, I think. One's big and one's small, so he insists on a section in about ten weeks.'

'Did he mean desperate?'

'No, Nellie. He meant their sizes don't match. He says they're not identical as far as he can tell, and he's usually right. He didn't want to poke around too much, but he thinks the neck of her womb's tight enough for now.'

'But she mustn't walk?'

'That's right. She's still calling herself bedpan Bertha.'

Mel dashed to her mother's side, or almost-side, as she stayed out of the cage.

'Are you all right, mam?'

'Am I buggery. I've got to stay flat for a few days, and that means my big baby's pressing on my little one. It's all wrong. The poor tiny thing'll be squashed flat by the other hulking great heavy-weight boxer. Seriously, I'm fine, Mel. What will be will be. But when I look in Keith's eyes, a bit of the shine's gone. He's terrified.'

Mel disagreed. 'He's fine. As long as you do as you're told, he'll carry on being fine.' She wanted to tell Mam about Peter, about his fears and his confusion, but this wasn't the best time. She'd always confided in Mam. Well, almost always. The messing about with Peter in Rachel Street had been an exception, but even that had come out in the end. 'If Miss Morrison hadn't died, and if we hadn't got so badly upset about losing her, and if there hadn't been papers to sign and the will to deal with, you'd have gone to Willows weeks ago. That doctor up there is rubbish, and you'd have lost the babies, Mam. The wind always brings some good, doesn't it?' Though the wind had brought no good to London in December...

Lying in bed had clearly failed to suppress

Eileen's powers of deduction. 'Have you been pulled through a hedge backwards, or is this the new haute couture style? You're crumpled. What happened?'

'Erm ... chasing about in the park on our way home.'

Eileen delivered a hard stare. Merchants girls did not chase about in the park on their way home, and she said so. 'Try again, madam.'

Mel knew she had to tell the truth. There came a point when everybody ran out of imagination, and a certain look in her mother's eyes often marked the edge of Mel's territory. 'Peter,' she said. 'Don't you dare sit up, Mam.'

'But isn't he supposed to be the other way?' The tone was dropped when the last three words were spoken.

'He is the other way, and you're the only one who knows apart from me, so say nothing to anyone. But he has plans to fool some poor girl into taking up with him so that he'll look as if he's not. Every girl at school wants him. He's good at sports, clever in the classroom, and he has a gorgeous face. But he's basically honest. I was the only one he trusted enough to be given the full story. And in his way, he loves me. But I'm not spending time pretending to be his girlfriend. He talks about us getting married and having children. I told him a wife and children are not there to be a safety curtain while he runs round being whatever he needs to be.'

'Quite right, too,' Eileen said. 'And when he goes to prison, the poor woman will be left there having to explain to her kids why their dad's done a disappearing act. You're well out of it.'

Mel pondered for a moment. 'I do care about him. I do think it's terrible that people like Peter get sent to jail just because they aren't attracted to the opposite sex. Who are they harming?'

'Women and children. They get wed, have kids, then bugger off to prison or with another man.'

'And the law sends them in those directions. It wants changing. It's going to change – I'm with him on that one.'

'So it's like the ten-day week you were going to invent?'

'No. This one's doable. Anyway, it's not your worry. Just concentrate on hanging on to these babies, even if they are going to be boys.'

'The big one's a girl, according to Dr Ryan. I wanted to know how she knows, and she said she doesn't know how she knows, but she knows.'

'You sound like Gran.'

A huge sigh was followed by, 'I know. I don't know how I know, but–'

'Stop right there, Mam.'

'But it comes to all of us.'

'We all end up sounding like Gran?'

Eileen laughed while her daughter left the room. But seriousness returned quickly. Why were her babies threatened? Had Tom Bingley upset her to the point where Keith's children might be hurt? Yet Mel was right; had Eileen moved to Willows, where the doctor was daft, this might have happened without any persecution by Tom. Had Miss Morrison's death had an adverse effect, had yesterday's sardines been all right, was the little baby giving up and trying to get out past the big one?

Was the big one healthy? Eileen had known plenty of large people whose health had been less than perfect.

Mel returned. 'Gloria just phoned, Mam. Her dad's going away because of nervous exhaustion. Apparently, it's people who don't seem nervous or exhausted that get nervous exhaustion. So how does his doctor know he's got it? I mean if it doesn't show, how do they know? How does he know?'

Eileen swallowed. 'You're sounding like my mother now. It'll show in his work and in his general behaviour.' *He's going away because of me.* No, she couldn't say that out loud, could she? *He thinks enough of me to stop his life for a while and take himself off.* Or had Dr Ryan put him up to this? Elizabeth Ryan could be fierce if she set her mind to it.

'Gloria's upset.'

'She will be; he's her father.'

'It's the war,' Mel declared. 'He's been doing too much. A lot of people are doing too much.' She carried some books to the davenport. 'I'm in charge of you while I do homework, so behave: it's moral philosophy.'

'Is that religion?'

'Debatable. Mam?'

'What?'

'You know when they sort of got back together again – Dr and Mrs Bingley, I mean.'

'Yes?'

'Well, it stopped. They're still in the same bed, but all the giggling's finished.'

'Nervous exhaustion.'

Had circumstances been different, Mel might have asked the question, but she didn't dare. Was Gloria's dad still carrying a torch for Mel's mother? Did nervous exhaustion translate into a broken heart? This was not the time for such research, so she stuck with moral philosophy which was, on the whole, much easier.

Marie was not happy. Her husband's doctor had declared him unfit for work, and he was to be admitted to a private nursing home in Southport. According to Liz Ryan, Tom had been overdoing things for some time, and he needed a long rest in order to recuperate before too much damage occurred.

So this was the reason for his neglect of her, was it? After the treatment in Rodney Street, a honeymoon had ensued, and Marie was now the one who missed being loved. Sometimes, she caught him looking at her with longing in his eyes, though he seldom made an effort in her direction. There was another woman. But no, there couldn't be. Had he fallen in love with someone, he wouldn't have been so ... happy wasn't the word; he wouldn't have been so complacent about going off to stay in Southport. According to Tom, Southport was suitable only for retirement, death and seagulls. Thus he had been known to dismiss an elegant and much loved seaside town, and he now intended to reside there for the foreseeable future.

The suitcase was half filled and on the bed when he lost his complacency. He turned the case over and emptied its contents on the quilt. Who the hell did Liz Ryan think she was? Eileen's threatened miscarriage was nothing to do with him, and he was being forced to enter a low-key psychiatric facility because of it? He sat down. 'Marie?'

'What?'

'I'm not going. She can't make me go, because I'm not certifiable.'

Marie sat next to him. 'What's happening to you ... to us? We were fine. Do you think more hypnosis would help? We were doing so well, both of us–'

'No.' He didn't want to open up again. He didn't want to admit to anyone that he was almost completely defeated by love. And how the hell could he love someone attached to a Liverpool accent? And to another man? 'It wouldn't help the exhaustion, Marie, but a few weeks off work might. I don't need to go to Southport. There's a beach here I can exercise on as long as I don't fall over a dragon's tooth and land in the barbed wire. Exercise helps with these symptoms. You're here. My children are here. There's a dog I can walk. And have you seen the state of Gloria? She doesn't know whether she's coming or going.'

Marie had seen the state of Gloria.

'I refuse to leave her, so I need to get this sorted out immediately, if not sooner. Back in twenty minutes.' Tom kissed the top of his wife's head and walked out. Straightening his spine, he began the short walk to his doctor's surgery. He was going to see Liz Ryan. She needed to be put straight, and he was the man to do it.

'I am not and never have been Eileen Greenhalgh's doctor. You can't lose me my job. I shall stay away from my surgery as advised, because I admit to being very tired. I'll rest and exercise until I feel better, then it'll be back to work. No convalescent home for me, Liz.' He stood tall at the other side of the desk. Liz, seated, felt small, and she knew that his intention had been to dominate the situation physically, mentally and through sheer dogged determination. He feared no one. She should have remembered that.

She glared at her patient. They both knew she wouldn't report him; they both knew he was a good doctor who needed respite. 'Stay away from two things. Liverpool, and Eileen Greenhalgh. You are putting yourself at risk in Liverpool. And you are putting her at risk here. It isn't love, Tom. It's obsession.'

'Yes, ma'am.'

Liz sighed heavily. He didn't know how close he was to emotional collapse. People in such a state were often unaware of their true situation. 'If you go anywhere near that poor woman's house, I shall make it my personal duty to separate you from medicine. I know she's never been your patient, and she would have managed you and your idiocy had she not been pregnant. But if her health worsens because of you, I shall report you. So.' She picked up a pen. 'A letter witnessed by my lawyer will be delivered to you, and you will sign the delivery sheet. My copy will be kept safe. Go near her after this written warning from your doctor and hers, go near her while an injunction forbids it, and you'll be in next Christmas's mincemeat.'

'There's no need for all that,' he blustered.

'Oh, but there is. She went to pieces earlier in this very room. "He won't leave me alone" and "I'll never get away from him" were her words. There is need. Where she is concerned, you are a predator. You are not the Tom Bingley I know. You're on the verge of emotional collapse and you may lose control of your behaviour.'

'But I'm not on the verge of anything, Liz.' Eileen was frightened not of him, but of herself. There was hope.

Liz tapped the table with her pen. Cupid was careless with his arrows. Never in a month of Sundays would she have expected Tom to fall for someone like Eileen Greenhalgh. She was extraordinarily pretty, but she was not Tom Bingley's type. There again, that was often how it happened. An intelligent and relatively sane man would come across someone who was nothing like his wife, and the arrow went into his chest and stayed there. The same applied to women.

'Eileen was drawn to me. It didn't happen in one direction only.'

'I see.'

'Do you? Look, I don't want to shock you, but she wasn't putty in my hands – she was magma, red hot lava. And I did the right thing, stayed where I was, got help for my frigid wife, carried on working, rescued people and so on. Let no one say I didn't fight for the status quo.'

The helpless doctor could hear the change in her patient's tone. Certification was not a possibility, because he wasn't mad, and other medics wouldn't support such a drastic step. Liz and Tom had worked in tandem for years, each helping the other when the workload became too great. Because she knew him, she was acutely aware of the changes in him. Other people might not see what she saw. He was utterly sane, miserably so. But the emotional seesaw he rode might tip at any time, and another patient of hers could suffer when he finally snapped. 'Go away,' she ordered. 'And I wasn't kidding about the law. You will receive a copy soon.'

The look he awarded her might have turned a lesser woman to water, but Liz maintained her solid state. It was going to be just a matter of time; he had better wait until after those babies had been delivered safely, God willing. But what if the births weakened Eileen? What if he started hanging about on the bombed playing field behind Eileen's house? What if...? There was no point in what iffing. The bloody man had gone anyway.

A few weeks later, Elsie Openshaw arrived in Crosby. She was driven across by Mr Marchant, friend of Miss Pickavance, art tutor to Philip Watson. Elsie had seldom travelled in a car, so she was round-eyed when she reached St Michael's Road. 'But ... I mean ... there's all kinds of... I saw ... what the blood and sand have they done to Liverpool?'

'Oh, that,' Nellie replied with all the nonchalance she could muster. 'They'll not kill this city, Elsie. The folk down there are tougher than shoe leather.'

'And they all talk funny. They're neither for'ards nor back'ards.' Elsie went through to visit the patient. Nellie looked at Keith, Keith looked at

Nellie. 'Can laughing cause a miscarriage?' he asked.

'I doubt it. She's far enough gone, lad. The twins'd be in with a good chance if they got born now.'

Two eavesdroppers stood in the hall. They knew that Elsie was hilarious, and that she was completely unaware of the fact.

Her strident tone, complete with broad, flat vowels, made its way out of Eileen's retreat. 'Your wife's trapped,' Nellie mouthed. Keith nodded his agreement.

Elsie was in full flood. 'You do. Just you think on. You do know who I mean. He was there the day you came with Miss Pickavance. His wife's got a caliper – one leg shorter than t'other. He's a long, lanky thing with a hernia, called Malcolm. His daughter lives in the Edge near us, lost all her teeth in an accident, got a spiral staircase fitted just to be different. I wouldn't care – she doesn't even own the bloody house. Spiral staircase, indeed. She'd have been a sight better cleaning up her doorstep – it's not seen donkey stone in years, hasn't that.'

'Oh, Elsie,' moaned Eileen. 'I'm so glad you came. You cheer me up.'

'Well, I don't know how, I'm sure. You're easy suited if you can laugh at Malcolm Bridge and his hernia. Ooh, I nearly forgot. Are we doing lemon, white or pale lilac?'

'Eh?' This single syllable from Eileen arrived crippled, as if it needed fitting with a surgical support.

'Your wool. Matinee jackets and bootees.'

'Any of those colours will do.'

Elsie lowered her tone, though she remained audible. 'You've done very well after losing your pericoolium.' She had been at the medical books again. 'That's the proper word for it. At least it weren't play centre previous.'

'Placenta praevia,' Nellie mouthed on the other side of the door. 'She's worse than me, because most of mine are deliberate.' They went away for a quick giggle, then returned to sentry duty.

'No,' Elsie was saying, 'no, that's her cousin. Mind, there's a tale to her and all. Monica, she's called. Very thin, lazy eye, gets a squint if she takes her specs off. Lived tally with a bloke from Blackburn with a thumb missing and one of them hanglebar moustaches. He came home early one day and found her in bed with the boss from the Co-op down Halliwell way and a lamplighter. They were playing tries and turns. But no, that's Monica.'

'I thought she'd stopped gossiping,' Nellie whispered.

'Anything outside the three-mile limit is fair game,' Keith replied quietly.

'And doesn't Elsie know anybody normal and in one piece?'

Keith shrugged and pinned an ear to the door.

'It were their Vera. Beautiful hair, she had, all waves and curls right down her back.'

'What about her head?' the invisible Eileen managed.

Keith and Nellie did another soft-shoe shuffle towards the front door. 'I can't take much more,' Nellie said. They returned.

'So she leans across the table, all casual, like,

sticks a knife in his chest and carries on eating her toast while he bleeds to death. It were her best tablecloth and all, so she whips it off and sticks it in cold water. It's a bugger to shift, is blood. Then she has a second cuppa, combs her hair, puts her hat and coat on and goes to the police. "I've killed him," she says.'

'God,' breathed the patient. 'Did she hang?'

'Did she hell as like. When the police doctor stripped her off, Vera were one big bruise. She had twenty-seven broken ribs, cos some were broke twice or three times. Poor girl came a flea's whisker away from having a punctuated lung. Then there were the burn damage from ropes and fag ends – he used her as an ashtray. Happen he were practising his boy scout knots and all. He were very big in the scouts at one time.'

Keith and Nellie fled to the kitchen. Now they had a war, a pregnancy, a teenage girl and an Elsie to deal with. Oh, and a bigger puppy. Eventually, they ran out of laughter. 'I suppose it's only fair.' Keith set the kettle to boil. 'They're overrun with Scousers at Willows, so why shouldn't Liverpool be blessed with an Elsie?'

Nellie thought about that before answering. 'She'll not be used to it. Bangs, thuds, explosions and sirens – all part of our lives now. Nearest she's come was when they exploded a stray bomb over Affetside way. It was all controlled by the UXB squad. That German lad still writes to Hilda, you know. She reckons he'll never go home.'

Elsie stood in the doorway. It might have been fairer to say that the doorway framed her, because she filled it. 'That daughter of yours has a very strange sense of humour, Nellie. She laughs in all the wrong places. But I'll give her this, she's saved them babies, God love her. And that dog won't leave her side, will he? Eeh, it's a smashing house, is this. I bet it'll look lovely when it's done up and painted proper after the war.' She went on and on, even when the others had stopped listening. 'It's nice round here,' was the last line in her monologue.

Nellie smiled to herself. This was the Elsie she had missed; this was the friend whose eccentricities would see everyone through the war. Elsie wasn't everybody's cup of Horniman's, but she was interesting, and free entertainment was one of the few unrationed items available these days. 'How long are you staying, Elsie?'

'Till I've counted them babies' fingers, toes, ear 'oles and eyes.' She cast a glance over Keith. 'Aye, they'll be grand as long as they get their mother's looks and brains. If they take after you, they'll just have to do their best, won't they? Can I have a butty? Or a bit of toast?'

The next few days and weeks would merit a title – 'Remembering How We Fed Elsie During a War'. Elsie took for granted all the little extras she managed to acquire at Willows. Here, for the first time, she was forced to live with true rationing; here, she began her weight loss programme.

Elsie Openshaw took up walking to fill in the time between meals. It didn't take her long to realize that her life at home had been one long meal interrupted only by sleep, shoppers, and people wanting the services of the Royal Mail.

Spoodle was a good excuse. Reluctant at first to leave Eileen in what he recognized as her hour of need, he had to be dragged along on his lead, and Elsie was just about ready to give up when he finally decided to go with the flow. Humans, he had discovered, always won in the end, so fighting was useless, tiring and a waste of breath.

Each day, they walked a little further until, after a couple of weeks of gradually lengthening journeys, they finally reached Nellie's beloved river. Immediately, Spoodle pulled so hard that he took the lead with him, leaving Elsie to scream while the dog chased his sister along a beach made narrower by dragons' teeth and barbed wire.

'Hello, stranger.'

She turned and studied the man. 'Oh, it's you. Spoodle's buggered off, and now there's two of him, and they're in all the muck. See? Over there.'

'Pandora's from the same litter. She'll come back to me, and he'll follow. How are you? Oh, and the food at Christmas was delicious.'

'How am I? Bloody starving's how I am.' She opened her coat. 'See this frock? It fitted when I got here. I'm becoming emacicated.'

Tom Bingley didn't laugh. 'You look better for the weight loss.' She would probably be healthier, too. 'Are you staying with Eileen and Keith?' he asked, a coating of nonchalance applied to the words.

'I am. Well, with Nellie, really. But I'm stopping till I see them babies. She's done well, has Eileen, keeping to her bed like that when she's not blessed with a patient nature. She can sit up now, like, but she must have been scared when it first kicked off. Any road, Nellie's mistress of the bedchamber, and I'm the bloody dog walker.'

'So am I, Elsie. I had to take a break from work. There's been a lot of pressure and stress. Not just my job, but the raids in town. It's been a bitter time.'

She wasn't surprised, and she told him so. The noises at night, bumps and thumps and bangs were enough to send anybody pots for rags. 'I thought I were going to be dead at first. Nellie explained things to me, but it's still only seven or eight miles away, so I'm a bit feared, cos we never see nothing up yon where I come from. Best excitement we get is tupping, and Jay Collins falling off a ladder when his sugar's low. Even that doesn't happen a lot now.'

'Diabetic chap?'

'Aye. Here comes trouble.' Two filthy little floor mops with legs arrived. The pups were breathless and covered in the muddy sand that gets dredged up by a tidal river. 'What the blood and dolly mixtures are we supposed to do now?' Elsie asked.

'My house,' Tom replied. 'Nearer than Nellie's. A quick rub down for the dogs, pot of tea for us, and a cake of sorts. Marie does her best, but I've ordered some chickens, then we can have our own eggs. And I've turned over the back garden for vegetables.'

'Aye, well keep your hens off that lot. Inquisitive little buggers, they are, so watch your veg. And if you fancy a chicken supper, I'll do the deed for you.'

Tom hadn't thought that far ahead. Eggs were one thing, murder was another. He swallowed.

'You make me laugh, you townies,' said Elsie. 'It's all right for the butcher to kill, but you'll not dirty your hands, eh? And you a doctor, and all.'

They walked back to St Andrew's Road, a feat for which they deserved medals, since the two pups decided to take up French knitting, and their leads became intertwined in a pattern that might have been pleasing had there been no mud involved. By the time they reached Tom's house, all four members of the posse were as black as sweeps.

Tom dealt with the spoodles while Elsie cleaned herself up and made tea. But the best laid plans often fell apart in the presence of Pandora and her brother. Within minutes, the whole house was marked. They didn't like the bath. They didn't like Lux Flakes, green soap, or human shampoo. They ran muddy, slightly muddy, damp and wet through across beds, rugs, chairs and sofas. They skidded into the kitchen, banged into Elsie's lisle-stockinged legs, turned, ran on the spot because their feet found no purchase on the slick floor, and were finally returned to the bathroom by an angry Boltonian female. 'Didn't you close the door, you daft bugger?'

'I didn't think,' he answered weakly.

'Out,' she commanded. 'Make the tea. And may God have mercy on your soul when the missus gets back.' But he wasn't going anywhere. Nothing on earth could persuade him to abandon Elsie to the machinations of two canine lunatics. He sent her away.

The missus, when she returned, thought the situation was hilarious. She staggered through the house with mops and cloths, pausing at the bathroom door to listen to her beleaguered husband. His voice rose above loud splashes and unhappy yelps. 'There has to be a tranquilizer for dogs,' he shouted. 'Put the bloody sponge down. No, we do not eat loofahs or pumice stones.'

Marie slid her body into the room, taking care not to open the door to its full width. Tackling one pup each, they managed the task, but only just. Wet through and laughing, they sat side by side on a flooded floor, clothes sodden, towels dripping, two very wet spoodles shaking water from their curls and up the walls. 'Bit of a mess,' she managed, tears dampening further the soggy atmosphere.

Tom pressed a hand against his aching stomach. 'Can you imagine a Great Dane or an Irish wolfhound?' he howled.

She hit him with a wet washcloth. 'Shut up.'

The door opened and Elsie stood in the gap, arms folded, head shaking sadly. A pair of soggy dogs shot past her and down the stairs. 'Hello, Mrs Bingley. I've found some big towels. You two had better sort yourselves out while I look for them two buggers and dry them off. Then I'll light a fire.' She wandered off, muttering quietly about daft Scousers, stupid dogs and the bloody muck in the bloody Mersey.

'That was fun,' Tom said seriously. 'Fun is what we lack.' He stood up, locked the door and made love to his wife in a dirty, waterlogged space alongside the bath. There was a near-stranger downstairs, and their surroundings were rather less than perfect, but it was glorious. Except for one thing.

When he reached the point of no return, for one exquisite moment, he thought of Eileen.

Dear all,

I have been remiss. So many letters from Mel, but I find myself quite caught up in life – who said it was quiet, peaceful and/or boring in the county? The new greenhouses have been erected on Willows land, while the planting at Home Farm was achieved in record-breaking time, since Neil Dyson now has an assistant, one Robin Watson – be proud of him, Eileen.

While his greenhouses are primarily for tomatoes, Robin intends to grow exotic flowers after the war. He is tender with blooms, and he says that brides should have more than just roses in their bouquets and sprays. So, like his older brother, he seems to have an artistic eye, though he says he'll get a female to front the wedding business. At that point, several others jumped on the bandwagon to offer hairdressing, wedding cakes and bridal attire, so perhaps we shall rename the hamlet Weddings Ltd.

But a great deal of my time has been invested in Philip, who blossoms like one of the rare orchids his brother might grow. Mr Marchant and I arranged a show for him, and we sold everything! Yes, even in wartime, he is valued. People who invest in him now will reap the benefit in later life, because Philip's talent is unique.

Which leaves just Bertie, your baby for the moment, Eileen. That boy can calm a horse from a distance, can break one for riding in under a week, and now has paid work in two stables where staff have gone to war. He rides daily, and is becoming accomplished.

I asked him once about his long-term future. He

declared his intention to serve the King at any of the palaces. The King's horses deserve the best, and he is the self-proclaimed greatest horseman ever born, so there you have it.

The most touching thing happened. When Philip sold his paintings, he gave some of the money to Bertie for riding boots, jodhpurs, coat and hard hat. Bertie, very solemn-faced, took the money and bought the things he needed. As he chose second-hand except for boots, he was able to give back change. 'For paint and stuff,' he said. Philip took the change and used it well. They are all good friends, and I believe their move to the country was for the best.

Appreciation of life here is widespread. Many of the other Scotland Roaders have settled well, but their parents have mixed feelings. When they visit their offspring, they often come to me almost wringing their hands because their So-and-So doesn't fancy going home when the war ends. God alone knows what lies ahead, but I think we are in for fun and games when hostilities cease – as long as we are victorious, of course. Like your three boys, most of the evacuees are at impressionable ages, since country folk took children who were old enough to be useful. They are useful; they are also falling in love with a way of life.

Eileen, I am so glad that you have come this far with your twins. I can scarcely wait for you all to come home. Nellie and Elsie, our two wise women, are missed, as is Keith. By the way, I am learning to drive and have bought a little Austin, so don't worry about keeping the car. Your need is greater than ours, because you are so near to Liverpool and so close to giving birth, and that vehicle might get you out of all kinds of difficulty.

The six willows are thriving, the land is healthy, and our best bull has been in great demand lately. We are taking no fees. Instead, we get produce, poultry and piglets. The Ministry has accepted the idea for the duration.

Eileen smiled when she reached this point. Black market dealings went on, of course, though Miss Pickavance would never allow such information to stain paper.

Please continue to take care of each other. Don't worry about the boys. They are well behaved, busy and happy. Oh, and Jay's diabetes is under control, Gill and Maisie are doing well, and the Dyson family continue to cope with the Land Girls. Beautiful blossom in the orchards; all's well with the world, or it will be when I see those babies.

Love, Hilda.

Nineteen

Smoke and grit often drifted their way along the Mersey to pay a polite visit to Crosby and Blundellsands. Nellie didn't want to think about it, but Mel kept everybody informed whether they liked it or not. She was like a walking book of statistics: so many houses flattened in Bootle, so many in Liverpool; the number of dead, gravely injured, walking wounded. Dusty gardens and windowsills were evidence enough, but Mel had to make cement and lay everything on with a trowel. Even Elise told her to shut up, while Keith usually left the battlefield before it became unbearable.

By the end of April, Eileen was sitting in a chair. Every time she wanted to stand, Keith threatened to send for ten big lads and a crane, because she was heavy, and her centre of gravity seemed to have shifted. 'She'll disprove the Newton theory soon,' he pronounced. 'At least the bloody dog's got it right now, but Eileen's a law unto herself.'

'She always was,' Nellie would say before going into detail about her daughter's wilder days. Tales of truancy, unsuitable boyfriends, and visits to Southport when she should have been in church poured in a seemingly endless stream from the mouth of this adoring mother. 'If her dad had been alive it would have killed him' or 'Her father must have been spinning round the cemetery on roller skates' were typical of her concluding remarks.

Occasionally, the voice of the accused drifted from the used-to-be-dining room. 'Shut up, Mam, or I'll tell Elsie about the time you went three rounds with Bootle Betty and pulled her wig off in Jackson's chippy' was one of the many ripostes offered by the expectant mother. She was going into Parkside soon. She was not happy; she was going to be cut open by a man who was five feet tall in his shoes, and she hoped he could reach her babies without a ladder, since she was very tall in the belly area when lying down. She was fed up.

Nellie and Elsie had taken up walking together while Keith minded his wife. They went daily to the beach, calling in at St Andrew's Road to collect Pandora, and, a few times a week, Tom Bingley came with them. He was working part time; he also went into the city to help in the evenings. Unlike Mel, he produced no information unless asked, thereby proving himself a truly professional man.

Surprisingly, Nellie was becoming very fond of Pandora's 'dad'. There was a great deal more to the man than met the naked eye. He talked about the twins with pride in his tone, mentioned his wife frequently, and indulged in lengthy sessions of private thought while gazing out towards the bar, an invisible seam where river became sea. She wondered whether he still longed for Eileen, but was proud of him for maintaining his dignity. In moments while dogs ran free, she frequently glimpsed the edge of his pain when he turned from the Mersey to address his companions. He suffered. Every death, every mutilation stayed with him. The man cared about people, loved Liverpool.

Today, he awarded Elsie Openshaw a broad grin. 'They won't know you back at Willows. You must have shed at least three stone.'

The 'emacicated' woman laughed. 'Mel's took all me clothes in. Eileen couldn't, cos she's not allowed to do much. What I want to know is, what happens to all me loose flabby bits?'

He thought about that. 'Your neck – cover it with a scarf or wear high-necked clothes. My wife has an imitation pearl choker; it's too big for her. I'll ask her for it, and you can wear that for posh.'

'Aw, you're kind. Isn't he kind, Nellie?'

For some temporarily obscure reason, Nellie wanted to cry, so she ran off to separate the spoodles from a huge length of seaweed. She'd never had a lad of her own, and wasn't old enough to be his mother, but he was fast becoming a son. 'I nearly broke his eye socket,' she told the pups while trying to relieve them of the slimy brown-green lasso to which they had become emotionally and physically attached. 'Then I sent the lads in. He's lovely. So much pain. See, Pandora and loony Spoodle, I know what she saw in him. Ten years younger, and I'd have been tempted meself.' Tom was hurting badly; he wasn't ready for patients, wasn't ready for Liverpool, but even those who battled against the tide had to work while there was a war on. If she and Elsie hung around for much longer, they'd have to work in Crosby for a while, because that was a law imposed by the coalition.

Two seaweedless puppies scampered off in search of more mischief. Nellie turned and saw Tom standing with his arm round Elsie's shoulder; Elsie was becoming fretful about her wrinkles, and the doctor in him was offering comfort. This was a good man who happened to be a randy bugger and selfish when it came to bodily needs. Clever blokes were like that. They worked hard, played hard and ... well ... they needed relief. 'God forgive me,' she mumbled. 'Stood standing here thinking about a man's private doings. I'm as bad as me mucky-minded daughter.' Still, she thought as she walked back to her friends, he was exciting.

'Ah, my other girlfriend,' he said when Nellie was back in the fold. 'Let's go back to my house, see what Marie has to offer by way of food, and we'll have an orgy.' He pondered momentarily. 'No, Elsie can't have an orgy, because she's on a diet. That leaves just you and me, Nellie. You look for grapes while I get the togas and massage oils.'

She understood her daughter. She knew now how strong Tom's magnetism was; at the same time, she saw a very similar quality in Keith. They were different, yet the same. Nellie loved Keith; she also loved Tom in her way. Even at the age of fifty-five, she had weakened slightly at the mention of togas and massage oils. Yes, Eileen had done well to resist.

Peter had not resisted. No longer a virgin, he lay sobbing in the arms of a girl he truly loved. This part of the park, behind the bowling club shed, was usually deserted, so he could weep in comparative privacy.

Mel, feeling unbearably sad, didn't know what she was. Sister, mother, lover, friend, adviser, priest, psychologist? 'Are you hurt?' asked the mother. Sister dried his tears, adviser urged him to compose himself before going home, lover kissed him on the forehead, friend held his hand. The priest prayed, while the psychologist reminded Peter that nothing had changed. Mother just tried not to be shocked, and the friend simply stayed by his side, because she would be around when all the other alter egos had left.

'It has happened,' he moaned.

Mel held on to him. 'Peter, you're homosexual. What a horrible, cold word that is. It reminds me of something surgical, perhaps for removing

growths. Look. Have you been hurt?'
He shook his head.
'Raped?'
'Not really.'
Mel blew out her cheeks. Not really? Surely a person knew? Surely there was no space for confusion? 'Look, soft lad. Were you willing like Barkiss in what was it? *Great Expectations*? No, *David Copperfield*.'
'Sort of.'
The adviser was running out of patience, though the mother, sister and friend remained sympathetic. 'Peter?'
'What?'
'Tell me about it. Blow your nose first; you look like a tap in want of a washer.' He didn't. As ever, he looked good enough for royalty.
'It was the lad who draws the white lines.'
Mel swallowed hard. 'He's got pimples on his neck and he always smells of grass and that chalky paint.'
'I know.'
'He probably needs help doing up his shoelaces.'
Peter raised his head. 'I enjoyed it, and I hate myself. I enjoyed you, too, so am I one of those bisexuals?'
'The wheel fell off mine,' Mel said almost absently. 'Sorry, sorry. Didn't set out to be flippant, but it does sound like something with handlebars. That means the best and worst of both worlds, Peter. Please don't make things any more confusing.'
'You wouldn't have me even if I was bi.' It wasn't

a question.

'No, I wouldn't. I want an extraordinary career, and a very ordinary home life, preferably with servants. My man will be my man, nobody else's. But no matter what, I'll always be your friend.'

Peter pulled away and hugged himself. 'I can't do it,' he whispered, his body rocking to and fro.

'Can't do what?'

'Live it, be it, do it. You want us to move to London and work in law. Right?'

Mel nodded.

'And you want us to tackle the statute books, stop the persecution of people like me.'

'Yes.'

'And when I go to jail? When the big, fancy lawyer doesn't exist any more because he's a pervert?'

As usual, she had an answer even for that. 'You find a nice, educated and lovable man with as much to lose as you have. Pragmatism rules. You buy a London house and make it into two flats. You have parties and occasionally you take a woman to the cinema, the theatre, the ballet. He does the same. No one needs to know that you live and sleep together. Confirmed bachelors, you see. Separate bedrooms, separate wardrobes, separate bathrooms, separate girlfriends.'

He knew his power over the fairer sex. 'They fall for me.'

'And you explain that you don't feel the same and you don't want commitment. Oh, what's the matter with you? Invent a dead fiancée. Dad went through twenty years after his Annie died. Where do you keep your imagination, Peter?

You're clever enough. No one need know.'

Very slowly, he raised his head. 'I'll know.'

'And?'

'Living a lie.'

She jumped up and stood in front of him, hands on hips, eyes blazing.

'Listen, Twinkletoes. We all do that. We all wear different hats for different situations. When I stand in court and argue for a murderer, how much truth will I be spouting? And will I tell them my truths: that I remember hunger, no coal for the fire, three brothers who stole and ran for bookies? No. Cambridge is the line. After that, it's Amelia Watson for London, Mel for my friends and family. How big a lie is that? And if I go for politics, I shall be elegant.'

'You're already that.'

'That's the point – I'm not. I have manufactured me. I'm a lie.'

She didn't understand, Peter decided. There was a huge difference between her lies and his. No. She did understand, and now she was saying so. What she meant was that his lie must become a habit, a part of life to which he could become inured, because it was an elemental necessity when it came to survival.

'It's too deep,' he said. 'Sexuality defines us at a level that's essential – of our essence. People hate queers.'

A part of Mel wanted to shake him till his bones fell apart and rattled. But that was the Eileen-and-Nellie side of her, the bit that reacted in an instant and flew off the handle. In the depths of her soul, she knew what he meant. On an earlier occasion, he had outlined his reasons for giving up the idea of medicine. A doctor was always vulnerable, and would definitely lose his licence if discovered to be different. A lawyer might just get away with it.

Getting away with it. Peter shook his head slowly. He would have to live the life of a liar, a man who denied his own heart and soul, who lived in shadow, who dared not be completely visible. Getting away with it. Did he want that? With so large an untruth, he would be painting himself into a corner from which there could be no exit Always, there would be a chance of footprints.

'I don't hate you. I don't hate queers.'

'You're not people; you're Mel.' He gazed at her. 'If I grow out of this, if I turn out to be a woman's man after all, will you have me?'

'No.' That sounded cruel, she decided. 'You've become a brother. And we both have a long way to go. Four years until university, more years of study, finding a job, somewhere to live. And a war, by the way. Our lives will change. One way or another, you'll get past this. Only the stupid get caught – I learned that much from Scotland Road.'

He was tired. There was at least one High Court judge behind bars, and that man was not the only clever one doing time because of love. Unnatural love, the world termed it. How could anything be deemed unnatural when it was part of the mind and soul of the person who contained it? Isolation was the only answer. Becoming his own jailer was the sole solution.

'Did you feel love for the line-painter?'

'No. It was mechanics, like you said about us. Love would make it amazing.'

'Be careful, then.'

They wandered homewards. Once again, Mel experienced a strange feeling when Peter turned left into St Andrew's Road. Something was happening. He was walking away again, and she was troubled. She had experienced this before, yet now an extra element deepened her discomfort. He disappeared through the gateway of the family home; a cold hand gripped Mel's heart and tried to squeeze the life out of her.

Why couldn't things be simpler? Why couldn't he be normal? She smiled at herself; Peter was one of the most normal people in her life, and she needed to get a move on. She had to finish an article about ten ways to cook a potato; Gloria had done her bit. It was Mel's turn to keep the young of Liverpool cheerful. Strangely, she wrote her funniest pieces when she was sad. Tonight, her writing would be hilarious.

Nothing had changed; Keith still adored her, even now when she had all the charm of a beached whale, plus swollen ankles she hadn't seen for weeks and a temperament as unpredictable as the weather. He'd threatened more than once to sit her on the draining board, though he had voiced sincere worries about denting her kitchen. When she'd begged for a ride in the car, he had told her he wasn't allowing her to break the springs, and overloading a vehicle took too much petrol, so she could stay where she was.

A bond that could have been weakened by enforced containment had been forged even closer. Eileen was learning the rudiments of chess; Keith was tackling Scouse. They argued in the usual way, with humour and love balancing the scales, and the kissing didn't stop. Both missed the act of love; both accepted the rule for the sake of their unborn children. 'Anyway, you'd roll off Mount Ararat,' she often said cheerfully, patting her swollen abdomen. 'And if I sat on you, you'd be circumcised by accident.'

Every day, he talked to his children. The little one was Frankie, a boy who would be baptized alongside his sister in St Anthony's church on Scotland Road, because Keith had promised before marriage that any offspring would be placed in the jaws of Rome. 'You see, Frankie, Helen's taken up all the room. This is good practice for when it comes to wardrobes. Women have ninety per cent of the space, while you'll get the bottom right-hand corner and half a drawer in the tallboy.'

Helen, Keith's most beautiful girl, was told to slow down a bit, because her brother, confined to the bargain basement, was having to make do with all kinds of cheap stuff, while she got the cream of the crop. He taught them the theory of relativity; Nellie was their grandmother, Eileen and Keith were their parents, while Einstein was just a scientist, and didn't count. They had three brothers and a sister; they had a spoodle, two houses, two gardens and sixteen chickens.

'You'll have them daft before they're born,' Eileen told him.

'This family has standards. We do daft. We do

nothing else but daft. How many pairs of knickers?' He was packing her bag for Parkside.

'Twelve.'

'How long will you be away?'

'Five feet five inches, same as I am now.'

'Eileen!'

'I am staying with my children until both can come home. I want four cotton nighties, my towelling robe, and my Christmas nightdress and negligent, as Mam calls it. I don't know why she does it. She knows the right words.'

'Yes, she does. Toiletries?'

'They're in my little blue bag. I hid the best soap and tooth powder so that Mel wouldn't use them.'

'Books?'

'I don't care.' She didn't. Caring about the birth of twins and surviving surgery took most of her thinking. 'Not *War and Peace*. I don't like it, and I'll not be away long enough to read the first chapter. I have tried, but it's a boring book. The baby clothes are in the tartan holdall.'

Keith sighed quietly. Waiting rooms and patients' sitting rooms at Parkside had been given over to casualty as part of the war effort. He would have to stay outside in the car while his wonderful Eileen was being cut open, while his children got lifted out from the warm, dark space they knew into a bright, noisy, war-torn world. Although he had begged and pleaded to go into theatre scrubbed and gowned, no one would heed his request. Fathers didn't count, it seemed. Fathers took their pleasure, left women pregnant, then disappeared on a ferry to somewhere exotic, like the Isle of Man.

'Keith?'

'What?'

'I've got you a ticket.'

'Eh?' Still on the way to the Isle of Man, he scratched his head.

'Mr Barr fixed it. You can sit in a corner away from me and all the cutlery and, once the babies are wiped down, you'll be the first real person to hold them.'

'What?'

'I'll be asleep behind a screen. They'll both be laid on me for a minute so they'll know their mother's scent, then they'll meet their dad. Mr Barr says dads should be involved. Quite modern for an old bloke, he is. Sometimes, when it's a normal birth, he lets the father cut the cord. Not all men can face it, but it's a significant moment and a privilege that shouldn't be withheld.'

He gulped. 'I'll be there? I'll be with you?'

'Yes.'

He gulped. 'Did I ever tell you you're wonderful?'

'No, never.'

He opened the cage and joined her in bed, winding his body round his wife and two children. Now an expert at these particular logistics, he wondered whether he would need to relearn the art of lying in a straight line. 'You're wonderful.'

'And you're crying, soft lad. You know, I took you on trust, because I hadn't known you for long, but I wanted you. It was a bit like remembering tomorrow, and that's silly. "He's the one,"

I kept saying internally. I'm glad I took that chance. Are you?'

'I'm glad you took the chance, yes. But I was absolutely certain. I don't take chances. You were my future; you still are. And they're going to cut you open–'

'Oh, shut up, Keith.' She didn't want him to know her terror. 'These two are so near the surface – you could cut them out with a butter knife. But the docs won't let you watch the procedure, as they call it. You leave them to their knives and forks, keep your mouth shut and your mask on.'

Keith the kisser was alive and well. His embrace reminded her that she continued a woman, that her body still belonged to her in spite of a couple of temporary non-paying guests who seemed to have claimed rights of residency. 'Don't worry,' she whispered when he released her. 'It will be fine. In fact, once these two are freed from jail, there'll be no peace. It's all nappies and bottles. They don't encourage breastfeeding after a section, and there will be two of them. There will. Both move, I promise you. And we'll be exhausted. Kids are a mixed blessing.' But she was better placed now. There'd be no running wild in an overcrowded community, no police, no bookies.

'Mrs Bingley's given you a lovely present. It's a very posh twin pram.'

'Oh.'

'It looks new. I think she's cleaned it to within an inch of its life, and she's put sheets and blankets in it, too. Sweetheart, be gracious.' He waited for a response. 'You and Marie are good friends, aren't you? She visits you, and you get on.'

'Yes.'

'So what's the matter?'

It was stupid, and she knew it was stupid, but she didn't want anything of Tom's, didn't like the idea of placing her twins in the pram that had contained his children. 'Nothing's the matter. We can afford our own pram.' It was hard enough having to listen to Elsie and Mam talking in the next room about Tom Bingley, often singing his praises. Mam was two-faced.

'Eileen?'

'I know, I know. My motto is accept anything but blows. Raggy little Rose, someone else's clothes, begging on the corner for anything but blows.' She smiled. 'I'm not that person any more. I'm Queen Eileen. And it's nothing to do with money or owning a house. I married a king. Get your guards to keep him away from me.'

'There's an injunction, love.'

'For the duration of the pregnancy, yes.' She would be at her most vulnerable in Parkside. The injunction would be useless the minute the twins left the womb. He was a doctor. He might have patients in the little Catholic hospital. Her family could not be by her side all the time, and a medic had the right to enter Parkside in the middle of the night if he so chose. There was no danger of his hurting her physically, but he might well upset her.

Why? Why could she be upset? Because she felt sorry for him, and pity was closely related to love. Behind the predator was a man, an ordinary, well-educated man. She knew he could have made her laugh; she knew that had he not been married, she would have been forced into a quandary. The two men, so far apart on the surface, had a great deal in common. In spite of all that, the certainty that she had married the right one remained firm. But she needed to stay away from Mr Might-have-been. The imbalance of hormones didn't help, and a woman recently delivered of a child was extra emotional.

Keith seemed to read her thoughts. 'Don't worry. I'll be living in the car.'

'You have to eat.'

He tutted. 'We've a cupboard full of National Dried. I'll make myself some bottles.'

'Bathroom?' she asked.

'I've got nappies.'

It was in moments like this that Eileen realized the depth of her love for her husband. A sensible, organized man, he still managed to retain a lunacy that was essential as far as she was concerned. 'Getting a wash?'

'I'll stand naked in the rain.'

'The penguins will die of shock.'

'Naw. They'll hang on to their rosaries and pray for a repeat performance.'

'I love a confident man.'

'And I love you.' He proceeded to deteriorate into the gibbering idiot who spouted lovey-dovey nonsense mixed with lewd terms concerning what he would do to her once she got back to normal.

'But we haven't got a trampoline, Keith.'

'I'll make one. And a hammock. You just have

to approach these matters scientifically.'

'Right,' she said.

He awarded her one of the more dazzling of his smiles. 'And after that, if we're still breathing, we'll have chips.'

'Not ribbon spuds?'

'God, no.' Because of Mel's research into ten different ways to cook potatoes, they had been plied with heaps of ribbons. The offerings would have been acceptable if the girl had heated the fat to a reasonable temperature. 'We'll stick to the chippy,' he said. 'By the way, who's Bootle Betty and why did she wear a wig?'

'You don't want to know...'

Marie was in a mood. Marie didn't have many moods, so Tom was perturbed. When the children had left for school, he remained at the breakfast table, arms folded while he watched her. She was scurrying. She never scurried unless something had gone wrong at the WVS. And she wouldn't look at him.

He untangled his arms and pretended to read a very slim newspaper until she left the morning room. From the kitchen, the sound of dishes being murdered floated on air heavier than lead. He was in no hurry unless the phone rang, because he was on call this morning, with just an afternoon surgery today.

Marie washed everything so cruelly that she thought glaze and silver plate might peel off. Men? Bloody men? She had taken enough, she was leaving him, she wanted to kill him. All that messing about for nothing in Rodney Street, all that soul-baring, had been a waste of time.

'What's the matter?' he called.

'Shut up!'

Shut up? Three words, he had spoken. Just three. She was the one making all the noise. 'Marie?'

She entered the arena, hands soapy, a tea towel worn casually over the left shoulder, curls tumbling into her eyes. 'Not Marie,' she announced before blowing upwards in an attempt to achieve clearer sight. But disobedient tendrils returned to their encampment of choice. 'Eileen,' she screamed.

'What?'

'It's not a what, it's a who.'

'And?'

'And we made love, you fell asleep, I went to the bathroom.'

'I am with you so far.'

'No, you're not!' She hit him with the tea towel. 'I'm lying there after visiting the bathroom, feeling glad that your depression's getting better and we're together, then thinking about what I need to do today, and you're talking to her in your sleep.'

'Oh.'

'You love her,' Marie accused, white-hot fire behind the words.

Tom stared hard at her. 'There's a difference between love and sexual attraction. It's window shopping. Men do it all the time.'

'In bed? Talking to your urchin in your sleep? "It will never be over"? What the hell is the matter with you? She's going into Parkside tomorrow, and I'm visiting her at home before she leaves, so–'

'Don't say anything to the poor woman, please.'

She swiped him again with the damp towel. 'I'm not the stupid one here. She's pregnant, and I won't hurt her. But you set one foot inside that hospital or in her house, and you'll find all your belongings on the pavement outside my gate. Because it is my gate, my garden, my house. I bloody paid for it in more ways than one, you cheating bastard.' She was proud of herself, her vocabulary was growing daily.

'Be reasonable.'

'I'm not the unreasonable one, either. Not stupid, not unreasonable. You're using me and seeing her. I'm moving back into the spare room. Why are you smiling?'

'Because you're beautiful. A mess, but beautiful.'

She didn't know what to say. Furthermore, she wasn't given the chance to organize her thoughts, because he swept her up and threw her over his shoulder. She beat him with both fists, but he carried on up the stairs and threw her onto the bed, ripping at her clothes until she was naked apart from her tea towel.

Tom was kinder to his own garments. Every time she tried to escape, he pushed her back where she belonged. If Keith Greenhalgh could manage this, so could he. 'Stay exactly where you are,' he ordered. When he joined her on the bed, the fighting continued. Between blows, he managed to whisper in her ear.

'Filthy words,' she answered, slapping his face.

'Have a few more.' He started to whisper again.

It happened. While he tortured her tiring body, Marie lost all her anger, only to replace it with impatience. 'Please,' she moaned.

'Please what? According to you, I please only myself.'

'Stop tormenting me.'

'Ah. I see. Which is the greater torment? This, or this?'

She grabbed his wandering hand. 'I don't know.'

'Say the word, the one you didn't like when I used it.'

She whimpered. 'I can't.'

'Then I'm going downstairs.'

So she said it. Loudly.

'Hang on,' he said gravely. 'The neighbours will hear, and they'll start forming a queue.' At last, he had defeated the lady in her. He was sorry, desperately sorry, that he couldn't control his dreams. The depression was lifting, and he would soon be back at the surgery full time, so everything was in order, except for Eileen bloody Greenhalgh. Tom immediately devoted himself to making life happier for his wife, and perhaps made rather too good a job of it, because she was saying the forbidden word. Repeatedly.

He collapsed on her and regained the ability to breathe sensibly. 'That was good,' came his understatement.

'We must fight more often, Tom.'

'Marie?'

'What?'

'Will you clean the blood off my back?'

'But I didn't scratch you ... did I?'

He nodded. 'We finally found the tigress in you. Once or twice in your life, you have an experience so intense that you fight back. The divide between pleasure and pain is very fine, isn't it?'

'I thought I was going to die,' she admitted.

While she went to the first aid box, he turned and stared at the wall. Loving two women wasn't easy. Loving Eileen was impossible, because he hadn't seen her for weeks, wasn't allowed to see her. Loving Marie was a gentler business altogether, though the past half-hour had been lively.

She returned, still naked, lint, cotton wool and ointment wrapped in her now notorious tea towel. 'Perhaps I should thank Eileen,' she said wrily.

'Don't bother. She'll be gone soon and she's only in my subconscious. You're my wife.'

'God help me.' She cleaned his back.

The news travelled up-country to the very few, those top brasses unacquainted with anyone working in the media, anyone with a second cousin twice removed who had a friend in the media, anyone descended from a long-dead ancestor who had ever written for a newspaper. It was top secret, though the news leaked here and there. Hitler, whose camp housed a few spies for England, was to change his prime target. Poor old London might get a bit of a rest, since the city of Liverpool was now top of the list on der Führer's agenda.

The common people got no warning, because little could be done at such short notice, and it was possibly only another rumour anyway. A few more big guns arrived at the docks, barrage balloons were made secure, and members of the Home Guard marched up and down the beaches for an hour or so every morning.

Elsie and Nellie were not best pleased, since Spoodle and Pandora had a marked tendency to become involved with feet, and they were kicked aside more than once. Nellie wasn't having that. She dressed down the whole parade, praying loudly that England would never need to depend for survival on fools, geriatrics, and people who kick puppies. 'You'll have to stop now, anyway,' she roared. 'You've two at the back what need crutches, and that one on his own a mile behind wants a wheelchair.'

Elsie dug her friend in her ribs. 'Give over, Nell. It's not their fault.'

Nellie was uneasy. Something was changing, and she couldn't work it out. It was a bit like the night when Heinrich had dropped out of the heavens at Willows. 'The sky was the wrong colour,' she whispered to herself.

'You what?'

'Nothing.' This day was the wrong shade of grey. Under a flawless blue sky, Nellie Kennedy saw only the dull monotony of gun metal. She shivered.

'Are you getting a chill, Nell?'

'No.' She wasn't cold at all. But somebody somewhere had just walked over a million graves.

Twenty

THURSDAY

'So this is it, then.' A terrified Keith held on to his wife's hand while Sister Mary Dominic hung onto him. This was definitely it. Eileen was going to disappear behind a screen with Mr Barr, an anaesthetist, and several Augustinian penguins. 'Are you feeling all right? Are you ready for it, sweetheart?' he asked, panic trimming the words. She was on a trolley. She was wearing a stupid gown that was open all down her back. And apart from the enormous bump, his Eileen looked like a frightened little girl about to have her tonsils out.

'Let me go, now, sweetheart,' Eileen begged quietly. 'This is the theatre door.' He was going to start. In her very bones, she knew he was going to kick off and score an own goal. 'Don't you be making a show of me,' she warned. 'Make a show of me, and I'll suspend your membership. And no, I'm not talking about a hammock. So think on and pull yourself together. Sister? Tell him. Tell him I've got no choice, because he sure as eggs won't listen to me.'

Mary Dominic, all four feet and ten Irish inches of her, tore Keith's hand from Eileen's. She glared at him while pinning a small, silver-coloured medal to his shirt. 'That is the Immaculate Conception,' she advised him sternly, 'to whom I shall be praying. However, my prayers to Our Lady will be delivered via St Jude, as I shall pray also to him. He's the patron saint of hopeless cases. And I have never, in all my born days, seen a case more hopeless than you.'

Keith fixed the tiny nun with steely eyes. 'This woman is my life.'

'This woman is a crowd. There are three of her. We need to read the Riot Act in order to achieve dispersal.' She pushed the trolley through the first set of doors. 'There's your chair, Mr Greenhalgh. Use it.'

'But–'

'No buts. You are now in theatre. Mr Barr has allowed you in. I, however, would never have let you through the outer doors. Now listen to me. When I wedge open the inner doors, which are transparent, by the way, you will hear and see all you need to hear and see. Now shut up before I find sutures and sew up your speaking equipment good and proper, but. I'll be with you in a tick. Do not follow me. I have a black belt in liturgy.'

He couldn't see a thing. He could hear them all greeting his wife, but his view was a cream-painted wall with a crucifix on it. 'I'll be waiting, Eileen,' he shouted. 'I love you.'

She had been whisked away, but her guard returned and sat next to Keith. 'There we go now, son. Even this difficult bit isn't difficult, as it lasts just a few minutes. Will we have a bet? I say two girls. If I lose, you may keep my medal. If you lose, I'll take from you a pound for Africa.'

'I thought Africa would cost more than a quid; a fiver, at least.'

'Very funny. The money's for starving babies.'

'Right.'

She laughed. 'Now shut your mouth and open your ears. The second she goes under, the babies will be out. We don't want the anaesthetic getting to them. So. What are they? Come on with you, get the bet placed before the race begins.'

'One of each,' he replied.

She prayed.

Within two or three minutes, the first cry arrived. 'Thanks be to God,' Mary Dominic muttered.

A second pair of lungs proclaimed loudly that they'd been all right in there, and why had they been disturbed? 'Jesus, Mary and Joseph, bless this earthly family and stop the tears of the blithering idiot next to me.' She turned to him. 'You haven't even seen them yet. What use are you going to be if you can't turn the tap off?'

'Will they bring them to me?'

'And give the poor little souls another shock at the sight of you? Pull your mask up. I shall bring them in a few minutes. They need to be with Mammy for a while after they're weighed, measured and tested, then I'll get them for you. Straighten your face, you've a forehead like a ploughed field.'

'Will Eileen be all right?'

'She'll be grand. Irish, strong as a horse, stubborn as a mule and fast as a flea. She told me earlier about the draining board for when she's naughty. You've a great way of dealing with the besom, so. Ah, you'll all be lovely, and that's for certain sure.'

After what seemed like hours, Mary Dominic went and fetched the babies. 'Keep your medal,' were her first words. 'One of each, you lucky boy. I'll still take the pound for black babies, but.'

'They're the same size,' Keith managed finally.

The nun nodded. 'He's cunning. He hid bits of himself all over the show; I think he must have had a cupboard. Six pounds, he is. The little girl is over seven, but it's not as much difference as we suspected. Aren't they beautiful? Caesars often are, you know, because they're lifted from one bed to another, no struggle to be endured. Will you stop weeping. See? You have me at it now.' She sniffed and dried her eyes on a handkerchief.

Keith couldn't take his eyes off his children. Perfect features in miniature, downy blond hair, five delightful little toes on one kicked-free foot. 'The day I married your mam was the best of my life so far. Till now. Hello, Francesca Helen. Hello, Francis Keith. We'd a few discussions about your names, but you're Helen and Frankie. I'm your dad. Your mam's unconscious, probably been on the Guinness again, the dirty stop-out, and this little lady is a nun. She's a bride of Christ, and she nags. Like your gran.'

Mary Dominic sniffed. 'Are you Catholic?'

'No. But I married one, so I go to church with her most Sundays when she's not confined to barracks, walk her to the altar, take a blessing instead of Communion bread. She has her doubts, but she hangs in there. A priest's been bringing

Communion to the house.'

Mary Dominic aired the opinion that a person without doubts was a person without a brain. 'You are with God, Mr Greenhalgh. You'll be a wonderful father. And they've the first of May for a birthday, which is the start of the month of Mary, who is fastened to your clothing. I want a pound for Africa.'

'I'll give you two.'

'Good lad.'

Keith carried on weeping when his children were moved to the nursery. Mr Barr emerged, congratulated the tear-stained new father and told him that Eileen would sleep for a while. 'She did well to go those extra weeks, Mr Greenhalgh. Oh, and the sisterhood's had a little meeting. They're putting a camp bed in your wife's room, because they know you won't go home. And you're to get to the office and phone Eileen's mother and her daughter, put them out of their misery.'

Keith shook the great man's hand. 'Thank you. Thank you so much.'

Nellie, Elsie and Mel had a party courtesy of Crawford's Cream Crackers, some mousetrap cheese, and two bottles of sparkling wine left by Miss Morrison. 'She'd have loved this day,' said Mel, who was inebriated for the first time in her life. 'She always said the house needed children. I miss her. I miss my mam. I miss my Keith-dad. I even miss my brothers. It's coming to something when you miss your brothers,' she told Elsie.

Nellie entered. 'Right, that's all at Willows informed.' She glared at Mel. 'How many glasses of that have you had, madam? Because you're drunk. Your eyes are all over the place like glass marbles.'

'One glass,' replied Mel. 'Only one.'

'Two, she's had.' Elsie apologized to Mel. 'Sorry, love, but you don't want to be ill.'

They stayed up late mostly because of Nellie's excitement, partly because she wanted to keep an eye on her oldest grandchild, who might be sick in her bed after taking drink, who might die as a result of inhalation, who was already fast asleep in an armchair.

The doors to hell opened fractionally at about eleven o'clock. Sirens screamed. People in the city sighed, put their kettles on, made tea, lifted children from their beds, carried them and tea-filled billy-cans to shelters before yet another raid. In Crosby and Blundellsands, few people bothered to move. It was just one more night, just a gesture so that folk would remember that Hitler and his forces were keeping an eye on the city and its environs. But doctors, nurses, firemen and ambulance drivers left the cosiness of bed or armchair and began the drive from outer to inner Liverpool. Nellie, Elsie and Mel went into Eileen's cage. But they heard and felt the assault, and were still awake when the all-clear sounded at one in the morning. 'My God,' Nellie sighed. 'That felt like they meant it.'

In Parkside, which was nearer by three miles to Liverpool, a new mother was disobeying the nuns. With a pillow under each arm, she supported her babies, cupped their heads and put them to her breasts.

'You'll have pain. You've been cut,' declared Mary Dominic.

'She's made her mind up,' Keith said.

'I've made my mind up,' came the echo.

'The feeding of a child pulls at the womb,' insisted the tiny Irishwoman. 'You've been cut.'

Eileen raised her eyes to heaven. 'Saints preserve me,' she muttered. 'I know I've been cut, Sister Mary Dominic. My belly probably looks as if it's been thrown together by a blind tailor – I don't know, because I can't see it. This milk is my children's birthright. It's the best thing on God's earth for them, it's free, and I am full of vitamins. Even a couple of weeks at the breast will help them.'

A siren sounded. The nun took a whistle from her pocket and blew hard.

Eileen smiled. Her twins were clearly not of a nervous disposition, since they simply lifted up their arms in response to the blast. 'They're not deaf,' she said as they continued to suckle. Mary Dominic apologized. She was in charge of blackouts, and the whistle served as warning to all the other sisters.

Keith went outside for a few minutes. He heard them long before he saw them, and he knew immediately that this show was not the same as previous incursions. Anti-aircraft fire was deafening; those three miles nearer to town made a lot of difference. Incendiaries floated down in their hundreds, the resulting fires acting as beacons for the pilots above. Bombs vomiting from underbellies of Heinkels exploded all over the city; there must have been fifty or more planes. Then God's heavens opened, and the Germans eased off. In spite of the rain, Liverpool burned.

Inside again when the planes had gone, Keith eavesdropped at Mother Superior's door. She was whispering to her sisters. There had been a hundred or more incidents in the city, none in Bootle, some on the Wirral. He heard the words Cazneau Street, North Market, Batty's dairy, and the names of many other shops in the city. 'But, as far as I can tell, we are receiving no casualties here tonight, thanks be to God,' was Mother Benedict's final statement. Keith's flesh crawled. This was the start of something new.

He cuddled his son while Eileen cooed over Helen. 'That was noisy,' she said, stroking her daughter's cap of silky hair.

'We're nearer,' Keith said.

'I know we're nearer, love. It felt different. There were a lot of them, too.'

Each bomb they dropped was estimated to weigh an enormous amount, but Keith wasn't going to tell his wife that, not when she'd just had surgery, not while she had six children to worry about.

Take us home,' she ordered.

'Don't talk daft, sweetheart.'

'And when they come back and kill us all? We're only about four miles from the edge of Liverpool.'

'And you've got stitches, and you were in theatre just a few hours ago having two babies removed.'

'We'll have more than bloody stitches if we get a direct hit. Mr Barr can see me at home, and Dr Ryan will look after me.'

'No.'

She tilted her head to one side. 'That sounded very firm and decided.'

'Because it was,' he said. 'Look, I know they're fine, but they're still slightly premature. They've to go back to the nursery in a minute, because they're due for being stared at. That Sister Agatha never sleeps, or so I'm told. I hear she doesn't even blink in case she misses something. You've done right by the twins so far. Just a few more days, darling. Please.'

Eileen sniffed. He knew she melted when he used that word. Nobody in Scotland Road ever said it; darling was for film stars. And for her, of course. 'All right,' she said. 'But don't go blaming me if we're all killed.'

'I won't.' He returned to the task of examining his son's hands. They had dimples instead of knuckles, but Frankie had a hell of a grip for a newborn. 'He'll be good for the tug of war team.'

Eileen snorted. She had married a madman.

FRIDAY

My dear Aunt Hilda,

Your adopted niece is under the caged kitchen table with mattress, pillow, blankets and Spoodle, so please excuse the untidy writing. I am rather squashed, and Miss Morrion's precious Victorian writing slope doesn't quite fit at a decent angle in my small shelter, so I can only hope that this letter is legible. The dog is no help. Chewing the end of the pen while I write is his idea of audience participation, but what can I do?

I am trapped, but safe, I hope.

With the head teacher's permission, I had the morning off. Dad picked up Gran and me, and took us to Parkside. Mam is very well indeed, and calling all the shots. She clearly got back to what's laughingly called normal in a very short space of time. My lovely stepfather is besotted with the babies – we all are. According to Mam, little Helen is the image of me, God help her. Frankie is gorgeous. When someone holds him, he cuddles into the person, and he seems not to care who picks him up. Helen is more choosy; she prefers her parents. But they are so delightful. They took me back to my childhood, because I wanted to dress them up like I did my dolls.

Despite warnings about stitches and pain, my dearly beloved mother insists on breastfeeding. Sister Mary Dominic, nominated by Mam as the dwarf prison guard, is very funny. Under five feet in height, she buzzes around like a bee in a flower and gets under everyone's feet and on everyone's nerves. She stings, too, when she puts her mind to it. Dad has found the kitchen, and he has threatened to put Sister MD on the draining board or in the sluice room with all the bedpans. She giggles when he says such things. Were she not a nun, I'd swear she flirts with him.

I tried to phone you earlier, but our lines are out of order, and I'm unsure about when we'll be reconnected. There is no point in writing anything other than truth, so I must tell you that our city took some hard knocks last night and, as I write, it's happening again. With my parents and the twins currently in a building a few miles nearer to Liverpool than we are, I can only worry. Germany has altered its strategy. The bombers are coming in from many directions to circle the docks and the city before dropping fire bombs followed by very high explosives. Even with a full moon, they still dropped incendiaries. Three or four planes flew over this house about an hour ago. Elsie resorted to praying – even borrowed Gran's rosary, and she isn't a Catholic.

My dear, sweet aunt, I know that hamlets have no churches, so please take as many people as you can to Bromley Cross, Harwood or Affetside – anywhere with a church. It doesn't have to be Catholic. All prayers are needed now, because I fear we are ear-witnesses to a blitzkrieg, which translates as lightning war. London has already suffered this, as have other towns and cities. Pray for Liverpool, I beg you.

Love, as always, Mel xxx

She pushed the writing slope out of the shelter, laid herself down, cuddled Spoodle and courted sleep. But the boom of anti-aircraft guns kept her awake, as did the slight shivering of the land on which the house did its best to stand. It was like a hundred aftershocks following an earthquake; would it ever end? After four hours, the all-clear sounded.

Sighing, Mel drifted towards sleep, Spoodle re-located at her feet. Four hours. How much damage might have been done in that time? Tomorrow would tell, tomorrow would… At last, she slept.

SATURDAY 3 MAY 1941

The terrible news drifted up the coast along with debris, ash, soot and bombed-out people looking for billets. By about noon, rumour and fact were finally becoming separable. Because of a bright full moon, incendiaries had been rather de trop except when cloud had drifted across the main source of light. Providence had clearly been on the side of the Germans last night, but the city stumbled on.

Bootle, a village nearer than Crosby to Liverpool, had taken a hammering. Flour mills, timber yards, factories, warehouses, shops, houses and arterial roads had been eradicated. Homeless and disorientated people wandered the streets long after sunrise, some carrying a chair, a picture, a cushion – sad little bits and pieces collected from a place they had loved. They searched, not only for somewhere to settle their bones, but also for family members, some of whom would never be seen again.

Emergency services in Bootle could not get through the rubble on Southport Road, Stanley Road, Balliol and Knowsley roads. Vehicles were abandoned while teams struggled on foot to reach mounds under which people were buried. Alive or dead, when lifted out, they were covered in the crumbled debris of shelters or of the homes that had provided a lifelong refuge. Nowhere was safe any longer; no one could be certain of seeing tomorrow.

In the city, the Dock Board building had been hit, while the White Star Shipping Line offices were badly affected by fire. The central repository of the diocese of Liverpool was in ruins, and many valuable books, tracts and records had disappeared in the flames. St Michael's Anglican church was damaged beyond repair, as were many houses and small businesses. All day long, fires smouldered. Rescuers and clearance teams did their best but behind every hearty word of encouragement, every slap on the back, the dread remained. Tonight would be the same. The strutting, power-crazed leaders of Germany intended to crush a proud city. Liverpool was not especially big but it boasted the largest docks in the world, and the docks were the real target.

But what the Luftwaffe might never see if the planes flew too quickly or too high was visible all over Liverpool on this Saturday. Cleared pavements bore painted words: *HA, YOU MISSED ME, THIS SHOP IS CLOSED PENDING ALTERATIONS, HITLER BLEW UP OUR LAV,* and *ME MA SAYS YOU OWE HER SOME NEW TEETH AND A TEAPOT.* An old Jewish man used luminous paint to execute a massive Star of David in the middle of a road on which all buildings had been flattened. 'Mazel tov, mate,' called a passing Irish docker. Like their Cockney cousins, this lot never gave up.

Young lads risked life and limb to climb onto ruins already bombed, tying strips of white sheeting to bits of chimneys and gutters in the hope of drawing attention to the already destroyed. With any luck, these derelict piles might get hit again. The number 16 appeared here and there as a reminder to the enemy that this number of German bombers had been shot down last night by the RAF. Ebullient on the outside, determined to the bone, Scousers were intelligent enough to recognize the might of the enemy. But they weren't going to run away, because this was their city. An old sailors' tale intimated that residents of Liverpool lived with their backs to the city, their eyes on the sea. But sneak behind their backs, and one way or another they would have your blood. They had pride by the ton; they also owned an anger that was measurable on no man-made scale. And to balance all of the above, they were humorous, cheeky and quick.

On the wireless, the clipped, correct BBC announcer spoke of damage to a northern port. Even the royal family didn't talk as daft as that. It was like listening to a foreigner, an alien who wasn't qualified to talk about Liverpool, about England, about the planet. Elsie blamed tight underwear. 'They all talk as if they've been neutralized,' she said. 'Their dangly bits is squashed.'

Nellie almost choked on her tea. 'Do you want to go home, love?'

Elsie bridled. 'For one, I still haven't seen them babies, and for two, it's my war now. No.' The arms continued tightly folded. 'I'm going nowhere till Hitler's been dealt with. Shouldn't be difficult; they say he's only got one dangly bit.' She picked up a carving knife. 'Let me at him.'

'Who are we killing now?' asked Mel as she led Spoodle into the kitchen.

'Hitler.' Elsie's tone was fierce.

'That's all right, then. I'm posting a letter, then going to Sniggery Woods with Gloria and Pandora.' She didn't want to be near the river, didn't want to look left in case she saw what she couldn't bear to see in her city. She left the two older women to their job of putting the world to rights over a pot of tea and a rack of toast.

Outside, an unfamiliar smell hung in the air. It was a bit like the morning after bonfire night, but heavier. Mel rushed round to St Andrew's Road, waited while Gloria found her dog, and had a word with Dr Bingley. Yes, the twins were born, Mam was safe, and Dad was sleeping on a camp bed when he wasn't chasing nuns. 'At least one has fallen in love with him. He parked her in front of a statue of the Sacred Heart last night because she keeps telling Mam to stop breast-feeding.'

'Because of the section?'

Mel nodded. 'Caesar mothers aren't supposed to feed. She won't listen, so we must hope for the best. But Sister Mary Dominic will carry on shouting haematoma, and Mam will carry on ignoring her. Mrs Bingley's going to visit today with Elsie.'

His wife would be welcome, but he couldn't go. Keith Greenhalgh was standing, sitting or lying on guard, and Tom was the enemy. He was also tired, since Liverpool had been lively and deathly last night The general opinion was that tonight would be the same, so he needed a rest.

The girls walked to the woods, releasing a pair of enthusiastic dogs as soon as they reached the path leading to the trees. Two bundles of black and white curls disappeared in a trice. They loved this place, which housed squirrels, rabbits and, on occasion, Boy Scouts cooking sausages. Today, the dogs' behaviour was different. They returned to the girls and whined, clearly asking to be followed.

Gloria and Mel found Peter hanging from a tree, movement in his legs proclaiming him to be alive. Without a word, Mel pushed her hand into his pocket, withdrew a jack-knife, climbed upward from bough to bough and severed the thin rope with one cut while Gloria took his weight. Brother and sister crashed to earth; Mel jumped out of the tree.

'Why?' sobbed Gloria. 'What's the matter with you; what the hell did you think you were doing?'

'Wrong rope,' Mel scolded. 'Washing line's not up to the job, and part of it was up the side of your face, stupid. You couldn't hang a picture on a nail, even with a spirit level.' She was scared to death. She could not imagine life without Peter. But she wasn't going to baby him – oh, no. The need to hug and comfort him had to be denied, since she could not allow him to continue in self-destructive mode.

Gloria, shocked and terrified, stopped weeping. 'Mel? This is serious.'

It didn't look serious. A very attractive boy, spread-eagled on the ground, was being drowned by two spoodles. Wagging happily, they circled him, washing his face, neck and hands, chewing on his hair and breathing heavily into his ears.

Mel folded her arms and tapped a foot. 'You selfish, spoilt wastrel. Your mother lives in a house filled with drugs, and she might be tempted to follow you into the hereafter when you break her heart. Your sister would be bereft, while your father, a man only just out of depression, could well slip all the way back to a mental hospital.'

He started to cry.

'Why?' Gloria screamed again.

Seconds ticked by. 'Will you tell her, or shall I?' Mel demanded. 'Because you owe her an answer.'

'Tell me what?' Gloria asked, her voice calmer.

Peter said nothing.

'Right.' Mel sat on the stump of a lightning tree that had been struck down years earlier. 'This isn't the first sign of your brother's cowardice, my friend. When we had all that kerfuffle about him and me, he was trying to be my boyfriend so that no one would guess the truth. He used me as a shield. After we'd ... been together, he confessed all. Your twin prefers boys, and he's too weak to stay alive and fight for his own rights and for the rights of other people like himself. I had the feeling that he might try something dramatic.' She recalled the occasions on which she'd watched him walk away, remembered an icy hand tracing a line down her backbone.

Gloria blinked rapidly. 'He's queer?'

Mel nodded. 'He's terrified of jail, and I understand that. We had a plan. He, I and other open-minded people were going to change the world. But soft lad here can't cope.' She stood up. 'I'm going home. I've had enough of him.'

Gloria's jaw dropped. 'You're leaving me here? With him? But what if he goes and ... what am I supposed to do with him?'

'He's your bloody brother. Why the hell would I want to keep company with somebody who's contemplating suicide? It's a mortal sin, for a start.'

Gloria, knowing that Mel didn't believe in mortal sin, realized that her best friend was using reverse psychology. It wasn't a bad idea. It might not be a particularly good one either, but Gloria could think of nothing better. 'Hang on while I get this rope, Mel. I'll come with you.' She gathered up Peter's washing line.

'Stop,' Peter begged.

'It speaks.' Mel glared at him. 'Well?'

'Don't tell them.'

Borrowing her friend's supposed strength, Gloria approached her twin. 'I'm not telling anybody anything. Just thank God you made such a pig's ear of it that your neck's not too noticeably marked.' Still shaking, she held her ground. 'I'm not going to break anyone's heart for you. Do it yourself when you're ready.' She began to walk away, turning after a few steps. 'It's not your fault, by the way. You can't help the way you're made.'

He lay still. *It's not your fault. It's the way you're made*. Females were always full of glib answers. *While I'm all shit and self-pity.* Why him, though? Why had he come out queer? Apart from the boy who painted lines for lawn tennis and rugby, Peter knew no one in this situation. His parents were normal, as was his sister, but...

In his head, Mel spoke. *You're just a different kind of normal,* she had said weeks earlier. He sat up. There was a war on, and his contribution so far had been worrying about his precious reputation, his own safety, his future, his exit from a world that could not be forced to love him. It was all me, me, me.

Of course, she'd provided an answer to that, as well. *We're all selfish. It's an age thing. We go spotty, disobedient and daft. But most of all, we go selfish.* Oh, how he loved her. How could he– 'Get on with it,' he hissed between gritted teeth.

Peter Bingley got on with it. He mounted his bike and rode the seven miles. The sky was dark with smoke. People ran when they could, walked round rubble when they had to, dug with shovels and with bare hands, every one of them searching for life below the piles, shouting, shining torches into blackness and debris.

In the heart of Liverpool, Peter dug with the best of them, lifting out injured and dead, young and old, male and female, dogs, cats and a little trembling rabbit. On the end of a rope ten times stronger than the one he had used this morning, he was lowered into a cellar where he found an intact and silent little girl. When they pulled him and the child out, tears streamed and made a clean path down his filthy cheeks. A warden led him away to a shed and forced him to sit and drink sweet tea. 'Yer all right, lad. You done well. That kiddy was shocked into silence. She could have starved down there. She's the only one left, because her mam and her brothers were killed, and her dad's out there somewhere on a ship.'

'What a bloody mess this is,' Peter managed.

'You talk nice, son.'

'Posh school. Crosby. Merchants.'

'Well, bloody good luck to you, that's what I say. What you going to be, like?'

'A lawyer.'

'Good. You can start by suing the Dock Board for us. We want the death penalty.'

'Fine.' He left the hut and worked for another

four hours. As he rode home, his legs could scarcely turn the pedals. Yet he felt ... good. Because on that third day in May, Peter Bingley grew up. Oh, and he acquired a baby rabbit.

Wabbit was just about old enough for solid food, though he chose to try suckling. Pandora, who took a fancy to the black and white intruder, accepted the circumstance without too much fuss. 'They match,' Tom said sleepily. 'Same colours. And she may produce milk – stranger things have happened.'

Today's human hero, cleaner after a bath, slept soundly in a rocking chair.

'I'm proud of Peter,' Marie said. 'Somebody took a photograph of him. He could be in the paper. That reminds me, Tom. Did you post the last lot to Phil Watson?'

'I did.'

Marie continued to smile benignly on her sleeping son. He had saved a little girl and a sweet rabbit. 'God bless him,' she sighed.

Gloria simply sat and held her twin brother's hand. They had been born together, raised together, and as a pair they would face the war, his secret problem, and whatever else lay on the stony road ahead. 'That sweet rabbit is eating its way through Dad's shoelace,' she said.

But Dad, too, was asleep.

'I'll try to make him stay at home tonight. He's so tired.' Marie moved the shoes. Tom did too much. He could not or would not unload his mental burdens when he got home, refusing point-blank to discuss the war work he was not supposed to do, since he had been instructed to stay at home for his patients' sake. In his head, he carried the weight of some terrible scenes. Time after time, he left a locum on call so that he could do battle for the city of Liverpool. She had two heroes now, husband and son.

'Mum?'

'Yes, Gloria?'

'The Pendleburys kept rabbits. They may have a hutch.'

Marie beamed. 'Telephone them, dear.'

'No line, Mum. They've fixed most of Liverpool Road, so Dad's locum has a phone at the practice, but we're still out of order.'

'Oh yes, I forgot. Would you go along and ask about a hutch?'

Gloria walked along silent roads. It was as if this cusp that divided Crosby from Blundellsands held its breath, no sound, no movement, no life. They were waiting to be bombed. She thought about the truly threatened a few miles down the road. Saturdays were almost as holy as Sundays in Liverpool. Me mam and me dad came, as did our Auntie Flo with her new feller from the gasworks, Uncle Fred with our Steve, our 'arry and our Edna, what was just out of jail for shoplifting what she never done, and it never rained but it poured, eh?

Floors of landing houses were scrubbed early on Saturday mornings. Even in wet weather, landing house kids were thrown out while the job was done. They could be picked out at a glance, shivering in shop doorways, walking to the swimming baths with rolled-up towels whose original colours were long forgotten or kicking a ball, or fighting in a tangle of limbs.

That was their culture, the rhythm they had invented, their own music, their own passion. Mel had often been heard to mutter, 'It'll be the poor who suffer most They're the ones I'll be batting for; not as a lawyer, but as a politician.' Mel was right. They were sure as hell suffering now. Extended families were forced to separate, because houses were gone, and people were becoming careful and wary. Saturday family gatherings were few and far between. A whole way of life had been stolen.

Mr Pendlebury promised to bring a hutch later on. 'Go home, Gloria. The Bosch are getting confident, and I shouldn't put it past them to arrive in daylight. They've been doing that for months down south.'

She walked home. Soon, all windows would be blacked out, all doors closed. This wasn't living; it was an existence, no more. Many children had never seen a banana, an orange, a pineapple. Food was so scarce that hunger was a constant companion. Hemlines had ascended to knee level in a bid to save cloth. The cotton mills were concentrating on calico for shrouds, a thought that made Gloria shiver.

She wasn't to know yet that this was the day on which all levels of the *Divine Comedy* would be visible. The descending circles of Dante's *Inferno* would be displayed, all the way from its seething rim down into the deepest realms of torment. But Wabbit would have a hutch, a surrogate mother, some greens, and a carrot. For now, that was

Gloria's sole concern.

For the people of Liverpool, Lewis's department store was sacrosanct.

Blackler's was high on the list, too, so the loss by fire of these two large emporia would be bemoaned for some considerable time to come. All seven storeys of Lewis's were destroyed, while Blackler's, already seriously lacking in windows, was also burned to death. Among the shop's contents, ten thousand pounds' worth of fully fashioned silk stockings had recently been delivered, and they melted alongside everything else in the building. This crime alone would be judged massive in the opinion of the city's already angry women.

Tom heard about these events, but he was on the dock road with several people who had been seriously hurt in a collision involving four vehicles. In truth, no one needed telling about the fires; even from the edge of the city, the devastation was visible. More news arrived. The William Brown Library had been eradicated along with the music section, and every book had been consumed by flames.

Tom placed two dead children on the pavement. They could wait there until an ambulance came. Minutes earlier, they had probably been sleeping in the car, but they would never wake again. His stomach rumbled angrily, though he could not have eaten to save his life. Dead children had always been the worst part of his job. He patched up a couple of adults, stepped back when ambulances arrived. At least three more were dead, but he could now leave them in safe, respectful hands. Because something was developing in the area of Huskisson Dock Two, and as he ran along the road his eyes remained riveted to the sight.

At about a quarter past eleven, a burning barrage balloon had freed itself from its moorings and floated gracefully past Tom, the ambulances, the suffering and the dead. It landed, after a few pirouettes, on the deck of SS *Malakand* and became entangled with the rigging.

'Oh, bugger,' said a nearby dock worker. 'That ship's packed with explosives.' After a further fifteen minutes the fire had been extinguished by the crew, but here came the Germans. They dropped firebombs and high explosives onto dock buildings, and burning debris fell on the steamer, igniting it from stem to stern. The order to abandon ship could be heard above anti-aircraft fire and falling bombs.

There was nothing Tom could do but wait while the crew obeyed the captain's orders. Many stayed on the quayside and fought to scuttle their ship, but she refused go down. He was probably wasting his time, so he backtracked into the city. The wind was up, the water mains had been blasted out of existence, and fire-fighters stood with dry hoses, many of the men in tears. Tom touched the arm of the nearest. 'Can I do anything?'

The man allowed a hysterical laugh to leave his dry throat. 'No. They've even burned Sammie, and all the fish boiled to death.'

'The museum?' Tom enquired.

'What sodding museum? We haven't got no museum no more. Even Sammie, poor little

Sammie. All the kids loved him.'

Tom blinked. Sammie the seal had been everyone's favourite. 'I want to hit somebody,' he whispered.

The fireman pointed to a colleague. 'Hit him,' he suggested. 'He's an Everton supporter.'

Fire raged and closed in on the city centre from all sides. And still a few loiterers circled, great iron birds spewing bombs, hatred and flame on a dry, windswept city. Over six hundred incidents had been counted by the time SS *Malakand* blew in the early hours. She scattered herself just about everywhere within miles of her mooring, yet only four people died, two of them a civilian couple on their way home via the dock road.

Tom, exhausted by lack of sleep and food, decided to call it a night. The all-clear had sounded, the city was a blazing wreck, and he had worked non-stop for five hours. The damage was unbelievable, yet it was only too real. A total lack of water due to bombed mains, coupled with a skittish wind, had taken away the core of Liverpool. But not its heart, never its heart. The pulse was in the people, in their intelligence, their humour– *Hit him, he's an Everton supporter.* Even while they wept, even when their clothes were almost on fire, that cheeky, confident banter floated to the surface. 'God help them all,' he muttered as he stepped into his car.

Forced to follow a tortuous route in near-darkness, he could only hope that the moon would continue to offer some glimmer of light. Roads that led directly to Crosby were not easily reachable; every few minutes, Tom had to negotiate a way past rubble, craters, abandoned vehicles. Mel's voice, mingled with Gloria's laughter, echoed in the sad, dulled chambers of his mind. *I miss Wagner,* she had said. *But it seems unpatriotic to listen to music favoured by a psychopath. I shan't give up Beethoven, though, not even for England. And Pandora's eating one of your mother's best shoes...* Mel summed up what he meant, what he felt about the people of this city. She was strong, passionate, smart and down to earth. As was her mother.

He stopped the car and closed his eyes. This going home business was too complicated for an exhausted man. While he nodded, the moon played hide-and-seek behind cloud or smoke, and as he neared sleep Tom didn't hear the ominous rumble, didn't see the nearby wall of a house peel away from its foundations. He and his car were buried; and the moon came out to play once more.

SUNDAY

Eileen, who resembled a question mark when standing, was now allowed to walk a few paces. According to Sister Mary Dominic, this would keep her blood on the move. 'We don't want to be having an embolism now, do we?'

'You can please yourself,' was Eileen's reply. 'I am not having one; a bag of chips with plenty of vinegar will do me, ta.'

'And you'd be straighter if you let us put the twins on the bottle. You've stitches, there could be adhesions–'

'Give over,' Keith advised. 'She does what she does, and nothing shifts her.'

'I'm learning that. She's a madam, a bold girl.'

Eileen stood still. 'Shut up, both of you. Wasn't there enough noise in the night? You've half a ship planted in your rockery for a start. I'm telling you now, we're going home. I mean, look at us, six o'clock in the blinking morning, three hours' sleep. Sister, go away. I've had enough. And no, I haven't said me morning prayers.' Eileen's mood was real; she wasn't acting up on this occasion. Liverpool was gone. With a sky as red as last night's, the whole of the centre must have been destroyed.

The nun left the room, and Keith followed with towel, toothbrush and shaving equipment. The wing was full of women, of course, so his shower had to happen at the crack of dawn. But in the corridor, Mary Dominic stopped him. 'We've a ... what you might call a situation, son. Away to the office. No one can hear us down there. You'll be all right for one day without the ablutions.'

A bemused Keith followed his new friend into the den of Mother Superior; Mother Superior, a fierce lady who always avoided him as if he were a pile of dog muck, was out, and Keith breathed a sigh of relief.

His little pal almost disappeared from view when she sat in Mother's chair. She moved a few things on the desk before speaking. 'Keith, you know how we closed down public rooms here and upstairs as our bit of war work?'

He nodded.

'Well, we used just upstairs at first. We tried not to affect maternity, but upstairs got busy, so we had to bite the bullet and use every room we had. You see, those who come here are in need of a priest or a vicar – we don't mind which. Very few walk out. This must not be told to any of the new mothers.'

'So they're dying?'

She sighed. 'We sometimes manage the odd miracle, because surgeons do their best in the theatres above. But, for the most part, our patients leave by a back door in a hearse and in the night. That's just to spare our mothers and babies. With this little lot down here at the start of their lives, it seems wrong to have the dead in the same building, but we have a Christian duty. Now, pin back your ears, this isn't going to be easy...'

Bad news travels fast, and truth hurts.

On Sunday, the fourth day in May, the whole Merseyside area of West Lancashire was in mourning. Many of the dead were still under rubble, as were several living souls. Even where fires had burned themselves out, the fabric of crumbled buildings remained hot, sometimes too hot to touch.

This time, the BBC named the city. This time, nothing could be hidden, though the media did not go into too much detail. The most moving moments came when Manchester arrived in all kinds of vehicles, and when North Wales emptied itself into the centre of Liverpool. People cared, and that mattered. A pair of proud Liver Birds supervised a city that was no longer there, a city to which non-residents had come to help clear up.

It would have been easier to count the few buildings that remained, and most of those were singed. The cultural area was destroyed. The overhead railway, known locally as the Dockers' Umbrella, was a tangle of metal. Wool and tobacco warehouses were no more, and Post Office engineers laboured with miles of wire, since the telephone exchange had been eliminated. Oil and fat works continued to burn, and the destruction of Inland Revenue premises was the only occurrence that gave rise to subdued laughter. Unfortunately, an employee ventured inside and found all records intact in a fire-proofed strong room. Fortunately, his excitement was so great that he ran out to spread the good news, forgetting to close the doors behind him. The strong room was burned out, and all records were lost.

Into the city cycled Peter Bingley with his father's camera. Dad hadn't come home, so Peter had expected to find a mess, but this was ... this was murder on a vast scale. Temper rose like vomit in his throat, and he was forced to breathe through his mouth in order to still his stomach. There were no church steeples, no bell towers, and very few shops remained. Oxygen was lacking, too. Where was Dad? How could he find him in the midst of such devastation? Taking photographs was no easy task, as his hands shook. But Phil Watson had to record this in his paintings. 'And I'm giving up German,' Peter muttered under his breath.

All punctuation marks, all points of reference had been removed. Where was he? Paradise

Street, Lord Street, St John Street, Canning Place – all burned out of existence. The words 'Turn left at Lewis's' would not be used for some time to come. 'We'll get you,' he told a murky sky. 'By God, you're finished.'

He started to search for his father. He found bodies, injured people, bits of people, blackened, charred figures that had once been people – one of those might easily have been Dad. After an hour or so, he became an automaton. Amidst the Welsh, the Mancunians and the people of Liverpool, he was just another silent worker. Occasionally, someone would shout, 'Anybody in there?' Apart from that and shifting rubble, there was little sound, not even birdsong.

He went to the warden who was minding Dad's camera.

'All right, son?'

'I have to go home, because my father's missing and Mum's frantic.'

'You get yourself away and back to school tomorrow. We're going to need brains like yours soon enough.'

'Be safe,' Peter ordered. 'And it's been a pleasure to talk to you.'

The man smiled through layers of soot. 'They done us good and proper this time. Trial by fire, eh?'

'Indeed.'

'Ta-ra, then, lad.'

'Liverpool will be back.' Peter picked up the camera. 'Because the Liver Birds are still here. As long as they stay where they are, there'll always be a Liverpool. It's the law.'

'And you're the lawyer.'
'Something like that.' He set off homeward.

Elsie ran in and placed herself opposite Nellie at the kitchen table. 'Buggering bastards,' were her first words.
'You what?'
'They've done that place with the daft name – Bootle, is it? It's not there any more. And all the shops in Liverpool and the libraries and museums and art galleries and docks and–'
'Slow down,' Nellie ordered.
'Toffee factory, Bootle town hall, Scott's Bakeries and twelve WVS dead with a direct hit. Oh, and some hospital called Mill Road Infirmary–'
'Elsie!'
'What?'
'You'll be having a stroke. Begin at the start.'
Elsie inhaled deeply. 'Right. You know her with the funny legs lower down?'
'You mean her ankles?'
Elsie groaned. 'Lower down the road. You know who I mean. Her pins don't seem to like each other; they stay apart. The lads could use her as goalposts at a football match. Frizzy hair, blue mac with a hood, had to get her wedding ring cut off with roomy-tied arthuritis.'
'That's Alice.'
'Right. Well her husband's high up in the Home Guard, and he came home skriking his eyes out. That big bang were a ship blowing up. It took Hodgkinson's Dock with it.'
'Huskisson.'

'Aye well, I were near enough. He's come back with all these tales. There's nowt left, Nellie. We have to get Eileen and the babies home. Telephone them and ... oh, I forgot. No phones.'

Nellie stood up. 'It's too far for either of us to walk, and I can't get hold of Keith to ask him to come and get us. No. We just have to wait.'

'She's got bunions and all.'

'Who has?'

'Her with the legs lower down...'

Keith pushed the wheelchair out of the lift. He and Eileen were greeted by Mary Dominic, a doctor and a priest. This was the floor on which the dying breathed their last. It stank of disinfectant and fear.

'Stay with me,' Eileen begged her husband. 'Don't leave me. Promise.' She was trembling like a dry leaf in an October wind.

'I promise.'

The priest took charge of Eileen and her chair; the other three followed at a slight distance. When she reached the bedside in a single room, Father Murray stayed with her, while the rest stood back near the door. Although the moment was meant to be private, Eileen wanted witnesses. And she ached, because she had to say goodbye to a man who wanted her and only her. He had refused to see Marie or his children; he was suffering multiple organ malfunction, and would soon drift into a final sleep.

Mary Dominic whispered in Keith's ear. ''Tis a terrible thing to ask of a newly delivered mother.'

Keith lowered his head by many inches. 'Shut

up, Sis. It has to be done.'

Tom's head was swathed in bandages. Gaps had been created for mouth, nose and eyes. Eileen sat and waited for him to speak.

'You came,' he said eventually.

'Of course I came. You knew I'd come.'

'You've left him?' The eyes glared at her.

'Yes.' That wasn't a lie, because she'd left Keith at the door. 'What about Marie?'

Feeble fingers pulled at a sheet. 'Who?'

Again, Mary Dominic whispered to Keith. 'That'll be his kidneys. The brain often goes odd when kidneys are affected.'

'He remembers my Eileen well enough.'

'Be brave, but.'

Tom asked about where they would live, and Eileen told him about two cottages knocked into one; that, too, was the truth. Miss Pickavance was making a lovely home for the family, an enormous kitchen across the back, two living rooms, three bedrooms and a bathroom. 'The doctor at Willows is rubbish, and he's being forced to retire after accidentally overdosing some poor old girl to death. You can take his job.'

'Do you love me?'

Eileen glanced at the priest, who simply nodded. 'I love you,' she said.

'And when I get out of here, you'll be waiting?'

'Oh, yes. I'll wait for you.'

Tom sighed. 'We've always known, haven't we? Right from the very start.' He drifted, spoke to people who weren't there, shouted orders as if he were in town saving the injured. Suddenly, his eyes opened. 'It will never be over,' he said, the words spoken clearly.

'You're right,' she told him. 'This is for ever.'

He fitted then, jerking about so violently that the doctor and Father Murray had to hold him down. A trickle of blood emerged from a corner of his mouth. The convulsion did not run its course, but stopped abruptly, because Dr Tom Bingley was no more. Eileen hung on to his hand. 'God be with you, Tom.' Tears streamed down her face. She turned to Father Murray. 'Bless me, Father, for I have sinned.'

The priest put an arm across her shoulders. 'My child, the lies you just told are your passport to heaven. Sometimes, there's a fine line between good and bad. He died in happiness. You helped him over and away from a broken body. God bless you.'

There wasn't a dry eye in the room. Even the doctor was blowing his nose while the priest performed the last rites on a man who had not been Catholic.

'There are more lies to be told,' the little nun announced. 'Mother and I will go to Mrs Bingley and pretend we didn't know who he was with all the bandages applied in the ambulance; also that he died without regaining consciousness. Sometimes a small sin is necessary for the greater good. Take her back down, Keith. She's done enough hard work for today.'

PART FOUR

1942

Twenty-One

A nun playing French cricket on Hilda Pickavance's huge front lawn was a sight few could resist. With her long black skirt hoisted up to knee level, the godmother of Frankie and Helen Greenhalgh belted the ball and ran like the wind. She had turned out to be a brilliant godmother, because she wasn't all rosary beads, children's prayer books and holy pictures; she loved the babies, saw them whenever she could, played with them and sang to them.

Guiding Keith, her best friend outside the convent, through the portals of Rome had been a source of great joy for her, though Keith had been forced to manufacture time for just himself and the priest. Asking a cleric about sexual behaviour had been no walk in the park; had Mary Dominic been present, the questions could not have been asked.

Father Murray had been impressively unfazed. 'You love the woman. But at her rate of reproduction, you could end up with a football team, plus a long bench filled by reserves. Go with the all-forgiving God to Father Flint in Bolton when you leave me behind, continue these lessons, heed your conscience, and keep that lovely wife of yours happy. Remember, the lies she told to a dying man were a great kindness. Need I say more about sin and humanity?'

Also on the lawn at Willows on this bright July day, Mel, Gloria and Peter tried to play a game whose rules changed by the minute. Mel confronted the good sister, of course. 'You're not playing properly, Sister Domino.' Domino was the nun's predictable nickname.

'Away with your bother, you bold child. I caught that ball.'

'You didn't. You threw your body at it, then fiddled about till you had it in your hand.'

Eileen, who watched her elder daughter fighting a losing battle, had finally let go. Her gorgeous daughter was now a very welcome cuckoo in the Bingley nest, because Gloria needed her, as did Marie and Peter. All four Watson offspring had turned out well balanced, industrious and amusing. Almost by accident, the boys had found themselves; as for Mel, she had always been focused. Nothing further would happen between Mel and Peter, since the poor lad had his own cross to bear.

Eileen watched the hilarious game. Mary Dominic contested every decision and continued to play unfairly. Stella and Patty, daughters of Neil and Jean from Willows Home Farm, were clearly bemused. They had no idea when it came to dealing with an unscrupulous Irish–Augustinian penguin. So they played the game and said little. Eileen nudged her husband. 'Your girlfriend's a lying, cheating cow.'

'I know. I must own every starving village in Africa because she cons me all the time.'

'Not difficult.'

He hit his much-loved partner with a cushion.

On the other side of the lawn, Nellie and Elsie

were making plans. They lived together now behind the post office, and they wanted extra space to make a tea room. When the war was over, they were going to expand. 'Mind you keep that weight off,' Nellie insisted. 'If we're expanding into scones and cakes, I might have to stick a plaster over your gob, or you'll be the expanding one.'

As ever, Elsie had an answer. 'You do scones and teas while I sell local produce. I hope you're right about advertising. I hope people come.'

'Your teeth are loose. They're clacking away like castanets.'

'Shut up.' Nothing changed; they still fought like cat and dog, still respected each other.

Phil Watson, who had been caught out on his first run, promoted himself to the level of umpire. The nun was cheating. What the hell was he supposed to do about a dishonest bride of Christ? He did nothing. Walking away from the game, he sat and picked up a sketch pad. It was a picture worth recording; the Yanks were here, God love them, and civilians had begun to relax a little. He laughed. The spoodles, having grown bored with the back garden, shot into the scene, and Pandora got the ball and ran off with it. 'That'll put a stop to her,' Phil said sotto voce. Nevertheless, his sketch retained its title: *Sins of Domino.*

Eileen and Keith's fourteen-month-old twins staggered about behind curtains kindly donated by thriving willow trees. Keith had given up on the hammock idea, so he sat with his wife on a rug. He was going to invent a double swing, upholstered, of course. 'I could cover it in waterproof material,' he announced apropos of nothing at all.

'What?' his precious wife enquired.

'The double swing.'

'Right.' Eileen decided to leave him to his inventions. So far, nothing useful had been produced, but inventing was his hobby, and she had banished him to the shed with his diagrams and tools. She didn't want her toddlers becoming acquainted with saws and screwdrivers.

Across the grass, Marie Bingley had returned from a solitary walk and was chatting to Nellie and Elsie. Miss Pickavance sat nearer to the house with her four stalwarts. Over the duration, she had grown close to Jay, Gill, Neil and Jean. Little Maisie Collins darted about in a pink tutu, a tiara and wings. She was being a fairy with a magic wand today; tomorrow, she might well be a cowboy – Maisie did not discriminate.

'Where's the rest of our brood?' Keith asked.

The sun was making Eileen sleepy. 'Well, Bertie will be with a horse somewhere, and Rob's bought a soil-testing kit. I can't imagine soil taking exams, but there you have it.'

Keith stretched out on the blanket, dragging his wife with him.

'There's a nun present,' she said. 'Don't start with the kissing, and watch the twins – I'm having forty winks.'

He whispered in her ear. 'Sister MD would lift her skirt higher for me.'

'Behave yourself.'

'She loves me. She wants me. I can see it in her eyes.'

'Then she's as daft as I am.'

With his gaze fixed on Frankie and Helen, he asked the question for the first time since the event. 'Did you have feelings for him, darling?'

'Yes, I did.' She paused, saw that final fit, watched and listened while Mother Superior lied to Marie. She remembered the touch of his hand, the sound of his voice, those eyes blazing out through the gap in the bandages. 'But you are my breath, and you know it. Without you, I'd be half of nothing.'

'Nothing?'

'Absolutely. He was brave, Keith. He had spirit, and I'm glad I knew him. But he wasn't for me, sweetie. I admired his cheek and his courage.'

'God, yes. He died for Liverpool, for England.'

'And behind all the bluster and the elegant doctor with his posh suits and shoes, he was very like you. He started off wanting my body, then he fell in love. But I didn't love him, you see. I fell in love postally. Is postally a word?'

Keith laughed heartily. 'Did you keep all my letters?'

'Of course. And you kept mine, because I found them in the dresser. We must read them aloud sometime. Yes, the postman led me astray.' She fell asleep.

He stared down at her, thanking God for bringing him to his senses. She had become a mother again, and his love had shifted for a while. Awe had replaced desire, and he had treated her like something delicate and priceless created by Fabergé. For some reason best known to womankind, Eileen had found the whole business hilarious. In the end, she had forced herself on him. Once recovered from sexual assault, he and she had returned to normal, or for what passed for normal between him and his beloved spouse.

Asleep, she was an angel; awake, she was exciting, unpredictable, passionate and crazy; this was definitely his kind of girl. She still spent the odd five minutes on a draining board...

Frankie and Helen gravitated towards their beloved Dada, curling at his feet and falling asleep in an instant. One by one, the Watsons joined them, Mel hot from running, Bertie in his riding gear, Phil with pad and charcoal, Rob moaning about acid and alkaline. Always welcome in several homes, the sons of Eileen and Lazzer slept where they landed. Nellie and Elsie made space when required. The boys had bedrooms in Willows, and there was a spare room in the newly renovated Greenhalgh double cottage. If the place got full, the dining room had a folding bed. But no matter where they rested their heads, these three boys always had Sunday lunch with Mam and Keith. It was a law they obeyed joyfully, because they had the best parents available to humanity.

The St Michael's Road house in Crosby was closed and shuttered. Eileen would make up her mind about it after the war, when it could be returned to its former pristine glory, black woodwork and white walls. Mel and Peter were no longer a worry; they were forging ahead at school, outstripping all comers, aiming for the stars. Gloria, too, had bucked up, and she promised to be a pretty and clever woman. All was well, Keith reminded himself. The Americans were not only strong in number, they were also fresh, not yet fatigued by battle.

Eileen woke, while the rest of the various groups stopped talking. Mary Dominic made herself decent, and all awaited the arrival of a vehicle that rumbled its way up Willows Lane. No one present had ever before been so close to an American Jeep. Major Joseph L. Chalmers jumped out and waved his driver off to park the vehicle closer to the house. He ran to Marie, picking her up and spinning until she was dizzy. Marie ignored his rank; he was her GI Joe.

He placed her on the grass, awarded her a huge kiss, then beamed at the pure Englishness of the scene. 'Beautiful,' he said. Marie steadied herself, led him round and introduced him to those he had not already met. He spotted the Watson/Greenhalgh clan and said, 'There's the girl who introduced us, Marie. That Liverpool girl. My sisters will blame her when I stay here with you and try to become the English gentleman. If your country will have me, that is.'

'Of course they'll have you. There she is, Joe. There's our Mel.'

But Amelia Anne Watson was having one of her moments. She walked behind the screen provided by the largest weeping willow. With her vision of the world fractured by trailing branches, she peered out at the people she loved, at an environment she had come to enjoy. Everything was so green and fresh, so untouched by hostility. This was how life should, could and would be. Even Peter was calm here in the bosom of

Lancashire's rolling generosity. He had settled into his own uncertainty, had decided to wait until the light dawned and pointed out his true way home. 'I'm happy,' she said to herself. 'Everyone here is happy.'

While she watched, the tree whispered to her. Magical trees, beautiful gardens, contentment. Willows was filled with wonderful people, and she was a lucky girl. Well, she would be when the war ended, when clothes came off ration, when Gran stopped moaning about the shortage of tea, when sweets were more plentiful, when… She laughed. A few flies in the ointment? No matter. The willows were healthy, the land was fruitful and an American Jeep was parked on the drive.

Mel stretched out in the shade, closed her eyes and dreamt of a better future. And the willow continued its whispering.

The publishers hope that this book has given you enjoyable reading. Large Print Books are especially designed to be as easy to see and hold as possible. If you wish a complete list of our books please ask at your local library or write directly to:

Magna Large Print Books
Magna House, Long Preston,
Skipton, North Yorkshire.
BD23 4ND

This Large Print Book for the partially sighted, who cannot read normal print, is published under the auspices of

THE ULVERSCROFT FOUNDATION

THE ULVERSCROFT FOUNDATION

... we hope that you have enjoyed this Large Print Book. Please think for a moment about those people who have worse eyesight problems than you ... and are unable to even read or enjoy Large Print, without great difficulty.

You can help them by sending a donation, large or small to:

The Ulverscroft Foundation,
1, The Green, Bradgate Road,
Anstey, Leicestershire, LE7 7FU,
England.
or request a copy of our brochure for more details.

The Foundation will use all your help to assist those people who are handicapped by various sight problems and need special attention.

Thank you very much for your help.